SAM HAIN

Hamid Amirani

PARADOX

Copyright © 2024, 2025 by Hamid Amirani

First published as an ebook in 2024

This revised edition published in 2025

The moral right of the author has been asserted.

All characters and events portrayed in this book are fictitious.

Any resemblance to real persons, living or dead, is purely coincidental.

All rights reserved.

No part of this book may be reproduced, stored in a retrieval system, or transmitted in any form or by any means, electronic, mechanical, photocopying, recording, or otherwise, without express written permission of the publisher.

A CIP catalogue record for this book

is available from the British Library.

ISBN 979-8-29613443-1

Cover design by Sam Cooper

ACKNOWLEDGEMENTS

Thanks to Jon Kirk at Palamedes for all his help and expertise.

Chelsey-Ann Stuart and Nicola Dunklin for their feedback.

For their inspiration and influence, I wish to thank Anthony Horowitz and Joe Dante.

PROLOGUE

PART I

"You have lied to me for the last time. You have betrayed me for the last time."

His voice had a timbre the pair weren't used to. He'd been angry before, but this was something new.

"I warned you not to sign your names again. I warned you I would punish you."

The woman finally swallowed the reservoir of saliva that had accumulated from her desperate attempt to not show fear. "What are you going to do?"

"I'm going to torment Sam."

The pair looked at each other and broke into hysterics.

"Fuck him!" she chuckled in unwisely hasty relief.

Speaking up, the man joined in with the premature jubilation. "Do what you like!"

Their captor observed them laughing raucously without making comment. He did this until he could tolerate the moronic pair no longer.

"Oh, shut the fuck up."

In a flash, the pair were dead, vacuous grins etched on their faces in a manner that would leave a neutral observer in no doubt that they had been profoundly stupid, annoying individuals.

Looking at the corpses, he sighed.

"Humans really piss me off."

PART II

Detective Wallace Morton crouched next to the SWAT Commander. The six-foot, athletic 47-year-old veteran of the Portland, Oregon Police Department was thriving on the adrenaline from the imminent arrests. He had on his dark blue Armani suit, a luxury he allowed himself, figuring that if he had to deal with scum every day – and that was just some of his colleagues – then he might as well look and feel good doing it.

Eight SWAT officers, each armed with standard department issue firepower, were positioned in the foliage, all eyes fixed on the isolated cabin next to the woods. The cool afternoon air, along with the serenity of the surroundings, made for a police operation that was unusually pleasant in its ambience.

Pleasant, but at the same time verging on the nauseating for the man who'd been on the case for five months. The whimsy of the wagon wheel gable that adorned the cabin roof juxtaposed with the knowledge of the grotesque individuals who inhabited the rental turned Morton's stomach. It was now apparent that this wasn't just an operation to capture monstrous people; it was also to detoxify an elegant abode from its interlopers.

"I'll take point," Morton said quietly.

The SWAT Commander looked at Morton as though he had just said the time is half past spaghetti. "Excuse me?"

"I've been on this case for too long. I'm going to see it through to the finish."

"You'll get your credit, Detective. I'm not interested in taking that from you. None of us are."

"I'm not talking about a pissing contest."

"Then what are you talking about?"

"I want to be the first to look them in the eye and either arrest them or shoot them. You guys are here in case things get messy."

The SWAT Commander, himself a veteran, was sufficiently thick-skinned and more bemused than offended. "Preventing a situation from getting messy is kinda what we're about, Detective, not being your back-up. I'm not even a hundred on assisting you like this, you here without a partner, something I still have my doubts about by the way."

"Really? You want to do this now? I told you already I work alone. When we're through, get on the phone to my Captain and he'll confirm."

The Commander looked at his team and then back at Morton. "This feels sketchy as fuck."

"Save it for later," Morton shot back before he started heading towards the cabin, gun in hand.

"Shit!" The SWAT Commander signaled to his officers. All moved in formation behind him with their customary precision, deftly honed from years of practice and in-the-field experience.

As Morton closed in on the door, he raised his gun. He glanced back to check his personal cavalry were ready in case things went shit shaped. The SWAT Commander gripped his shield, which was designed to protect a point man from gunfire, but it was now superfluous, as Morton effectively doubled as his shield.

The cop nodded and turned back to the door. Making time for exercise and watching his diet meant he had maintained optimum physical condition throughout his years on the force. Most of his fellow officers his age would have a problem trying to kick in a cabin door. Morton had no such fear. He struck the door with a thunderous kick that sent it flying open.

"POLICE! NOBODY MOVE!" Morton yelled as he entered the cabin. He immediately stopped.

The cabin was empty.

A rush of disappointment coursed through his body.

Morton raised his hand to signal the scene was clear. The others entered, guns still trained in case of any surprises.

"Check the bathroom and bedroom," Morton ordered in a despondent tone. "But they're not here."

Four officers went to explore the rooms, while Morton sunk into the dirty couch. The cabin was beautiful on the outside, but its interior was a grim, dirty, raggedy tragedy of neglect and poor hygiene that let you know the kind of people its inhabitants were. The floor was littered with empty beer cans, takeout boxes with putrefying remnants of glazed noodles and carrots, and – most revoltingly – scrunched up napkins. Morton shuddered to think what vestigial particles lay in them.

The misery didn't stop there. The wall panels were scarred with knife slashes and stabs, two wooden chairs lay broken on the floor – one leg covered in dried blood – and the decrepit hearth of the fireplace was home to discarded needles and syringes, though the few spots of the mantelpiece that weren't coated in dirt revealed once-opulent marble stonework, which helped the fireplace retain some dignity.

That is, until Morton's eyes alighted on the mantel shelf, which he saw had been reduced to serving as a retirement home for a further pile of needles, syringes, and beer cans.

The SWAT Commander looked at Morton with a small degree of sympathy from one professional to another. "My condolences, Detective."

Morton glanced up at him. He couldn't tell if the burly SWAT man was being sarcastic, but he chose to accept it. "Thanks."

"Detective!" The call came from one of the officers in the bedroom. "You need to see this."

Morton immediately sprang up. He and the Commander ran into the bedroom where they saw the two officers standing on one side of the stained, shabby bed. Nothing appeared out of the ordinary, other than the foul state of the bed with its dirty, straggled sheets, equally grimy pillows that were missing cases, and a broken headboard decorated with specks of dried blood, a mise en scène so revolting that a hobo who hadn't slept in a bed for ten years would say "No, I'm good."

"What?" Morton asked, his momentary excitement rapidly ebbing away.

"Over here," said the officer who'd called to him.

Morton walked around to where they stood and now saw what they were looking at. To the right of the bed, scrawled in capital letters on the wall in blood, was the name *MIKE*.

"*Mike?*" Morton said.

The SWAT Commander came over and looked at the bloody signature. "Another serial perhaps?"

"A rival. Fantastic. That's all I need," Morton said. He gazed around the room as he pondered his next move. He noticed a very thick and antique-looking leather-bound tome resting upright against the adjacent wall. The cop wandered over and picked it up. The title of the book made him shake his head. "Of course. Fucking idiots," he muttered to himself.

"Ah, jeez!" one of the officers who'd gone to inspect the bathroom uttered outside the bedroom. He peered in at the doorway. "Don't, whatever you do, go into the bathroom. It's gross."

The hitherto silent officer now spoke up in response to Morton. "But if it's a rival, where are their bodies? Why kill them but not leave them here so we know this Mike was the one who did it? I mean, that's why these types leave their names, right? For the fame and the media? Zodiac, Son of Sam."

"There are two possibilities," Morton surmised. "One: They've been kidnapped and are still alive. Two: They're dead. And we're looking for a rival serial killer who wants the world to know him as… Mike."

ONE MONTH LATER

Thursday

8:14pm

The small Northern Californian town of Millvern, population just over 5,000, is a startling amalgamation of the past and present. It's as though innocent 1950s Americana had partially intruded upon modern day. You can find an internet café next to a mom-and-pop bakery next to a shop selling cellphones next to a good old-fashioned adult bookstore.

The town's union of Americana and modernity had effected an aesthetic that the local Sheriff thought could be called *Apple PiPad*. He was quite pleased with himself for coming up with that neologism. He just wished he had an opportunity to use it when someone was around.

The residents of Millvern all knew about Nancy Dirgle, the 85-year-old owner of the local laundromat. Even those who had no cause to use a laundromat knew about Nancy. If you took the archetype of the sweet old lady who finds the word *damn* a step too far and then searched for its direct antithesis, you would find Nancy. Her notoriety stemmed from her habit of peppering her every utterance with swear words, mainly *fuck*. And from being relentlessly offensive.

She was also known for closing her laundromat every day at six for two hours, during which she would have her dinner and copious amounts of whiskey. Some residents doubted that Nancy actually imbibed any alcohol, because her demeanor never changed – she was consistently, continually, and continuously objectionable.

On this evening, 30-year-old Brit Drew Langer was waiting outside the laundromat. He looked at his watch again and sighed in frustration, pushing his round glasses up the bridge of his nose. He wore a dark blue t-shirt, black trousers, and a dark grey shirt; he'd always been fond of simple, dark colors.

Just then, Nancy appeared from around the corner and ambled to the entrance. The first thing one would notice about her was her ridiculous blonde wig that sat on her head awkwardly. Then your attention would be drawn to her face, an intricate map of wrinkles, the result of scowling for most of her 85 years. In contrast to Drew's stygian hues, she wore the kind of cream-colored trousers that people her age are fond of, a cream sweater, and a cream cotton cardigan. A cream coat completed her ensemble. The lightness of her attire didn't extend to her personality; the old, dirt strewn pair of sneakers she had on did.

"Finally," Drew said.

"Oh, fuck you, boy," Nancy hit back in her Texan drawl. "You should be grateful I'm opening at all. Goddamn ungrateful fucker."

"I've paid to use your service."

Nancy couldn't believe her ears. Had this punk just talked back to her?

"Watch your mouth!"

Not long ago, Drew would have just humored the cranky woman, but a recent experience back home in the UK had been somewhat of a learning curve, the conclusion of which was that he wouldn't tolerate abusive behavior again.

"How about you just open the fucking door?"

Nancy was again momentarily speechless. Seeing that her verbal ripostes weren't having the desired effect, she just turned to face the door and dug into her trouser pocket for the keys. "Where the fuck are they?" She went into her other pocket. "Oh, hell. Don't tell me I left them at the diner. I ain't going back there." She searched her coat pockets.

Nancy sensed Drew watching her expectantly and was about to say *If they ain't here, you gotta come back tomorrow,* but she was still smarting from his willingness to give as good as he got.

She reached into her inside coat pocket and there was a jangle of keys. She retrieved them and unlocked the door's two locks.

They entered and both immediately noticed the loud thudding coming from one of the large dryers towards the back.

"What the fuck is that?" she said. Then, quieter: "Did you put something weird in your load?"

"What? No, that's not mine. I haven't even used a dryer yet."

"What the hell is that racket?"

Nancy approached the dryer that was the source of the alarming noise.

Drew went to the washing machine holding his clothes, but a sense of unease came over him. He turned and looked over at Nancy as she neared the dryer.

She opened the door. The body of a dead man in a nice suit flopped halfway out of the machine.

Drew uttered a shocked grunt.

"Goddammit!" Nancy looked at the deceased man as though she'd just received a parking ticket.

"I'll call the police," Drew offered.

"You do that."

Drew took out his cellphone. He went outside to make the call, while Nancy headed towards the back office where she had a stock of whiskey and biscuits.

Neither of them had noticed that, above the dryer, on the faded shade-of-vomit yellow wallpaper, the name *MIKE* was scrawled in still freshly dripping blood.

But that wasn't all. Had Nancy turned around at that moment, she would have seen something to which her reaction would have been composed entirely of *fuck* and every variation thereof, including but not limited to *What the motherfuck, you fuck?!*

Friday

10:34am

Sam Hain's parents had always had a sense of humor. That is to say, they were a pair of witless idiots whose organic stupidity was compounded by being prolific crystal meth users, obliterating what few viable braincells were previously functioning.

Being fucking stupid wasn't enough, though. Leo and Polly Hain were also obsessed with the occult. That obsession led to them naming their son Sam, as they thought it incredibly funny to have a kid whose full name sounded like Samhain, the ancient Gaelic festival that marks the night when the barrier between the corporeal and the discarnate wanes; the forerunner to Halloween. When a passing acquaintance – everyone they'd known had only been an acquaintance, and any whose brains weren't addled were quick to make sure their acquaintance was passing – pointed out to Leo and Polly that their son's name was a homophone, a confused and then indignant Polly declared their son wasn't scared of gay people, which, ironically, was true, but not for the reason she said.

It will be of no surprise, therefore, that Sam had an unhappy childhood. Growing up in a dilapidated one-story house in Marion County, West Virginia, it was television, schoolteachers, and friends that raised him in the absence of sentient parents. He didn't care about their favorite hobby, because it usually meant they'd be gone for days on end getting high while fucking in a graveyard, which he found almost endearing in its lack of imagination.

But their fixation with the occult, trivial and juvenile to begin with, grew more unhinged as he got older. It came to a head one fateful night when he ran away at the age of 17 and never looked back.

Making his way to a neighboring county, he found Jess Dalton, a friend from school he'd stayed in touch with after she moved at the end of the previous semester. When he explained to them what happened, Jess's parents said they wouldn't inform the authorities. He rejected their suggestion of adopting a new name, as he didn't want the hassle that comes with taking on a new identity. Besides, he was confident that his parents wouldn't report him missing, given what they'd tried to do.

Taking pity on Sam, Jess's parents let him stay and he was enrolled at her school. He was introduced as Jess's cousin, which seemed a good idea at the time, but became a source of frustration when they fell for each other and wished they could openly kiss during break times at school, though it did occur to Sam that, in parts of the Bible Belt, cousins kissing was an everyday, acceptable sight.

At home, Sam felt it best not to push his luck, having been saved from the streets by Jess's parents, and therefore they kept their relationship a secret. Her parents were pleased that the two spent every evening doing homework together and not playing video games. For their part, Sam and Jess mastered the art of fucking as quietly as possible. Jess would cover his mouth when he reached climax to muffle his vocal exhalations of ecstasy. She didn't need his help on that front, as she was more adept at self-control.

After graduating from college and moving to San Francisco, Sam flitted from one job to another, one abortive career to another. He tried being an office manager, a desk clerk, and, in an exercise in irony, a careers advisor.

It was when he saw a friend's husband kissing another woman and telling his friend of the infidelity that Sam hit upon the idea of becoming a private investigator. People would always cheat and people would always be suspicious of their spouses. Of the latter, there would always be those with expendable income who would pay for the services of private investigators. Sam made no personal judgment on those who were cheating. He was realistic about the main pitfall of monogamy being the inevitable tedium of sex with the same person. He might sympathize with some of the cheaters, but he always served his clients' needs.

Except for one occasion when he felt he had no choice but to lie. His surveillance target was a 32-year-old housewife who was meeting her personal trainer during the day for extra personal training. Sam was unusually sloppy on that assignment and was spotted by the woman, who angrily confronted him. He confessed what he was doing. He was ready to tell her that this didn't change anything and he had a duty to tell her husband, so it came as a surprise when she asked him how long he'd worked as a private investigator and how many cheating wives and husbands he'd followed. After the second anecdote, she suggested they continue the conversation over a coffee.

Sam told her about his cases, and she told him about sex with her husband getting boring. All the while, Sam couldn't take his eyes off her. She was a beautiful woman with long blonde hair and a figure that attested to her regular workouts with her personal trainer.

He thought he wasn't bad either. At five nine, slim but not especially muscular, and with a defined jawline, Sam was handsome but without the arrogance or overly chiseled features that afflict alphas.

After the third coffee, she suggested they continue the conversation back at his place.

Sam didn't work out of a rented office; he saved money by using the spare room in his apartment as one. He gave the housewife a quick tour of his apartment before they went to sit in the living room to drink some white wine. She told him about the malaise of being a housewife, and he told her about his deranged parents. They sympathized with each other's past and present plights. After the fourth glass, she suggested they go to his bedroom and have sex.

Sam reported back to the client that his wife was not being unfaithful.

Now 35, Sam was in his seventh year as a private investigator. One of the attractions of working for himself was getting out of bed when he wanted. There was one case where the husband suspected of adultery left the marital home at six every morning, supposedly to go to the office. Sam hated early mornings, so he ended up just sleeping in his car across from the house every night.

Dressed in a t-shirt and trunks, he emerged from his bedroom and headed straight to the kitchen and opened the fridge. He took out a bottle of Diet Pepsi and chugged. An ex-girlfriend was dumbfounded by this, but Sam explained it was a habit from his childhood that he couldn't drop. The ice-cold carbonated liquid hitting his tongue was an exhilaration he could not resist first thing in the morning.

Bottle in hand, Sam went downstairs to retrieve his mail. There was only one letter. He opened it on his way up and stopped when he saw the contents. He looked behind him – quite unnecessary but an instinct he'd developed in his occupation – saw no one was around, and hurried back to his apartment.

He sat on the edge of his bed and removed the contents of the envelope: a typed note and $500 in clean, fresh $100 bills. He held one of the notes up, and then realized he had no idea how to discern a fake note from a real one.

Putting the money aside, he turned his attention to the note. It was brief, simple, and direct. And all in capitals, probably for dramatic effect.

DEAR MR HAIN,

PLEASE GO IMMEDIATELY TO MILLVERN. VISIT THE SHERIFF AND ASK HIM ABOUT THE LAUNDROMAT MURDER. IT IS IMPERATIVE THAT YOU INVESTIGATE. ENCLOSED IS $500 FOR YOUR TROUBLE.

He read the note several times, trying to glean something more than its surface message, but all he could think was that *The Laundromat Murder* would be a terrible title for a murder mystery.

Friday

11:25am

Showered and dressed, Sam got into his car for the six-hour drive to Millvern. He had no live cases on the go, and the bizarre anonymous note, as well as the cash, left him no choice but to find out where it might lead.

He had all he needed: a shoulder bag with enough clothes to last him a few days away, basic toiletries, his handgun, his P.I license, a notepad, and his cellphone. And that started ringing just as he was about to put on his seatbelt.

"Hello?"

"Morning. Am I speaking to Sam Hain?"

"You are."

"Hello, Mr. Hain. My name is Detective Wallace Morton. I'm with the Portland Police Department."

"Maine or Oregon?"

"Sorry?"

"Which Portland?"

"Oh, excuse me. Portland, Oregon."

"How can I help you, Detective?"

"I need to speak to you about your parents."

Sam's heart sank and he sighed. "Look, can you tell them I'm 35 and I want nothing to do with them."

"Sorry? No, you don't understand. I'm trying to find them and I hoped you might be able to help."

"I have no idea where they are. I haven't seen them in eighteen years and I want to keep it that way."

"Even so, if you don't mind, I'd like to talk to you in person and just ask a few questions."

"In person? However you got hold of my number, you must know I don't live in Portland."

"I know. I'm actually here in San Francisco. Could we meet for a coffee?"

He'd come all the way to San Francisco just to ask him about his parents? Sam immediately knew this must be serious, but he couldn't be bothered inquiring any further at that moment. "I'm sorry, Detective. I'm on my way to Millvern to investigate a case that's just landed on my desk."

"Oh, yes, I gather you're a private investigator."

"Great detective work!"

"Uh, yeah, thanks."

Sam detected a note of mild offense in Morton's voice and smiled.

"If you need to talk to me, I'll be there."

"OK, that's do-able."

Sam was about to end the call when he realized he hadn't said the obvious. "Detective, if you find them before then, feel free to shoot them. I'll even speak in your defense if you need me to."

"I'll take that as a joke."

"Sure, OK."

Friday

6:07pm

Having stopped off at a roadside diner for lunch, Sam arrived in Millvern shortly after six. He noted the genteel feel of the town square as he drove around, observing the twenty-four-hour diner called Eat All Day, a name that, judging by the girth of some of the people in the neighborhood, had been taken literally, a bowling alley called Just Bowl Me, which he found adorable and was certain had been given that name by people completely oblivious to its connotation, a Tex-Mex restaurant called Tex's Tex-Mex, because it was run by a guy called Tex, and a red neon arrow on a wall pointing pedestrians in the direction of the adjacent alleyway, where he briefly idled his car and saw a pole dancing club with an equally garish neon sign announcing the establishment as Tex-Sex. It appeared that Tex was quite the entrepreneur with a diversified business portfolio.

Sam also saw the laundromat, which was called Laundromat. After the other places, the name came as a disappointment.

He parked outside a bed & breakfast, though he intended to decide later exactly where he would stay. Eager to get a start on his inquiries, he searched for a newsstand. Immediately he saw the headline on the front page of the local paper: *Man Murdered in Town Laundromat.*

Sam speed-read the article, but it provided nothing of substance beyond the basic fact of the murder and that the victim had not been identified. He was about to put the paper back when he realized he'd almost missed something quite important. The murder took place only the previous evening. The letter to Sam was postmarked yesterday morning – before the murder.

He asked the newsagent for directions to the sheriff's station. Crossing the square, he noticed a TV crew assembled outside the laundromat and the reporter, a bubbly and enthusiastic young woman, interviewing Nancy. Sam stood a short distance back and observed.

"Did you scream upon discovering the dead body?" the reporter asked Nancy.

"Scream? I ain't no fucking sissy."

"Ma'am, you can't swear. Let's go again. Two, one… Did you scream upon discovering the dead body?"

"No, I told you, I ain't no fucking sissy!"

"Ms. Dirgle, you cannot swear on prime-time news."

"You keep asking me the same goddamn question and I keep telling you I ain't no fucking sissy."

The reporter turned to her camera operator. "Cut it. There's no point."

Nancy wasn't done. "Why would I scream? I've seen dead bodies before."

The camera operator's interest was piqued. "Were they already dead when you saw them?"

"Fuck you!"

Sam took out his notebook and scribbled down a note: *Laundromat, Dirgle – angry and cranky. Possibly homicidal.*

Shutting his notebook, he continued on his way to the sheriff's station.

Friday

6:42pm

In the twenty-five years that Don Jockton had been Sheriff of Millvern, there had only been one murder, and it was a case of mistaken identity. A cheating husband had hired a hitman to kill his wife, a tall, buxom blonde called Veronica. The hitman ended up killing his mistress, also called Veronica. Also a tall, buxom blonde. At trial, the husband argued that it wasn't his fault the wrong woman had been killed and he shouldn't be held responsible just because he had a type. When the judge pointed out that this didn't mitigate a murder for hire, he said he'd like to sue the hitman for failing to deliver the service promised. At that point, the man's lawyer quit the case.

Sheriff Jockton was a sturdy fellow of 53 with salt and pepper hair and a friendly face that at times wavered on the border between amiable and dim. Unlike most divorced men his age, his temperament and outlook on life weren't encumbered by a debilitating bitterness or vengeful attitude towards members of the opposite sex. Whatever their differences, he and his ex-wife at least agreed that their 26-year-old daughter, Melody, who lived in Chicago and ran her own deli, had been worth them meeting and getting hitched.

The Sheriff was in the middle of deciding whether he should check if the Medical Examiner had any news for him about the laundromat John Doe or if he should make another cup of coffee when Sam entered the station. The officer of the law settled upon the coffee and got to his feet when he saw Sam approach the front desk.

"Is it an emergency?" he asked of the visitor.

"Excuse me?" Sam replied.

"I was just about to make myself a coffee. Can it wait or is it an emergency?"

Sam, looking at him with arched eyebrows, said: "If it was an emergency, I would have dialed 911, I wouldn't have ambled into your station."

"That's great. Just wait a minute."

Jockton disappeared into the back of the station, and Sam took a seat on one of the chairs in the reception area, figuring that this Sheriff's idea of a minute was more likely to be ten.

It didn't turn out to be quite that lengthy a wait, however. Jockton returned to the front desk five minutes later with his coffee and sat down. Sam stood up and made his own return to the desk.

"Now, what can I do for you?"

"I'm a private investigator," Sam said, showing his license. "I'm here about the laundromat murder."

Jockton put his coffee down melodramatically. "How do you know it was a murder?"

"Because I saw the newspaper headline that a man was murdered in the laundromat last night."

"Oh, yeah, that's right." Jockton resumed drinking his coffee. "And what does this have to do with your good self, may I ask?"

"I think the killer has contacted me."

Jockton again put down his coffee, this time standing up after doing so. "What?!"

"I got a letter this morning asking me to come here and investigate the laundromat murder."

"How do you know it's from the killer?"

"Because," Sam said, digging into his inside jacket pocket and removing the folded letter, "the letter was sent yesterday morning. Before the murder."

Sam handed the letter over to the Sheriff, who proceeded to read it out loud. Jockton, initially affecting an overwrought aspect of professional seriousness upon reading the opening words, couldn't help beam with pride when he saw the part that said *Visit the Sheriff and ask him about the laundromat murder.* He paused before speaking those words louder than the beginning of the letter, and recited the rest in a rush to get to the end so he could hand the letter back and say to Sam: "Well, you did the right thing coming to me, Mr. Hain."

"So, you're OK with me investigating?"

"The killer, if this letter *is* by the killer, obviously knows me and sees me as a challenge to him." Sam resisted the urge to roll his eyes. "I'm guessing he's one of those perps who has a sneaking admiration for certain members of law enforcement like myself and likes to play games. By asking you to come and help me investigate, he wants to… play games." Jockton immediately regretted not having thought that through better. "I was about to go down to the morgue. You're welcome to join me."

"Thank you, I will."

Jockton finished his coffee. "Ronny!" he called out.

A moment later, a man in his late twenties emerged from a back office. Deputy Ronald Rundle, who struck Sam as having time-jumped from

1955, limped slowly to the front desk. Sam imagined Ronny was married to a cute girl called Bonnie who baked cupcakes and they had a son called Johnny who played little league.

"Yes, Sheriff?"

"You'll have to excuse my Deputy, Mr. Hain," Jockton said, looking a little embarrassed in front of his new friend and colleague. "He hurt himself last week coaching little league at his son's school." Sam smiled. The Sheriff turned to his Deputy. "Man the front desk while I go to the morgue to look at the John Doe."

"Will do, Sheriff."

Jockton retrieved his jacket and came around front to meet Sam in the reception area. "Let's hit the road."

As they began to depart, Sam turned around and took a couple of steps back towards the desk. "Deputy, just out of interest, what's your son's name?"

Ronny, surprised by the question, replied: "Jimmy."

"Classic name. Did you choose it or your wife?"

"My wife Becky chose it."

Sam smiled again. "Well, it was nice meeting you."

He rejoined Jockton at the door. *Close enough,* he thought.

Aw, what the hell. Sam felt he could call it three for three.

Friday

7:05pm

In the car ride to the county morgue, Jockton elected to provide a running commentary on the surroundings, much like a tour guide except that Sam hadn't requested it and he wouldn't be giving a tip at the journey's conclusion.

"We got pretty much all you need in a modern town, all the hi-tech stuff the youth love. But in some ways, time has stood still here. Some of the places you see around here like Eat All Day and the bakery have been around for generations. It's nice to have the old with the new. I guess you could call our version of Americana *Apple PiPad*."

The Sheriff, beaming again, glanced over at Sam for his reaction and was disappointed to see the absence of one.

"OK," Sam said flatly.

Jockton cleared his throat and switched on the car radio.

***

Laid out naked on the morgue autopsy table was the man known for the time being as John Doe. John Doe was Caucasian, six-feet-one, 145 pounds, aged about 34, and had neat, short black hair. Physically, he was in good shape; not athletic, but trim. Facially, he was handsome and blemish-free in that bland, non-descript, Ivy League kind of way. John Doe was so white-bread, Sam reckoned the guy would have bled vanilla. The only thing that spoiled this otherwise polished specimen was the single, deep stab wound in his chest.

Standing with Sam and Jockton was the 38-year-old Medical Examiner, Chuck, who had a habit of running his hand through his hair when speaking. "We didn't find anything on him. Not a speck of his killer's DNA. No fibers. Nothing. Cause of death is, as you'd expect, the fatal stab wound in his heart."

Sam took a closer look at Doe's flawless hands. "Not even any defensive wounds."

"Yeah, no defensive wounds," concurred a nodding Jockton, to which Sam had to, again, resist the urge to roll his eyes.

"He probably knew his victim and didn't have time to react," Sam continued.

"Yeah, there were no signs of struggle at the laundromat," Jockton said.

"And no one knows him?"

"Well, that's the thing, Mr. Hain… What's your first name, by the way?"

"Sam."

"Yeah, that's the – Your name is Sam?"

"Yes."

"Sam Hain? As in Samhain?"

"Oh, here we go. Look, my parents were fucking morons with a hard-on for the occult. They thought, with their surname, it would be hilarious to call me Sam. It wasn't my choice."

"OK," Jockton said, looking at Sam with a slight hint of apprehension.

"Sheriff, I'm not a bad guy because of my name. Can we please carry on?"

"Yes. So, yes, here's the thing, Sam. I don't recognize this fella. Neither does my Deputy. And we know most folks around here."

"So, he was a visitor to Millvern."

"He had no ID on him. Nothing. We've run his prints and we got nada. Ronny checked his details against missing persons. I wanted to do it, but Ronny's better at the computer stuff than me. Again, donut. This fella is a total mystery. That's just the first unanswered question."

"How the killer got in the laundromat is the second," Sam said.

"Yeah, Nancy Dirgle locked up the laundromat, went for her dinner. There was no forced entry. No broken windows. Alarm didn't go off. So, those are the two unanswered questions at the heart of this mystery," Jockton finished with a look of satisfaction.

"There's a third."

"Sorry?"

"Who killed him."

"Oh, of course," Jockton said, embarrassed.

"Unless he did it to mislead you, we at least know his first name is Mike," Chuck volunteered.

"Mike?" Sam repeated quizzically.

"Oh, yes," Jockton said. "I forgot to mention. The killer signed his name at the scene in blood."

"Yes, I can see how you'd forget a small detail like that," Sam said, resisting the urge to call Jockton a fucking pinhead.

"And no," Chuck said, "the blood wasn't the victim's. And there's no DNA match on the system."

"The killer cut himself to sign his name?" Sam asked with mild revulsion.

"I doubt it. He wrote it in huge capital letters. That amount of blood loss, he would have needed emergency treatment," the M.E. informed him.

"Please tell me you've checked all the local hospitals," Sam asked, looking at Jockton skeptically.

"Yes. Ronny has checked. Nada. So, as I was saying: yes, who is the killer who knows who I am."

"The killer knows you?" Chuck asked.

Jockton filled him in on the details of the letter Sam had received.

"But that sounds more like the killer has a special interest in you," Chuck said to Sam.

Jockton cleared his throat. "Excuse me, Chuck, but the killer specifically told Sam to come see me about the murder. He's got an interest in both of us."

"Do you know anybody called Mike?" Chuck asked Sam.

"Excuse me, Chuck, but I was just about to ask Mr. Hain that!" Jockton lied indignantly.

"I've known many Mikes over the years, but the only one I know now lives in San Francisco and works at an investment bank. I can give you his info, but I guarantee he's got nothing to do with this."

"Fine. I'll take his details later," Jockton said.

"Have you interviewed Nancy Dirgle yet?" Sam asked.

"Ronny took a statement from her. I'm going to talk to her tomorrow."

"I think we should speak to everyone who used the laundromat yesterday. And the guy who was with Dirgle when she found the body."

"Good idea. I'll set up interviews with them for tomorrow at the station."

"No, not at the station."

"This is a murder investigation!" Jockton said incredulously.

"I know, but station interviews can put people on edge and make them lawyer up just out of fear even if you tell them they're not under arrest. If we, say, use the diner for the interviews, it's just a relaxed conversation with local folks whose help we really need."

"Oh, I see. Yes. Yes, you're right."

"That's the best way to get answers from them. A bit of that old Millvern *Apple PiPad* Americana," Sam said with a smile, giving Jockton a friendly fist bump on the shoulder. The Sheriff beamed in response, as Sam had expected. Early on in his interaction with Jockton, Sam had, for a fleeting moment, considered the possibility that the Sheriff was the killer and had authored the letter as a way to garner himself attention and feed his ego. Sam dismissed that as ridiculous, and now he was absolutely certain Jockton wasn't the culprit. The guy wasn't so much an open book as he was a fully annotated volume, complete with appendices and recommended reading list.

Friday

8:30pm

Jockton gave Sam the list of visitors to the laundromat from the day before, which he managed to compile after being subjected to a stream of invective from Nancy, behavior that he had become inured to long ago and now constituted Millvern's mood music.

List in hand, Sam went looking for a place to stay. The bed & breakfast he'd parked outside was booked up, so he went searching. As soon as he saw the name of the first place he found, he knew there was no need to search any further. It was called Let Me Be Your BB. Regardless of whatever was to transpire in the coming days, Sam decided he now officially loved Millvern.

Sam was settling into his room when his phone rang. The number came up as *Some Cop,* which is how he'd saved Morton's number after their conversation that morning.

"Hello, Portland, Oregon," Sam said.

"What?" Morton replied.

"Sorry, I couldn't remember your name, Detective."

"Wallace Morton. And I'm not in Portland, as you may remember. I'm actually calling to let you know I'll be arriving in Millvern tomorrow afternoon."

"Well, Detective Morton, you have my number. Call me when you're here and we'll have a good old chat about my gruesome parents. Even though, as I told you before, I don't think I can be of much help to you."

"Sometimes even the most seemingly insignificant piece of information can be the proverbial key to unlocking a seemingly impenetrable mystery, Mr. Hain."

"Not really."

Friday

9:33pm

Sam had accepted Jockton's offer to buy him a drink at the local bar. He first grabbed a quick meal at Eat All Day, where he saw Nancy coming in for a later-than-usual dinner on account of her laundromat being a crime scene and therefore not open for business, and having spent the best part of the evening telling local reporters to get fucked. The waitress, a sweet looking girl of college age, came over to take Nancy's order. She hadn't even reached the table when Nancy virtually spat: "I'll have the fucking chicken dinner."

Entering the surprisingly named Samphire – surprising because it was the sort of name he'd expect for an upmarket New York bar and because most of the businesses in Millvern had adorably charming names – Sam made his way through the Friday night crowd of drinkers comprised of college students and nine-to-fivers to the bar, where Jockton was engaged in conversation with the barman.

"Sam!" The Sheriff greeted him like they were old buddies who'd known each other for years. Sam surmised that the combination of the murder with its attendant Delphic elements and his own arrival in town had provided Jockton with more stimulation than he was used to, hence an overfamiliar attitude that he found exasperating.

"Good evening, Sheriff."

"Call me Don!" Jockton turned to the barman. "This is Sam Hain. He's a private investigator from Frisco who's assisting me with the laundromat murder." Before the barman could greet Sam, Jockton continued: "What would you like, Sam?"

"Beer, thanks," Sam said, wanting to add *And less of the old buddy, old pal of mine shtick.*

Taking their drinks to a booth that Jockton had reserved, Sam listened politely as the veteran cop regaled him with the story of the mistaken identity murder. That being the sole homicide case in Jockton's career, Sam wasn't instilled with much confidence in the Sheriff's ability to bring any prowess to investigating the John Doe murder.

When Jockton finally asked Sam something, he wavered on how much he should disclose. He already knew he'd have to divulge everything about his parents to Morton tomorrow, so the idea of providing even an executive summary of his life now, let alone the whole story, wasn't enticing. Instead, he settled for telling Jockton he had been a private investigator for seven years helping people with personal problems, which he felt was more elegant than saying he followed cheating wives and husbands.

"So, here we are, two detectives and neither of us has much experience in solving murders!" Jockton roared with laughter. Sam was surprised by this self-aware admission.

"I'm sure we'll be fine," Sam said. A completely trite response, but it's all he felt the moment justified.

Jockton took a look at his watch. Sam resisted smiling when the Sheriff announced: "I best be going."

Jockton finished his beer and was about to stand up when a female voice said: "Sheriff!"

Sam looked up and saw a very attractive blonde woman in her thirties. For a moment, he forgot basic etiquette and stared at the intruder into their conversation, mesmerized by her looks. She wore her hair tied back and had on bright red lip gloss that was a potent counterpoint to her deep black nail polish. A black skirt, designer blue flats, white blouse, and black jacket completed her style. He snapped out of it before she or Jockton could notice. And he had barely looked at her legs.

"Miss Katz!" This time, Jockton's enthusiastic greeting was apposite, as she was someone he *had* known for a while, though the jury was out as to whether they could really be called buddies. Lengthy duration of acquaintance notwithstanding, he felt, as Sheriff, he should address her formally.

"So, am I in trouble?" she joked.

"Why would you be in trouble?" Jockton replied.

"Twelve o'clock tomorrow at Eat All Day. Ronny called me."

"Katz?" Sam said. He reached into his inside jacket pocket and retrieved the list of people they were to interview the next day. "You're Chloe Katz?"

"Sounds like I *am* in trouble!"

"Miss Katz, let me introduce to you Sam Hain. He's a private investigator from Frisco. Sam, this is Chloe Katz, a teacher at Harwood College."

"Should I be worried you have my name on a list, Sam?"

"You're one of the people we're interviewing, I mean chatting to tomorrow about the laundromat."

"Yeah, you don't need to worry, Miss Katz," Jockton assured her. "You're not a suspect."

"You said *we're* interviewing?" Chloe asked Sam.

"Sam is helping me with the investigation," Jockton explained.

"Since when do you require outside help, Sheriff? And from someone who isn't even a cop?" Sam liked the feisty edge to her, and the twinkle in her eye told him there was no condescension underlying her question.

"Well, that's confidential for now," Jockton replied. He got to his feet. "Well, night, kids!" Sam was delighted when he saw Chloe immediately slide in to take the Sheriff's place in the booth.

As Jockton departed, Sam felt a newfound appreciation for the Sheriff. Perhaps he'd been too harsh on the guy. He'd been certain that Chloe's arrival would give Jockton an excuse to hang around longer. Whether the Sheriff had left because he genuinely wanted to go home or because he did have the emotional intelligence to discern that Sam would prefer to talk to Chloe alone, Sam wasn't sure, and it didn't matter in any case. He'd left and now Sam could get to talk to this woman who fascinated him.

Even if he just came away from Millvern with a new friend rather than a girlfriend, he didn't mind. His philosophy was to go with the flow. He'd learned long ago that, by taking this attitude, it immediately lifted any sense of pressure or angst about getting a date. That mindset, in turn, fed through to his demeanor, giving him an air of relaxed, natural confidence that, ironically, was more likely to get him a date than the laser-like focus many men adopted that usually resulted in failure, something he knew from experience and could speak of with authority.

Seeing Sam's beer was almost finished, Chloe asked: "Can I get you a drink?"

"Sure. I'll just have another beer. Thanks."

She nodded and signaled to one of the bargirls, who came over and took their order.

"I don't know about you, but I hate ordering at the bar. All the waiting and the assholes who get their drinks but stay there, taking up space! That's why I like coming here. You can order from a booth," she said.

"You're speaking my language," Sam said, deciding there and then he really liked Chloe. If nothing else, this would be someone he'd love to hang out with.

"So, Sam, are you going to tell me what your connection is to the murder? Or are you going to keep it confidential like the Sheriff?"

"I'm afraid it has to stay confidential for the time being," Sam replied, hoping it didn't sound pompous.

"You're not the killer, are you?" she asked with the same twinkle.

"No. And I would tell you if I was." He immediately regretted making the joke, worried how she would take it, but he relaxed when she laughed.

"I should hope so. It's the least you could do if you were."

The bargirl brought over their beers, which they clinked in a *cheers* and drank.

"What do you teach at the college?"

"Hair and beauty. It's a community college. Don't judge."

"Why would I judge?"

"You tell people you teach at a college, they assume it's something legit like English literature or science. At a legit college."

"What you're doing *is* legit."

"Thank you. But the college isn't." She laughed again.

"Really? That bad?"

"We're not talking cream of the crop when it comes to the student body."

"I'll take your word for it."

"And you? How long have you been a private investigator?"

"Seven years." Sam hesitated as to whether he should tell Chloe the nature of his investigative work. Remembering his mantra not to overthink these situations, and given Chloe was honest about her job, he decided to just tell her. "My cases have mostly been cheating spouses and… no, just cheating spouses."

"That's a recession-proof industry."

Sam lifted his beer. "Here's to adulterous husbands and wives." They clinked their glasses. Sam could no longer deny the obvious to himself. He was very attracted to Chloe. He had that fluttering in the pit of his stomach that he only got when he was aroused. But figuring it was way too early to even think of asking her out, and reminding himself that even pondering that scenario was contravening his philosophy, he decided he would finish his drink and head back to the bed & breakfast.

"Another round?" Chloe asked.

"Yes," Sam replied immediately.

They continued drinking and chatting into the night, long after most of the students and office workers had left. With only a few other patrons left in the bar, one of the bargirls called out for last orders.

Chloe decided to order cocktails for the both of them. "You like Long Island Iced Tea, right?"

"Of course." Sam actually did, but he would have said that even if he didn't. Some stereotypically male weaknesses he still retained.

Now that the bar area was clear, Chloe got up and went to buy the drinks. Sam used the opportunity to look at her legs as she slinked across to the bar.

She returned a few minutes later and laid down the cocktails. Instead of taking her seat, she let her hair down. The motion of her blonde locks falling gracefully was the propulsive force that carried the fragrance of her shampoo across the air, hitting Sam and intensifying his arousal. She lifted her glass and went to sit down on his side of the booth. Taken aback, he moved up to give her room. Putting her arm around him, she said: "We'll have these and then go back to your hotel."

Sam froze. He wasn't sure if he'd heard correctly, and he certainly didn't want there to be any misunderstanding. "What?" is all he could muster.

Any ambiguity evaporated when Chloe placed her hand on his face, turned it towards her and gave him a long kiss.

"OK, but it's a bed & breakfast," he said.

Saturday

0:17am

Chloe put sex into three categories.

It had been a long time since she had made love to someone; the kind of sex she would have in a serious relationship.

Not as long ago was sex: the fast, meaningless encounters; the snatched moments here and there; a blowjob in a restroom; an overnight liaison.

But what Chloe had missed for the longest time was a top drawer, A1, premium grade, high caliber session of fucking. No pretense of anything less or more. Just raw, sweaty sex. Among friends, she was wont to say that she liked getting a good dicking. Tonight, at the Let Me Be Your BB bed & breakfast, it was Sam giving her the good dicking she'd longed for.

Sam, too, had gone without for a long period. Lovemaking, though undeniably exhilarating, frightened him a little because it meant commitment, a fear that he was well aware meant he typified a stereotype of men, especially those in their thirties.

What he regarded as just sex was the quick, anonymous, bump uglies-and-go on nights out clubbing or going to house parties.

But the thing he had missed most was good old fashioned, hard, relentless fucking. The make-your-whole-body-shudder-in-euphoria, lose five pounds of sweat from the exertion, scream your lungs out at climax kind of sex.

In this place, at this time, these two were made for each other.

All thoughts and mental images related to the murder forgotten, Sam had escaped into pure carnal abandon. Now on their third round, he gazed into Chloe's eyes as he held her breasts. Taking control, she rolled him over onto his back to get on top. She thrust energetically astride him. Sam shut his eyes and began to lose himself in the moment.

Then he heard a light, quiet but nonetheless discernible chuckle. His eyes shot open. Chloe's eyes were shut and she appeared to be blissfully adrift in ecstasy. She didn't look like someone who had just chuckled. Even so, Sam had to inquire. "What is it?"

Opening her eyes, she frowned in confusion without losing momentum or rhythm. "What's what?"

"I thought I just heard a laugh."

"What?"

"You didn't hear anything?"

"No. Now shut up or you'll kill the mood."

Sam closed his eyes and continued their meeting of body and mind. He tried to forget what he thought he had heard.

No. Not thought. *Had* heard.

Great. Now every time he would recall this night, the first thing that would come to mind would be a phantom chuckler.

Don't be absurd, he thought. He knew very well that the first thing he'd think of is Chloe and their spectacular night of sex.

And then the chuckle.

Saturday

10am

Before arriving at Eat All Day, Sam stopped off at the laundromat to look at the killer's signature. He'd made a bet with himself the evening before that either Jockton or his Deputy had already washed it off. It came as a pleasant surprise when Jockton told him he could view it in the morning.

Sam arrived and saw Deputy Ronny waiting to let him in. As Ronny limped over to greet him, Sam thought it was pretty shitty of Jockton to make his injured Deputy do something he could have easily done himself. Not wishing to take up any more of Ronny's Saturday morning, Sam offered to lock up and return the keys to Jockton. A very grateful Ronny thanked him, though it did occur to Sam that, as a general rule, a police officer shouldn't be so trustworthy of someone he'd known for less than a day.

Wishing Ronny a pleasant afternoon watching his son play little league, Sam went in to see the bloody autograph above the dryer where Mr. Doe's body had been discovered. He took a photo of the scene on his phone and then headed across the square to Eat All Day, where Jockton was waiting for him.

The owner had kindly agreed to close his diner for half the day so that Jockton could talk to persons of interest, though his kindness didn't extend to acceding to the Sheriff's request for free food and drinks to put the suspects – persons assisting the investigation – at ease.

"Morning, Sam!" Jockton said with the same overfamiliarity that had irked Sam the night before. This time, though, the Sheriff's inappropriately simpatico effusiveness had taken on a quality of quaint goofiness, a pronounced shift in Sam's conception that was, he was well aware, due entirely to Jockton's timely departure after Chloe's arrival.

"Good morning, Sheriff."

"I told you to call me Don!"

"Morning, Don." Sam took a seat at the table adjacent to Jockton's. "Who's up first?"

Nancy Dirgle

It's difficult to pinpoint the precise moment in Nancy Dirgle's life that turned her into the colorfully offensive person she was now. True, she had never been a bundle of joy to begin with, but she also had never always existed in a perpetual state of volcanic hostility, a state that, once fully attained, she steadfastly refused to adjust according to circumstances; such subtle social maneuvers that most people are habituated to held no appeal for Nancy. Whether it was a party or a dinner or a court hearing or a funeral, her interactions with others was uniform in venom and loathing, all of it derived from her ingrained presumption that everyone she encountered was to be immediately despised regardless of whether that individual could prove otherwise.

But before she had reached that state, Dallas-born Nancy Hales, as she was then at the age of 24 in 1963, met a man. For Garland Dirgle, the assassination of President Kennedy wouldn't be the only tragedy in Dallas that year.

Nancy met Garland when she worked in a secretarial pool for a law firm. He was the senior partner's son and would often drop by the offices to flirt with the secretaries, mainly because he was unemployed and had nothing else to do. Nancy watched with contempt as Garland devoted attention to a particular secretary on a given day and, when his interest wasn't reciprocated, moved on to another the next day. His efforts always met with polite refusal; polite because he was, after all, the son of one of their bosses, and refusal not just because an unemployed fellow with the charisma of a pencil didn't scream eligible bachelor to the secretaries, but because he was very, very unattractive.

Despite his own shortcomings, Garland had immediately ruled Nancy out for being too plain. That changed once he'd exhausted flirting with all the other girls in the pool. When he finally made the decision to engage her in conversation, he was shocked when she too responded with icy disinterest. He honestly thought she'd be grateful for any attention.

Nancy mentioned their encounter to her parents during dinner that evening. They were aghast at their daughter's refusal to even consider Garland as a suitor.

"You're not going to do better than him," her father said.

Nancy looked at her mother, hoping for support.

"Your father's right. Garland is an ugly, idle dolt with no prospects. You won't find anyone better."

"And don't forget," her father continued, "his dad has money. You won't want for anything."

And so, Garland's luck changed for the worst when she agreed to go on a date with him. Soon after, they married and began a life of domestic misery. They argued relentlessly and had sex rarely, which Garland thought was supposed to be the other way around in a marriage, and when he said as much, a friend told him he'd obviously never spoken to any married people.

When Nancy told Garland she was pregnant, he spent the next five days crying. His father had to talk him down from the roof of the law firm, which was redundant, given it was a low one-story building.

Everything changed when Mary Dirgle was born. In some volatile marriages, the birth of a child can sometimes be the inciting pivot to achieving harmony, the new parents mutually bound by their responsibilities. And Nancy and Garland did feel optimistic for the first time upon the arrival of their baby. Nancy felt optimistic because now she could divorce him and get alimony payments. Garland was optimistic because now he could divorce her and get his father to make the alimony payments.

And that is exactly what they did. Nancy took custody of Mary, and Garland announced to his family that he was going to take a year or two off from dating, to which his father responded: "Like you have a choice."

Nancy was also sworn off relationships. Instead, she focused on raising her daughter and making a living. She took a job at another firm's secretarial pool even though Garland's father offered her a raise to stay on.

"But I divorced your son," she told him. "Why would you want me to continue working for you?"

"Because you being here makes it awkward for Garland and he won't want to come to the office every day. Please, Nancy. I'm begging you."

But Nancy wanted a fresh start. And so did Mary by the time she was five. Nancy was delighted that Mary hadn't taken after her father. She wasn't so happy that she had taken after her. Mary was a forthright, determined, and independently minded girl who gave as good as she got, but without her mother's coldness or then-burgeoning animus towards everyone. Nancy didn't like clashing with anyone, much less her own kid. On one such occasion, Mary complained that her mother didn't read bedtime stories to her like other kids' parents. When Nancy said she's not that kind of mom, Mary asked: "Could you find me someone who is?"

Nancy did make one half-hearted attempt to soften her attitude to her daughter, but found herself cringing painfully when struggling to say "I love you, sweetheart."

When Mary turned seven, Nancy dropped her off at Garland's family home and said he could have full custody, before jumping into a cab and disappearing from their lives forever.

Garland's father came downstairs to find the little girl standing in the cavernous entrance hall with a battered suitcase by her side and his son sitting on the floor in tears. He put his hands on her shoulders in a warm, reassuring manner and said in a soothing tone: "Mary, I know you might feel scared, but you don't need to worry one little bit. And I know you don't remember much of your father. But you don't need to worry about him one little bit either. Because I have lots of money and I'm going to hire a nanny and maid to raise you."

Nancy settled in Millvern, where she got a job at the laundromat. She formed something approximating a friendship with the owner, Judith, which, for Nancy, meant saying hello in the morning and goodnight at the end of the day without adding *asshole* and *motherfucker* respectively.

Judith started the laundromat with her late husband. As she advanced in years, she began to rely on Nancy more in running the business. Their partnership lasted until Judith died. Nancy was shocked when she was told Judith had bequeathed the laundromat to her in her will. As committing acts of kindness were alien and distasteful to Nancy, it never occurred to her someone else might do such a thing.

Now 40, Nancy had her own business. After considering selling it, she came to the realization that she might actually enjoy being in charge of running things and having the authority to tell people to go fuck themselves whenever she wanted. And she had done just that for the last forty-five years.

Saturday

10:06am

Before Jockton could respond to Sam's question, the door flew open and Nancy came into the diner like a tornado, only less pleasant.

"Let's get this shit out of the way right quick!" she said, taking a seat three tables back from her interviewers. "Now what the fuck do you want to know?"

"Good morning, Ms. Dirgle," Jockton began. "This is Sam–"

"I don't give a good goddamn who the fuck this petal is. I ain't got all day." Sam covered his mouth as though he was ruminating thoughtfully when, in fact, he was trying to conceal his laughter. "Get on with it!"

Jockton confirmed with Nancy what was already known, that she had closed the laundromat at six and come here for her dinner, returning a little after eight to find a young man waiting, who later identified himself to Deputy Ronny as Drew Langer, and she found the corpse inside one of the dryers.

Now, the Sheriff moved on to the pressing details that he hadn't ascertained. "You didn't recognize the victim?"

"No."

Sam was taken aback by her reply. She'd managed to answer a question without saying *fuck*.

"And you'd never seen him come into the laundromat before?"

"No."

Again, Sam was startled.

"And never seen him around town?"

"No."

Sam was beginning to get spooked.

"Now, Ms. Dirgle, did anything out of the ordinary happen on Thursday leading up to the murder? Anyone causing trouble or arguing?"

"If anyone gives me shit, I throw them out on their fucking ass."

And she was back.

"I know you do, but I was asking if anyone did."

"No, they didn't."

"Ms. Dirgle," Sam spoke up. He knew there was no point in what he was about to ask, but he wanted to amuse himself.

"What, petal?" she replied with a vicious smirk.

"Do you have CCTV?"

"Sissy TV? Is that what you said, petal? Yes, I got one of those fancy, hi-tech, modern movie camera gadgets that all you petals own."

"So that's a no."

Nancy looked irked by Sam's swift reply. She was used to people indulging her sarcastic remarks for longer than that.

"The thing is," Jockton resumed, "we just can't figure out how the killer got in. There was no sign of a break-in, the windows are intact, and the alarm didn't go off."

"Why are you telling me, Sheriff? Figuring out that shit is *your* fucking job."

"Has anyone threatened you recently, Ms. Dirgle?" Sam asked, looking forward to her reply.

"Petal, do I look dead to you?"

"I'm sorry?" he said, genuinely confused.

"Did the killer kill me or that guy lying in the fucking morgue?"

Sam, annoyed with himself that he didn't catch on to her meaning immediately, shot back: "Yes, but this could have been a warning to you of some kind. The fact he killed his victim in your laundromat for no apparent reason except, perhaps, as a message to you."

"Then the killer is a bit of a bitch, ain't he, petal? He wants to murder me but he just kills some guy I don't even know to scare me? What kind of sissy move is that? You tell me, petal. I figure you'd know. Do you know? Huh, petal?"

Sam, sufficiently entertained by Nancy, decided to end his line of questioning with "I don't, but thank you for your help, Ms. Dirgle."

"OK, petal." She turned to Jockton. "Can I fucking go now?"

"Just a couple more questions."

"Then get a move on, goddammit!"

"Do you know anybody called Mike?"

"No. Next."

"We'll be talking to Mr. Langer and the other people who visited your laundromat on Thursday. How well do you know them?"

"That sissy boy come round a few times. That young girl with the floozy make-up only started coming last week. Some brat I ain't never seen before came by in the morning. And Kenneth. I like him 'cause he don't try to talk to me. I'm sick of people who try to chit chat with me. Chit-chat. Yeah. Shit-chat more like."

Sam looked through his list. "By young girl you mean Chloe?"

"I didn't ask for her fucking passport and birth certificate, petal."

"Yes," Jockton said, turning to look at Sam, "she means Miss Katz."

"How long has she lived in Millvern?" Sam asked him.

"About five years or so."

"And she's only just started using the laundromat?"

"I'd love to hear you two petals talk about the floozy, but I'm gonna go now if it's all the fucking same to you."

"Thank you, Ms. Dirgle," Jockton said with the polite smile he'd learned to deploy whenever dealing with her.

She stood up. Sam couldn't resist releasing one last bait. "It was very nice to meet you, Ms. Dirgle."

"Oh, that's just so fucking sweet of you, petal."

Holding back his laughter, Sam waited until she was outside before erupting.

"Yeah, that's our Nancy," Jockton said.

"I still wouldn't rule her out as the killer," Sam said.

Drew Langer

Drew Langer couldn't understand why more people weren't misanthropic. Unlike Nancy Dirgle, London-born Drew didn't express his misanthropy openly or indiscriminately. While she hated people irrespective of personal experience, Drew still maintained civility and the belief that there were still some individuals, however few in number, whose lives were not spent in service of providing the grounds for his or anyone else's misanthropy. It's just that it never surprised him when someone turned out to be a shit.

His disdain for society was informed by years of experience interacting with the odious, and it had led him to the epiphanic realization that the animal kingdom was infinitely superior to the human one. That's why he would react so viscerally to dolts casually describing violent criminals as behaving like animals. That kind of unthinking descriptor for the perpetrators of awful crimes wasn't just an egregious slight against animals, it was also indicative, he believed, of an intellect that relied upon stock cliches instead of active thought. Animals behave according to evolutionary instinct in order to survive, not with malice or sadism. People, the ones supposedly with higher brain function, behave despicably, carrying out acts of violence for pleasure or financial gain or from some pathological and ideological drive, whether misogynist or religious in nature, often both, since misogyny and religiosity had been fuck buddies throughout history. For Drew, it would be a compliment to be likened to an animal. Behaving like humans, on the other hand, was an insult.

His most recent experience that had further entrenched his philosophy was in his last job back home in the UK, where he was a proofreader and had to contend with a colleague called Sarah Thornflood, whom he'd later come to privately nickname Sarah Shitblood.

From the beginning, there were little titbits in conversation with Sarah that he found obnoxious, but nonetheless amusing. Like referring to herself as blessed. Who the fuck does that? Or when she mentioned she didn't like ever being told that she'd done something wrong. It was this remark that Drew would later remember when her behavior towards him turned antagonistic and bitchy.

These titbits weren't limited only to her delusions of grandeur. There were occasional revelations about her past that he found odd. Like going straight from living at home until 26 to buying a house with her partner. She had never gone out into the world to get life experience living with others or alone. He had done that and everyone he knew had as well.

When it came to Sarah and society, she let her views be known freely. He couldn't stomach the conceited, pachydermatous, Thatcherite brand of condescension she oozed so revoltingly; the worldview that the poor somehow deserve to be poor, completely ignorant of the fact that many people, including her, are, at any point, potentially one or two paychecks, one or two shock mortgage rate rises, or one or two disabling illnesses away from complete destitution through no fault of their own.

It didn't stop there. On one occasion, she said overweight people shouldn't expect to get treatment for free on the National Health Service when it's their fault for being fat. He thought this was a tad uncharitable, and supremely hypocritical, given how sickeningly pally she was with their very overweight older colleague, Sue, who worked from home.

To her list of odious personality traits, he was also able to add sycophant, or, rather, hypocritical sycophant towards their boss, Miriam.

Drew often noticed that, when he made a comment to Miriam, Sarah would immediately parrot it.

Except when politics was being discussed. Miriam made no secret of her loathing for conservatives and Conservatives. There was always radio silence from the usually chatty Shitblood when this topic came up. When Sarah's behavior later on exposed her as a vile little nark, Drew regretted not casually letting Miriam know that the toadying phony was a true-blue Thatcherite who stood for everything Miriam despised. It was the equivalent of having a nuclear weapon in his back pocket and, to this day, he regretted not using it, especially given that Shitblood regarded David Cameron as the greatest prime minister in her lifetime, a man who was alleged to have stuck his member in the mouth of a dead pig as part of a ritual among his fellow entitled posh twats at Oxford.

The marked change in her attitude towards him began with a generally cold atmosphere in the office, and then escalated to her saying "Can you not type so loudly, it's really annoying." Drew, not having an ego delineated by delusions, had no problem in apologizing, but she couldn't leave it at that. "It's not like you'll send it out any quicker, you still have to finish it." He would later regret not telling her to shut the fuck up.

Mystified by her obnoxious attitude, Drew tried to think back on what he might have inadvertently said or done that could have elicited this shitty behavior. He surmised one possibility. Checking his email history and then cross-referencing the company's intranet database of past documents, his suspicions were confirmed. Some months back, doing admin duties and collating monthly management information for clients, he had stumbled upon a note littered with grammatical and spelling errors. He flagged this to Miriam in an email, and she agreed it didn't look good. He hadn't checked who was assigned the proofreader on that document, as it was neither here nor there. But what neither Drew or Miriam were aware of at the time was that the MI reporting system only saved the raw transcripts and not the corrected, proof-read versions that were sent to clients. So, there was nothing to actually worry about. When he did the cross-reference, his theory turned out to be correct. Sarah had been the proofreader. Miriam must have innocently relayed Drew's flagging of the note to her, and Shitblood, having made it abundantly clear that even the slightest criticism was anathema to her, obviously thought this was an intentionally malicious act on his part.

Her behavior continued to deteriorate, most of it passive-aggressive. And then came the incident that, to this day, he wished he'd told Miriam about.

Miriam was working from home, and Drew, Sarah, and another colleague, Rita, were in the office. A grammatical issue came up regarding a document. Sarah, communicating with Miriam via online chat, was questioning the issue. When Miriam responded definitively, Sarah, with her standard issue smirk and dripping the arrogance that had long become her trademark, laughed and shook her head, as though Miriam was a child. Drew felt offended on Miriam's behalf. Here was this talentless brat in her twenties behaving like she knew better than their boss, who had been doing the job for years.

The turning point that confirmed for Drew beyond all doubt that Sarah was a nasty piece of work was when Miriam mentioned to him that she was aware he had once said, in a moment of frustration, that he sometimes gets criticized for things that others in the company get away with. It had been a silly thing to say and he apologized, but thinking back on when he made the remark, he remembered it was only him and Sarah in the office.

The fucking lickspittle nark.

He thought it utterly egregious of Shitblood that she was now an infantile, high school level snitch. And it was this moment that Drew, all this time later, still regretted not responding to in kind by informing Miriam about Sarah's overweening attitude on the grammatical issue and about her slimily Thatcherite ideology.

After this, Drew began to regard with more contempt those aspects of Sarah's character that he had previously only found weird. He knew that this was perhaps petty, but he was also cognizant of the basic fact that people, when wronged, will derive schadenfreude from the flaws and failings of the person responsible for the injustice.

He noticed that every time he passed Sarah during her lunch break, she was on the phone to her partner.

On more than one occasion in the online chat, she mentioned to her BFF Sue that she was staying at her parents' house that evening because her partner was away.

And many times she recounted a previous evening's visit to the theatre with her parents.

Now, all the pieces finally fell into place – living at home until 26, calling her partner every lunch break even though she would be home with him that evening, going to her parents when he was away, and frequently going to the theatre with her mother and father. Drew realized that this objectionable dullard suffered from an extreme form of dependence, to the extent that she couldn't even venture out of the parental home into the world to live alone or with other people as part of life experience, couldn't go a few hours without needing to speak to her partner, couldn't bear to be by herself for even one night and needed the cocoon provided by mom and dad, and relied on her parents for a chunk of her social life.

He was also certain, inferring from remarks she'd made, that her partner was the only relationship she'd ever had, which, in itself, was hilariously sad. Bad enough she'd never lived outside of her parental bubble, but to settle down with the first and only guy she'd met was really pathetic. Drew felt a bit sorry for him; that he had chosen this stinky, onion sandwich eating right winger to be his life partner.

In turn, it occurred to Drew that these flaws explained other facets of Sarah's behavior in the workplace. From the beginning, she had been an oversharer in the office. Everything from ordering a new pillow for her partner to detailing her mortgage application. Drew now saw that this oversharing was Sarah's way of overcompensating for her shortcomings that she must have been painfully aware of. This was made very apparent in how her every pronouncement in the online conversation was characterized by a peculiar bombast, as though she was the first adult in history to be doing things like getting a mortgage. It was as if she wanted validation for doing grown-up activities that left her giddy in the belief it somehow ameliorated those shortcomings from her past.

After further clashes, he knew remaining at the company wasn't a viable option. The situation was beyond repair and he wasn't prepared to continue working in a toxic atmosphere with a cretin.

Now in the US on a three-month visitors' visa, he occasionally looked back on his time at the company and on Sarah. Sarah the smug fuckwit with delusions of grandeur. Sarah the Thatcherite hypocrite who had the audacity to brag one morning that she had given money to a beggar when she had already let slip her contempt for those who weren't as *blessed* as her.

Sarah, the needy, oversharing, arrogantly sneering, greasy nark.

Saturday

11:08am

Drew came into Eat All Day holding a cup of coffee he'd bought on his way over, having guessed correctly that the diner wouldn't be serving anything while the interviews were taking place.

"Good morning, Sheriff," he said, taking a seat opposite Jockton. He looked over at Sam quizzically.

"This is Sam Hain, he's a private investigator I've enlisted to assist with this case. Please don't ask why, the reasons for that are confidential," Jockton said, causing Sam to finally roll his eyes.

Drew took a sip of his coffee and put down the cup. "Don't you normally do these things at the station?"

"Well, you're not under suspicion of anything, Mr. Langer."

"I'm glad to hear that, but I assumed you do all interviews like this at a station."

"If you really want that, I'm sure we could arrange it," Sam said.

Drew assessed Sam for a second and, perceiving the hint of joviality in his tone, took the remark with good humor. "Let's do that for the next murder." Sam rocked in his chair with laughter, but Jockton didn't look amused. "That was a joke, Sheriff."

"This is a serious situation, son. Law enforcement doesn't have the patience for jokes about a case like this."

Drew regretted trying to cut wise with the Sheriff and wondered if he'd made trouble for himself. Luckily, Sam was on hand to help.

"Relax, Don. It's just his British sense of humor."

Jockton relaxed. "Oh, I was trying to place your accent."

"I'm from London," Drew said, equally relaxed now. "Have you ever been?"

"I've been to London, Ontario," Jockton replied.

Sam smiled to himself, while Drew was unsure quite how to respond to that non sequitur. "Oh… Well… They're very different places."

"Are you on vacation here?" Jockton asked.

"Sort of. I'm on a three-month visitors' visa. I'm in California for about a month and then I'm headed to the East Coast."

"In that case, may I welcome you to the United States. I hope you have a wonderful time here. You'll find we Americans are good, kindhearted folks."

Drew glanced at Sam as though to say *Is this guy for real?* Sam couldn't meet his glance, as he was looking down and pretending to rub his face with the palm of his hand to conceal his laughter.

"Thank you, Sheriff."

Picking up his pen, Jockton began the interview. "Where are you staying?"

"I've got a room at Let Me Be Your BB."

Sam's eyebrows arched. If anything suspicious was to emerge about Drew, it would at least be easy to keep track of him.

"You've got a room for the whole month at a bed & breakfast?" Jockton asked.

"The owner let me have it at a discount in return for helping her with some chores."

"And is that where you came from when you arrived at the laundromat?" Sam asked.

"No, I'd gone to see a film at the Cinemount with my friend Inessa."

"We'll need Inessa's details," Jockton said.

"Sure."

"How long have you known this lady?" Jockton continued.

"About a week. We got talking in a bookstore."

"She lives in Millvern?"

"Yes."

"And what movie did you see?"

"*The Maltese Falcon.*"

"Oh, great flick. What time did it start and finish?"

"We got there around five thirty. The ads started at five fifty and I think the film started at six."

"Only ten minutes of ads?" Jockton asked with surprise and a little hint of suspicion.

"It's a repertory cinema. They only show trailers."

"Oh. I don't visit those. I figure if I'm gonna fork out twenty bucks for a movie ticket, it should be for something new."

"The tickets were seven dollars each."

"You don't say! Well, hell, I may start going there. Do you know if they ever show old Burt Reynolds movies like *Smokey & The Bandit* or *Cannonball Run?*"

"I don't know, Sheriff, I've only been here for two weeks. But I think they usually only show classics."

Sam, getting weary and in need of a refuel before the next interview, decided to hurry things along. "When did you get out of the movie?" he asked.

"At about seven forty. Inessa went to meet a friend for dinner and I headed back to the launderette to put my clothes in the dryer. Which, obviously, I never got to do."

"*Launderette?*" Jockton repeated.

"Sorry, laundromat. We call them launderettes in Britain."

"And when did you arrive at the laundromat?" Jockton asked.

"Just after eight. I told your Deputy it was locked and I had to wait for that annoying old hag to turn up."

"You mean Nancy Dirgle?" Jockton asked with a faint smile.

"Is there more than one annoying old hag who runs the launderette? Literally all I said was 'finally' when she turned up and she mouthed off at me. I wasn't going to put up with that, so I basically told her to get knotted."

"Get knotted?" Jockton looked confused.

"Oh, that's right, you don't say that over here. It's a British expression."

"Meaning?"

"What do you think it means, Sheriff? Given the context?"

"I'm not familiar with Britishisms, that's why I'm asking."

"What I actually said was 'How about you just open the fucking door?' So, I didn't actually literally tell her to get knotted, but it's basically what I meant." Jockton hesitated before writing that down. "Next time, I'll be more direct and just tell her to fuck off."

"Next time?" Suspicion returned to the Sheriff's tone.

"The next time she mouths off at me, Sheriff."

"Oh, gotcha."

Sam looked at his watch and felt the rumble in his stomach. "So, you went in and you heard the noise coming from one of the dryers," he said.

"Yes. The hag – Nancy – opened it and the body fell out. I went outside to call the police. I waited till your Deputy arrived. He took my statement and my contact details. I wanted to get my clothes to go to another launderette – laundromat – to have them dried, but he said it was now a crime scene and he couldn't let anyone in. So, I just went to get some food and went back to my room at the B&B."

Jockton rifled through his papers and retrieved a photo of the John Doe. He held it up for Drew to see. "Do you recognize him?"

"No."

"You've never seen him before?"

"In the two weeks I've been here, I've never seen that man before, no."

"Do you know anyone here called Mike?" Sam asked.

Drew shook his head.

"OK," Jockton said, "I think that about covers it, Mr. Langer."

"Do you know if I can collect my clothes? I know they'll be damp and stink by now, so I'll need to take them somewhere else to get washed again."

"I'm sure my Deputy can sort that out for you."

"Thanks." Drew got up. "It was nice meeting you both. Good luck with your investigation."

"Thanks," Sam said.

Jockton nodded. As Drew turned to go, the Sheriff said: "One thing I always liked about the UK…"

"Yes?"

"Mrs. Thatcher. Gosh, what a great lady. Don't you agree?"

"Well… I agree that that's how you feel about her."

Chloe Katz

"What do you think about the Middle East?"

Chloe Katz was taken aback by the question. She had been cornered by a group of students in the hallway of Rees College as she was heading towards the exit after finishing for the day.

"Sorry?" she asked in genuine bewilderment as she faced five hostile looking students, three male, two female, each staring at her with palpable venom.

"What do you think about it?" the male student repeated.

"I'm not sure what you mean. Why are you asking me?"

"Why do you support violence?" one of the girls asked.

"Excuse me?!"

"Isn't your name Katz?" the girl asked.

"Yes."

"Exactly."

The penny dropped. "Wait. Are you asking me because I'm Jewish? You think that makes me answerable?"

"We just want to know what you're doing to help," said another male student.

"Why are you asking me?"

"You're not answering the question," the second girl said.

"You're asking me all this because I'm a Jew?"

"Still not answering."

Chloe, growing uncomfortable at the way she was surrounded by this group, tried to maintain a calm composure, as well as show defiance. "So I understand: would you go up to a random Iranian and ask them the same thing?"

"We knew it! You're a fucking racist!" barked the student who'd first interrogated her.

"Are you innately obtuse? You're being racist towards me! Why am I answerable for what goes on in the Middle East?"

"Because you're a fucking Jew," said the third guy, turning red from his slip of the tongue.

"He didn't mean that," the first male student chipped in.

"I heard what he said," Chloe said.

Just then, a fellow member of staff came into the hallway and the group stepped back from Chloe.

"We'll see you around, *Katz*," the second girl snarled, putting an emphasis on Chloe's surname while smirking, and they walked off.

Chloe had heard from Jewish friends about this kind of thing happening, even in supposedly civilized settings like dinner parties, where self-satisfied antisemites who passed themselves off as ostensibly progressive would hold forth on issues that inevitably concluded in them asking a Jewish guest where they stood on the Middle East – not as a sincere question borne organically from conversation but as a challenge to that person to prove his or her worth as a human being – or querying why it should be so controversial to question if the Holocaust happened (concurrently dismissing, and with not a little intimation of sadistic disingenuity, that all claims of antisemitism and hate crimes against Jews are made up for political ends), a view that put them in the company of the far right, their commonality only differentiated by the so-called progressive's capacity to use language to code their antisemitism, in contrast to the far right's willingness to be overtly racist, quite apart from their limited ability to couch their hatred in calculated verbiage even if they wanted to.

There were further incidents like this one for Chloe. And as much as she didn't want to give her tormentors the satisfaction of having won, she pondered if there was any point in remaining there. When she heard that the students who harassed her held a protest on Holocaust Remembrance Day at which their chief organizer said the Nazis couldn't have been antisemitic because they held a rally at Nuremberg and "there's nothing more Jewish than a berg," she concluded there wasn't. That experience tempered any moments of frustration she may have had at Harwood College, which, for all its flaws, wasn't nearly as bad as Rees and its contingent of bullies.

As if being stalked by racists hadn't been bad enough, that period in her life was also tainted by a series of bad dating experiences. Not for nothing had Chloe given men a wide berth prior to her meeting Sam. No matter how many ill-fated or stillborn relationships she had, she never failed to be astounded by some of the things that would come out of men's mouths.

There was the guy who at first appeared to be potential long-term dating material. They'd been on five dates and slept together on the third. He was chatty, friendly, and good looking, all fine attributes and all obliterated on their sixth date during dinner when he said that now they had a good thing going, he'd expect to see her four times a week.

"Excuse me?"

"For this to work, I want to see you at least four times a week."

"Are you kidding?"

He didn't break into a smile. He wasn't kidding. "I thought you were serious about us."

"Four times a week?"

"At least."

She wanted to say something more profound, but all she could say was "Are you kidding?"

"No, I'm not kidding."

Again, words escaped her and she just repeated: "Four times a week?"

Now it was his turn to repeat himself. "At least."

Chloe burst out laughing. He remained stony faced. "No, you have got to be kidding."

"Stop saying I'm kidding."

"I don't know what kind of relationships you've had, but I do not see anyone that often."

"Why not, if you love them?"

"Love?!" Now Chloe was getting scared.

"Of course."

"This is only our sixth date!"

"Yes. And it's time to get serious."

She looked around the restaurant to see where the ladies' restroom was located in relation to the exit and their table in case she needed to escape without being seen.

"I'm sorry, but I don't think this is going to work."

"So that's it? You're not going to give love a chance?"

"I guess it's my loss."

The next morning, Chloe received an email from her beloved with a full itemized list of everything he'd spent on their dates and demanding a full refund, saying "I don't like having my time wasted by women like you." She blocked him online and threatened to go to the police when he tried to call her at work.

Her night with Sam had come as an enormous relief. Mainly because she hadn't had sex in a while, but also because she felt they were definitely on the same page. Neither wanted anything more than sex, and he didn't give off any vibes of being needy or gross. She'd approached it as a one-night stand, but had such a good time that, walking home early in the morning, having been careful not to wake him up, she decided she was willing to extend it to another night.

Or however many nights he was going to be in town.

Saturday

12:02pm

After the interview with Drew, Sam and Jockton took a short break to refresh themselves. Since the diner owner wasn't around and had refused to provide any ready-to-eat nibbles, Sam sprinted across the road to get a sandwich and a drink from a local store. The Sheriff wasn't hungry; he only needed to use the restroom.

Sam was finishing his soda when Jockton emerged from the restroom. "You ever had one of those dumps where you feel like you've just lost half your body weight?" he asked Sam.

Sam, glad he'd finished eating, replied: "I'm not sure. But what I *am* sure of is that I don't say out loud every single thought that crosses my mind."

"That sounds a good principle," the Sheriff replied, Sam's point doing a departing 747's trajectory as usual. Sam began to question whether he'd been wrong to reconsider his initial impression of Jockton. But just then, the door opened and Chloe came in and Sam remembered why he'd felt some appreciation towards the Sheriff.

"Afternoon, Sheriff!" she said.

"Good afternoon, Miss Katz."

"And afternoon, Mr. Hain."

"Miss Katz," Sam said with formal detachment. He and Chloe exchanged knowing smiles. As she took her seat, he remembered the joke by Robin Williams about how men have a brain and a penis but only enough blood to run one at a time and he realized he wouldn't be of much use during this interview, and so would just let Jockton do all the talking.

"Thank you for coming," Jockton said. Sam made an adolescent-level joke in his head and smiled.

"I'm happy to help, Sheriff."

"This won't take very long. You told my Deputy that you used the laundromat on Thursday afternoon. That right?"

"Yes."

"Nancy Dirgle mentioned you started using the laundromat last week."

"Yes, my washing machine has broken down. I'm still deciding whether to get it repaired or just buy a new one. In the meantime, I'm using the laundromat."

Sam now felt guilty that he'd regarded with suspicion Chloe's sudden recent usage of the laundromat after living in town for so long. He wished he could sometimes switch off the private investigator side of his brain, though thanks to his current state, neither side was functioning. He was at least relieved that Jockton had broached the subject without mentioning him.

"Oh, good, that explains it. Sam was wondering why you'd used it."

Son of a bitch.

Chloe looked at Sam with a surprised smile. "Really?"

Sam looked for the twinkle that usually accompanied her feisty remarks and was relieved to find it. "Just crossing all the t's and dotting all the i's," he said, reaching for the most boring, generalized, bland response he could think of.

"OK," Chloe said, biting her lower lip, which only made Sam's arousal even more profound, to the point that his erection was now verging on the painful, though not quite in the category of priapism.

"Did you see anything weird while you were at the laundromat? Anyone arguing with Nancy or anyone else?" Jockton asked.

"No. It was very quiet. Well, except for Nancy. That is one angry woman. Boy, does she like to swear."

"Yes, she does," Jockton said. "So you didn't see anyone else?"

"Only some old guy who was coming in as I was leaving. He gave me a funny look. I don't know what that was about."

"Moving on to the evening, can you tell us where you were from six to eight?"

"Yes, I was getting my hair and nails done at the Ms. Me salon."

Sam smiled. *Ms. Me. I love this town.*

"For two hours?" Jockton asked.

"Are you married, Sheriff?"

"I used to be."

"And you're surprised?"

"I never really asked my wife how long she spent at hair salons."

"I was actually there till about eight thirty. The lady who owns the salon likes to finish every day with a glass or four of wine and she asked me if I wanted some."

"Thanks. I'm sure she'll verify all that no problem."

He then asked if she recognized the photo of John Doe and if she knew anyone called Mike and she replied no to both.

"Well, I think that's it. Thank you, Miss Katz."

"That's it?" She looked at Sam. "Don't you have any questions for me, Mr. Hain?"

Sam cleared his throat and sat forward. "No, I think the Sheriff has covered everything."

"OK, Mr. Hain," Chloe said with a smile, her red lip gloss once again working its magic on Sam.

After she departed the diner, Sam received a text from her: *Your place tonight, 9pm? I'll bring some refreshments.* Sam felt immense relief that she had made the move, as he'd been reluctant to suggest another night in case it put her off and killed the memory of the night before. He replied: *Sure. I'll bring some drinks too.*

Chloe smiled upon reading his text. Sam naively assumed Chloe meant some alcohol, perhaps even champagne. He was partly right. What she actually had in mind was something that would fulfil a long-held fantasy of his.

Kenneth White

Kenneth White held some unconventional views pertaining to the world, like believing that Earth is 6,000 years old, dinosaur fossils are a hoax, and evolution is a lie. That is to say, he was very stupid.

It will be of no surprise, therefore, that 65-year-old White was an evangelical creationist, although his rotund, red-cheeked visage indicated that he viewed the decree against gluttony as purely discretionary.

His religiosity wasn't all that defined White. If the frightening cult that had developed around the forty-fifth and forty-seventh occupant of 1600 Pennsylvania Avenue had membership tiers, he'd be a fully paid-up member of all of them, including the *For Kids* subscription, complete with *My First Insurrection* coloring-in book and a *Jews Will Not Replace Us* badge.

As a concomitant of his deranged worldview, White viewed science as evil. He enjoyed telling anyone who would listen that evolution should be spelled *evilution*. He beamed with pride over his joke, though, ironically, the word pride triggered him greatly.

Despite his self-proclaimed commitment to a belief in science as evil, it did cause problems for him on a practical level. He refused to own a washing machine or to visit doctors, the former because his purchase would contribute to the wealth of those responsible for creating what he called "satanic technology," the latter because he regarded any trust in medical science as a betrayal of one's faith and that all anyone needed to do when sick was to pray.

His late wife shared his unshakeable faith, even when she started vomiting and suffering diarrhea on a daily basis, and their daughter, who didn't share her parents' religiosity, begged her mother to go to the hospital. Mrs. White told her daughter that the hospital was staffed by devil worshipping Democrats who would inject her with a vaccine in order to download tracking technology into her body. She also wanted to tell her daughter who else in Millvern was satanic, but before she could do that, she threw up one more time and died. It was later confirmed that Mrs. White had died of a gastric infection that could have been easily treated within days of her contracting it.

There were certain limits to White's anti-science stance. He owned a TV and a computer, which he described as the creations of godless liberals and Jews respectively, but he justified it to himself and his friends on the grounds that he needed them in order to watch the man to whom he'd sworn eternal loyalty and to communicate with fellow travelers.

He rationalized visiting the laundromat on the basis that he hadn't paid for the godless machines, and he would pray at home over his clothes to cleanse them from having been washed in what he called "the devil's drum." One of his friends, who could be classed as several tiers below White in cult membership status, asked why he didn't just handwash his clothes himself if he was so opposed to washing machines. White lacked a satisfactory explanation, burdened as he was by an awareness of his hypocrisy; a hot, needling awareness that, had he been honest with his friend, he just couldn't be bothered to handwash his clothes, and he would certainly never admit that washing machines were convenient. He'd had to make a choice of which satanic technology to own, and being able to see the man whom he and his friends believed was sent by god to save America was a non-negotiable priority. Visiting the laundromat was his way of untangling the cognitive knot that had resulted from his mental gymnastics.

Kenneth White was indeed a special kind of cretin.

Saturday

12:44pm

Sam looked down at the flyer.

ALL ARE WELCOME IN THE KINGDOM OF JESUS

EXCEPT *HOMOSEXUALS*

WICKED SINGLE WOMEN

ATHEISTS

JEWS

AND DEMONCRATS

BECAUSE GOD IS LOVE

Sam folded the flyer that White had placed in front of him and carefully dropped it on the floor behind his chair. Ordinarily he would have a few choice words for the author of that kind of material, but he had to remind himself he was there to do a job.

Jockton folded the one he'd been given, but just smiled and put it in his pocket.

White, dressed in green corduroys and a blue polo shirt, now took his seat after fulfilling what he felt was his duty.

"Thank you, Mr. White, but you don't need to give me that every time you see me," the Sheriff said.

"The truth needs repeating," White replied.

"Thanks for coming by. This won't take very long. This is Sam Hain, he's a private investigator–"

"Sam *what?!*" White interrupted.

"Sam Hain."

White looked at Sam for a moment and then bolted out of his seat, pointed at him, and thundered: "DEMON! DEMON! DEMON!"

"Oh, not this shit again," Sam said.

White continued to yell. "He's the killer! He's the killer! He's the killer!"

Sam looked at Jockton with a world-weary expression that was an entreaty to explain to the evangelical moron about his name.

"Relax, Mr. White. You can trust Mr. Hain."

"He's turned you too!"

"He hasn't turned anyone! Calm down and sit down. Please."

White, now trembling from rage, gripped the back of his chair. Sam wondered if he should prepare to duck in case White used the chair as a weapon.

"Mr. White, would you just sit down please!" Jockton demanded.

"Do you have your firearm?" White asked.

"Yes, of course I do. Why?"

"I'll sit down if you bring out your gun and have it ready in case he tries anything."

Sam rolled his eyes. He'd already known from the flyer that White was a hateful simpleton, but he didn't expect this.

"OK," the Sheriff said. He took out his gun and looked at Sam in embarrassment. Sam cut Jockton slack and nodded to indicate he understood it was only to placate a very thick person. Jockton placed the gun on the table. "OK?" he asked.

"Take off the safety."

For the first time, Sam saw a glimmer of mature anger in Jockton's demeanor. "Mr. White, I've got my weapon out like you asked, but do not give me orders or tell me how to do my goddamn job. Now sit down!"

Sam smiled in gratitude. Jockton may have, on occasion, been goofy as fuck, but he'd come to Sam's defense more than adequately.

White gave Sam another dirty look and then resumed his seat.

"As I was trying to tell you," the Sheriff continued, "Mr. Hain is a good man. His name is just… it's just a coincidence it sounds that way. That's all."

Don't mention where I've come from.

"He's a private investigator who's come from San Francisco to help with the investigation."

Motherfucker.

White shot Sam another lethal look. "San Francisco. Of course. The satanic city. The devil's depot."

Jockton, now getting weary too, said: "What?"

"A place of faggots, dykes, and the godless."

"That was originally going to be the city's motto before they settled on *Gold in Peace, Iron in War*," Sam said. White looked confused. Sam realized the fanatic had taken what he'd said literally.

"Mr. White, I don't like or tolerate language like that. Please refrain or I will arrest you for hate speech and breach of the peace," Jockton said firmly. Sam felt relief that Jockton didn't share White's bigotry. He'd been fifty-fifty on whether the Sheriff's charming goofiness beclouded any prejudices.

"So he *has* turned you. I knew it!"

"Last warning, Mr. White." This time, the Sheriff's tone appeared to silence White. For the moment, anyway. "OK, let's get this over with. You told Ronny you came into the laundromat on Thursday afternoon. That right?"

"With the grace of god, I entered the laundromat on Thursday afternoon, and with great reluctance, I made use of the devil's drum."

"The what?" Sam asked.

White ignored him.

"The what?" Jockton asked.

"I do not believe in owning satanic technology. But as I need to stay clean for the lord, I compromise by having my clothes washed here and then I bless them at home to cleanse them of evil."

Sam was speechless. He couldn't even bring himself to make a sarcastic comment. He was simply shocked by the elaborate idiocy of the man sitting a few tables away.

"But Mr. White, I know you own a TV and a computer."

"That's okay, because the lord wants me to see speeches by the real winner of the 2020 election."

Sam sighed. He should have expected that.

"Did you see anything strange while you were in the laundromat?" the Sheriff asked.

"I arrived, using my legs powered by the lord, just as that Jewess was leaving."

Sam sat up straight. "Excuse me?" White again ignored him. Raising his voice, Sam said: "What did you say?"

White smiled as he continued to ignore him.

"Mr. White, Mr. Hain is assisting with the investigation. You have to answer his questions too."

White slowly turned his head to look at Sam. Still grinning, he repeated: "The Jewess."

Sam considered him for a moment and then asked: "Did you get your brown shirts cleaned?"

"I don't own brown shirts," White responded, looking confused.

"OK, Mr. White, for the remainder of the interview, could you just stick to answering the questions?" Jockton demanded.

White turned his gaze back to the Sheriff. "I washed my clothes and took them home to pray over them and let god's air dry them in the garden."

"And you didn't see anyone arguing with Nancy or with anyone else?"

"It was only Nancy and I. I wanted to spread the gospel about Demoncrats and…" – he looked at Sam – "You know *who*."

Sam pictured landing a punch on White's face and blood streaming from his broken nose. It provided him with some momentary catharsis.

"But I know that she doesn't like to talk to anyone, so I just handed her a flyer as I always do and she threw it away as she always does. She'll learn one day."

Jockton showed him the photo of John Doe. "Have you ever seen this man before?"

"I do not know this man. But he died because the lord willed it."

Sam began to wonder if White would answer like this if asked about his bowel movements. Would he say: *The lord enabled me to relax my sphincter and expel the feces from my body that he created?*

"Where were you between six and eight in the evening?" Jockton asked.

"The lord, in his eternal wisdom, guided me to a wholesome restaurant where my sister and me praised the heavenly father before eating a wholesome American meal of steak and potatoes. None of that liberal vegan garbage," White said, looking at Sam, who, by this point, wasn't showing any reaction to his barbs.

"Last question," Jockton said with immense relief. "Do you know anyone called Mike?"

"The only Michael who matters is the Archangel Michael."

"That's great, but we're asking about a Mike who may be involved with this murder."

"It's very possible that the lord sent the Archangel Michael to kill this man for being a sinner."

"OK, for the last time, Mr. White, can you please just answer my question. It's just this one question and then you can go. Do you personally know anybody called Mike?"

"I know Mike Spran. He lives among good god-fearing folk in Fayette County, Alabama. Folk who like things how they used to be and will be again. Good, clean folk who love their god, their guns, and their true President."

"OK," Jockton said, finishing his handwritten notes and feeling a euphoric rush that this ordeal was finally over. "Thank you. That's all."

White stood up slowly and eyed Sam again. "The lord will deal with you, demon."

"Does this mean we won't be friends?" Sam asked.

Again, White looked very confused. "You want to be my friend?"

Rob Laurenson

"If you think you're going to wear that t-shirt in this house, you've got another thing coming, young man!"

Fifteen-year-old Rob Laurenson looked at his mother, Iris, nonplussed by what he perceived to be a completely disproportionate reaction. Dressed head to toe in black – shirt, denims, sneakers, and, of course, the t-shirt itself, whose death metal image of a skull engulfed in flames provided the only contrast to the black – and having dyed his spiky dark brown hair jet black, he looked the kind of teenager conservative parents feared would become school shooters, though their concern never went as far as wanting to actually prevent such teenagers easily getting hold of weapons to become school shooters.

At just over six feet, with blue eyes that focused on the recipients of her gaze like a laser, immaculately coifed blonde hair that was tied back with almost scientific precision in a bun, thin pink glossed lips, and starkly white face powder, Iris Laurenson was at once an attractive and austere 50-year-old who tended to dominate all those around her, including her husband, Todd, and most of her children except Rob. She didn't literally think he was a potential spree killer; she just didn't like the aesthetics of his appearance, which she felt spoiled the otherwise sparklingly polished American heartland family archetype she and the rest of her family represented.

"It's just a t-shirt."

"It's a t-shirt of a grinning skull on fire with flames and all sorts of horror over it."

"And?"

"What do you mean *and?!* And you're not wearing it in this house. It's disgusting!"

Rob shrugged his shoulders and went to turn around to leave the very expensively Italian-furnished living room of the six-bedroom mansion he lived in.

"Don't turn your back on me, Rob!"

"Aren't you overreacting a bit, Mom? It's just a t-shirt."

"You can wear that when you're with your friends–"

"I do."

"But you're not wearing it when your father and I are around."

"So you're cool with me wearing it anywhere else?"

"Yes."

"But not around you and Dad."

"Correct."

"Why? Does it hurt your eyes?"

"Excuse me? Are you trying to cut wise with me?"

"No, I'm just asking what the big deal is."

"The big deal, young man, is that you're living in your parents' home and you abide by our rules."

"Fine!"

"Don't take that tone with me."

"I said fine. What's wrong with saying fine?"

"And one more thing."

"Yeah?"

"If you're going to keep that t-shirt, you're going to have to take responsibility for it."

"Well, yeah, obviously. It's my t-shirt."

"Don't cut wise. I mean it's your t-shirt, you can go to the laundromat in town to get it washed."

"Are you fucking serious?"

Iris had long got used to her son's tendency to swear. The first time he did, she did a very convincing imitation of a thermonuclear weapon going off, but her opposition to his choice of language was gradually worn down by sheer force of attrition and, in the end, she just had to accept it. "Yes, I'm *fucking* serious. It's your choice. You can either get rid of it or you can keep it but take responsibility for getting it cleaned somewhere else."

"That's some serious bullshit, Mom."

"You want to be a grown-up, you better learn to act like a grown-up."

"OK. Does that mean I can invite Lucy over to spend the night in my room and do grown-up things to each other?"

Iris targeted her son with her laser focused gaze. "Quit while you're ahead, Rob."

Saturday

2pm

White's early arrival for his interview meant Sam and Jockton had a long break before their final interview, scheduled for two in the afternoon. Sam wanted to avoid making boring conversation with the Sheriff, so he went for a walk to get fresh air and buy a bottle of wine for his evening with Chloe.

Walking back to Eat All Day, he thought the case over and how none of the people they'd interviewed was a suspect. Even Nancy, despite her sociopathic tendencies, wasn't a viable suspect, as she had a solid alibi for the time the murder took place, and, pending checks to verify their accounts of their whereabouts, so did Drew, Chloe, and White. After the way his interview had started, Sam had hoped White wouldn't have an alibi, but by the end it didn't matter, as he could tell that the creationist lacked the faculties to plan and execute shoplifting a candy bar, much less a perfect murder.

Getting out the list Jockton had given him, he looked at the last name at the bottom. He hoped this Rob Laurenson was the killer and they could get this all wrapped up quickly.

Sam resumed his seat in the diner at 1:59pm. At precisely 2pm, the doors opened and in walked Rob, wearing his black shirt buttoned up, accompanied by Iris and two men, both dressed in finely tailored grey suits, one with a blandly handsome countenance not dissimilar to John Doe save for a more lived-in look, and the other a little older, with slick-back hair and wearing an ostentatiously gold watch.

Lawyer, Sam guessed with confidence about the older man.

The arrivals took their seats across from Jockton, who was momentarily lost for words.

"Good afternoon. I wasn't expecting so many people," Jockton said.

"We weren't going to have you talk to Rob without us and our lawyer present," Iris replied.

"Did you need to bring your son?" Sam asked.

The others all turned to look at him.

"Rob *is* their son," the Sheriff explained.

You could have fucking told me that earlier.

"Oh. Sorry," Sam said.

Turning back to the Laurenson coterie, Jockton continued: "Rob isn't under suspicion. We just want to ask him a few questions."

"We always have Mr. Jonathans with us for anything involving the police," Iris said, making Jockton shudder from her lasers.

Jonathans took out his mobile phone and began recording.

"Are you filming?" Jockton asked.

"We're not idiots," Iris said. "We know to protect ourselves."

"There's really no need, Mrs. Laurenson."

"Keep going," Iris directed her lawyer.

Having let Jockton take the lead on the interviews with Chloe and White, Sam decided he'd steer their last interview, not least to get it over with quickly. "The owner of the laundromat said you came in around ten in the morning," Sam asked Rob.

Jockton shuffled in his seat, irked that Sam had started the questioning and before he could formally introduce him.

"Who are you?" Iris asked with more suspicion than the situation warranted.

"This is Mr. Hain. He's a private investigator who's assisting me with this investigation."

Sam was relieved that Jockton omitted his first name and, thereby, avoided the potential risk of another outburst from superstitious dimwits.

"Yeah, I did," Rob answered.

"Why?" Sam asked, perplexed.

"Why what?" Iris fired at Sam.

Sam could tell this interview was going to be particularly excruciating. "I'm going to assume your family own a washing machine."

"Three of them," Todd volunteered.

"So why did you use the laundromat?" Sam asked the teen.

Rob looked at his mother, who fired up her lasers. "Tell him," she ordered. He slid his chair back and began unbuttoning his shirt. "What are you doing?" she inquired, her eyes wide in trepidation. The others also looked on in bewilderment. Rob undid the last button and held his shirt open to reveal his skull t-shirt underneath.

"I don't believe it!" Iris squealed.

"What, we're not at home," Rob protested.

"I'm sorry," Sam said, "I don't understand."

"We won't let him wear that disgusting t-shirt around the house and we won't let him wash it there either. He wants to be all grown-up and take a stand, he needs to take responsibility and get it washed in his own time at the laundromat."

Sam let out the biggest sigh he'd made up to that point during his visit to Millvern. He really had had his fill of the people here and their weird notions and irrationalities.

"Excuse me?" Iris said, offended. "What's that supposed to mean?"

Sam sought to quickly restore the situation: "I'm sorry. We've been interviewing people all day and I'm just tired."

"He's right to make that noise," Rob said. "It's fucking stupid that you make me use the laundromat."

"You see how he talks? It's all this death metal stuff he's into, with the black clothes and the gory t-shirts."

"A lot of teenagers do that," Sam said.

"Thank you!" Rob said.

"Are you a parent, Mr. Hain?" Iris asked.

"No."

"Then I'll thank you to keep your opinions to yourself. I'm his mother and I think it's disgusting."

"I'm just saying a lot of teenagers are into metal. And even more who aren't swear."

"Swear?! Swear?! That's not the half of it!" Looking at her son, she said: "Tell them the disgusting lyrics you listen to." Rob shrugged. "I caught some of the lyrics on his phone during breakfast. Get out your phone."

Now it was Rob's turn to sigh as he retrieved his phone. "It's just a song."

"It's not a song, it's noise. He listens to a band called *Cuntfuckery*. Can you believe that?! I'm sickened to even say the name."

Sam smiled, while Jockton just looked on, pissed off that his interview was being derailed. "This really isn't necessary," the Sheriff said. "We'll take your word for it they're disgusting."

"No, he wants to be all grown-up, he should be willing to say out loud the sick, obscene things he likes to listen to."

"Got it," Rob said, finding the track in his phone's music library.

"Go on. Tell them. Read out what I caught you listening to. It's foul. You should be ashamed."

Rob looked at his parents and then down at his phone. *"I ate his intestines for dinner/ The meal was three-course/ I ran out of condiments/ I used my own blood as the sauce."*

Sam rocked with laughter.

"You think this is funny?!" Iris asked, aghast at his reaction.

"They're just lyrics, ma'am. Just a form of creative expression."

"Thank you!" Rob said again in gratitude at Sam's support.

"That's not the kind of music I want my son to be listening to."

"What do you want me to listen to, redneck country shit?" Rob hit back.

"You'll have to leave all this music and black clothes behind when you go to Harvard or Yale. You'll be representing your family then. And when you eventually run for Congress."

"I don't wanna go to Harvard and Yale and I'm not gonna run for Congress. I'm gonna start my own band and tour the world. I'm gonna fuck at least one woman on every continent, just like Lemmy."

Sam smiled again. He liked this kid.

"You hear how he talks to his own mother?" she said, shaking her head.

"What Lemmy really said was he had 'carnal knowledge' of women on every continent," Rob added.

"Well, at least say that then," Iris said.

"I'm 15. The fuck would I say *carnal knowledge?*"

"If we may get back to the interview," Jockton said. "Now, Rob, did you see anything strange while you were at the laundromat? Or anyone having an argument with the owner?"

"The only strange thing I saw *was* the owner."

"Shush! Don't talk about her like that," his mother said.

"What, that bitch could start an argument with a wall. I didn't even say anything to her and she yelled at me."

"Did anyone else come in while you were there?" Sam asked.

"No. But I was listening to music on my headphones, so maybe someone did and I didn't notice."

"OK," the Sheriff said. "Now, where were you between six and eight in the evening?"

Before Rob could answer, Iris put a hand on his shoulder and leaned over to whisper to the lawyer, who whispered something back.

"OK, you can answer," she told Rob.

"I was at a party."

"What?!" his mother thundered. "You said you were going to hang out at Chad's house."

"I did. He was having a party at his house."

"You didn't mention anything about a party."

"Chad didn't mention it either. I turned up, thinking we were gonna sit down and watch C-SPAN so I can start learning for when I run for Congress, and all these kids from school were there. He lied to me, Mom."

"Cutting wise again," she said, shaking her head.

"How many people were there?" Sam asked.

"I don't know, man. I don't go to a party and count how many people are there. The fuck."

"Yes, I agree, that's a stupid question," Iris told Sam.

"Mrs. Laurenson, I'm asking so we can verify what he's said."

"So he *is* a suspect! I knew it!"

"No, he's not a suspect. It's just standard procedure," the Sheriff tried to reassure her.

"More than ten, less than a hundred, I guess," Rob offered.

"Fewer," Iris corrected her son.

"The fuck?" Rob said quizzically.

"When you're talking about numbers, you say fewer, not less."

"And that's really important right now, is it, Mom? The fuck."

Shaking her head again at his language, Iris told Sam: "Chad's parents have CCTV in their home, so I'm sure you'll see my son is telling the truth."

"They do?" Rob said, perturbed. "Do they have it in the basement too?"

"I don't know. Why do you ask?" Iris inquired, furrowing her brows.

"No reason," he said quietly, looking away.

Concluding the interview, Jockton showed Rob the photo of John Doe and asked him if he knew anyone called Mike. Rob didn't recognize the victim, but said he knew two guys at school called Mike and they were both at the house party.

Sitting back in his chair, Sam sighed again, this time less intensely and this time because he was relieved that the interviews were done. "We're finished. Thank you."

Jockton, annoyed that Sam had stolen his big finish, nonetheless said: "That concludes this interview. Thank you for your cooperation."

"OK," Iris said, turning to their lawyer, "You can stop recording now."

"I'll email you the MP4 later," Jonathans said.

Iris and Todd stood up, followed by Jonathans and Rob.

"Hey man, want me to Bluetooth you that song you liked?" Rob asked Sam.

"That's enough out of you!" Iris told her son.

"No, just tell me the title, I'll look it up," Sam said.

"The band is *Cuntfuckery* and the song is *Cannibal Cuisine Part II: The Vanquishing of Your Guts.*"

Saturday

3:36pm

Sam drove back to Let Me Your BB after agreeing with Jockton that they'd resume the investigations on Monday morning. He parked and was about to get out when his phone rang. It was *Some Cop* calling again.

"Hello, Detective Morton," Sam answered.

"Hello, Mr. Hain. I'm calling just like you asked."

"You're in Millvern?"

"Yes. Would you like to meet somewhere for a chat? I just passed a diner called Eat All Day. How about we meet there?"

"I've just spent several hours there and that's the last place I want to go."

"Another diner perhaps?"

"No, I could do with fresh air. There's a green space in the middle of the town square. I'll see you there in fifteen. Bring me a Diet Pepsi."

"What?"

"I'm thirsty and I'm giving you my time. See you in fifteen."

***

Morton was waiting on one of the benches in the town square's small space that constituted greenery when Sam strolled up. He was surprised to see the cop holding two bottles of Diet Pepsi. That made way for a second surprise:

Morton's suit. Sam had met many cops and none of them had worn luxury tailoring.

"You actually got me the drink."

"You asked. And I thought I'd be friendly," Morton replied.

They shook hands and Sam sat down, taking the bottle that Morton held out for him.

"Don't you worry about getting blood on that?" Sam asked, nodding at Morton's suit.

"Blood?"

"Is it Armani?"

"Yes, it is. And no, I don't."

"I bet your fellow officers love you dressing like that around them."

"I don't care much what other people think about me, Mr. Hain."

Sam nodded, having a drink. He sat back against the bench, reveling in the relaxation of meeting in the open, a meeting he was certain would be swift and inconsequential. "Like I said on the phone, I don't think I can be of much help to you, but ask me whatever you like."

"You told me on the phone you haven't seen your parents in eighteen years, yes?"

"That's right."

"And I think you said you're 35."

"Yes."

"So you last saw them when you were 17?"

"Yes, I think you'll find the arithmetic works there, Detective."

"Only 17?"

"Yes, Detective, only 17. I remember because it was me."

"What happened? Did they have you move in with another family member?" Morton knew some of what had happened, but he wanted to see if Sam would be honest and if the information he'd been given was correct.

Sam bellowed with laughter, which Morton was a touch offended by, though didn't let on. "Why is that amusing?"

"No, it's just the idea that it was their choice we part ways."

"Can you tell me what happened?"

Sam provided the cop with a brief account of his childhood and his parents' sociopathic natures up until the night he ran away, all of which matched what Morton had been told by his tipster.

"Why did you run away?" The one detail Morton lacked was the specific circumstances, and only because the tipster didn't know either.

"They wanted to make me the star of their first home video."

"And?"

"It was going to be called *Snuff: The Movie*."

"Fuck."

"They were gonna use a cheap handycam too, so calling it a movie was way off base."

"And you've never seen them since?"

"No, Detective. Now can you tell me what this is all about?"

"For the last six months, I've been investigating serial murders in Portland. You may have heard about it on the news."

"I don't watch much news. I find it depressing."

"Right. Anyway, your parents are the serial killers."

Sam didn't say anything for a few seconds, absorbing what Morton had just told him. He then sat forward and looked at the cop. "You think my mother and father are serial killers?"

"I do, yes."

"And you've been investigating for six months?"

"Yes."

Sam bellowed again, almost spilling his drink.

"You just told me they wanted to kill you. That they're obsessed with the occult. Why do you find it so hard to believe they're serial killers?" Morton asked, getting increasingly irritated by Sam's outbursts of laughter.

"Yeah, they're pieces of shit, but serial killers? Detective, my parents have never had the self-discipline to maintain regular personal hygiene, let alone a killing spree and evade capture. They're not criminal geniuses."

"I know they're not. They signed their names in full at almost every murder scene."

"Yeah, that sounds like my parents," Sam sighed, leaning back against the bench.

"There was no pattern to the victims. They've been men and women of different ages, social class, and locations within Portland. And there were zero forensics at every murder save the last one. The only thing that connected them, the only reason we even know they're serial murders and not isolated crimes, is the signature of Leo and Polly Hain in blood at almost every scene."

"Almost?"

"Yes, well, you see, there were two murder cases beforehand that had zero forensics but were treated as separate cases. There were no names left at those scenes. It was only with the first murder where your parents wrote their names that a cross-reference with similar recent killings flagged up those two murders and we realized your parents had been behind all of them."

Sam shook his head. "So, my mother and father finally settled upon a career."

"We made their names public, asking for anyone who has information to come forward. That's why I was surprised you didn't know about this already."

"Like I told you, I don't watch the news. Did you get anything?"

"No. You're the only link we have to them."

Sam sat forward again in advance of departing in a few seconds. "I'm sorry I can't be of any help to you, Detective. I wish you luck in finding them. All I ask is, when you do, don't mention me. Better yet, just shoot them. Save everyone a lot of time."

"Well, that's the thing, Mr. Hain. Your parents have disappeared."

Sam resisted the urge to laugh again. "You mean you just haven't found them. That's not the same thing as disappearing."

"No, Mr. Hain. The last murder was over a month ago. I tracked down where they were staying and they weren't there. They've never gone more than four weeks without claiming a new victim or victims. They've either been abducted or murdered. I think the latter because of what I found in their cabin."

"Oh?" Sam said, his interest piqued.

Morton got his mobile phone out, pressed a few buttons, and held the phone up for Sam.

A visceral tingle coursed through the landscape of Sam's stomach when he saw the photo of the bloody signature in the cabin bedroom.

"This is all I've got to go on. And whoever this Mike is hasn't struck again either."

Sam looked up from the phone at Morton. "Until now."

Saturday

4:31pm

Morton looked at the name above the dryer, and then looked at his phone. He nodded slowly. "Yeah. It's the same guy."

Sam had forgotten to return the keys to Jockton, so took it upon himself to let Morton view the crime scene. He called Jockton en route to the laundromat to inform him of Morton and their visit. A very put out Jockton, pissed off that Sam had both forgotten to hand him back the keys and gone right ahead without seeking his permission, huffed that he'd join them shortly.

"Looks it," Sam agreed.

"Whoever killed or kidnapped your parents killed your John Doe. And knows who you are to have sent that letter. Unless…"

"Unless what?"

"What if your parents aren't missing and they're really *Mike* and it's them who murdered John Doe and sent you the letter to lure you here?"

Sam looked at Morton to ascertain if his initial impression that he's not a moron had been wide of the mark. He concluded it hadn't been and, in turn, knew laughing would, on this occasion, be unwarranted. "There are three things wrong with your theory, Detective. One: a plan that convoluted would require thought that my parents are incapable of. Two: if they knew where I live, they'd have just tried to kill me there. And three: – the smoking gun of why it's not them – the letter is typed and contains coherent, intelligible sentences."

The door opened and Jockton came in. He walked right up to Morton to shake his hand. "Afternoon, Detective. I'm Sheriff Don Jockton."

Shaking Jockton's hand, Morton replied: "Detective Wallace Morton, Portland PD, Homicide. That's Portland, Oregon."

"Always nice to meet a fellow officer of the law, Wallace," Jockton said.

Sam cringed at Jockton's default overfamiliarity, which he could see didn't sit well with Morton at all.

"OK, Sheriff."

"Call me Don!"

"No, I'd rather call you Sheriff."

Jockton's chirpy smile, which he always believed to be disarming, faded. Feeling rather wounded by this cop's bluntness, he decided to discard the pleasantries and be more formal. "Has Sam filled you in?" he asked entirely unnecessarily. His query was purely to let Morton know that he and Sam were practically buddies.

"Yes, Mr. Hain has been very helpful. We agree that we're both searching for the same man."

"All three of us," Jockton corrected him.

"What?"

"You said *both*. All three of us are searching for the same man."

Morton folded his arms as he looked at Jockton and asked: "Are you a fucking idiot, Sheriff?"

Sam smiled, wishing he had Morton's courage to be so direct.

"Hey! That is uncalled for! I am a fellow officer of the law and should be shown due respect!"

"You were not present, Sheriff, so why would I say all three of us?"

A now red-faced Jockton just shook his head. "Still uncalled for."

Feeling a little sorry for the Sheriff, Sam decided to move the conversation on. "Well, now it will only be the both of you. Because this is where my investigation ends."

"What?" Jockton spluttered, dismayed at the prospect of his new buddy leaving town.

"What are you talking about?" Morton asked.

"I came here because I got an anonymous letter asking me to investigate and giving me some money to do it. Now that I know this Mike has either abducted or killed my parents, I have no interest in pursuing the John Doe murder further. I want nothing to do with a case that's connected to my parents."

"Hold on, Sam," Jockton said. Before he could continue, Morton interrupted.

"Wait a second, Mr. Hain. There has to be a reason the killer wrote to you."

"Yeah and I don't care what it is. For all I know he's holding my parents captive and thinks that I would give a shit. Well, he's wrong about that. Or – *or* – he killed them, in which case he's done both you and me a favor."

"But he knows where you live. Doesn't that worry you?" Morton asked.

"No. If he wanted me dead, he'd have just killed me already. Why send me on a case about some random guy I don't know? In fact, no one knows. He's virtually a ghost."

"You haven't ID'd the John Doe?"

Jockton saw this as his opportunity to show his formal professionalism and jumped at it. "His fingerprints aren't on the system. No one around here knew him. No one's been reported missing. He doesn't match any missing persons in a hundred-mile radius. And he had no ID on him. It's like he just appeared out of nowhere."

"*Out of nowhere.* Thanks for that, Sheriff," Morton said sarcastically. He may have found Jockton's remark a pointless cliché, but he couldn't have known just how close to the truth the Sheriff was.

Turning back to Sam, Morton continued: "There must be a reason the killer wants you to investigate. Don't you want to know why? If nothing else, you can find out for certain if your parents are dead."

As Sam considered his next move, a thought occurred to Jockton. "Detective, if Mike murdered in Portland and now here, doesn't that make this a federal case?"

"A federal case? Did you hear that on some TV show?"

"It's across state lines," Jockton persisted.

"At this point, we don't know if Leo and Polly Hain are in fact dead. I don't want to get the FBI involved just yet. So, cool your jets, Sheriff."

Jockton, newly offended by the cop's attitude, looked to his buddy Sam with hope. "Come on, Sam. The killer wrote to you. He told you to come find *me.*" The Sheriff placed emphasis on the last part for Morton's benefit. "And we've got a victim who's a complete mystery. Don't tell me you don't want to find out what's going on."

Sam remembered he'd be meeting Chloe that evening. Continuing with the case would enable him to see more of her while he was in town.

It was settled.

"OK."

"Great decision, Sam!" Jockton beamed.

"Good," Morton said unemotionally. "I'd like to see John Doe's body now."

Jockton resented the prospect of escorting Morton to the morgue.

"Will that be possible, Sheriff?" Morton asked.

"I'm sure my Deputy can help you with that."

Poor Ronny, Sam thought.

The door flew open and in stormed Nancy. "How much fucking longer, Sheriff, goddammit!"

"Tomorrow, Ms. Dirgle. You can reopen tomorrow," Jockton said.

"About goddamn time! I'm losing business here because of you and your goddamn murder!"

Morton folded his arms as he observed the angry woman in astonishment.

"Detective, this is Nancy Dirgle, the owner of the laundromat," Jockton said. The Sheriff knew there was no point in saying the next part, but he'd started, so he might as well finish. "Ms. Dirgle, this is–"

"I don't give a good goddamn who the fuck this petal is!"

"Petal?" Morton repeated, bewildered.

"Was I talking to you?!" she barked.

Morton took a step forward and flashed his badge. "Detective Wallace Morton, Portland PD, Homicide!" he said in a loud, firm, and definitively authoritative voice that rattled Nancy.

"I don't give a good goddamn where you're from, petal!"

"And I don't give a shit what you think! I'm here on a case and you will conduct yourself properly or I will arrest you for breach of the peace!"

Nancy was stunned. First that sissy boy talked back to her outside the laundromat, now this petal from out of state was talking back to her. She missed the good old days when she made everyone around her quake in fear.

Bruised by Morton's warning, Nancy turned around and headed out of the laundromat. She slammed the door shut as her way of regaining some dignity.

"Yeah. That's our Nancy," Jockton said.

"Are you sure she's not the killer?" Morton asked.

Saturday

5:04pm

Sam accompanied Morton back to his car after the Detective told him there was something he wanted to show him.

As Morton unlocked the trunk, he looked up at Sam and asked: "Is that Sheriff for real?"

"Yes, he's for real."

Morton shook his head and opened the trunk door. He delved inside and lifted out the heavy book he'd found in the cabin. He handed it over to Sam. "I found this in their bedroom."

Sam looked at the weathered cover of the mammoth volume. He saw the title and laughed, shaking his head. "Assholes to the very end," he said. "But why are you giving me this?"

"I thought you might find something in there that could help the case. You know them best."

"Yeah, but I don't know about any of this shit. I mean, you don't believe this stuff, do you?"

"No. But it doesn't matter what I or you believe. The fact is your parents do or did. And there might be something in there that will tell us where they've ended up."

Sam flicked through the pages randomly. "How old is this?" he wondered out loud.

"It's on the second page."

Sam flicked back to the start of the book. "Wow. Holy shit that is old."

"Just take a look when you can. Anything that sticks out, let me know."

"OK. But I really doubt this is gonna help us." Sam bounced the weighty book in his hands, pondering its provenance. "A book this old, and on this subject. They wouldn't have come by this in a regular bookshop. I wonder who they had to kill to get their hands on this."

SIX MONTHS BEFORE

The Red Hex

In the neighborhood of Centennial, Portland, OR, The Red Hex was the sleazy dive bar that other sleazy dive bars aspired to be. If there was a genealogy for piss-stained, low-down, greasy, grimy shitholes to grab a drink or an STD, The Red Hex was the progenitor. It was the place that the most rank, low-rent, putrid, pukey, seedy, trailer trash bars looked up to as their hero. They trembled in awe of its skanky aura.

It will be of no surprise, therefore, that it had become Leo and Polly Hain's favorite hangout since moving to Portland. Aged 61 and 63 respectively, the Hains were the antithesis of a sight for sore eyes. Both looked much older than their years, partly from excessive meth use, partly from bad genes, and partly from being living proof of the aphorism that, as awful people age, their awfulness shows in their faces. When Leo smiled, far from making his visage more palatable or himself appear friendly, it made him look like the traditional renderings of Jack the Ripper as a smirking psychopath, minus the elegant top hat, suit, and doctor's case.

Their clothes were equally wretched: unwashed, heavily stained, and frayed. Leo's beer belly spilled out at the bottom of his ketchup-stained brown sweater, and he had on dark gray slacks that were once green. Unlike her husband, Polly was skinny and gaunt. Her faded purple t-shirt, flecked with dark spots that might have been food or dry blood, hung on her frame like she was a rotting clotheshorse, and she wore ripped jeans that were ripped through misadventure as opposed to intentionally for fashion purposes.

Leo had given up long ago trying to comb over his receding hairline or dyeing the grays out and accepted his thinning black hair on his oily pate.

Polly still had all her dark brown hair, which she had given up long ago trying to maintain in any sort of style and settled upon short, uneven layers and an equally uneven and formless back, on account of Polly cutting her own hair, giving her an appropriately frantic and unbalanced look.

On this evening, the pair were drinking with a guy they'd recently befriended, Eddie Wynchover. At 29, Eddie, with his hollowed-out features and almost vampiric pallor, was borderline anorexic from prolonged heroin use. But though he didn't share Leo and Polly's fondness for crystal meth, he did their obsession with the occult. Not that Eddie was aware of this. The Hains had been very careful not to let slip their hobby when they struck up a conversation with Eddie in The Red Hex a few nights before like a couple randomly chatting to a fellow barfly and not people who already knew all about him.

Leo looked around the establishment that he and his wife had frequented over the last three weeks and which they were now visiting for the last time.

A trail of vomit led from the men's restroom to the middle of the bar. A biker type, all tattoos and piercings, lay unconscious on the floor in one corner, blood streaming from a still fresh wound on his forehead. His attacker lay next to him, dead. A 14-year-old girl and her 21-year-old boyfriend were sat on stools at one end of the bar top, smoking crack in front of the bargirl, who watched and then took the pipe from the guy for a hit.

It was midweek and therefore a quiet night.

"I'm gonna miss coming here," Leo said.

Polly nodded and kept an eye on the bar, where Eddie was buying a round. "Do you think I should roofie him here?"

"No, do it at his place."

"What if he change his mind?"

"Carlos told me this son of a bitch never says no to a fuck. If he thinks you're gonna ride his dick, he'll take us back to his place."

Eddie returned to the table with three beers and sat down next to Polly.

"Have these, then back to yours, right?" Leo asked casually.

Eddie looked at Polly with the grin of an excited kid anticipating a cheeseburger and fries and not caring that the cheeseburger was rancid and the fries covered in old grease. "Absofuckinglutely!"

Polly and Leo smiled at each other. They were one step closer to getting the book they wanted so badly.

Sugar

Leo couldn't believe his luck.

There, in the middle of Eddie's miserable hovel, lying on an old, cracked glass table, was the book. All worries about potentially spending the night searching through the decaying, one-story gloomscape evaporated.

Sitting on a chair, he looked over at Polly and Eddie, who were laid on a couch, Eddie groping Polly all over with uninhibited glee as though all his birthdays had come at once. And the way he was carrying on, he looked as though all his ejaculations now and in the future were going to come at once.

With Eddie's back to him, Leo caught Polly's eye and nodded. She nodded back to signal her understanding.

"Sugar, would you get us something to drink?" she asked Eddie. He was busy burying himself in her bosom and didn't hear. "Sugar?" she repeated, this time pinching his neck just enough to be construed as playful rather than aggressive.

Eddie looked up at her. "What, baby?"

"Would you get us something to drink, sugar?"

"In a minute."

"Now, sugar. Bring us some drinks. And then you can get some of *my* sugar."

Eddie grinned. He got off the couch and headed to the kitchen.

Leo gestured over to the table. Polly almost squealed with delight.

Eddie returned, holding three cans of beer. "It's really cool of you to be so cool with me banging your lady, Leo," he said as he handed one of the beers to him.

"We're relaxed and shit," Leo replied.

Eddie dropped himself back on the couch, handing a beer to Polly and opening the last one for himself.

"Oh, sugar, I almost forgot. You got any drugs for after?"

"Uh, yeah, I got heroin. You guys do heroin?"

"We're into meth, but heroin's good too," she said.

"Alright!" Eddie put his beer on the armrest and got up. He headed to his bedroom.

As soon as he was out of sight, Polly got the roofie out of her pocket and dropped it into Eddie's beer. She and Leo shared a smile.

This time it was Leo's turn to pay a compliment when Eddie returned holding heroin paraphernalia. "It's cool of you to share your shit with us and shit."

"That's alright, dude. You letting me bang your lady, it's the least I can do."

Eddie plunked down on the couch again, taking his beer and putting the heroin kit in its place on the armrest.

"Here's to a night of good fucking," Polly said, holding up her beer.

Eddie did the same and all three drank their beers.

"Now," Eddie said, "I want some of that sugar your promised me."

Polly lay back and opened her legs wide. Eddie ran his hands up her jeans as he buried his face in her bosom again.

Leo watched in anticipation.

"You are so damn sexy hot, Polly," Eddie said, now rubbing her between her legs. "Are you wet down there?"

"Mmmm, yeah, sugar. You got me soaked," she lied.

"I can't wait to get that cooch. I want that…" His voice trailed off.

Leo sat forward with urgency.

"I want that, that…" Eddie's words now sounded slurred. He tried to lift his head up to look at Polly, but he only managed halfway before falling back into her bosom.

Leo stood up slowly and edged towards the couch.

"That… That coo… I want that… Coo…" Eddie stopped rubbing Polly between her legs and then stopped rubbing his face in her breasts.

Leo and Polly waited a few more seconds to make sure Eddie was out.

Polly wriggled out from under Eddie, who slumped face first on the couch.

"We did it!" she squealed, joining Leo at the table. The both gazed down at the book in awe.

"We fucking did it," Leo agreed.

Leo bent down and lifted the book they never thought they'd ever get their hands on. He held it in his hands and Polly slid her hand across the cover reverentially. The title was embossed in faded gold. There was no author's name.

THE DEMONIAN

MANUAL OF THE INFERNAL

Polly read the title and whispered: "The Demon Ian."

"Manual of the funeral," Leo added.

The Next Level

Instead of going back to their motel room to look through the book, Leo and Polly were too impatient and started immediately while still in Eddie's house.

The floor was like an assault course, strewn with empty bottles, cans, cigarette butts, discarded needles, and even a pizza box from the rare occasion when Eddie's heroin addiction hadn't completely obliterated his appetite.

Having cleared a spot on the floor for them to sit cross-legged, they spent the next hour reading portions of the book and marking which chapters to read at length later, not caring that they were spoiling the rarity with their scrawls.

Polly practically orgasmed when they found the chapter that had motivated their hunt for the tome. "It's there!"

"It's there," Leo concurred.

"Let's do it tonight!"

"We gotta read how to do it and shit."

"I know, but after that, let's do it."

"Pol, we can't do shit till we're in a new neighborhood."

"What the fuck are you doing?!" Eddie yelled.

Leo and Polly swung their butts around on the floor in shock. Eddie was standing, a look of fury on his face. Either Polly had been given low-quality shit or Eddie just wasn't very susceptible to its effects, but the Rohypnol had worn off.

"You cunts are after my book!"

"Calm down, Eddie, it ain't like that," Leo said as he stood up, followed by Polly.

"Bullshit it ain't! Get the fuck away from my book."

The pair moved away from the book, their minds racing as to their next move, though, in their case, said racing was akin to a contest between a growing blade of grass and a drying streak of paint.

"Who told you about it? Carlos? Was it Carlos? It was Carlos, wasn't it, the asshole."

Leo nodded.

Eddie's eyes darted around as he tried to recall where he'd laid down his heroin bundle. When he remembered, he turned to his right and reached down to the armrest to grab one of the hypodermic needles.

He took two long strides towards Leo and Polly, brandishing the needle. "You sonsa bitches are gonna get it. No one's taking my book!"

Leo whipped out his .38 and fired twice.

Two bullets entered Eddie's head and exited the other side, the impact sending him to the floor. Chunks of brain matter also hit the floor when the bullets exited.

Polly stepped across the room to Eddie's body. She knelt down and picked up a piece of his brain and held it in her fingers. She rose and turned to face her husband. She raised the piece of Eddie's brain to her mouth.

"What the fuck are you doing?" Leo asked in disgust as he went over to her side.

"I want to take our evil to the next level."

"Evil to the next… We ain't cannibals, you crazy bitch!"

"Fuck you, motherfucker!"

Such repartee had held their marriage together over the decades.

Polly dropped the sliver of brain on the floor, disappointed she wasn't able to advance the gradient of their evil. To make up for it, she rubbed her face with her bloodied fingers.

"How do I look?" she asked Leo, her cheeks glistening red.

"You know how to get me horny, baby," he replied.

He stepped closer till they were face to face. "I'm gonna pound the shit out of you," Leo promised, which was his idea of a come-hither.

"Fuck my cooch." And that was her idea of feminine wiles.

The pair went to the couch. Normally, after killing someone, they would flee the scene immediately and move on to another area, as they had done when they murdered Carlos after getting the information they needed out of him. But as Eddie's house was situated in a road where gunfire was white noise, they were in no rush to leave.

They took off their clothes and bumped uglies, uglies being the operative word.

Saturday

7:34pm

"You don't need to hover over me, Deputy Ricky," Morton said.

"It's Deputy Ronny, sir."

Morton looked up from the corpse of John Doe. "Fine. Can you wait over there please, I don't like having people watch over me when I work."

Ronny nodded and went to hang back in the morgue. Morton's tone had stung, but Ronny justified the alacrity of his acquiescence with the notion that one should be deferential to an officer of Morton's rank.

The cop resumed looking over the corpse. "Just one single stab wound… I can rule out the Hains."

"Sorry, Detective?"

"I wasn't talking to you, Deputy Randy, I was just thinking out loud."

"Uh, it's… it's Deputy Ronny, sir."

Morton ignored him. As he stared into Doe's lifeless eyes, he noted how glassy they were; not in the obvious sense of him being deceased, but Morton couldn't escape the feeling that these eyes had never actually observed material reality. He shook his head at the absurdity of such an observation. Even so, there remained a lingering feeling that, in life, John Doe had been something of a non-entity.

"Pretty vacant," Morton commented.

"What's that, Detective?"

"Nothing, Deputy Roddy."

Morton turned away from John Doe and headed to the door. Without looking back, he said: "Get your Sheriff on the phone. I need the keys to the laundromat."

"But I thought you've already viewed the crime scene, Detective."

"There's something else I need to check, Deputy Rudy."

Saturday

8:21pm

Doug's Emporium had provided porn to the men of Millvern since 1959, though founder and owner Doug Gillick was occasionally tempted to change the sign to say *Est. 1969.*

From its inception, Doug's Emporium had been frequented by local high schoolers and single and married men seeking out its supply of porn magazines and various lovers' guides. Loyal customers had continued to visit the store through the advent of videocassettes, which proved a boom time for Doug in the early '80s. They couldn't get enough of the new technology that enabled them for the first time to watch porn in the comfort of their own homes, except for the few poor fools who opted for a Betamax VCR instead of VHS.

With the arrival of the internet and the ensuing proliferation of free porn, Doug feared for his business's survival. Luckily, many of those high schoolers who were there from the start didn't own computers and had no desire nor intention to get online. They still visited Doug to get their fix of adult entertainment, and he had at the very least persuaded most of them to upgrade to a DVD player, some even to Blu-Ray.

Doug himself had bought an Ultra HD Blu Ray player for the forthcoming release of a '70s favorite. Originally titled during production as *Hoe-tel Kellyhornier,* the producers feared it was too clunky a title and not everyone would get the reference to the song by The Eagles, so it was changed to the more direct and easily understood, if derivative, *Becky Bangs Boston,* which was getting a beautiful 4K restoration from the original 35mm camera negative, with special features that included a director's commentary, spelled on the packaging as *Cummentary,* and a second disc with an extended Director's Cut, labelled on the packaging as the *Director's Clit,* the director in question having been a woman.

Unfortunately, the less successful, but he felt underrated, sequel, *Becky Blows Baltimore,* was only getting a standard 1080p transfer.

On this evening, 86-year-old Doug, still sprightly, was in his usual spot at the front desk, reading the sports pages of the local paper. There was only one customer in the store, a married man in his thirties who was browsing the Blu Ray shelves.

Doug turned the page and he heard a little chuckle. He briefly looked up at the customer and then went back to his paper.

A moment later, he heard another chuckle. Frowning, Doug looked up again, this time taking a longer look at the man, who had his back to Doug.

"Everything OK, sir?" Doug inquired.

The man turned around with a look of surprise. "Yes, why?"

"Just wondered why you was laughing is all."

"I wasn't laughing."

"I just heard you, sir."

"But I wasn't."

"OK, if you say so." Doug went back to his paper, adding quietly: "Must have been some ghost, right?"

The porn connoisseur turned his back to the front desk again and continued looking at the titles. An itch on his inner right thigh that had been growing in intensity was now too distracting to ignore, so he reached down to scratch it. *Oh yeah, that hits the spot.*

Doug flicked to the next page of his paper and he heard three short chuckles like the rapid-fire spray of a semi-automatic. He looked up and saw the man's right arm shaking vigorously and heard him utter a sigh of pleasure. "Oh yeah."

Even at 86, Doug could get out of his chair and around to the front as fast as he wanted. And he did, yelling: "That's it, you goddamn freak! Just 'cause I sell adult entertainment don't mean you can pleasure yourself in my store!"

He stomped over to the man, the poor guy's face a portrait of confusion and indignation. "What the hell are you talking about?!"

"You think it's funny to jack off in my store?"

"I wasn't jacking off! What the fuck do you think I am? I don't do that in public!"

"You goddamn right you don't! Now get out!"

Shocked at the accusation, the man headed to the exit. "I'm never shopping here again!"

"You weren't shopping here at all, you were getting to third base with your hand!"

Doug saw the guy out and shut the door.

He returned to the desk. Settling back into his chair, he looked at his watch and wondered if he should close early. Still pondering his decision, there came another chuckle.

Doug stood up, a panic-laden trickle running down his spine. He decided to close up for the night.

Saturday

9:44pm

Sam sipped the glass of champagne, closing his eyes to relish the feeling of the ice-cold liquid going down his throat.

Chloe sat next to him on the bed in his room at the B&B, holding her own glass. They kissed.

"I feel bad," Sam said. "You got us champagne and I just got us a bottle of white."

"Don't feel bad."

"Yeah, but I should be the one to buy champagne."

"Careful, Sam. You don't want to ruin things by talking like this is a date."

Damn.

He really needed to be careful. He'd met someone who was on the same page as him when it came to casual hook-ups and he'd almost fucked it up. He cursed the last vestiges of the behaviors that had been mainlined into him and other men from youth with respect to the conventions of going out with women, in this instance the entrenched role of the man paying for everything, something that he felt was outdated for a standard date, let alone a hook-up.

"Yeah, you're right," he said, almost adding *Sorry* before wisely remembering that an unnecessary apology was also not a good look.

Chloe had another sip of her champagne and looked at Sam with the mischievous grin that never failed to get him horny. "So, Sam, I have a question for you."

"Shoot."

"Are you vanilla?"

"Am I vanilla?"

"Please tell me you're not one of those men who repeats what's just been asked of him."

"No, I'm not. I just... I'm not sure what you mean."

"I'll put it this way. Are you vanilla when it comes to refreshments?"

A second passed and Sam couldn't believe he'd just been on the verge of saying *Vanilla when it comes to refreshments?* Another second passed and the penny dropped. "You're not talking about drinks, are you?" he asked.

Chloe smiled and shook her head. She leaned across Sam, her right breast brushing against him, and took her handbag that was perched on the bedside table. She opened it up and delved inside. Sam watched as she removed a small bag containing a white powder.

"Do you like coke?" Chloe asked.

"I love it," he said immediately, scarcely able to believe he'd met someone who was so on his wavelength and then some.

And then some came next.

"I want you to snort and lick it off my clit."

Time stood still for Sam.

"Are you psychic?" he asked rhetorically.

Chloe laughed and said: "Why do you say that?"

"I've so long wanted this. Drinking champagne and doing lines of coke off a beautiful woman's clit."

Oops. Had he gone too far by calling her beautiful?

"You naughty, hedonistic little boy," she teased, licking her red glossed lips.

Phew.

***

Chloe, now only in her bra, lay back on the pillow and shut her eyes. She held her glass of champagne by her side.

Sam, down to his boxers, carefully laid a line of coke across her labia. He began by tentatively licking some of it off her clitoris. Chloe convulsed with pleasure. Sam, closing one nostril, snorted the rest of the line. Again, she convulsed.

Clasping one hand on her inner thigh, he trickled out another line of coke and licked the whole line off, once more eliciting a shudder of ecstasy from Chloe.

She lifted her head just enough to have another sip without spilling the champagne.

Sam snorted another line of cocaine off her labia. Lost in the moment, he pictured the scene as though an observer: a tableau composed of champagne, a beautiful naked woman, and cocaine on labia.

But it was his current perspective that hit certain nodal points in his brain chemistry that, apropos of nothing, triggered the mental image of his close-up of her clit as a 35mm film frame in a 2.39:1 aspect ratio, resplendent with native, baked-in photochemical grain that he found infinitely superior to the hideously antiseptic and lifeless look of digital video.

Swept up in the intoxicating bliss of the moment, Sam thought that this wasn't so much just two adults engaged in sexual activity as it was a sexual liaison as live art.

He cringed hard. Had he really just internally called what was happening art? The coke must have taken effect.

Sunday

0:32am

Sam and Chloe followed the cocained cunnilingus with two very sweat inducing sessions of sex.

All spent, Sam put his arm around Chloe and began drifting off to sleep. There came the usual hypnagogic deluge, caught between awake and asleep.

There were the typical nonsensical scenes derived from the day's events and conversations reconstituted into a jumbled sequence, like a conservative Congressman in a diner asking for a condiment to go with his bowl of intestines and asking the waitress if she was a Jewess.

Drifting further towards sleep, one fleeting scene was even accompanied by a voice saying "See you soon, Sam."

Sunday

1am

The laundromat stood silent. Only a ceiling light remained on overnight.

The bloody signature had finally been washed off so Nancy could reopen for business in the morning.

Lying splayed out on the floor was the corpse of a man in a nice suit.

Death had once again come to the laundromat. And once again, it had arrived with all the sound and fury of a meeting of carpet sample enthusiasts.

Except that this was merely the calm before a very bloody storm.

Sunday

11:03am

"This killer seems to have a hard-on for the laundromat," Sam said.

He stood over the corpse that lay face down on the floor. Morton and Jockton stood next to him. The three had headed straight over after the call came through to the sheriff's station about the discovery of the body. Nancy had come in at around ten thirty to get ready for reopening at eleven when she found the body.

Sam resented having his Sunday morning lie-in interrupted, not least because Chloe had stayed this time rather than heading home while he was asleep. He was woken up by a call from Jockton, and as he headed towards the bathroom to take a shower, Morton had pounded on his door, suggesting they head on over immediately. Sam was about to accuse Morton of following him, but then remembered the cop mentioned he was staying in the same B&B. Sam tried to insist on taking a shower first. It was one of his personal lifestyle rules that he couldn't function for the day ahead if he wasn't revitalized by a morning shower. Morton said he'd go on ahead without him in that case, which really irked Sam. From his immaculate appearance, he could tell that the cop had got showered, shaved, and dressed long before the call had come in.

"Alright, gimme a minute," Sam told the cop. He splashed water on his face, brushed his teeth and changed his underwear before joining Morton in the lobby.

And now in the laundromat, he stood bleary eyed and feeling uncomfortable that he'd stepped out into the world without his normal morning refresh. It brought to mind that he never understood how some people could face the day without a morning shower. He was trying to focus on the murder scene, but all he could think of was going back to the B&B to stand under the invigorating force of the shower's jet.

But as he stood there, there was one consolation in having got ready in a haphazard manner, and that was he could still smell Chloe's perfume on himself.

"Should we turn him over? See his face?" Jockton asked.

Morton greeted that question with the same look he'd greeted almost everything that had come out of the Sheriff's mouth. "No, we wait for the paramedic to come and remove the body from the scene. Then we examine him at the morgue."

Like the first victim, this man was dressed in a neat, crisp suit. And as with the first victim, the name *MIKE* was written in blood, though this time on the floor immediately in front of the deceased man's head.

"His hair's wet," Sam said. He kneeled down and saw drops of brown liquid on the floor. He touched one of the drops. "It's still warm."

"Yeah," Jockton responded, "Nancy said she was pissed off to see another dead body and threw her cup of coffee over it."

Sam stood upright and looked at Nancy, who was standing outside the laundromat drinking a whiskey and muttering to herself angrily. "No customers yesterday, so at least we don't have to do interviews again," he said with relief.

"No CCTV, no witnesses, we got nothing to go on," Jockton complained. "And again, the killer got in without forced entry. How in the heck is he doing it?"

"Let's find out," Morton said.

"Huh?" Jockton said. For once, Sam shared the Sheriff's reaction.

Morton turned and headed to the front of the laundromat and came to a stop at the first dryer to the right of the entrance. He reached up and grabbed hold of an old detergent carton that had been left on top of the dryer with its top flap wide open.

Sam and the Sheriff joined Morton, who put his hand inside the carton and took out a small black device that fit perfectly between his fingers.

"What's that?" Jockton asked.

"This, Sheriff, is a 4K spy camera with an SD card for recording," Morton replied.

"You clever son of a bitch," Sam said.

"That I am."

Sunday

11:15am

Sam, Jockton, and Morton were gathered in the back room of the laundromat.

Morton sat at the table where Nancy had her bottles of whiskey and biscuits laid out. He cleared a space for his cellphone and inserted the SD card.

Sam and Jockton stood behind him, waiting excitedly for what the footage had in store.

Morton accessed the video file and pressed play. The footage began with Morton stepping back from the camera. The wide-angle lens showed the expanse of the laundromat.

"When did you do this?" Sam asked.

"Is this from when you and my Deputy got the keys because you said you needed to check something?" Jockton asked, at the same time answering Sam's question.

"Yes," Morton replied.

The video showed Morton exiting the frame, leaving the laundromat empty. Morton pressed the thirty-second skip forward function. After a minute, he jumped forward in longer chunks until it was night-time and then resumed the shorter skips.

The cop could sense the other two getting impatient. "Hold on, we're getting there."

"I didn't say anything!" Jockton said, feeling bruised.

Morton went back to jumping further ahead in the footage until they saw the body on the floor.

"There!" the Sheriff said giddily.

Morton skipped the footage back until the floor was empty and then let the video unfold.

All three watched closer than they had ever watched any footage in their lives. Even closer than the time Sam and some friends watched a DVD of *Basic Instinct* when they were 14.

In the dimly lit laundromat, timestamped at 01:00, without making even the slightest sound, without displacing even one speck of dust, the dead body of a man appeared, splayed out on the floor.

Sam, Jockton, and Morton simultaneously felt something they had never experienced in their lives. It was like a collision of an electrifying thrill with a sheer ineffable horror that made them feel they had stepped outside the bounds of normalcy and were poised to succumb to catastrophic lunacy.

"Go back," Sam requested quietly and quite unnecessarily. Morton had already pressed to skip thirty seconds back. Jockton held on to the back of the chair, thinking about whether he should retire soon.

The video played and the three men watched. Sam wondered if the man had been killed out of frame and had merely fallen onto the floor. Morton hoped a closer review would show a glitch in the recording. Jockton thought a visit to Italy might be a nice way to start his retirement.

They watched and, as before, out of nowhere, the body of the man appeared on the floor of the laundromat. This time, Morton let the video continue. If the inexplicable appearance of the corpse had caused emotions the men had hitherto never endured, what they saw next would catalyze in them an existential crisis they could never have foreseen.

Immediately in front of the dead man's head, large globs of blood from nowhere hit the floor and, as though guided by an invisible pen, wrote the name *MIKE*.

The men remained silent while the footage continued, now uneventfully.

About twenty seconds passed before Morton turned to look at the other two. "We all saw that, right?" the cop asked.

Sam nodded slowly, thinking of the book Morton had given him.

Jockton was staring at the wall.

"Are you OK, Sheriff?" Morton asked with genuine concern.

Jockton replied by throwing up on the floor.

Sunday

11:45am

There were certain predictable things Sam had expected that Sunday morning. Having a shower, getting dressed, and eating breakfast were among them.

What he had not and could not have expected was having his entire conception of reality and the world overturned. There was no way around it – they'd all seen the same video – and as much as he didn't want to accept what the footage represented, he had zero choice.

Sat at a long table in the sheriff's station meeting room with Jockton and Morton, he held the mug of coffee that Deputy Ronny had brought him in mid-air as though he was a life drawing model, not a drop of it having passed his lips. Jockton and Morton hadn't touched theirs either. Ronny had tried to elicit some information from his boss when they entered the station looking like walking catatonics, but Jockton just shook his head. After handing them coffees they hadn't requested, he went to sit at the front desk so they could talk in privacy.

Not that anyone had talked yet. Each man was in his own way trying to come to terms with the implications of the video recording.

Sam realized what his dumbfuck parents believed in was actually real. It was a given that anything comprising their worldview occluded Sam from believing in it as well purely by dint of *them* believing in it. But this went well beyond his thick parents; he would have dismissed anyone taking the occult literally.

Morton, reclining with his hands in his pockets, considered the potential consequences of the video becoming public. Consequences like hysteria among the masses and, more dangerously, leaders in the global religious firmament seeking to capitalize on it to terrorize and stoke their already indoctrinated and gullible flock and to intensify their political influence, as though they didn't already have a horrifying degree of power in the political sphere, especially in Washington.

Jockton, staring up at the ceiling, wondered what he should have for dinner that evening.

"So...," Sam finally broke the silence, "Looks like... I think it's safe to say that we are... Yes, I think we can say we are dealing... With this case, we are dealing with something... supernatural."

Morton looked at Sam and simply said: "Looks that way."

Sam looked over at Jockton, who was still staring up at the ceiling. The Sheriff sensed he was being watched and, as though prodded awake, he abruptly sat forward and slapped the table. "It's not!"

"What?" Sam asked.

"Don't you see?" Jockton continued. "It's a trick of the light. Whoever killed the man is just trying to mess with us by making it look like the body came out of nowhere! The blood too."

Morton removed his hands from his pockets, sat upright and pushed his coffee aside. He looked at Jockton and said: "Did you just have a lobotomy while we weren't watching?"

"Uncalled for! I'm telling you it's not supernatural. It's a prank by the killer."

"This isn't *Scooby-Doo!* You can't fake a six-foot man and blood appearing out of thin air!"

"He could have used special effects."

"When the fuck would he have had time to add CGI to a recording made on my spy camera?! Look, Sheriff, if you're having a breakdown, just tell us and we'll drive you to the local mental health facility."

"I'm just spitballing possibilities, Detective, there's no need to be offensive."

Sam put down the coffee he'd been holding and cleared his throat to indicate he was present again. "I think we should go examine the body."

Sunday

1:17pm

Sam wondered if he was in a time loop. After the video, such a possibility didn't seem ridiculous.

Laid out naked on the morgue slab was the man known, for the time being, as John Doe #2. John Doe #2 was Caucasian, six-feet-one, 145 pounds, aged about 34, and had neat, short black hair. Physically, he was in good shape; not athletic, but trim. Facially, he was handsome and blemish-free in that bland, non-descript, Ivy League kind of way. John Doe #2 was so white-bread, Sam reckoned the guy would have bled vanilla. The only thing that spoiled this otherwise polished specimen was the single, deep stab wound in his chest.

"Another milquetoast. This Mike has a type," Sam said. "Well, except for my parents."

Chuck, running his hands through his hair, yawned and said: "It's the same as before. No DNA and no fibers. The kill was as clean cut as the victim."

"All these theatrics, the bloody signature, and he just kills them with one single stab?" Morton said. "It doesn't make sense. I'd expect more than just a stab."

"Are you saying you wish it was a more violent death?" Chuck asked.

"Is idiocy in this town contagious?" the cop replied. "That's not what I said."

Chuck, unfazed, replied: "That was a perfectly reasonable inference, Detective. Why would it follow that a killer leaving a signature in blood has to have committed a very violent murder?"

"It's not just the signature," Morton replied. Before he could continue, Sam shot him a look that reminded the cop Chuck wasn't privy to their recent discovery. And nor should he be.

"What else is it?" Chuck inquired. "You said theatrics."

"Umm… Nothing, I just meant serial killers tend to be more elaborate in their killings. I'm sorry if I offended you."

"No, you didn't offend me. Amused me, yes."

Jockton, who had stayed quiet up to that point, took a step forward. "I'm hungry. Let's go have lunch."

Sunday

1:44pm

Rob entered Eat All Day with Lucy, his cute 15-year-old blonde girlfriend. Rob had on a different death metal t-shirt, this one depicting the Grim Reaper grinning and holding a blood splattered skull, and Lucy was wearing black lipstick, black eye shadow, and mascara, a gothic counterpoint to the unexpected '50s style white skirt and blouse she had on.

Rob nodded hello to Sam, who was sitting with Jockton and Morton, drinking coffees. Sam nodded back with a friendly smile. As Rob and Lucy passed the table where the men sat, he overheard the word *demon*.

"Demon?" Rob stopped in his tracks to ask.

Sam, thinking quickly, explained: "We're just talking about some song lyrics."

"Oh, nice! Demons. Gnarly."

"Yeah," Sam said, hoping Rob would move on.

"What's the band?"

"I'll tell you later. Off you go, kid."

"Cool. Later, man."

Rob and Lucy moved on to find a table. As they went, Lucy could be heard asking: "Who was that?"

"That's the private detective I told you likes *Cuntfuckery*."

Once the teens were out of earshot, Sam continued. "When I get back to my room, I'll start looking through the book to see if I can find out what we're dealing with."

"I knew bringing that would pay off," Morton said.

"So we're going with this being a demon? That's for definite?" Jockton asked.

"Yes, Sheriff. I'm sorry we're not going with your *Scooby-Doo* theory, but maybe we'll come back to it if this one doesn't work out."

"Give him a break, Detective," Sam said. Now it was Jockton's turn to feel grateful that Sam had come to his defense.

"Don't tell me you believe that special effects crap?" the cop asked, beginning to question Sam's sanity as well as his smarts.

"No, I don't, but is that really any harder to believe than a demon? If it was the other way around, you'd be getting a 5150 hold."

"Thank you, Sam," Jockton said, briefly fantasizing about being the one to put Morton in the hold.

"OK, fine," the cop said wearily, realizing Sam had got him on that point.

After a moment's silence as the men drank their coffees, Jockton said: "It's a funny thing being the only one in a religious family who ain't a believer. My momma, regular churchgoer, grace before dinner, 'kill the homos' and all that, she'd always try and get me to go to Sunday School. She'd say 'Don, if you don't go to Sunday School, you will have plenty to fear.' I had to tell her I already had plenty to fear because the pastor who taught Sunday School liked kids a bit too much if you catch my drift. She didn't believe me, of course. She said no man of the lord would do such things. Yeah, that was my momma. A real fucking piece of shit."

Sam smiled faintly, surprised that he and the Sheriff had things in common.

"So you went?" Morton asked. "And the pastor hurt you?"

For a second, Sam pondered if Morton was asking that in the malicious and cruel hope that Jockton would confirm so, but he didn't detect that attitude in the cop. It did appear to be a sincere query.

"Hell no. But he didn't last long anyway. One boy told his uncle what the pastor had done. Not his parents, 'cause they were hardcore like my momma and would never have believed him, but lucky for the boy, the uncle was in the marines and fallen in love with some woman he met in Bali called Lusitania or something who was into atheism. Or maybe paganism. Some such anyway, but he said she opened his eyes. So, anyway, the boy told his uncle and one night he went to the pastor and cut off his dick."

Morton almost choked on his coffee, sending it down the wrong pipe mid-swallow.

"He what?" Sam asked on the verge of laughter.

"Yeah. I think they managed to sew it back on in the hospital but they told him it would never work again. Now my momma, of course, my momma defended him to the end of her days, saying he was innocent. Yeah… A real piece of shit my momma was."

"Where was your father in all this?" Sam asked.

"He died in 'Nam. He finished his tour of duty and was all set to come back, but he asked to go on another one. I think he just wanted to get away from momma… Can't blame him, really."

"What about you, Detective?" Sam asked.

"What about me?" Morton replied. He was never comfortable being the focus of a conversation, preferring the reliability and familiarity of his usual role as interrogator.

"You know about my parents, and now Don's. What about yours?"

"My parents are in their seventies, they're healthy, happy, and now married to other people."

"That's it?" Sam asked.

"Yes. I didn't have a shitty childhood if that's what you're asking. My parents are very nice and very boring. Except when it comes to each other. Then they hate each other's guts."

"Funny thing about my momma, though," Jockton said, as though he'd never ceased his previous reminiscing. "All those years I wasn't a believer. And now seeing this video. I'm thinking she was right after all."

Sam, having briefly tuned the Sheriff out, said: "Wait, Don. Are you saying this is somehow proof of a god?"

"What else do you call it?"

"Hold on. How does it follow that what we saw is proof of an anthropomorphic cosmic deity?"

"Err… Could you repeat that please? I'm not sure about the last part."

"What I'm saying is that what we're potentially dealing with has no correlation to religious fairytales."

"We're all agree it's a demon, right?" Jockton asked.

"Yes," Sam replied.

Morton stretched out his legs to recline in his chair, put his hands in his pockets and sighed. "I thought you were still going with *Scooby-Doo*."

"Well, that's in all the religions. It's in all the books," Jockton continued.

Sam, feeling the few positive perceptions he had of the Sheriff starting to ebb away, said in the tone of a schoolteacher: "No, a bunch of stories and superstitions are in those books. The fact that they use the term demon is irrelevant, Don."

"How can it be irrelevant? Your parents' own book refers to demons."

"That's just a name, Don. Yes, it's a name derived from the long history of religious bullshit, but the name has nothing to do with the reality of the thing itself."

Getting exasperated, Morton said: "Really? We're doing this? A debate on etymology and nomenclature? Not like there are murders to solve."

"I don't get –"

Before Jockton could complete what he was about to say, Morton interrupted: "There's a lot you don't get, Sheriff."

"If you don't mind letting me finish!" He turned back to Sam. "I was going to say I don't get how you can see something supernatural and not say it ties in with what religious texts have been saying."

"Don, say you were living in the middle of the 19th century, OK? So you're living in the middle of the 19th century and –"

"What year?" Jockton inquired.

"It doesn't matter what year," Sam said, trying to keep his irritation in check so as not to hurt the Sheriff's feelings more than the conversation necessitated. "Let's say 1850. OK? Are you happy? You're living in 1850 and somehow you suddenly wake up now in our time. Right? And you go out for a walk and you see cars and people talking into a device they hold in their hand, and you see planes and helicopters, and you see a something that looks like a mirror except it shows people inside the mirror and they're doing things like shoot laser guns and fight dragons. Now, how do you think you'd react? Do you think you'd look at all that and be amazed at how technology has progressed? Or – *or* – do you think you'd look at all that and think they're acts of god?"

"Well, I don't know about that, Sam…" Jockton trailed off.

"You know how people first reacted to thunder? They thought it was an act of god. Now we know better. They thought shooting stars were missiles thrown by angels. Now we know better. This is no different. We don't know what it is, but the answer isn't a bunch of stories written by men."

Jockton sat back in his chair, feeling chastised and not a little hurt. Taking a more conciliatory tone, Sam continued: "Look, Don. I understand that the video has shaken you and made you question your understanding of the world. That's to be expected."

"And now we're onto existential angst," Morton commented, appearing to address the ceiling.

"I guess you absorbed more of your mother's dogma than you thought," Sam said.

"Sorry?" Jockton replied, discerning something of an insult in the comment.

"That wasn't a dig. I'm just saying your kneejerk reaction in reaching for the most ridiculous explanation tells me your exposure to her superstitions had something of an effect."

"To be fair to the Sheriff," Morton volunteered to both Sam and Jockton's surprise, "we're in a nation full of rubes who believe that kinda shit. No, make that a planet. Some of us can be exposed to idiocy without long-term damage. Some… can't."

"Excuse me!" Jockton interjected with self-righteous outrage. "Don't talk like I'm not sitting here!"

The diner door almost blasted open from the force of entry. Sam and everyone else turned to look at the arrival and saw Nancy head straight to her usual table, shoving past a customer's chair, and sit down. Opening her handbag, and without looking up to even see if a server was available, she yelled: "I'll have the chicken fucking lunch."

Morton turned back to look at the other two. "I still wouldn't rule her out as the killer."

SIX MONTHS BEFORE

Summon

After getting out of Centennial, Leo and Polly headed to the neighborhood of Sunderland, where they found themselves a cheap motel.

Forest Creek Motel was neither near a forest or a creek, and it was barely a motel. The room itself was grungy, with an old double bed, a corner desk and chair, and ensuite bathroom. The Hains were used to going low-cost and squalid, but even they were taken by surprise by the TV – a 29in CRT that still had a *Merry Christmas & Happy 1984 from TV Hut!* sticker on the side.

They wasted no time in getting down to what they'd been itching to do for so long. Delayed gratification wasn't something that came naturally to the pair. They'd almost killed a random guy at a gas station to sate their hunger, but a passing police car had nixed that. Now sitting on the bed in the motel room, Leo and Polly had the *Manual of the Infernal* open to the chapter on summoning a demon.

The error Sam had made was in assuming his parents' literal belief in the occult was there from the beginning. In fact, for a number of years, Leo and Polly's obsession didn't go any further than the conventional and archetypal trappings of black magic and devil worship, the aesthetics and performative aspect of the sub-culture being the primary signifiers of their interest. Hence the goofiness of fucking in graveyards or indulging in edge play, cutting each other during sex to lick one another's blood.

It was only when they began mixing in more fervently dedicated and unhinged circles that they started to hear about a notorious book that supposedly contained spells and instructions to manifest the darkest and most dangerous entities. Leo and Polly were enraptured by the stories they heard of people through the centuries using the book to conjure up demons, creatures, and ghosts, and the atrocities that followed, including the spectacularly brutal deaths of the individuals who had done the conjuring, something that, true to form, didn't register with the pair. It reached the point where the Hains could think of nothing except finding the book, a marked change from the default where the Hains could think of nothing.

They travelled from state to state, following any leads they stumbled upon when encountering fellow occultists. One anecdote almost threw them into despair when they were told the most recent owner of the book had moved to Japan. Leo was all set to pack his bags when Polly reminded him they didn't have passports, had never had passports, and didn't know how to get passports. Besides, there were multiple arrest warrants out for them across six different states, so any passports would require fake ID, something they couldn't afford.

It was to their great relief that they later heard the owner had returned from Japan and died in mysterious circumstances. Mysterious because the police couldn't quite understand how the man had managed to get into his bedroom to die in bed when his bowels were on the sidewalk outside.

The Hains murdered two people during their search for the book. Carlos became their third victim when they tracked him down to Salem, Oregon. Leo and Polly were thrilled just from being in Salem alone. It therefore came as a crushing disappointment to them when they discovered this wasn't the Salem where the 17th century witch trials took place. Leo suggested they kidnap Carlos and take him to Salem, Massachusetts and kill him there, an idea that even Polly found absurd.

After torturing Carlos to find out where his friend Eddie had moved to with the book – Carlos himself having no interest in the book or the occult

– they put two bullets in his head and headed straight to Centennial in Portland.

In the motel room, Leo and Polly re-read the first page of the chapter for the fifteenth time. They wanted to get this right.

"You ready? We should do it now, yeah?" Polly asked.

"Yeah, let's do it. We gotta say it at the same time, so don't fuck it up."

"Why you gotta say that, Leo? Why do I gotta be the one to fuck up?!"

"I didn't say you'd fuck up, I said *don't* fuck it up!"

"OK, you son of a bitch! Let's do it."

Leo and Polly held hands and began reciting together: "Oh spirits of the never world, overlords of the night dummy neons, we–"

Polly broke off from reciting.

"What's wrong?" Leo asked.

"I just remembered something," she replied, flipping the pages.

"What are you talking about? Do you wanna do this shit or not?"

"There!" she said, hitting the middle of the page with a finger.

"What? What is it?" Leo asked like a whining schoolkid who can't have more cake.

"It says something about some demons can't all never be not controlled and you might get destroyed."

"Oh, he's gotta say that shit. His lawyers probably told him to put that in so he don't get sued if shit goes wrong. He's gotta cover his ass."

"You reckon, hon?" Polly flipped to the start of the book to check the year of publication. "This came out 1245. He's dead by now."

"He might have cast a spell to live forever or some shit."

It never occurred to Leo and Polly why a book published in the first half of the 13th century was written in contemporary English. Their lack of inquiry was powered by the same intellectual void that made them wonder why there was no email address or website listed anywhere on the book.

What they didn't know is that the *Manual of the Infernal* transmuted its text in accordance with the era in which it was being read. It was for the same reason no author was listed. Because it had no author. The book was a creation of the very forces that its pages spoke of. It was a living integer that was designed to draw in adherents who sought to dabble in black magic for their own ends, only for it to wreak carnage upon them. Were those forces to articulate in current vernacular their motivation behind setting a vicious trap for these unwitting adherents, they would say it's for lols.

Leo and Polly went to start the spell again, but were astounded to see the words had changed. Before, the spell began: *Oh spirits of the netherworld, overlords of the night dominions, we mortals seek that you grant us a demon to do our bidding.* Now, for some reason they couldn't fathom, the language had become much simpler. So simple, in fact, that a 4-year-old would be able to understand it. In other words, them.

"It done changed!" Leo said, both confused and excited.

"It's a magic book, that's why!" Polly said with excitement that verged on the orgasmic.

Finally, they recited together the newly phrased spell: "Give us a demon to do whatever we want."

TO THE

DIABOLICAL DOMAIN

The Bloody Vista

When Leo and Polly woke up, they thought they were still fast asleep and dreaming. That had to be the only rational explanation for what they were seeing. It wasn't just because they didn't wake up in bed in their motel room. It was also because they were flying high above a blood-soaked terrain that was littered with what appeared to be several hundred thousand naked corpses, their entrails filling the gaps between each body.

If they could have observed closer, they would have seen that the corpses weren't quite corpse-like. Their mouths were all stretched wide open to a grotesque degree, from which emanated deep wails of pain, and their black eyes blinked impossibly fast. Some of the half-dead raised a hand, reached into their mouths, and tore out their tongues, which they held aloft like a trophy. Most hideously, the entrails on the ground were wriggling on their own accord.

The pair were separately locked into their own particular flight paths over which they had no control. Being pushed forward at what felt like 1,000 miles an hour by an invisible force would have been sufficient cause for them to scream. Seeing the topography of death below made them both want to rip their eyes out. So, they looked ahead instead. That provided no respite either, for in the distance, against the black sky, a series of volcanoes were violently active. But they weren't emitting molten lava. The volcanoes were spewing gigantic fountains of blood.

Rapidly approaching the mountains, Leo and Polly screamed until they thought their throats were going to tear open. Getting closer, spurts of blood from the mountains struck them. The blood was hot and burned into their cheeks.

The unseen power that was guiding them took the Hains up over one volcano and plunged them down face first at maniacal speed. Leo and Polly resigned themselves to the inevitability of their imminent deaths. They couldn't scream anymore even if they wanted to, as they felt their bodies dissolve in the eruptions of hot blood until there was only darkness.

The Green Corridor

Out of the darkness, the Hains now found themselves standing in a corridor of pharaonic length. If scale and emptiness could be so imposing as to terrify an observer, this seemingly endless corridor had reduced Leo and Polly to tears.

The walls, ceiling, and floor were painted Paris Green, a deliberate selection by the Domain for its own amusement. Even the Hains couldn't help but notice the incongruity of the superficially pleasant color with the overwhelming sensation of nauseating horror deep in their bowels that the corridor's length was causing. This awareness only served to remind them of the long trails of wriggling viscera across the vast expanse they'd flown over, which exacerbated the sensation.

They moved achingly slowly along the wide corridor. Not out of choice. Just as they had no control when they were flying, they couldn't go any faster than the pressure of their environment allowed. The agonizingly enervated pace threw up the terrifying possibility that they would have to go the entire length of the corridor like this. Almost in unison, Leo and Polly turned their heads to see what lay behind them. They wanted to scream when they saw it was equally interminable in the other direction, except, when they tried to open their mouths, it felt like they were attempting to lift a 100lb weight plate.

Adding to their torment was the suffocating nature of the corridor, since there were no doors and no windows. An invisible source illuminated the path, as there were no lights anywhere. The ceiling was as barren as the Hains' minds.

Leo wondered what would happen if he just stopped walking, so he did. His body started to shudder with such savagery that he was certain his bones were going to rip through his skin. He immediately resumed walking, and the tears continued to flow as he pondered the very real prospect that this was to be their eternal imprisonment.

Polly tried again to open her mouth so she could call Leo a son of a bitch, in the belief that he must have fucked up the spell, but it was still impossible. And even though she'd seen what happened to Leo when he stopped walking, she wanted to try it for herself. She did, and she too felt her entire body shake with insane ferocity, so carried on walking.

As the hours passed, Leo and Polly began to lose their basic cognitive faculties, though it would be hard for someone to tell the difference. No longer able to form even rudimentary thoughts, like Polly wanting to tell Leo *I'll shoot you in your dick* or Leo wondering why it was necessary to wipe his ass after taking a dump, the pair had become drooling savages who would be deemed too backward for an incestuous hillbilly orgy.

Just seconds away from wanting to eat their own faces, Leo and Polly were jolted back to their previous only significantly limited state, as opposed to drastically limited; the one where they'd fit right in at an incestuous hillbilly orgy.

Mike

As Leo and Polly had come to discover, the normal earthbound laws of physics didn't apply in the Diabolical Domain.

Not that that's how they articulated it to themselves. Leo thought: *This place is fucked up and shit!* Polly thought: *What in the shit is going on in this fuckass house?!*

After reverting to their normal sentience in the corridor, everything went pitch black and they found themselves stumbling in the dark at the same plodding pace.

Freaking out that this complete black void would be their prison, the floor gave way and they plummeted in chaotic bursts, by turns rapid and glacial. The jarring effect of the sudden shifts made them feel as though their necks were going to snap. And they still couldn't open their mouths to scream.

The Hains hit solid ground. But it only felt solid for a second. Still enveloped in darkness, this floor too was breaking apart, as they felt themselves sinking, and braced for another drop.

But as an invisible source slowly dimmed their environment into visibility, they saw that the floor was solid. To their revulsion, Leo and Polly saw the flesh of their bare feet flopping in slow-motion, detached from the bones within. It was of no small import that something had disgusted the Hains. After all, they had committed murder and seen each other naked. They were repulsed even more when they realized what was happening to their feet was happening over their entire body. The flesh of their faces drifted forward slowly from their skulls, never quite coming off entirely, just jiggling fluidly.

Though they couldn't see because of the bedclothes they wore, Leo and Polly felt the flesh of their torsos, arms, and legs reacting the same way. Leo panicked when he sensed his dick flopping more than usual.

They mistook what was happening as the start of a degenerative process and they braced themselves once again for imminent death. But this was the Diabolical Domain's laws of physics in action. Their bodies were merely reacting to the atmosphere.

Once the pair saw there was no advancing deterioration, they took in what was around them. Where the corridor had been green and endless, this was almost entirely black and merely 10x12 in size. Almost entirely, because long streams of blood were rippling up and down the walls on either side of them. The streams didn't go anywhere, they were in a state of perpetual motion. The room was equally suffocating, though, from the absence of doors and windows.

Rooted to the spot, too scared to take a step forward should even the slightest movement shatter their bones, Leo and Polly just stared ahead, once again resigning themselves to the prospect of this being their prison.

"WHY HAVE YOU SUMMONED ME?" a deep and unsettlingly sinister voice boomed. The voice reverberated all around them and made them shiver. The pair assumed they still couldn't open their mouths to answer.

"WHY HAVE YOU SUMMONED ME?"

Leo was astounded to find he could open his mouth, and even though the flesh of his face was jiggling just a few centimeters adrift from his skull, he was able to speak, and at normal speed too, making for a bizarre and uncomfortable kinetic contrast. The Diabolical Domain liked to fuck with its visitors that way.

"We just wanted… A demon… We just wanted a demon to…" Leo trailed off.

"Oh, fuck you, Leo, I'll do the talking," Polly said, aggravated and out of patience. "We wanted a demon to do whatever we want. We got this book, the demon Ian, manual of the funeral, and we summoned a demon."

A long silence. And then the voice said: "WHAT WAS THE BOOK CALLED AGAIN?"

"The demon Ian, manual of the funeral. Are you Ian?" Polly asked.

A longer silence.

Then: "NO, I'M NOT IAN."

"What's your name?" Leo inquired.

"YOU CAN CALL ME… MIKE."

"Mike? Demon Mike?" Leo asked in a disappointed tone.

"JUST MIKE."

"That's your real name?"

"He told you his fucking name, Leo!" Polly ranted.

"MIKE IS NOT MY REAL NAME. IF I TOLD YOU MY REAL NAME, YOUR EARS WOULD BLEED."

"So, are you gonna do our bidding like we ordered you to?" Polly asked as though she was talking to everyone she had ever met.

"WHAT DO YOU SEEK OF ME?"

Leo decided to jump in before his wife could: "Rob banks. We want you to use your demonic powers and shit to steal as much dough as you can for us."

An even longer silence greeted this last remark.

Leo and Polly looked at each other, squirmed in disgust at what was happening to each other's face, and went back to staring at the black wall ahead in excruciating anticipation of an answer.

"THAT'S... THAT'S IT?"

"Yeah! Maybe we get you to kill some people for us too, but right now we want you to get us cash money!" Polly said, barely able to contain her thrill at their sure-to-be-imminent wealth.

Another frustrating silence followed and the Hains waited for Mike to give the final confirmation that it was a greenlight for their demonic bank robberies command.

"OK."

"Really?!" Leo said, clapping his hands and feeling grossed out when the skin on his hands just flapped against each other gruesomely.

"YES."

Before they knew it, Leo and Polly were back in their motel room bed. They looked at each other. Everything was back to normal; normal being a relative term when it came to the Hains.

Polly beamed at Leo and squealed: "Well, that was easy!"

They hugged each other. But as Leo embraced his wife, he was absolutely certain that, just before they were bounced back to their motel room, he heard Mike say: "FUCKING MORONS."

Cash Money

"Polly and Leo Hain! This is the police, FBI, DEA, and ATF! You are surrounded! Come out with your hands where we can see them!"

Leo and Polly, who had been watching TV and eating leftover Chinese takeout on the motel bed for breakfast, ran to the window, a noodle hanging from Leo's mouth and satay sauce dripping from Polly's chin.

Assembled outside in the motel courtyard were twenty heavily armed law enforcement officers, from uniformed Portland PD cops to bulletproof-vested FBI, DEA, and ATF agents. A line of snipers was stationed across the courtyard on the opposite landing, rifles aimed straight at the pair.

"What the fuckass is this shit?!" Polly screamed.

"Polly and Leo Hain!" the cop with the megaphone repeated. "This is the police, FBI, DEA, and ATF! You are surrounded! Come out with your hands where we can see them!"

"What do they want with us?!" Leo whined in agitation. He turned to move away from the window and came to an abrupt stop when he saw six mammoth open sacks on the floor that were so full of cash, $100 bills were falling out of each one. And each bag even had a giant dollar sign on it, something that money sacks never have. "Jesus fucking Christ!" His agitation went down several notches.

Polly, still peering out the window, turned to see what Leo was talking about. "Where the hell did that come from?!" she yelled.

"Where do ya think?! It's Mike! He did what we told him!" Leo jumped up and down and clapped his hands in delight. "We're fucking rich!"

Polly wasn't quite ready to join in the celebrations. "But how do those asshole cops outside know about it?!"

"Polly and Leo Hain! This is the police, FBI, DEA, and ATF! You are surrounded! Come out with your hands where we can see them! This is your final warning!"

"What we gonna do?!" Polly asked. "You think I should cast a spell to kill them?"

"I CAN MAKE THEM GO AWAY," Mike's voice boomed all around the motel room. The Hains jumped in fright at the unexpected intrusion. Leo's agitation revved up again.

"Yes! Make them go away, kill them!" Polly barked. "Do as we order you and kill 'em! I don't give a shit how you do it!"

"NO."

Polly heard what Mike said, but still felt compelled to ask the pointless rhetorical question: "What did you say?!"

"YOU HAVE A SIMPLE CHOICE. EITHER YOU AGREE TO DO MY BIDDING FROM NOW ON AND I WILL MAKE THEM DISAPPEAR, OR I LET THEM FILL YOU WITH A THOUSAND BULLETS. YOU HAVE TEN SECONDS TO DECIDE."

Struggling to cope with his pendulous emotions, Leo succumbed to tears, and Polly screamed in frustration while punching the wall. They both knew they had no choice, and they both felt something they weren't used to, and not only weren't used to but were now enduring at a corrosively gut-churning depth: regret.

"Alright!" Leo conceded, struggling to see through his tears.

"FIVE SECONDS."

"I said alright, Mike!" Had Leo been capable of more than rudimentary thought processing, he would have realized Mike's inaction was due to Polly's failure to provide an answer one way or the other.

"TWO SECONDS."

Finally, Polly shrieked: "OK, you son of a bitch!"

Outside fell silent. Leo edged towards the window and saw all the officers had vanished. "They're gone," he announced with such relief that he thought he was going to collapse.

"What the fuck!" Polly shrieked.

Leo swung around to see the sacks of money had vanished as well. He wanted to cry again. "Mike, where's our money?!"

Another of Mike's silences followed, but this time Leo wasn't going to wait. "Cut that shit!"

"WE HAVE A FEW THINGS TO DISCUSS. LET'S TALK."

Insight

The Hains were once again taken on the odyssey to the Diabolical Domain, except that this time Mike hurried things along, which meant the Hains flying at breakneck speed over the blood-soaked terrain, resulting in them breaking their necks.

Still alive, their heads lolled down and they saw the wailing, blinking, naked bodies. They couldn't avoid the spectacle by raising their heads to look ahead at the bloody volcanoes, but before they could shut their eyes, two of the living corpses reached into their mouths, tore out their tongues, and, instead of holding them aloft like trophies, hurled them upwards. Each diseased looking tongue smacked Leo and Polly in the face and stuck, the one on Leo pointing up so that the tip was touching the area between his eyebrows, and Polly's one pointing down so that the tip was touching her lips. They couldn't move their hands to rip the tongues off.

Continuing at demented speed, they plunged down into a volcano, felt the searing blood burn their flesh, but when they emerged back in the green corridor, they were frustrated to find the rancid tongues were still stuck to their faces and their heads still lolled down. This indignity, and the prospect of walking slowly for several hours with foul smelling, decomposing tongues clinging to them, instigated in them the first stirrings of something epochal in the life of the Hains. It was still taking shape when, to their relief, they were pushed through the corridor at the same berserk speed until everything went dark and the floor gave way.

There was no falling by turns rapid and glacial. It was a straight, manic plummet to the floor of the black room. Standing there again, the stirrings came to fruition: the notion that they could have ordered a demon to do whatever they wanted now seemed utterly, mind-blowingly naïve. This marked the first and last time Leo and Polly Hain had any insight into their own behavior.

"Where's our money?" Leo asked, grimacing as his flesh reacted to the atmosphere of the Diabolical Domain and made the severed tongue quiver away from his face and back again. As it did so, the bottom caressed Leo's nose and he felt its decaying odor go right up his nostrils. He retched in disgust. Leo wanted to rip the tongue off his face, but he couldn't move his hands like he could the last time he was in the room. Mike was really fucking with them.

"Yeah, where's our fucking money?!" Polly asked. The tongue on her face quivered too in reaction to the Domain's atmospheric composition and the tip flitted against her mouth. She felt its full fetid force and retched.

"THERE NEVER WAS ANY MONEY."

"We saw it! We... We... Can you make the tongue disappear? Please?" Leo asked, shifting his tone mid-sentence from aggrieved to pleading.

Mike chuckled and the sound of his laughter reverberated around the room.

"This ain't funny," Leo complained.

"IT IS TO ME."

Leo and Polly simultaneously felt the tongues slither down their faces. As one last insult, the tip of the tongue on Leo's face licked his lips and the one on Polly's face briefly entered her mouth and licked her tongue. The Hains heaved as though about to spew. The tongues dropped to the floor, where they rapidly decomposed into a brown sludge and evaporated.

"We saw the sacks," Leo resumed, desperately hoping this was all a dream and he'd wake up and find that he and Polly were yet to summon Mike.

"YOU SAW WHAT I MADE YOU SEE. LIKE YOUR BRAINS, THE SACKS NEVER EXISTED. OR THE PEOPLE OUTSIDE."

"You done mean to say those cops and agents were fake too?!" Polly whimpered.

"THAT SHOULD HAVE BEEN OBVIOUS."

"It ain't wasn't obvious! They were outside and had guns!" she said infuriated.

"YOU NEVER STOPPED TO ASK WHY THE FBI, DEA, AND THE ATF WERE INTERESTED IN A BANK ROBBERY? THAT SHOULD HAVE BEEN A CLUE NONE OF IT WAS REAL."

"You tricked us!" Leo complained, reverting to his aggrieved tone.

"TRICKED? WHY WOULD THE FBI BE INVESTIGATING A SMALL LOCAL ROBBERY, DRUG ENFORCEMENT A STASH OF CRYSTAL METH, AND THE ATF A COUPLE OF HANDGUNS?"

"You know," Polly said, wiping the remaining satay sauce off her chin, "you don't talk like a demon talk."

"MET A LOT OF DEMONS HAVE YOU?"

"Uh…" Polly trailed off, as she had no answer. She wanted to say *fuck you*, but figured saying that to a demon wouldn't end well for her.

"Mike," Leo began, "you saying if we knew the cops and feds were fake and shit and we never agreed to what you said, nothing woulda happened to us?"

"NO, I WOULD HAVE STILL MADE YOU DO MY BIDDING."

"That ain't fair!" Leo shouted, angrily banging his fist against his side, but since all physical movement here was in slow-motion, he had time to remember there would be no catharsis, and so the loosened skin of his fist merely bounced against his side and rippled back over the bones. "Shit!"

"IT WASN'T INTENDED TO BE FAIR. IT WAS AN INTELLIGENCE TEST AND YOU FAILED. SPECTACULARLY."

Polly, getting ever more furious, raged: "Then why say you were gonna rob the bank for us if you ain't never was not gonna not do it?!"

"COULD YOU SAY THAT AGAIN WITHOUT SO MANY DOUBLE NEGATIVES?"

"What?"

"I JUST PLAYED ALONG. I WAS NEVER GOING TO DO YOUR BIDDING. ROB A BANK? A BANK?! IS THAT THE LIMIT OF YOUR IMAGINATIONS?! YOU SUMMON ME TO STEAL MONEY?!"

"We was gonna get you to kill some people too," Leo responded quietly.

"THE BOOK WARNED YOU WHAT WOULD HAPPEN."

"The demon Ian said not all demons you can't not control. We figured that was some lawyer talk," Polly also said in a quiet, defeated voice.

"*THE DEMONIAN,* YOU INCREDIBLY THICK HUMAN! *THE DEMONIAN: MANUAL OF THE INFERNAL.*"

Polly just watched the perpetual streams of blood on the wall to her right, stung by the insult.

"What's gonna happen now?" Leo asked. "And when you gonna show your face and shit?"

"YOU'LL SEE ME WHEN I WANT YOU TO SEE ME. AS FOR THE OTHER… YOU'RE GOING TO KILL FOR ME. AND WHATEVER ELSE I TELL YOU TO DO."

"If we say no?" Leo asked.

"YOU HAVE A HABIT OF ASKING POINTLESS QUESTIONS. BUT SINCE YOU ASK. IF YOU REFUSE, I WILL HANG YOU UPSIDE DOWN BY YOUR ENTRAILS AND USE A HUNDRED THOUSAND DIFFERENT INSTRUMENTS TO CARVE YOUR FLESH INTO A MILLION PIECES."

"Instruments? You mean like a keyboard and shit?"

Silence.

"NO ONE CAN SERIOUSLY BE THIS STUPID, SURELY."

Sunday

5:30pm

Back in his room at Let Me Be Your BB, Sam sat up on the bed, resting against one of the pillows, made himself comfy and opened *The Demonian,* figuring he was in for a long evening of reading.

Reading the first few lines of the introduction, which he expected to be impenetrable due to the period in which it was written, he was taken aback by the modern syntax.

INTRODUCTION

The contents of this manual are highly dangerous. Only those of you who are skilled occultists and possess adequate knowledge should attempt any of the spells contained herein. Be warned: black magic is not for the faint of heart. You are putting yourself at great risk by experimenting with the darkest reaches of the discarnate.

Laying it on a bit thick with the cautions, he thought.

But very quickly he deduced there was no way a book published in the first half of the 13th century would be written like this. His heart beat faster when he arrived at the only possible explanation. An idea came to him to test his theory.

Looking up from the book, he said out loud: "Discarnate? What does that mean? I've never heard of that. This book is confusing."

He waited a good fifteen seconds and then looked down at the page.

The sentence now read: *You are putting yourself at great risk by experimenting with the darkest reaches of the ethereal and scary.*

If Sam had thought nothing could produce a more visceral reaction in him than the video recording, this moment proved him wrong. With the video, he witnessed the events second-hand. This book, which he now knew to be a living thing, was in his hands. And it scared the shit out of him.

Feeling queasy, and fearing he was about to repeat Jockton's earlier reaction, he wanted to close the book, give it back to Morton, and go home to San Francisco. But he knew that wasn't practical or viable. And as much as his hands were trembling, he still had work to do. Sam just wasn't sure if he could get through reading entire chapters without having a breakdown from the weight of the knowledge that this centuries' old primer on the unearthly was itself unearthly.

To alleviate the stress this task imposed on him, Sam skimmed through the pages to see if his parents had written anything in the margins. He couldn't see any illegible and childish scribbling for the first couple of hundred pages, so he tried a different approach by closing the book and holding it lengthways to see if any sets of pages appeared worn from repeated handling. Given it was in outstanding condition for a book that came into being over 700 years ago and had passed through who knows how many different hands, Sam made the reasonable assumption that the book periodically restored itself and that, therefore, any well-thumbed sections were from most recent use.

Sam saw a thickened set of pages in the middle and he opened the book to the start of that segment. What he saw produced in him a wholly unexpected reaction. For the first time in his life, he was grateful for his parents' rank imbecility.

At the top of the page, above the chapter heading *SUMMONING A DEMON,* they had written *This the spell we want!*

Sunday

7pm

"My parents summoned a demon to do their bidding."

Jockton and Morton had got a call from Sam asking them to join him at Samphire for a drink and an update.

"You read the book that fast?" Morton asked.

"I didn't need to. They'd marked the spell they wanted to use."

"Like with an asterisk or something?" Jockton asked, sipping his beer.

"No, they wrote *This the spell we want*."

"Yeah, that sounds like your parents," Morton said, having a drink of his expensive cocktail.

Jockton looked at Morton's Armani suit and the flashy cocktail and felt a prickling he couldn't describe, but he was definitely certain it was not in any way, shape, or form jealousy compounded by an inkling of an inferiority complex. Absolutely not.

"And what does the spell say?" the Sherriff continued.

"You want him to repeat a spell that summons a demon?" Morton asked Jockton. "Do you ever think before you open your mouth, Sheriff?"

"Hey! That is uncalled for!"

"Relax, Detective," Sam said. "I think the spell only works if you recite it in the presence of the book."

"Exactly," Jockton said.

"Like you knew that," Morton said.

"I didn't. But I assumed it's so."

"Sure you did," the cop said quietly.

"I heard that!" Jockton said.

"It just asks for a demon to do your bidding," Sam explained.

"So your parents got a demon to go murder a bunch of people in Portland?" Jockton asked.

"It would appear so, yes," Sam replied.

"And then these John Does?"

"No, not them. They're Mike's work, who I think it's safe to say is the demon they summoned."

"I'm confused," Jockton said. Morton would never say it out loud, but he agreed with the Sheriff, as he too was confounded. "If Mike did the Portland murders, why were your parents' names at the scene of every crime?"

"That's what I've been wondering about," Sam said, which Morton found greatly reassuring that it wasn't just him and Jockton who were perplexed. Sam turned to the cop: "Detective, was there anything about the murders that stood out? Anything unique?"

"Only that there were zero forensics at almost every crime scene. I mean, totally spotless. And the murders were violent and chaotic. You'd expect something to be found. And there were things that just didn't make sense at all as to how there could not be any evidence left. Like I told you when we first met, the only reason we knew your parents were involved was they signed their names."

"But not the first two you told me about. The ones you connected to them later."

"No, not those two. Which is also confusing as to why they didn't autograph those kills."

"That's it, then. It's as I thought. No way my parents could pull off flawless murders. Knowing them, they got a demon to go kill some people for them, but they wanted to take the credit."

Jockton, putting down his beer for a moment, asked: "Are you saying your parents got mad that Mike was committing murders that folks were calling genius and wanted the fame for themselves?"

"Yes, Don. They really are that dumb."

"But that doesn't explain your parents' disappearance and the John Doe murders," Morton pointed out. "That part makes no sense."

"Not quite. Think about it. They summoned Mike to go kill for them. But then they decide they want the notoriety, so they start signing their names. Imagine how Mike reacts when he finds out they're taking credit for all his work."

"Right. So he abducts them," Jockton suggested.

"Possibly."

"Or kills them," Morton suggested.

"Hopefully. And leaves his name at the scene so that we know another player is now involved in all this shit."

"But why murder these two random guys?" Jockton asked. "And why get you involved?"

"That's the part that's giving me a headache." Sam looked down at his beer and lifted it to his lips when he remembered what he wanted to ask Morton. "Why did you say there were zero forensics at *almost* every murder scene?"

"Not the most recent one, the last one. There was evidence all over the location. Fingerprints, DNA, fibers, the works."

"OK, now that really doesn't make any sense." Sam rubbed his forehead in frustration. "Mike isn't going to suddenly screw up for no reason."

"Because it's not him," Morton said confidently. "That's one, for whatever reason, your parents did. That's why the scene was a mess of evidence."

The door opened and Drew came into Samphire with his friend, Inessa, a bohemian looking woman of 37, dressed in a long, colorfully patterned skirt featuring elephants and giraffes interspersed with floral shapes, a midriff top, and a red scarf. A nose ring, handmade aquamarine earrings, and a pink tongue piercing completed her look.

Drew saw the three and headed over with Inessa.

"Hello Sheriff, hello Mr. Hain," Drew greeted them with a friendly smile. He didn't recognize the other man at the table, so just nodded his hello to him. "This is my friend, Inessa."

The three said *hello* with cookie cutter smiles, too preoccupied with the subject at hand.

"Hi," Inessa said. Sam saw her tongue piercing and remembered a girl he once dated.

"She's the one I told you about," Drew reminded Sam and Jockton, who nodded. "The one I saw *The Maltese Falcon* with."

"Yeah, OK, we get it. You've got nothing to worry about. We know you're innocent," Sam assured him.

"I told you I already spoke with the Sheriff yesterday," Inessa told Drew. "Chill. I'm not feeling any negative vibes from them."

"You two kids have fun now," Jockton said, trying to get them to go away.

"How's the case coming along?" Drew persisted, not getting the hint.

"It's great," Morton pitched in. "But we're having a private conversation, so you and your girlfriend can move along now."

Sam once again admired the cop's blunt style.

Drew, embarrassed, clarified: "Uh, Inessa's not my girlfriend."

"But who knows?" she said with a smile.

"Really?!" Drew responded with unconcealed fervor that made Sam cringe.

"Let's just chill and see what happens."

"Sounds good," Morton said. "Go chill and see what happens."

Drew finally got the hint, nodded at them, and walked off with Inessa.

Poor guy, Sam thought. *Now he's gonna spend the rest of the evening thinking about that one comment.*

"Where's the book?" Jockton asked Sam.

"Back in my room at the bed & breakfast, why?"

"Is there a chapter on how to destroy a demon?"

"I don't know, I haven't read the whole book," he replied, and he was in no hurry to.

"It's worth a look," Jockton insisted.

Sam stared down at his beer, ruminating and then shaking his head.

"What's on your mind, Mr. Hain?" Morton inquired.

"Nothing. It's just, of all the things I thought I'd be doing when I came to this town – scratch that – thought I'd *ever* be doing, dealing with a demon and researching how to kill one wasn't among them."

"Makes a change from following cheating husbands and wives, doesn't it?" Morton commented, playing with the cocktail straw in the empty glass. He hadn't used the straw, as he thought it was too feminine and he already had enough ribbing from colleagues over his drinking habits.

"How do you know that's what I investigate?" Sam asked suspiciously.

"I looked at your website. All your testimonials are from people who were cheated on."

Sam shrugged, thinking he'd prefer to be on a case that only involved horny marrieds fucking and nothing more.

Sunday

8:43pm

Chloe had texted Sam earlier in the day to tell him she was meeting a friend that evening, so wouldn't be hooking up that night. Although he certainly wouldn't have turned down another opportunity to spend the night with her, having the evening free would allow him to read more of the book, as uneasy and intimidating a task as that posed.

He stopped off at Tex's Tex-Mex for a quick dinner before returning to Let Me Your BB to look at *The Demonian.*

Very unhelpfully, the manual didn't have a contents page or an index. He would have no other option but to search through the 800-page volume for anything about killing a demon.

But an idea came to him just like before. Sitting at the small desk in his room, in front of a window that provided a guest's dream view of a brick wall, he closed the book, looked up and said: "I wish I could find a chapter on how to kill a demon. All I need is a clue or hint on where in the book I can find that information."

And like before, Sam waited fifteen seconds and then looked down at the book.

Nothing happened.

He waited expectantly, hoping the book would open to a relevant page.

Another fifteen seconds passed and still nothing.

"Well, it was worth a shot."

He flipped through pages at a brisk pace to check the chapter headings, but even that was made difficult. The absence of chapter numbers meant he couldn't be certain that he hadn't missed a chapter in between, so he ended up laboriously flipping the pages. Chapter after chapter, there was nothing like *How to Kill a Demon*. Instead, there were chapters such as *Finding Your Evil Within, Conjuring The Three-Headed Death Reaper Dragon, Visiting the Netherworld For The First Time, Spell To Undo Your Existence, Inviting Ghosts to Family Reunions,* and *Do Demons Have Sex?*

Sam was waylaid by the chapter on undoing one's existence, thinking it could come in handy if things ever got too difficult. Though it did occur to him that had he come into possession of this book as a teenager, he'd have used it straightaway.

He continued flipping and skimming and speed reading and searching, to no avail. He then had an epiphany, one that made Sam slap his forehead at how clueless he'd been. This book was a live entity that had to have been forged by dark, inhuman forces. It followed, then, that they would not include a chapter on how to destroy one of them. How could he have been so dense?! He couldn't blame Jockton, whose suggestion it had been to look it up, as Sam had gone along with it. Maybe Morton was right and idiocy in this town was contagious.

Monday

2:54am

Sam was a deep sleeper. It had to take a lot to rouse him.

He was surprised when he woke up for no immediately apparent reason and saw the bedside digital radio displaying the time as 02:54.

He turned to lie on his side, poised to go back to sleep, when a deep and unsettlingly sinister voice boomed: "HELLO, SAM."

Sam bolted upright in bed, grunting loudly in shock. He reached for the bedside lamp switch and pressed it. The light didn't come on.

He scanned the room, which wasn't entirely cloaked in darkness, as some light seeped in through the curtains. He thought he was going to faint when he saw the outline of a man stood in the corner of the room, diagonal to his bed.

"DO YOU KNOW WHO I AM?"

Trying to project an appearance of dignified calm, Sam answered: "Judging by your creepy voice and standing creepily in the dark, I'm gonna guess you're Mike the demon."

The man chuckled.

"Is that a yes?"

The man chuckled again.

"Wait. I recognize that laugh… Did you watch me have sex?"

He chuckled again.

"Oh, that's fucking gross!" Sam said, now genuinely relaxing. The visitor turning out to be a Peeping Tom had diminished his fearsome presence somewhat.

He chuckled yet again.

"So are you Mike? You're the one my parents summoned?"

Yet again, the man responded with a chuckle, following up with: "WHAT DO YOU THINK?" and another chuckle.

"Right now, you sound like someone who's easily amused."

Mike laughed even louder.

"There," Sam responded, adjusting his position to sit more comfortably now that he was no longer frightened.

"SO HAVE YOU FIGURED IT OUT YET?"

"That you're Mike? Yes, I already told you."

"NO. THE JOHN DOES."

"I don't know, you've got a thing for murdering white-bread blue bloods with no character?"

This time, Mike didn't laugh. Sam swallowed nervously. "Mike?

"WHY IS THIS CASE NOT TROUBLING YOU?" Mike's voice reverberated all around the room.

Sam waited for the reverb to fade out.

"Impressive. You come equipped with your own Dolby Atmos."

Mike, who hadn't moved at all, took a step forward. Sam felt his stomach lurch. "I WILL MAKE YOU FEARFUL. GO TO THE BATHROOM. NOW."

"Why?"

"NOW!"

Sam pulled the duvet back and slid across to get out on the other side of the bed to avoid passing Mike.

"What's in there, another Ivy League grad?" he asked as he approached the bathroom door. He looked behind him in case Mike was planning to give him a scare, but he hadn't moved from his spot.

Sam opened the door and went into the bathroom. He took in a deep breath in readiness for whatever lay in store and pressed the bathroom light switch.

Once his eyes had adjusted to the brightness, he saw Leo's decapitated head in the sink, and Polly's head attached to Leo's naked corpse in the bathtub. The bath curtain was drenched in blood. The sight made Sam's entire body jerk in revulsion. He looked up to avoid the literal bloodbath and saw Polly's naked decapitated corpse stuck to the ceiling.

Sam vomited all over the bathroom floor. He badly wanted to rinse his mouth with cold water, but with his father's head in the sink, that was a non-starter.

He switched off the light and emerged slowly from the bathroom. He reached out for the bedroom light switch, wondering if that would fail to come on like the bedside table lamp. He pressed it and the lights came on.

Mike was gone.

"That was a shitty thing to do. I did not need to see my parents nude."

No reply came.

"And if you thought that was gonna scare me, you're wrong."

Sam turned back to the bathroom and reluctantly went in. He knew he'd have to call Jockton and Morton about this. There was no way he could just leave two dismembered bodies till the morning. He pressed the light switch.

To his astonishment, his parents' corpses were gone. As was his puddle of vomit.

He went to the sink and turned on the cold-water tap. He rinsed his mouth several times, but still had the gross vomit taste at the back of his throat. He squeezed out half a finger's length of toothpaste and rinsed his mouth for a minute, gargling for a further twenty seconds before spitting into the sink. That still wasn't enough.

He went over to his wallet and got out his debit card. He remembered there was a soft drinks machine at the end of the corridor and he was really jonesing for an ice-cold soda fix to get rid of the gross taste in his mouth. He bought a Diet Pepsi and started gulping it down immediately. The carbonation slightly exacerbated the vomit burn in his throat, but he didn't mind.

By the time he was back in his room, he was halfway to finishing the bottle. He downed the remainder and let out a gasp of satisfaction.

Sam turned off all the lights and got back into bed. He pressed the bedside lamp switch and was relieved when it came on. Although it slightly dented his self-esteem to do so, he wanted it on for the rest of the night.

He closed his eyes and sighed: "At least he cleaned up the vomit too."

"YOU'RE WELCOME."

Sam started, knocking his head against the headboard.

"Son of a bitch."

FIVE MONTHS BEFORE

Random

"YOU ARE TO KILL A RANDOM PERSON."

Leo and Polly stood in the black room of the Diabolical Domain. It had been a month since Mike last spoke to them and they had started to believe he'd forgotten about them. They regretted getting their hopes up.

"Who?" Leo asked.

"YOU DON'T UNDERSTAND THE WORD RANDOM?"

"Yeah, I do!" Leo lied. "So… Who do you want us to kill?"

"FUCKING MORON. I OUGHT TO TORTURE YOU JUST FOR THAT."

"That's it? You just want us to blow some fucker away?" Polly asked.

"FOR NOW."

"Well, hell," she grinned, but then shut up. Even with her intellectually bankrupt mind, Polly realized that if Mike knew killing was not a problem for them and posed no threat of psychic trauma (which she phrased internally as *won't not make us go not batshit*), he'd hand out a genuinely severe punishment. "Well, hell," she repeated, this time with a look of dismay, "that's some sick shit."

"YOU BOTH HAVE A VERY LIMITED VOCABULARY, DON'T YOU?"

"Limited what?" Leo said.

"SO THAT WOULD BE A YES."

Attempting Murder

It's not entirely accurate to say that the Hains hated rich people. They hated anyone who was more successful than them regardless of the specifics of their wealth. They hated a schoolteacher or bus driver as much as a corporate executive or rock star. That said, the rich most easily and readily represented what they lacked in life.

It was this that motivated their selection of the affluent Forest Park as the location for their random kill. They drove to the neighborhood and parked two blocks away from the residential road where they were going to find a home to invade.

Leo and Polly strode down the road, looking in disgust at the rows of opulent houses with a BMW, Lexus, or Benz in the driveways, sometimes all three, and beautifully maintained lawns.

"I think we should take out all 'em fuckers," Leo suggested. "Every single house."

"How we gonna do that, you dumb asshole?! Cops be all over the place after the first guy we blow away."

"Not if we do it all quiet and shit."

"Shut up, Leo."

They passed a house and saw all the windows save for one on the ground floor were dark.

"What about this one? Don't look like lotsa fuckers in," Polly said with growing enthusiasm.

Leo saw the dark blue Benz in the driveway and said: "Let's do him."

They approached the front door, looking behind them all the time. Only the occasional car passed through the road.

"This gonna be good! Ain't no one not gonna see us!" Polly squealed.

Leo pressed the doorbell and they waited, weapons concealed in their pockets.

When the Hains had selected Forest Park as the location for the murder, what they had neglected to consider was dressing appropriately for an upscale part of the city. As it was, they had turned up in the same dirty, unwashed, and frayed clothes they usually wore.

They also hadn't considered that the residents of this neighborhood might have door cameras. As it was, the owner of this property had seen the disheveled visitors on his live video monitor and called the cops.

The pair continued to wait. But the capacity for delayed gratification not being among their skillsets, they were getting antsy.

"Fuck this, let's find another house!" Polly muttered as quietly as she could manage.

"You folks need any help?"

Leo and Polly spun around and saw a uniformed cop at the end of the driveway.

"No, sir," Leo said, adopting the synthetic subservient persona he always deployed when confronted with law enforcement. "We're just visiting a friend and shit. To take a shit. I mean, to use his bathroom."

Polly just smiled politely.

"Your friend lives here?" the cop asked.

"Yes, sir."

"Really? 'Cause we got a call from the owner of this house reporting two strangers on his doorstep acting suspiciously."

"Us, sir?" Leo asked with the disheartening realization that they wouldn't get one past this cop.

"Yes, you're both strange and acting suspiciously," the cop said, looking at Polly, whose fake smile had since morphed into a rictus grin.

Polly turned around to look at the door number and switched from phony cheerful to phony surprise. "Oh, Leo, you dummy! We at the wrong house!"

Leo, playing along, looked at the door number and said: "Well, shit! We done fucked up, Polly! Sorry, officer! We ain't visited our friend before in this part of town."

"What number does your friend live at?"

"Well…" Leo struggled to answer.

"Oh, Leo, you dummy! We in the wrong road too!" Polly laughed.

"Well, shit! You're right, Polly! This ain't even the right road! Sorry, officer, we're gonna get going."

Leo and Polly started to make their way down the driveway. The cop took a step forward and raised a hand. "I'm going to need your details before you go."

"What for? We not ain't done nothing," Polly said irritably, her commitment to her façade slipping.

Leo glanced to his right and saw that the cop wasn't alone. Another officer stood next to their marked police car further down the road, where they had arrived in a silent approach. Leo nudged Polly to keep cool and told the cop: "It's alright, officer. Whatever you need and shit."

"I just need your names," the cop demanded, getting out his notepad and a pen.

"I'm Frank Brown, and this is my wife, Maggie… White."

The cop stopped writing and looked up. "I just heard you call each other Leo and Polly."

The rictus grin returned to Polly's face, and Leo thought he was going to piss his pants.

"Oh…" Polly spluttered, "You see, them our middle names. Them names we like more than our firsts."

"So it's Frank Leo Brown and Maggie Polly White?"

"Yes, sir," Leo said.

"Not Maggie Polly Brown?"

"What?"

"You said you're married."

"Oh, I wanted to keep my name, officer," Polly said, putting her arm around Leo. "My Leo let me do that 'cause he loves me and I'm a fanny mist."

"Do you mean feminist?" the cop asked.

"That, yeah."

"OK. Brown and White," the cop said, writing the names down.

"Yeah, all our friends thought it was hilarious and shit!" Leo said. "They call us the breads!" Leo wasn't entirely lying there. He once thought he overheard someone refer to them as breads, but that person had actually called them brain-dead.

"Are you from Portland?"

"No, sir. Born, raised Marion County, West Virginia," Leo replied. Polly wanted to grab Leo by the neck and scream in his face before emptying her gun into his mouth. "But we're living in Portland now."

"I'll need your address."

"The Red Hex," Polly replied hurriedly. "It's a bar in Centennial. We know the owner. He's letting us crash there for a while."

"The Red Hex," the cop repeated as he wrote. "OK, I think that covers it. You folks have a nice evening. I hope you find your friend."

"We will. Thank you, officer, sir, detective," Leo said.

"Just officer," the cop said. "I'm not a detective."

"You should be, sir. You're a great cop, officer, sir," Leo insisted with his Jack the Ripper smile. Polly wanted to punch Leo in the face and scream at him to shut up and let the cop leave.

"Thank you. Have a pleasant evening," the officer said and walked off.

Polly kept her forced grin going for a few more seconds. "Let's get the fuck outta here," she whispered.

The pair headed back in the direction of where they had parked. When Polly looked back and saw the police car depart, she turned to Leo and screeched: "You fuckass idiot! You told him where we from!"

"So what? We don't live there no more!"

"They got computers! They can look up backgrounds!"

"Only if they got our real last names and shit, you crazy bitch!"

"Oh, fuck you, Leo! They gonna look up Leos and Pollys from Marion County and see our photos. They gonna put an ABP out on us!"

"You're the one who said my real name, Polly! And you told him about The Red Hex. So shut the fuck up!"

"You were fixin' to tell him the motel we're at! The Red Hex owner don't know us! It won't matter a shit if they go asking about us there!"

"I was not gonna tell him what motel we're staying at! I ain't that fucking dumb, Polly! We didn't do nothing anyway! They ain't gonna do anything just 'cause we was outside some asshole's house!"

"Now we gotta find another house. I still wanna kill a rich fucker."

"No, Pol, they all got cameras and videos and even video cameras. Let's just go find a house near the motel and take out some guy there."

The First Murder

Leo and Polly drove around Sunderland looking for the most rundown houses. They spotted a ramshackle one-story with a truck parked out front that had a Gadsden Flag decal on the bumper; that last detail made Leo and Polly feel an affinity with the intended victim.

They parked across the road and got out. "Let's surprise him by going in the back!" Leo said.

"Like when you done surprised me?" Polly asked, laughing.

"Ooh, you nasty, Pol!" Leo snorted in amusement.

They went down the dark alley beside the house that led to a wooden-fenced rear garden. The garden was a sorry sight, littered with the remnants of a long-ago barbecue. Half-eaten moldy hotdog rolls and empty beer cans lay below plastic chairs. In the center of it all was the filth-strewn and irreparably rusted grill, bedecked with ancient ashes and even chunks of burnt brisket. The last thing a normal person would think of upon seeing this is eating, so, of course, Leo took one look and got hungry.

Leo climbed the fence, getting quickly out of breath from the ordeal, and landed in the garden with a grunt. Polly followed.

They got out their guns, crouched down, and approached the rear door. It was dark through the windowpane, so they knew there wouldn't be anyone immediately within.

Closing in on the door, they saw it was ajar. Polly almost squealed in delight, but kept her composure, keen to save her energy for the murder.

The pair entered and found themselves in the kitchen. The kitchen doorway opened on to a lit hallway. Country music was blasting from a room further down.

Leo and Polly gripped their guns and went into the hallway, which led in a straight line to the living room.

Standing in the living room was 55-year-old Jake Bloodworth, a tall, rugged guy dressed in a camo outfit and heavy rough terrain boots, though he'd never actually been in any situation that required camouflage, or been on rough terrain. He was cleaning his AR-15 semi-automatic and listening to Jason Aldean on the stereo. Bloodworth had his back to the hallway and couldn't see the Hains coming towards him. But he did hear when Leo tripped on an empty glass bottle and fell forward, yelling: "Oh, shit!"

Before even turning around, Bloodworth instinctively slid his finger onto the trigger, as instinctively as the time he heard a noise in the middle of the night and shot dead his 12-year-old nephew who was getting a drink from the fridge, later narrowly avoiding a manslaughter charge on the grounds of self-defense based upon exigent circumstances wherein he perceived to be under threat. He turned around and let rip with the AR-15, riddling his own home with bullets. It was only in the course of that frenzy that he registered a man face down on the floor struggling to stand up and a woman screaming and firing her .32 equally frenetically but managing to miss every single shot.

Polly dived to her left, shooting her remaining ammunition.

Leo, still on the floor, aimed his .38 and got off a round, striking Bloodworth in the shoulder, who grunted in pain.

"You're fucking dead!" Bloodworth roared, grabbing on to his wounded shoulder.

Leo finally stood up and fired several more shots. Bloodworth's abdomen was ventilated by the bullets and he collapsed backwards onto the floor. He was still breathing and still grunting.

Polly got up and joined Leo in walking over to Jake.

"Who the fuck are you?!" Bloodworth asked, his fury undiminished by his injuries. "I don't even know you!"

"We're Leo and Polly Hain. And we're here to do a demon's work," Leo said smiling.

Polly grabbed the gun from Leo and, stepping into the growing pool of blood, fired the remaining bullets into Bloodworth's head.

Despite him being clearly dead, Leo picked up the AR-15, also stepping foot into the blood as he did so, and blazed a round into Bloodworth's corpse.

Leo dropped the rifle, a smile of satisfaction on his face, and crouched down to search the dead man's pockets for anything worth stealing, smearing his hands and sweater in the blood that was seeping from the bullet holes.

Polly went over to rest on the couch. She put her feet up on the table in front, staining it red, and spread her arms out on the backrest, nodding her head along to the music. She too smiled in satisfaction at what they both thought to be a successfully executed kill.

"He ain't got shit," Leo announced, rising up. He walked across the room to sit next to Polly, leaving a trail of bloody footprints. He put his feet up as well on the table and relaxed. "We did it though, hon. We straight up wasted that son of a bitch and shit."

Leo and Polly kissed. As they embraced, Leo's fingers, bloodied from searching Bloodworth's clothing, dotted Polly's t-shirt.

"You've never committed a murder before, have you?"

Since casting the spell to summon a demon, Leo and Polly had jumped in shock more times than they had in their entire lives prior to that point. And here they were, yet again, feeling themselves jerk violently from the unexpected.

Standing in the living room doorway was a man in a nice suit. He was Caucasian, six-feet-one, 145 pounds, aged about 34, and had neat, short black hair. Physically, he was in good shape; not athletic, but trim. Facially, he was handsome and blemish-free in that bland, non-descript, Ivy League kind of way.

"Not one you got away with," he continued.

"Who the fuckass are you?" Polly thundered, reaching for her gun and remembering she was out of ammo.

"Yeah," Leo agreed, "who are you and shit?" He eyed the AR-15 next to Bloodworth's body and wondered if he could grab it in time, since he was out of ammo too.

"You haven't guessed yet? What am I saying, of course you haven't. I'm Mike."

The Hains looked at the intruder askance.

"Bullshit," Leo said.

"Mike's a demon. Ain't no human," Polly concurred.

"OK," Mike said. "Here's proof."

Bloodworth opened his eyes and was on his feet in a second. Leo and Polly shrieked in panic. He lifted the AR-15 and roared: "I'ma blow you cocksuckers away!"

The pair leapt off the couch and headed for the hallway, but Bloodworth instantaneously popped up there, blocking their path.

"Do you want me to make him go away?" Mike asked.

"Yes!" the Hains screeched in unison.

Bloodworth appeared back on the floor, dead once again.

Leo and Polly, breathing heavily, returned slowly to the couch and slumped down.

"I've taken human form to... Hold on a second." Mike clicked a finger and the stereo exploded into a mini fireball that then vaporized. "I can't stand country music. As I was saying, I've taken human form to talk to you here in your earthly domain. This isn't my real visage, naturally. If you saw my true form, your eyes would bleed. Now, I was saying it's quite obvious you've never competently committed a murder before."

"No, we never entered a competition to murder anyone," Leo said.

Polly, who had discerned an insult but not the one Mike had actually made, wanted to brag that they had, in fact, killed several people over the years, but thought it better to pretend this was tortuous punishment for fear of him meting out a genuinely unbearable ordeal. So, instead, she replied: "Never! We hate killing! This some sick shit you making us do!"

"Drop the act, idiot. I know you've committed murder and robbery."

"How you know about that?!"

"Is that a serious question?"

"Yeah, we ain't never not told you nothing about it!" she said.

"So, you remember the part where you summoned a demon?" Polly looked at the floor in embarrassment. "You two can't commit a murder to even a rudimentary degree of proficiency to save what passes for your lives."

"What you talking about?" Leo asked rhetorically in response to the part he did understand and sincerely to the part he didn't. "Don't you see that son of a bitch on the floor? He's dead. We took him out."

"Yes, and in the process left so much forensic evidence, the cops will think a toddler did it. Which, let's face it, isn't too far from the truth."

"We did?" Leo asked, rubbing his slacks with his bloody fingers. "I don't see nothing."

Mike shook his head. "Is this how it's going to be? I'm going to have to clean up after every murder I order you to commit?"

"How many more these we gotta do?" Polly asked.

"I haven't decided yet. For however long I want."

Mike looked around the mess they'd made in the room. "Get up," he ordered. They obeyed and got up, a task that proved difficult for Leo, who found the exertion too much and promptly fell back on the couch.

"Leo, do you want me to drag you off the couch by ripping out your intestines, tying one end around your neck, and using the other end as a leash?" Mike asked.

Leo made another attempt and this time Polly helped him stay on his feet.

Mike clicked a finger and all the DNA and fibers that the Hains had both left and collected throughout the house vanished. "There."

"I don't see nothing different," Leo said.

"Look at your shoes, your clothes, the floor, the table, and the couch, you imbecile. You're welcome."

Leo and Polly looked and, indeed, their attire was back to just being dirty, and the bloody footprints and the bloodstains on the couch and table had disappeared.

Mike turned to leave the living room. "I'll be seeing you soon."

"Hey," Leo called after him. "Since you're here anyway and shit, could you send us back to our motel room? Save us the drive."

Mike looked at the pair and said: "I gather there's a certain phrase that you humans are fond of using at moments like this. I believe it's: Go fuck yourself."

Wallace Morton

If you were to ask Wallace Morton's colleagues in the Portland Police Department for their opinions of him, the responses would mostly go along four lines.

The first three were of him being too serious, too unapproachable, and too thorough. That last observation, which Morton once heard being said about him, he found hilarious and also revealing about the attitude of some of his fellow officers. Unlike his critics for whom this was just a job to do and go home, the Portland native saw being a detective as his métier and he always pushed himself to be painstaking. It pissed him off that all cops didn't take the same approach. Why be in this job if you're not going to do it right?

The fourth was that he came off as solitary with no girlfriend to speak of. This too he found funny. Unlike the oversharers you find in some workplaces, the Sarah Shitbloods of the world as Drew might say, Morton just chose not to go into every aspect of his private life. His Captain and a handful of other cops knew he was divorced, but nothing more. Morton got married at 37 to Melissa, a surgeon the same age as him whom he met when he brought a patrol cop with gunshot wounds to the ER. Morton made frequent visits to hospital to see his buddy, who made a full recovery, and soon after, he started dating Melissa.

One of the many things they had in common, along with being dedicated to their work, was that neither of them wanted to have children. Morton had made that decision many years ago, and a few relationships with long-term potential had fallen by the wayside as a result. Melissa sympathized, as she too had encountered some problems, not just in ill-fated relationships but also from people who had no hesitation being openly sexist by telling her *real women* have children, *real women* get married before 30, and *real women* don't have careers, and that was just from her relatives. Even the announcement of her engagement didn't put an end to their preachy bullshit. Her brother, himself married with two kids, asked why she was bothering to get married, since "the whole point of marriage is to have children, as the lord ordained." Melissa asked him if his wife knew he was fucking the 19-year-old babysitter, as ordained by his dick. He never brought the subject up again.

Morton's marriage to Melissa lasted five years. He was grateful that, at least, theirs wasn't the typical story of a marriage ending in acrimony and mutual loathing. In the end, they simply drifted apart and saw no point in continuing. Their friends were amazed at how calmly the divorce process was conducted. Amazement turned to shock when Melissa invited him to her divorce party and he turned up.

In the years since the divorce, Morton had the occasional fling, but he came to the conclusion that serious relationships just weren't for him. During a catch-up dinner with Melissa, she suggested the possibility he might be aromantic. After looking the word up online, he said he wouldn't go that far, but he certainly wouldn't get married again. "If anything, I'm married to my work."

While some people derive enormous personal satisfaction from seeing their children grow up, go to college, get married, and so on, Morton found closing a case and putting a vicious criminal behind bars indescribably satisfying. And to get that feeling, he had to dedicate himself wholly to his job.

Magicians

"There's bad news and there's bad news. Which would you like first?"

Morton, visiting the Portland morgue for an update, looked at Judy Younger, the 29-year-old Medical Examiner, and said: "I'd rather you just give me what you've got without resorting to clichés."

"You know, Morton, you're too grumpy for someone who wears Armani."

When Morton assessed the Bloodworth crime scene, he initially thought it looked reassuringly clear-cut. CSI officers collected twenty-five shell casings from the AR-15 and eight shell casings from an unidentified .32, along with their corresponding bullets. The bullets from the .32 were lodged in the wall immediately behind the body, and the AR-15 bullets were in the wall around the entrance into the hallway, reflecting the initial mutually failed attempts to kill. The lead in Bloodworth's body would surely be from a subsequent reload of the .32.

But when crime scene technicians examined the GSR on the floor under the body, indicating the downward trajectory of the headshots and bullets in the chest, they were baffled. A killer would have had to stand over the circumference of the pool of blood to achieve those entry wounds. And yet, there wasn't a single shoeprint in the blood and no bloody prints leaving the scene. Even if some feat of physical dexterity could explain that, there was no way the killer could have searched Bloodworth's pockets without stepping into the blood to kneel down.

"You've got two shooters," she said, chewing gum, a habit that Morton would ordinarily have found annoying but for which Judy got a pass, as he found her willingness to talk back and stand up to him – coupled with the ever-changing colored streaks in her black hair – currently blue – and her college-graduate-who-hasn't-quite-left-college-behind character rather endearing, a fact that would have shocked her, being so at odds with the perpetually professional and unsmiling demeanor he carried. He also enjoyed the occasional spectacle of cops, some more than twenty years her senior, trying to ask her out on a date, oblivious to her being a lesbian. Morton was well aware of how sober and businesslike he came off at work, so it was for his own private amusement that he would never tell any cop, ballistics specialist, or CSI officer who asked him if she was available that Judy was gay, and when they reported back red-faced from rejection, he'd act shocked at the revelation of her sexuality. They never thought the too serious Morton could have a mischievous side.

"The victim was shot thirteen times. I removed eight bullets that were fired from a .38 and five from the vic's own AR-15. No bullets hit him from the .32. Hence, two shooters. Hence, the absence of shoe prints in the blood now looks even crazier, Walls," Judy said, chewing her gum with relish. Morton never liked subordinates taking it upon themselves to call him by his first name, let alone a nickname of their own invention; again, Judy got a pass.

She stood over Bloodworth's body on the morgue table and talked Morton through the sequence of bullet wounds. "You know the shooters come in from the hallway. Vic is taken by surprise. One of the shooters must have tripped and fell and that's what made the vic turn and fire. One of the bullets from the .38 entered the vic's left shoulder from an upward trajectory about ten feet away," Judy explained, indicating that bullet hole on Bloodworth. "Shooter number two with the .32 gets trigger happy and misses all eight shots, and the first gunman fires four more shots from the .38 straight into the vic's abdomen, taking him down." Morton saw the spread of bullet holes in Bloodworth's stomach. "And that's when the shooters come right up and real close." Pointing to the three holes in Bloodworth's head, she said: "The last three rounds from the .38," and then nodding towards the wounds in his chest, she concluded: "And five rounds from the AR-15 straight into his chest."

"Overkill. It was either personal or just they enjoyed it," Morton responded. Staring at the corpse, he continued: "Two perps. And not a single bloody footprint between them. How the hell did they do that?"

"Not a single bloody footprint and not a single fiber transfer from when perp number one hit the floor. It's funny."

Morton looked at Judy. "Funny?"

"Well, the shooters started off like sloppy amateurs and ended like magicians. How often do you see two extremes within one crime scene?"

Morton almost did something he never did while on duty: smile. Almost. Instead, to show his appreciation, he said: "As you know, Judy, I don't work with a partner. But if I ever had to have one, you'd do a better job than the jerks in my department."

Judy, still chewing her gum that had long lost its flavor, smiled and said: "I won't tell anyone."

"That I called them jerks?"

"That you paid someone a compliment."

Flawless

Leo and Polly, dressed comfortably in the same clothes five days running, including underwear, watched the local evening news from the bed in their motel room, giddy in anticipation of their handiwork making the headlines.

And sure enough, the murder of Jake Bloodworth was the top story. The reporter outlined the case while Leo and Polly jumped up and down on the bed as though they were trying to hold in their piss.

The newscaster in the studio spoke to the reporter via a live link-up: "Gavin, I gather that this murder is proving something of a challenge for the investigating officers?"

"That's right!" Leo said jubilantly. "That's 'cause we did it!"

"That's right, Angie," Gavin the reporter replied from outside Bloodworth's house, which police had taped off. "My source tells me that whoever perpetrated the murder managed to not leave any forensic traces behind. Now, that might not sound too unusual in a homicide case, but my source said the circumstances of the crime scene are such that it's inconceivable nothing was found. As murders go, this one sounds pretty flawless."

"Son of a bitch!" Leo barked.

"What you so mad about?" Polly asked, shoving Leo, angry that he was spoiling the mood and her arousal.

"He said it's floor-less. Don't that mean it's good and shit?"

"Yeah! So what's your goddamn problem?"

"All that stuff he said about evidence, that wasn't us, Pol. It was Mike. He's the one getting the buzz, not us. He got rid of the blood and other shit."

"We wasted the guy. We went into his house. We blew him away. That's all that matters. Stop being such a whiny bitch."

"Oh, fuck you."

A stung Leo turned back to the TV, which was reporting on the aftermath of a school shooting in Texas. The Governor there was offering his thoughts and prayers.

His angry words had sparked Polly's arousal again. "You keep talking like that, Leo, I'ma blow you away."

"The fuck?" Leo said, sliding back an inch on the bed.

Polly grinned: "With my mouth, you dumb fuck."

"Ooh, you had me scared for a second, Pol. You got a nasty mouth and I like it. And I ain't talking about when you talk."

"I know."

"I'm talking about when you suck my dick."

"Yeah, I got it. I don't give a shit what some guy on the TV says. You made it floor-less."

"Yeah, I did fuck up his floor, didn't I?" Leo said, leaning in for a kiss, not minding the aroma of cheesy nachos, barbecue ribs and beer combined with halitosis emanating from her mouth.

Shits and Giggles

Leo and Polly stood in the black room, expecting to get their second order to go and kill a random person. So, they were understandably bewildered when Mike told them what he wanted. Now that they'd seen his human visage, he'd dropped the unseen scary voice approach and sat on a humble black throne to address them. Not for Mike the ostentatious adornments that some demons opted to have on their thrones.

"Go to a movie theater, talk loudly, make lots of noise, burp and fart, and when the others in the audience tell you to shut up, keep going louder than before. And when they beat the shit out of you, don't fight back."

Leo looked at Polly. Polly looked at Leo. Had they summoned a demon or a high school kid?

"You don't want us to kill a random guy and shit?" Leo asked. "Like, someone we don't know? Not someone we know."

"Congratulations, you've learned what the word random means. But no."

"Why you want us to go to the movies and act like assholes?" Leo asked.

"What do you mean *like?*"

"You want us to get beat up and not ain't not do nothing about it?" Polly asked.

"No," Mike said, "I want you to get beaten up and not do anything about it, you illiterate drop of precum."

"Why?!" Leo asked in desperation.

"For my amusement. For what you humans refer to as shits and giggles. You're the shits and this will give me giggles. And because I have a hold over you and you know you have to do as I say or you'll face something far, far worse."

"This ain't right!" Polly complained.

Mike stood up and walked slowly towards the Hains. "I know your instinct will be to ignore what I've said and to defend yourselves, and though it's tempting to let you do that so I can have the satisfaction of ripping the jawbones off your faces, I'm going to immobilize you for the duration of your visit to the movies."

"Which movie you want us to see?" Leo asked.

Mike looked at Leo. "Tell me something, Leo. Don't you ever get tired of asking fucking brain-dead questions?"

***

Leo wasn't happy. And not just because his and Polly's plan to summon a demon had backfired so spectacularly and they now had to obey him or face agonizing torture. He hated the very idea of letting anyone beat the shit out of him and being unable to defend himself.

Polly wasn't happy. And not just because she was married to Leo. She hated the very idea of making someone angry and being unable to let Leo take the fall.

They were in their seats in the movie theater, each with a big tub of popcorn and soda. If they were going to get the shit kicked out of them, they might as well have something to eat and drink first. It was a full house for the opening night of the latest *Fast & Furious* sequel, so it was a rare occasion where they were in the company of people who were almost around their level.

Twenty minutes into the movie and Leo was struggling to understand the story. He and Polly had their orders, but his frustration at the film's plot meant he wouldn't need to playact at least one aspect of the role he'd been given.

Even though this was a typically noisy Friday night audience for a moronic flick, most of the chatter was in reaction to what was happening on screen. As a relatively quiet scene played out, Leo said loudly: "This a confusing movie! I don't like this movie! This movie sucks! This be a hard movie!"

As the starting shot, it wasn't bad, and a few moviegoers in their row did crane their necks to see who had talked, but there was no further reaction.

So, it was Polly's turn.

"No! This done be a good movie! I like this movie! This movie got fast cars and things blowed up real good!"

A few more members of the audience looked in their direction, but this was relatively small fry.

It was time for Leo to up his game. He gulped down his soda and burped as loud as he could. This time, his behavior elicited a few laughs, but still no anger.

Polly took a handful of popcorn and threw it behind her.

"Hey! Cut that shit!" a man called out.

"No! We do what we like!" Polly yelled back.

Leo couldn't delay any longer. He'd been dreading what he had to do and it was time to get it out of the way. He lifted his ass halfway off the seat and let rip a fart of such mammoth power, people sitting on the other side of the theater heard it. And as soon as he farted, he followed it up by shouting: "Mmmm! That a big nasty fart! I did the big nasty fart! Yaaay!"

The people around them groaned in disgust and there were shouts of "Shut the fuck up," "Get the fuck outta here," and "You're a nasty motherfucker."

Leo wanted to stop, but he couldn't. They had to keep going until someone wanted to beat them up. So he lifted the tub of popcorn and the soda and hurled them behind him, roaring: "Fuck all of you and this movie! Yaaay!"

Polly was deciding whether to drink the remainder of her soda or to toss it into the audience when she saw the result of Leo's actions. Two men, both about six feet, with tattoos that ran the length of their arms and up around their throats, and a mountain range of arm muscles poking through their t-shirts, now stood by their row, popcorn clinging to their t-shirts and hair slick from soda. One grabbed Polly and the other grabbed Leo. The audience erupted into cheers and applause as the pair were pulled violently out of their seats and up the aisle by their feet. Neither could put up any resistance because Mike, true to his word, had immobilized them. The only thing they could do was grunt in pain from the carpet burns as they were dragged along face down.

Instead of heading for the exit back into the lobby, the bodybuilders dragged them towards the fire exit, which was a cold, concrete corridor with bleak sodium lighting that led to a door to the outside. There, the men slammed Leo and Polly against the wall and proceeded to punch them. Over and over.

As they turned progressively bloodier from the onslaught, the Hains' knees buckled. Leo was the first to collapse, whereupon his assailant continued by kicking him. Over and over. "If you wanna fart and throw shit, do it at home, you nasty motherfucker!"

Polly's assailant landed a blow that sent her to the ground and she was subjected to a flurry of kicks. "You're making us miss the goddamn movie, you nasty bitch!" her attacker roared.

Leo and Polly thought they were going to pass out from the beating. And even if they wanted to beg the men to stop, which they wouldn't because of pride, Mike had put a cerebral block that disabled them from saying anything.

The angry cineastes both finished with a triumphant kick and they dragged the Hains to the door, this time by their hair, and threw them out onto the street, where they landed face first in a puddle of urine. As Leo faded to unconsciousness, he felt certain Mike had deliberately placed the puddle of piss there as yet another insult.

***

All Leo and Polly could do was just stand there and take it.

For the last two hours in the black room, Mike had sat on his throne laughing uncontrollably while watching a loop of them acting moronically in the theater and getting the shit kicked out of them after. The loop appeared on a virtually diaphanous screen that hung in the air in front of the throne and was of such insanely high definition, it was like they were viewing events through an open window. It was bad enough reliving their humiliating ordeal again and again; seeing it unfold in a resolution that didn't exist anywhere in the world was rubbing digital salt into their wounds.

Mike paused to catch his breath and said, tears of laughter streaming down his face, "They really fucked you up! I think I'll visit those guys and shake their hands and – Oh, this part's my favorite!"

Mike clicked his finger and the picture skipped back ten seconds and then played in slow motion. Leo and Polly watched themselves falling through the air outside the movie theater and landing in the urine. Every single droplet of piss that was thrown up by the splash flew up in such rich detail and real-time lifelike brilliance that Leo and Polly thought they could almost taste the foul liquid. Then they realized they were just tasting some of the residue that was still on their face and dripping from their hair.

"I must say," Mike continued, "that movie you were watching didn't look nearly as fun as this."

Monday

9:30am

"Mike visited me in my room last night."

Jockton and Morton looked at Sam, the three of them assembled in the station meeting room, each with a coffee.

"Mike the demon?" Jockton asked.

Finally, after resisting the urge for so long since arriving in town, Sam had had enough of being falsely polite with Jockton and took inspiration from Morton's attitude. "No, Michael Jackson. He wanted to know if I have any sons he can have a slumber party with."

Jockton's face was a clash of shock and hurt, each emotion fighting for dominance. This only made Sam feel a touch of remorse and he wasn't sure if he should apologize, but Morton exploded into laughter, impressed by Sam's unexpected riposte. Sam, for his part, was also impressed, as nothing in Morton's behavior had hitherto suggested he was capable of smiling, much less laughing.

"I was only asking, Sam," Jockton said. "There's no need to be rude."

"What did he look like?" Morton asked, recovering his composure.

"I didn't see his face. It was dark and I didn't feel like going for a close-up look."

"Then how do you know it was Mike?"

"He showed me a vision of my dead naked parents."

"That's disgusting!" Jockton said.

"Yes, Don, my parents are disgusting."

"So they're dead?" Jockton continued.

"A vision?" Morton inquired.

"He told me to go into the bathroom and I saw my decapitated parents. I puked and Mike vanished. Then my parents vanished. And so did my puke."

"Then they could still be alive," the Sheriff opined.

"That's neither here nor there, Sheriff," Morton said, and turning to Sam, asked: "Did Mike say anything?"

"He wanted to know why this case wasn't bothering me more. And he asked if I'd figured it out about the John Does yet."

"Meaning?" Morton asked.

"Who knows? He was probably being cryptic just for the hell of it. I also found out he's a pervert who watched me having sex."

"A perverted serial killing demon," Morton commented, shaking his head.

"Only in America, Detective? Is that what you're thinking?" Sam asked.

"Only on this fucked up planet, Mr. Hain," Morton replied.

"You've been in town only a couple of days and you've already met someone?" Jockton asked, doing his best to conceal his jealousy.

"Is that relevant, Don?" Sam asked, irritated again by Jockton. "My personal life is not up for discussion."

"Do you know any occultists?" Morton asked Sam.

"No, why?"

"Since you say the book can't help, I think our next move should be to seek out an expert on black magic to see if there's a way we can destroy Mike."

"Well, I don't know any…" Sam trailed off. "Actually, yes, there is someone we could ask. But it's a long shot."

Monday

12:38pm

"Say what?"

Rob looked at Sam, Jockton, and Morton across from him in a booth in Eat All Day, wondering if these guys were either mocking him for his taste in music or trying to groom him for some pedo shit.

"Do you happen to know anyone who's an expert on the occult?" Sam repeated.

"We know a few people who are involved in the shadowy regions of society where the faint of heart fear to tread," Lucy, seated next to Rob, offered with a smile.

"Stop trying to be an edgelord, Lucy," Rob said.

"Hey!" his girlfriend said, playfully shoving him.

"Do you or don't you, boy?" Morton asked impatiently.

"No, I don't. We don't. The fuck you wanna speak to someone about the occult? Are these murders satanic?"

"We can't discuss the details of the case," Jockton replied with an air of authority that even to Rob rang hollow.

"You kinda already did."

The three men stood up. "Sorry for wasting your time," Sam said.

"Did you ask me just because I listen to death metal?" Rob asked.

"We asked because you seem like a cool kid who knows people," Sam replied.

"The fuck you did. You're as bad as my mom. Just 'cause I listen to heavy shit don't mean I'm gonna slice someone up or know people who do."

"Cool it, boy," Morton ordered forcefully, which dented Rob's bravado in front of Lucy.

As the three walked out of the diner, Sam said: "It was worth a shot."

"No, it wasn't," Morton replied.

"It was your idea, Detective. You can't blame Don for this one."

"Thank you, Sam," Jockton said.

"I know it was my idea. I can admit when something I've come up with hasn't paid off. It's called having integrity and insight," Morton explained.

"I should have known you laughing this morning was just a temporary glitch," Sam said.

FOUR MONTHS BEFORE

Premium

Since the turn of the 21st century, American television had witnessed a golden age unlike anything that had come before. Quality, talent, creativity; all were in abundance, and the term *premium* was used to describe the intelligent, epic drama series that took their time telling a story and didn't patronize the audience.

Leo and Polly weren't the demographic to whom these shows were aimed at. However, one evening alone in their motel room while Polly was out getting drunk in a bar and letting desperate, sex starved men finger her, Leo was surfing channels when he stopped at one such drama. He watched, struggling to make sense of what was happening but nevertheless discerning that this was one of those fancy shows that people with college degrees or who were gay watched.

Leo was about to switch channels when a violent scene got his attention. He stayed with it and, as the scene unfolded, a character began a lengthy monologue, telling the other character an allegorical anecdote that had a moral related to the present situation they found themselves in. Leo didn't understand it, but he got the impression that this is how smart criminals must speak. His pride was still hurt from Mike garnering all the glory for the Bloodworth murder, and now watching this, he got an idea for the next murder that excited him. He'd tell Polly when she got back from being finger fucked by the kind of men who still live with their parents.

***

The Rance family – father Louis, 53, mother Joanna, 50, son Melvin, 22, and daughter Esme, 20 – were sat around the dinner table, discussing what was going on in their lives while enjoying Louis's signature rigatoni that he had slaved away for hours searching for a restaurant of above-adequate epicurean standards to deliver. Joanna and Louis sat at opposite ends, and Esme and Melvin sat across from each other.

Melvin had moved into his own apartment the year before, but he always kept his promise to attend the weekly family meal unless his job as an investment banker took him away on travels. Esme was home for the week from Princeton, where she was studying anthropology.

"Guess who I bumped into at a party last week?" Esme asked, grinning. Before her family could answer, she said: "Plumeria!"

"Is she studying there?" Joanna asked.

"I thought you two hate each other," her brother said, luxuriating in the rich buttery taste of the rigatoni.

"No and no," Esme replied. "She was there with her boyfriend who's studying there. And I don't hate Plumeria. I never have. She's just never forgiven me for what I said about her cotillion two years ago."

"She's still mad about that?" her mother asked in astonishment.

"Sweetheart," Louis began, which always meant a criticism was forthcoming, "like I told you at the time, you can't go getting principled and outspoken at such a young age and about things that are important to other people."

"Dad, all I said was I don't agree with cotillions. They're outdated, regressive, and they have no place in today's world. I didn't say anything about Plumeria herself."

"She felt you were judging her," her father continued.

"No, she felt Esme thinks she's better than her," Melvin volunteered.

"Melvin!" Esme said.

"It's true, isn't it?" Melvin asked.

"Well, yes, but that's beside the point. Loyalty's a two-way street. It's like all the times I defended her against the kids at school making fun of her name counted for nothing."

"Hey, umm, Esme? Question. Do you judge me for working in banking?" Melvin asked. Esme looked at him and could immediately tell he was back to being that 14-year-old who liked starting shit.

"Can we just have a nice family meal please?" Joanna pleaded to her children.

"I'm just asking," Melvin said innocently, taking another mouthful of the rigatoni.

"No, Melvin, I don't," his sister finally replied.

"But you do think you're superior to me?"

"Well, that goes without saying."

A pause. And then the tension was relieved by everyone at the table laughing.

And then the doorbell rang.

***

Leo and Polly had received the order from Mike for a second kill. After their ill-fated trip to Forest Park, they knew that if they were to target another affluent neighborhood, they had to look the part. They splashed out on a suit and dress from a thrift store, ten dollars in total. Despite their effort, Leo in a suit and Polly in a dress were much like Michael Jackson's marriages:

unconvincing, implausible, laughable, and tragically desperate. It also didn't help that Leo's faded navy suit smelled of poverty, and Polly's dress was last fashionable in 1979.

Searching for a house in Bridlemile, they selected one in a secluded spot. The top of the road they were on bent to the left and right. To the right was the entrance to the local forest. Turning left, the road ended in a cute cul-de-sac where the only house, a sumptuous two-story, was situated.

The happily married killers ascended the stone steps that were nestled in between two beautifully maintained burgundy shrubs and walked up the winding path to the front door. Polly was skeptical about what Leo had in mind, but she agreed to go along with it since he never complained whenever she wanted to go out and get finger banged by desperate men.

Leo rang the doorbell and they both waited with phony grins in case they were being observed on CCTV. Both had their new weapons concealed, having disposed of their previous firearms, the one act of law enforcement evading efficiency they had learned over their many crime committing years, and were sweating from the anxiety of this potentially ending in another fuck-up. When they heard multiple voices inside, their anxiety magnified.

"There's people!" Polly whispered agitatedly.

Before Leo could respond with *We're awesome at killing and we ain't gotta be scared of more than one fucker and shit,* the front door opened and Louis Rance looked out at the two strangers with a polite but bemused smile. "Can I help you?"

"Yeah, you can," Leo answered. He took out his gun from his inside jacket pocket and said quietly: "Don't say shit or I'll blow you away. We're just gonna join you for a bit."

Louis was speechless. He had never dealt with a situation like this before in his life and he didn't know how to react. His instinct was to yell a warning to his family, but the gun being pointed at him by the malodorous man on his doorstep put paid to that option.

"OK," Louis finally said, now looking at the equally foul-smelling woman on his doorstep who was pointing a gun too.

"Good. Just go back in, quiet, and normal and shit," Leo ordered, taking a step forward into the entrance hall, forcing Leo to make way for the intruders to come in.

"Louis, who is it?" his wife called from the dining room.

Joanna, Esme, and Melvin had all stopped eating and watched the doorway expectantly. They simultaneously exchanged glances upon hearing more than one person approaching the room. Louis appeared, looking pale, followed by two odd looking individuals whose appearance and smell immediately set off internal alarm bells.

"Honey, who is this?" Joanna asked while looking at the man and woman with a friendly smile.

"Umm...," Louis began weakly. He turned to look behind him and saw that the two assholes who'd just fucked up his family meal had concealed their weapons. "These are... These nice folks are just going to join us for dinner, that's all."

Esme looked at the pair and deduced what was going on. "Oh, Dad, it's so kind of you to help the homeless!" Before her father could correct her, and before Leo or Polly could get indignant, Esme got up and pulled her chair out, saying: "Please, one of you take my seat. I'll go get more chairs."

Leo was desperate to tell her to go fuck herself and that he didn't want her pity, but he was adamant about conducting this in the way he had planned with Polly. He went ahead and sat down, and Polly, who was desperate to tell Leo he's a rude son of a bitch for taking the seat without asking her first if she wanted it, stayed silent, wishing to go through with their plan without any mistakes.

While Esme went to get some extra chairs, Louis took his place back at the table and smiled awkwardly at his wife and son.

"You folks from around here?" Melvin asked.

"No," Leo replied curtly.

"Where are you from?" Joanna asked.

"All over," Polly replied even more brusquely than her husband.

"Well, I'm Melvin. Nice to meet you, Mr. ...?"

"Hain. Leo Hain." Since they intended to kill them, there was no need for fake names.

"Nice to meet you, Leo," Joanna said, who then looked over at the woman stood there stiff and joyless.

"Hain. Polly Hain."

"And nice to meet you, Polly."

"Here you go," Esme said, returning to the room with two chairs. She placed one down next to Leo and went around to the other side and placed the other chair next to Melvin. She was about to sit down next to her brother when Polly took a step forward.

"No, I'll sit there."

"Don't you want to sit with your husband?"

"Your parents ain't not sitting next to each other now, is they?" Polly said with irritation in her voice that took Esme by surprise, given her family's hospitality towards these total strangers.

"OK, whatever makes you most comfortable." Esme went and sat down next to Leo, lifting her wine glass and breathing it in as a way to cope with the putrescence of the funk from the man next to her.

Polly took her seat next to Melvin, who felt he was going to retch but picked up on what his sister was doing and followed suit, seeming to Polly he was admiring the aroma of his wine for a prolonged period.

"This is excellent Merlot, it really is. I can't get enough of it," Melvin said, his nose so far into his glass that he was almost snorting the wine.

"Would you both like some of the rigatoni? There's some left in the kitchen," Joanna offered, hoping they'd say no.

"No," Leo lied, dying to eat but determined to see this through correctly. He'd show everyone he could be clever when it came to murder.

"Some wine?" Joanna asked.

"Alright, let's cut the shit and shit," Leo said, taking out his gun.

Joanna and her children shrieked in shock.

"Please don't hurt them!" Louis begged.

"You knew he had a gun?!" Joanna asked in disbelief.

"He said he'd kill me if I said anything. They just want to join us for a while, that's all. We'll have some drinks and food and they'll be on their way. Isn't that right?"

"No, we're gonna fucking kill you and shit," Leo replied.

Joanna cried out in despair. Esme and Melvin looked at each other fearfully.

Polly took out her gun, causing Joanna to wail again.

"We're cooperating," Louis pleaded calmly. "There's no need for violence."

"Not yet. We're just gonna sit here for a bit, talk and shit. You carry on doing what you doing," Leo ordered.

"You want us to eat while you point guns at us?" Melvin asked.

"Yeah," Polly said.

"Let's just do what they say," Louis said, trying to think of a way out of this situation.

"Go on. Eat and shit," Leo ordered.

"Which do you want us to do?" Melvin asked.

"Huh?" Leo said, scratching his scalp with his gun.

Melvin's suspicions were now confirmed. They were not dealing with smart criminals. "Do you want us to eat or do you want us to go to the bathroom?"

"Huh? I just said eat and shit."

"He's using *and shit* as an etcetera," Esme explained helpfully.

"Yeah, that thing," Leo said, pretending to understand.

The Rance family resumed their meal in a very uncomfortable silence, their appetite long gone thanks to the firearms being pointed from either side of the table.

The moment had come. Leo was excited to finally do what the TV show had inspired in him. "Let me tell you something," he began. Polly smiled proudly as the others stopped eating and looked at him. "One time, I went to the track. I placed a bet on a horse to win. I read all the tips and shit and I picked the one they all said was gonna win. So I placed my bet. Twenty bucks. I sit down with a beer and I watch the race. I watch it and the horse I bet on lost. He fucking lost. I lost my goddamn bet and shit. I was pissed. After the race, I go looking for the rider who lost. I found him and I said: 'Hey! You lost me twenty bucks!' So I took out my gun and I popped him. Two in his head."

The Rance family stared at Leo, none of them sure why he had just told them this and none of them sure what, if anything, they were supposed to say in response.

"Yeah. Makes you think, don't it?" Leo said, trying to fold his arms and remembering he was holding a gun and unfolding them.

"Yeah," Polly concurred. She looked at Joanna and then looked at Melvin next to her and Esme across the table, making sure they'd seen her make eye contact before continuing. "Let me tell you a story. I was at a house party. This was some many years back. I didn't ain't met Leo not yet. I go to this party and this fuckass guy told me I ain't invited. I said I don't care. He said 'who are you?' I said it don't matter who I am. He got his friends to throw me out his party. I went back to the house later when it was just him and I shot him. Killed him. He was dead. He died."

Again, the Rances were lost for words. The silence annoyed Leo and Polly. These people weren't reacting the way they were supposed to.

Leo decided to have one more go. "You know, sitting here, looking at you people and shit and thinking about things, I remember something. There was this guy I knew back in Marion County. That be Marion County, West Virginia. This guy lent me fifty bucks. I said I'd pay him back and shit. One week goes by. Two weeks. Four weeks. A month. And he's on my back about paying him back. So I just go round to his place with a couple of other guys and we bash his head in. He go to hospital. He didn't ask for his money back again. 'Cause he was in hospital, see? Yeah... Makes you think, don't it?"

"Think what?" Louis asked, his irritation having peaked. Even though they were brandishing firearms, these two had proven themselves to be somewhere near the bottom of the evolutionary ladder, which somewhat fractured their desire to be seen as intimidating. "All you've done is tell us about people you've murdered or beaten up."

Leo sat forward, seriously pissed that his plan had failed. "Oh, you people think you're so much betterer than us, don't you?!"

"Oh, there's no need to go all the way up to us as a benchmark. No, our turds are a sufficient apex in comparison to you," Louis proclaimed.

Leo looked to his wife for some help in understanding.

"I think he's insulting you, Leo!" Polly said.

"You catch on fast," Louis told her.

"Aw, fuck this shit and shit!" Leo barked. He slid back his chair to stand up, but did so with such uncontrolled anger that instead of sliding the chair, it rocked backwards, sending him crashing to the floor.

Joanna Rance didn't like guns; never had. And she had always resisted the notion of owning any for home defense for fear of accidentally killing a family member. However, after a friend of hers had narrowly survived a home invasion, she decided with Louis that perhaps one or two guns would be worthwhile in case the worst ever happened. In the end, they had a fully loaded gun concealed in every room of the house, their locations known only to the four of them. In the living room, the gun was strapped to the underside of the dinner table where she now sat. For the last ten minutes, she had been surreptitiously gripping the gun, waiting for the right moment to remove it from its holster. Upon seeing Leo fall to the floor, she pulled the gun out and stood up, pointing her weapon at Polly and screaming: "Don't you fucking move!" She didn't wait for an answer and just fired, hitting Polly in her left shoulder. Polly shrieked and got up in a panic.

Melvin stood up and went to restrain her, but she fired off a shot. The bullet struck Melvin in the throat. Blood seeped from the hole and he gurgled as he held his throat.

Joanna and Louis screamed on seeing their son's injury. She ran over to him, while Louis stomped over towards Polly, intending to punch her into a grave. Still unsteady on her feet, she fired again and struck Louis in the stomach.

Esme wasn't aware of what was happening with the others, as she had been alarmed when she saw Leo struggling to get up. She had got out of her seat and was holding her chair above her head. She brought it down and smashed Leo on the face. She continued to rain blows, turning his face bright red with blood. "You ungrateful fucking assholes! We offered you rigatoni and everything!"

Pausing her attack for a second, Esme looked around and saw her mother on the floor, holding her dying son, and her father doubled over in pain, clutching his belly. Esme's brain was still struggling to process the abject tragedy taking place in front of her when her rage glistened anew on seeing Polly approach from the other side of the table, one hand clasped to her wounded shoulder, the other on her gun. Esme mustered up all her strength and tipped the table up onto its side, sending all the plates, bowls, glasses, and cutlery smashing to the floor. Polly slid on the tomato sauce and wine and landed on her back.

With her back to him, Leo, struggling to see through the curtain of blood that was draped over his eyes, reached for his gun and fired three times upwards at Esme. The law of averages wasn't usually on the Hains' side, but this time, after the first two bullets missed, the third hit her right elbow. She swung around, squealing in pain. Esme looked down at Leo, who still had his gun aimed at her. The shock of being shot had immobilized Esme, leaving her an open target.

Louis, trying to ignore the pain from his bullet wound that had caused blood loss beyond the point of no return, appeared behind his daughter and attempted to pull her back, but he was too late. Leo fired and the bullet went into Esme's head, traveled through, exited, and entered Louis's head, coming to a stop in his brain. Father and daughter dropped dead to the floor.

Once Melvin passed his final breath, Joanna looked over and saw Polly writhing about in the pool of blood, sauce, and Merlot. The sight of this wretched monster triggered a ferociousness in Joanna that she had never felt in all her 50 years. She carefully rested Melvin against the wall and got to her feet. She still had her gun, but opted for another method of vengeance instead.

She marched over to Polly, who looked fearful, as she had dropped her gun out of reach when she slipped onto the floor. Joanna saw the bullet wound in Polly's shoulder and slammed her high-heeled foot down on it.

Polly felt pain like she had never experienced before and screamed as Joanna dug her heel even deeper into the hole.

"You OK, baby?" Leo called out from the other side of the table.

"Does it sound like I'm OK, you fuckass idiot?!" Polly screamed.

Joanna raised her heel a few inches and drove it back down, hearing the crunch of bone. Polly, screaming so loud that Joanna thought the windows might shatter, was tempted to beg for mercy, but she had her pride.

Joanna put all her weight on her right foot, eliciting more ear-piercing screams from Polly. Joanna had never been a sadist, and she would now reject any suggestion that what she was feeling was sadism. Her family had been taken from her in the most horrendous manner imaginable and she felt justified in giving one of the individuals responsible a taste of what they had served up.

"I'm coming, hold on and shit," Leo said, wiping the blood off his face. He was in agony from the blows that Esme had struck with the chair and he felt nauseous.

Joanna removed her heel from the bullet hole and a geyser of blood sprayed up. She leaned down and grabbed Polly by the back of her head. "I'm not done yet, you fucking illiterate, stinking, evil, badly dressed piece of shit!" She charged forward, dragging Polly with her. She rammed Polly face first into the upturned table. Joanna repeated this five more times, discharging all her anger and grief in vociferous and cathartic screams that punctuated each slam. After the fifth head smash into the table, Joanna let Polly slump to the floor. She appeared to have lost consciousness.

Joanna sat down on the floor, breathing heavily. She looked up and saw Leo, a bloody, disheveled mess himself, who had crept around from behind the table and was pointing his gun at her. What had earlier on frightened Joanna no longer held any threat for her. Her family was gone and she knew she was next. The inevitability was strangely calming.

"I was going to say if your wife wakes up, she might have brain damage," Joanna said. "But...," she continued, looking down at Polly, "I think that ship sailed a long time ago, don't you?"

Leo fired once, killing Joanna instantly.

He then scratched his head with his gun and wondered out loud: "What ship?"

Debrief

The first question that came to Polly after she came round was what was causing the excruciating pain in her shoulder. The second was why her head was throbbing as though it had... As if she had been... Like she had...

Polly always struggled to formulate similes, so she just settled for wondering why her head hurt so fuckass bad.

She sat up on the floor, too battered and exhausted to stand. The sight of the bullet wound made her grunt in shock. Taking in the carnage around her, she tried to piece together where she was and who had shot her and why. As far as she could tell at this moment, there had been some violence. She just wasn't sure who these dead people were. The house was much nicer than any she'd broken into before, which made her presence there all the stranger.

Polly then saw someone she did recognize. Leo was lying on a pile of shattered plates, where he'd rested after killing Joanna. He had spent the last ten minutes staring up at the floating leaf chandelier, debating whether it would be better if Polly didn't regain consciousness. When he heard a burp of mammoth bass and the scratching of fabric, he knew his wife had come round and that she was scratching her crotch.

"What... the fuckass... happened... Leo?!" were her first words to him, each one separated by an agonized exhalation.

Leo didn't immediately answer, figuring that, from her line of sight, she couldn't see his face and he could pretend to be asleep.

"Leo... I know you ain't... you ain't... ain't asleep, you son... you son... son of a... son of a... bitch!"

He slowly sat up. "We killed some rich people, don't you remember? I killed three of 'em and you killed one of 'em."

Polly attempted to stand up, and she did succeed, only to then keel right over, landing face first on a shard of the shattered salad bowl. She shrieked, rolled over, and sat back up, wiping the blood from the cut on her cheek, and wiping that off on the table. She maneuvered around, her feet shoving Joanna's corpse aside as she did so, and rested against the table. Clutching her injury, she ranted: "Why'd I only waste one? That ain't fair, you son of a bitch!"

"It ain't my fault you fell on your ass!"

"Who was they anyway?"

The question scared Leo. Had that woman really caused his Polly brain damage? "You telling me you don't remember shit?"

"Oh...," Polly said, feeling woozy and touching her forehead. "No, I don't not remember nothing."

Leo grabbed a handful of spilled rigatoni and shoved it in his mouth. His pleasure quickly turned to disgust and he spat the whole barely masticated lot out. It was only then he realized some of the red on the rigatoni wasn't sauce.

"So this *is* how it's going to be every time you kill for me," Mike said, standing at the doorway, one hand in his pocket and the other brushing some dust off his suit jacket.

Polly hit her head against the table from the shock of the sudden intrusion. "Son of a bitch!"

"No, I don't have a mother. Or a father for that matter," Mike said, venturing into the room.

Polly's memory was fully restored and she now remembered Leo falling on his ass first. "Leo, you lying son of a bitch! You was the one who fell on your ass!"

"I thought you can't remember shit!"

"That's my doing," Mike explained, coming to a stop just in front of the chaos. "I can't be doing with a conversation where everything I say is met with a moronic *huh* because she can't remember. I already get enough of that from the both of you when you do remember."

"What you mean by this how shit is gonna be?" Leo asked.

"We did good, didn't we?" Polly asked hopefully.

"No, my dear," Mike replied with a jaunty tone in his voice. "No, you didn't. You didn't do good, didn't you. You did bad. You did very bad, didn't you."

"Huh?"

"Right on schedule."

"Huh?"

"When I commanded you both to kill for me, it was not with a view to me being your clean-up man after every murder. It should not be my responsibility to keep you dumb fucks from being caught by the police because you leave more DNA than there is on a hooker's bed."

"You calling my wife a hooker?" Leo asked indignantly, forgetting who he was talking to.

Mike replied by making Leo's eyeballs fall out of his skull and roll across the floor, coming to a stop in front of Mike's shoes.

"I'm sorry! I'm sorry!" Leo wailed, looking up from his new position and seeing Mike tower over him.

Polly grinned. She didn't want her husband dead, but he deserved this for lying and for dominating the kills.

"Raise you voice at me again," Mike said, "and I'll carve you into a million pieces and make your wife eat them."

Polly wanted to say that was unfair, but then remembered what happens when you talk back to Mike, because she saw it just a few seconds before.

"Yes, sir," Leo replied. The eyeballs rolled across the floor and hurtled up and back into their sockets. He clasped his face with relief. "Thank you, sir."

"Enough of the *sir* shit, I'm not a human."

Mike stepped over to Polly, leaned down, and lifted her to her feet by her hair. She grimaced and squealed in pain. Observing the bullet hole in her shoulder, he asked: "Who did that?" Polly cocked her head and nodded to indicate Joanna's body. "Good for her. She defended herself and that's right. Not to mention you deserved it."

"Can you fix it? Like, get the bullet out?" she pleaded.

"Why, of course I can," Mike answered, the jaunt returning to his tone, this time accompanied by a smile. "Why, I'll remove it, clean the wound, apply a dressing, get you milk and cookies, tuck you up in bed, and read you a bedtime story."

"You will?!" Polly said, pleasantly surprised.

"No, you vomitous goblin, I was being sarcastic."

He nudged her across the room and gestured to Leo to get up. "The two of you go stand over by the door." They did as they were told.

Mike then clicked his finger. In a flash, the dining table and chairs were back in place, along with the meal, crockery, and cutlery. The Rances were back in their seats, albeit still dead.

The floor was pristine once again, and all the transferred fibers, DNA, blood, and wine and food stains that had collected on the Hains from the Rances and vice versa had disappeared.

Mike turned to look at them. "Next time, just go for one person to kill. What am I saying, you couldn't even kill one person right."

He shook his head and walked past them into the entrance hall, putting a hand to his nose as he went. "And for the love of fuck, would you take a bath once in a while. Just once."

Even though Mike had no need to go to the front door to leave, since he'd be transporting himself back to the Diabolical Domain imminently, he used the time it gave him walking there to continue insulting them. "As for your injury," he said, addressing Polly, "go to the hospital. Or don't. Do whatever you like. I really don't care. You can even die if you want. I'll still have your husband to go kill for me." He opened the door and stepped out, adding: "I'll be in touch about your next kill. Till then, you two can just… uh, you're not worth the effort of thinking up another insult." With that, he closed the door.

The Magic Bullet

"Do you believe lightning can strike twice, Walls?"

Morton looked at Judy, who was chewing gum and had switched to purple streaks in her hair, and said: "What did I say about cliches, Judy?"

"You said something, but I can't remember."

Morton suppressed the smile that was clawing its way to his face, put his hands in his pockets and said: "Just hit me with it."

When he examined the Rance murder scene, it had certainly appeared unusually tidy for the location of four murders, and there was also the question of why the victims had stayed in their seats as each was shot one at a time. But Morton had theorized a perfectly logical explanation. There was no forced entry because the victims knew their killers, or the killers gained entry under false pretenses – and there had to have been more than one killer because of the next point in his theory. There were no signs of a struggle because one or more killers made sure the Rances didn't move while another carried out the shootings.

Now standing in the morgue, he was perturbed by Judy's rhetorical question, which he understood to be a reference to the Bloodworth murder.

"You have at least two shooters. Bullets were fired from a .38 and a 9mm." Morton nodded, relieved that one part of his theory was confirmed. Judy moved across to the first body, Joanna Rance. "One bullet to the head from a .38. Simple." Again, Morton nodded, but he could tell Judy was building to a showpiece reveal.

Moving to the body of Melvin Rance, she continued: "One bullet to the throat from a 9mm."

Morton wanted to say *Just get to the lightning part,* but he just nodded and followed her to the third body, Louis Rance. "Two shots. One to the abdomen from the 9mm. And one to the head from the .38."

"OK. And?"

Judy moved to the last body, Esme Rance. "This is where the interesting part begins. Two shots. One to the elbow from the .38 and one to the head, which I now know was also from the .38."

"Two shots from the same firearm. What's the shocker here, Judy?"

"Cool it, Walls. Have I ever let you down? CSI recovered shell casings that account for all the shots fired, and the bullets that missed, and it threw up a mystery that I've only just solved in the autopsy. The back of Esme Rance's head has an exit wound. The bullet didn't lodge in her brain. And it wasn't found at the scene. But it hadn't disappeared either. You ready for this, Walls? It entered in a straight line into Louis Rance's head and lodged in *his* brain. I know it's the same bullet because her DNA was on it." Judy gestured towards the tray containing all the bullets she'd removed from the bodies.

Morton's stomach lurched. He knew the import of what she had just said, because he remembered where the victims were sitting when he visited the crime scene.

"Esme was sitting diagonal to her father to his right."

"Yeah, I got that already," he replied quietly.

"I don't need to say Oswald for you to understand what happened here."

"You just did." He shook his head. "Magic fucking bullet."

"You got it, Walls! Bullet enters Esme Rance's head, exits, flies all the way around in a 180, turns left, and goes into Louis Rance. That's impressive."

"It's also impossible."

"Says you. The facts say otherwise. And based on the forensics report, it just adds insult to mystery, what with the killers not leaving any evidence behind. But that's not so weird. You said they didn't have to force entry, and there was no struggle."

"Maybe they weren't shot where they sat and the killers moved the bodies after."

"And not leave any trail of blood? If they were shot in another part of the room, Esme in front of her father, blood would be dripping from her exit wound, her elbow, and the shot to his stomach. I don't care how meticulous the killers are, there's gonna be blood trickling from those injuries all the way to the dinner table. You know the blacklight didn't find anything."

"The elbow and stomach wounds could have come after they were moved."

"After they've already been shot in the head and they're dead? Are you OK, Walls?!"

"Cool your jets, Judy. Killers do crazy shit all the time that defies logic," he said more in a tone of malaise than conviction. "Tell me one thing, though. You don't normally test for DNA when you recover a bullet."

"You're right, Walls. But I had to because the number of bullets I took out didn't match with the number of wounds. Esme's headshot wasn't accounted for. So I knew one of the other bullets from the .38 had to have done double duty. I do know my job, partner! Didn't you say we might become partners?" she winked.

"Your lightning comment. Are you suggesting the same people who did Jake Bloodworth did this?"

"Not at all. The .38 bullets don't match the ones from the Bloodworth murder. There was no 9mm used there either. And I'm not a cop, but even I can see there's nothing to connect the two cases. Bloodworth was a hick with an AR-15, and the Rances were an educated, upper middle-class family."

"Two cases close together where there's no forensics and something impossible happens both times. What are the odds."

"No cliches, Walls! Come on, partner!"

"You know I don't let anyone else talk to me the way you do, don't you, Judy?"

"That's why I love you, Walls. Platonic, of course."

"Yeah, you didn't need to confirm that part."

"That reminds me. Would you quit telling guys I'm single and available?"

Morton felt hot embarrassment in the pit of his stomach. "Uh…"

"It's not like you to be lost for words, Walls!" Judy said. "What, you think I didn't know it was you?"

"I'm sorry. It was just…"

"I'm just fucking with you! I don't mind. I'm happy that you're just like the rest of us after all."

"What?"

"You're not the cold, gray dude some people have you down as. OK, everyone has you down as. I thought *Damn, Walls does have a lighter side. He gets his kicks sending guys my way for rejection.*"

"Thanks, Judy. You'd have every right to be pissed at me."

"No problem, Walls. And don't worry, I won't tell anyone."

"That I apologized for something?"

"That you have a sense of humor."

Mastermind

When Leo and Polly were scouting for a home to invade in Bridlemile, they saw the forest that was near the house they settled upon as their target. They agreed they'd visit the forest after carrying out the murders so they could fuck in pitch black darkness, just to give it an occult vibe, the location itself having no occult markers about it.

But that whim had to be abandoned when Polly was shot and Mike refused to help. They headed to a hospital in Sunderland, not far from their motel. It was the kind of hospital that often saw visitors to its ER with gunshot wounds for which they had no detailed explanation. The doctors there were accustomed to this and no longer bothered to ask how someone was shot in the leg while having a bath alone in their apartment or who was responsible for stabbing a young self-proclaimed entrepreneur who had *MURDER IS FUN* tattooed across his chest, accompanied by tattoos of machetes.

And the ER staff certainly knew not to involve the cops. Not because the docs arrived at that decision by weighing up the options and potential consequences, but because one visitor who required the removal of six bullets told the junior surgeon treating him: "Call the cops and I'll massacre your whole family." A threat that left the doc terrified, even though he didn't have any family and now would never have one just to be on the safe side.

With her shoulder patched up, they returned to their motel room and eagerly awaited news coverage of their latest escapade. And sure enough, the Rance murders were the top story on the lunchtime news the following day. The reporter, Gavin, outlined the case while Leo and Polly jumped up and down on the bed, spilling beer all over themselves.

Newscaster Angie in the studio spoke to the reporter via a live link-up: "Gavin, I gather you spoke to one of the detectives on the case and he had some interesting things to say, isn't that right?"

"What did he say?!" Leo asked jubilantly.

"He gonna say we were the shit!" Polly predicted.

"That's right, Angie," Gavin replied from outside the Rance house. "The detective I spoke to couldn't go into a lot of detail, but what he did say was that there was an aspect to this crime involving a bullet that defies the laws of physics. They can't explain it and it's proving a real brainteaser. He did say they believe there were at least two killers involved and that, whoever they are, they're criminal masterminds."

"Motherfuck that shit and shit!" Leo roared, spilling his beer on the bed that was already covered in cheesy nacho dust, BBQ sauce, and semen.

"What you bitching about now?"

"He said the killers is masterminds. He's saying we jerked off in the house!"

"That's *masturbate,* you dumbass!" In her impoverished lexicon, masturbate was one of the few words with more than two syllables that Polly knew.

"So what he calling us?"

"I think it means we did good. I didn't get the other stuff. Something about phys ed and the law."

Leo calmed down and scratched his balls, trying to make sense of the report. "Maybe the mom was a gym teacher and the dad was a lawyer."

"Yeah, I guess. The main thing is we the news!"

"We ain't though," Leo said, picking up his beer and grunting in disappointment when he went to have a chug and realized the last few drops had ended up on the bed. He eyed an unopened can on the other side of the room, but it was too far for him to walk, so he settled for picking up a stale nacho from the carpet and dipping it into the newly wet duvet. As he munched on it, he continued: "We ain't the news. If he saying we did good and shit, then he's gotta be talking about Mike."

"This shit again. Just quit your whining, Leo, or you won't get any head tonight."

"That ain't fair, Pol! I need to nut!"

"Then go nut in a towel!"

Leo turned back to the TV, which was reporting on the aftermath of a school shooting in Florida. The Governor there was offering his thoughts and prayers.

"I say next time we let 'em know who's doing this shit," Leo suggested.

"What you saying?"

"I'm saying we leave our names."

A gleam of excitement appeared in Polly's eyes: "You mean like Zodiac?!"

"Even betterer. We sign our real names."

"That is fucking amazing, Leo! I love it!"

"So you gonna give me head now, Pol?"

"Unzip your pants. I'ma blow your mind."

"Can't you just suck my dick?"

Monday

5:57pm

Sam was across the street from the laundromat, drinking a Diet Pepsi, and thinking about Chloe, cocaine, and clitoris, when he heard the commotion. He looked up and saw a huddle of bystanders gathered outside the entrance. Squeals, shrieks, and screams emanated from the crowd. He ran over, assuming another dead body had been found inside.

He forced his way to the front through the throng of smartphone holders recording the spectacle and immediately understood why the looky-loos were so horrified, albeit while still zooming in or adjusting their camera settings to ensure the best shot for upload later.

The inside of the laundromat was awash with blood that alternated between splashing up and down against the windows to spinning in a circular motion, each new rotation faster than before. Nothing else was visible and it took Sam a few seconds before he had the realization that what they were all witnessing was a macabre emulation of a washing machine. Mike was finally flaunting his abilities.

Sam's first instinct was to have the crowd disperse, but he had no authority, and though he'd have liked to believe at least one of the bystanders had been a good citizen and called 911, he knew it was far more likely that their phones had only been used for recording.

He got out his cellphone and called Jockton. "Don, it's Sam. I'm outside the laundromat. You need to get over here ASAP. Morton too."

Monday

5:50pm

It had been a slow day at the laundromat, the news about the murders having put off some potential customers. Nancy was thinking of shutting early and getting a chicken dinner at Eat All Day before heading home.

She took a swig of whiskey, ate a biscuit, and came out of the office. She locked the office door and turned around, all set to depart, when she saw a man in a nice suit who looked a lot like the dead assholes who'd hurt her business. By now, she would have been telling the newcomer to go fuck himself, but she was confused. She hadn't even heard him come in. The door's brass bell should have rung when he entered.

Mike stood in the center of the laundromat, waiting to see how this woman he'd seen and heard so much about would react to his arrival.

Setting aside the matter of his silent entry, Nancy resumed normal service: "We're fucking closed. Come back tomorrow."

"I'm not here to wash clothes."

"Then fuck off."

Mike looked at Nancy with fascination, stroking his chin with the back of his hand. "Have I said anything that can justify your aggression, Ms. Dirgle?"

Not another one. Not a-fucking-nother one. She'd had that sissy boy talk back to her. Then the petal cop from out of town. Now this asshole she wished was as dead as the men he resembled.

"This is my goddamn laundromat and I choose when to close, you got that, petal?!" she boomed.

"Your prerogatives as the owner of this business aren't the problem, or up for debate. I'm asking what entitles you to speak to people the way you do when they, and I, have done nothing to provoke it."

Was this petal fucking serious? She should have been digging into her chicken dinner by now, but here she was being questioned. She was particularly irked by his composed demeanor. If someone was going to talk back to her, as egregious as that was, she'd much rather they swear and get loud, as it was a form of interaction she was comfortable and familiar with. But here she was telling this guy to fuck off and he wasn't flustered at all. It was strange. And it even made her feel a little queasy.

"I talk to you and anyone else how the fuck I like, petal! It's my goddamn right as an American citizen! And I don't need no sissy in a suit coming into my business asking me questions! Now get the fuck out!"

"You know what I can't abide, Nancy?" Mike asked.

That's it. She was done with this shit. Nancy started walking across the laundromat, intending to pass this intruder and go to the door where she would usher him out in a storm of expletives.

But after the second step forward, she found she couldn't move any further. "What the hell is going on?!"

"What I can't abide is someone being offensive and unpleasant for no legitimate reason whatsoever."

This had gone beyond some petal being a pain in the ass. His unwavering demeanor, and her being unable to move, was scaring her and she didn't like it one bit. Because it's others who should be scared, not her.

"You've gone through your whole miserable, worthless life treating people appallingly, and I find that unacceptable. Granted, I'm a demon, so the argument could certainly be made that I'm a fine one to talk about what's unacceptable, but I think basic courtesy is the bare minimum anyone owes each other. Even I make the effort. If I'm going to annihilate someone, let's say, and I'm going to peel the flesh off their skull and use the skull as a drum, I will, at the very least, introduce myself with civility. If I was to greet that person with abuse and fury, they'd be entitled to respond in kind. But you, Nancy…," Mike, who hitherto hadn't moved an inch, said as he stepped forward, causing Nancy to feel terror for the first time ever, "nothing ever provokes you because nothing *has* to provoke you, and no one ever says anything that *could* provoke you. You're just offensive by default."

Nancy, still pointlessly trying to move from her spot, was sure she'd misheard something he said and was desperate to ask. "What did you say you are? A deacon?"

Mike laughed so loudly, it reverberated around the laundromat. "Pretty far from, Nancy. I said… I'm a demon. At least, that's the word you humans use. Silly word if you ask me."

Nancy didn't believe him. Why would she? Who would anyone believe a statement like that? This petal was unsettling and intimidating, but he was a petal nonetheless.

"Are you going to apologize?" Mike asked.

The idea of Nancy apologizing was so out of the realms of reality that she wanted to laugh but for the fact that this man had caused in her feelings she'd never had before.

"Ms. Dirgle," he said slowly, which made her shiver. "Are you going to apologize?"

No. This isn't how things are going to go. She was Nancy Dirgle. Nancy Dirgle doesn't have to put up with this shit. Other people put up with this shit. What was she thinking? Scared? Scared of this petal in a suit? No no no. This ain't that sort of day. Parlor tricks aside, for which there obviously had to be a logical explanation, this ain't how things are gonna go. Time to bring this situation back under her control. Time for normal service to resume.

"I ain't apologizing for shit, you fucking cocksucker! This is my business, my establishment, and you're gonna get the fuck out now! Shut the fuck up with your crazy talk, thinking it gonna scare me! You're nothing but a piece of shit sissy petal in a suit! So, fuck you!"

Silence.

Then Mike said: "You know the ironic thing? If you'd apologized, I'd have just left."

Mike clicked his finger and Nancy shrieked as a gaping hole tore open in her midriff and her insides spilled out.

Monday

6:05pm

Jockton sped over with Ronny as soon as he got the call from Sam. Morton arrived a minute after, and between the three of them flashing their badges, the morbidly curious dispersed.

But what now? The blood was still in a spin cycle and they couldn't just walk into the laundromat. They would just need to wait for it to end.

Then there was Ronny. They couldn't let him in on Mike. But he and the crowd had already seen the blood show. They'd have to come up with a cover story later, but for now, Jockton ordered Ronny to stay outside to keep any further onlookers away.

The blood slowed to a gentle cycle and then went up a notch in speed for what Sam hoped was its final spin. And, indeed, it was.

Jockton told Ronny to keep his eye on the road and not the inside of the laundromat. With the Deputy's attention elsewhere, Sam, Jockton, and Morton prepared to go inside. It was immediately obvious that part of Mike's theatrics was the excess of blood, more than could have come from the poor victim, whoever it was, which would mean the revolting prospect of wading across the laundromat three feet deep in blood, but upon hitting the floor, the giant splash decorated the walls in red, and the excess vanished amidst the splatter, leaving only the remaining real blood that had been shed over the floor.

And when it splashed on the floor, no longer veiling the interior of the laundromat, what they saw astounded the three men. Every time they'd thought this case had offered up the extent of its capacity to shock, they came in for another nasty surprise. They had expected to find another dead man in a suit. What they weren't expecting to see was Nancy suspended horizontally in the air, the center of her torso completely hollowed out and filled by a steel circular column that ran the length from the ceiling to the floor. It spun Nancy around like a NASA training centrifuge, emitting a mechanical hum.

"Well. I guess we can finally rule Nancy out as the killer," Sam said.

Jockton puked.

"Goddamn it, Sheriff!" Morton snapped. He sounded more annoyed with Jockton vomiting than with the baroque scene that confronted them.

"Mike's been busy," Sam commented.

Jockton coughed and wiped his mouth before saying: "Hold on, now. There's a lot of folks in town who had a reason to kill Nancy."

Sam looked up and only then saw what he'd missed before because it had been partially obscured by the blood that had spattered onto the ceiling. There, in big bloody capital letters, was the name *MIKE*. Sam gestured to the ceiling and the other two looked.

"He's a real showman," Sam said.

"I wonder if he heard me when I asked why he'd only killed the John Does with a single stab," Morton pondered.

"I doubt Mike is the thin-skinned type, Detective," Sam said.

"What do we tell the locals?" Jockton wondered out loud.

"I don't think anyone will be surprised to hear Dirgle was murdered," Morton said, hands in his pockets and watching Nancy spin. "You said as much yourself."

"I mean, how do we explain what those folks saw?"

"Just make something up, Sheriff. Can you do that? Sorry, pointless question. Say someone killed Dirgle and set up a wind machine and a vat of blood. That should cover it."

"We need to think laterally here on out about how to end this," Sam suggested.

"Think what?" Jockton asked.

"Outside the box, Don. This isn't a case of collecting clues and arresting suspects."

"How, exactly, do you suggest we think laterally about defeating a demon?" Morton asked, wondering what would happen if he touched the column.

"I haven't got that far."

Morton took out a quarter and warned: "Stand back." He didn't even wait for a response and tossed the coin at the column, taking several steps back in anticipation.

The quarter hit the steel and just fell to the floor.

"Disappointing," Morton intoned.

"Hey!" Jockton said angrily. "What if Mike heard you? Now he's going to do something even crazier for next time!"

"Yes, because I'm sure he was just planning to shoplift for his next spectacular and now he'll have to up his game because of me."

Monday

7:49pm

The vat of blood and wind machine story worked on the locals.

But Mike's extravaganza meant that Sam, Jockton, and Morton were faced with something that, up till then, they'd managed to avoid thanks to his initially unremarkable murders, but was now unavoidable.

They had to let Chuck, the Medical Examiner, in on their secret. There was no getting around it. Nancy's injuries and the steel column that had appeared out of nowhere could not be explained away. They also needed his help in removing her body. No one else could be allowed to view the scene.

Sam volunteered to tell Chuck. He and Jockton sat him down in the meeting room of the sheriff's station while Morton stayed behind at the laundromat to ensure no one entered.

"So, here's the thing, Chuck," Sam began. He was still forming the words in his mind, figuring how best to lead into the secret that had been kept from the M.E., when he realized there was a far easier, quicker, and undeniable way to tell Chuck what was going on.

"Yes?" Chuck asked with a yawn.

"One second," Sam said, getting his cellphone out of his pocket. Morton had sent him the footage of the second John Doe captured by the spy camera. He lined up the video to about twenty seconds before the money shot and handed his phone over to Chuck. "It's best if you just watch this."

Chuck yawned again as he viewed the clip, running his hand through his hair. "Can't you just tell me what this is about?"

"Just watch. Please."

Chuck continued to run his hand through his hair.

His hand stopped moving. He stared at the phone. Then at Sam. Then at Jockton.

"What is this? Is this a joke? You got me over here for a joke?"

"No, Chuck," Jockton replied. "You have my word this is very real."

Sam hoped this assurance from Jockton meant something to Chuck. He hadn't met him enough times to gauge whether the M.E. held the Sheriff in high esteem or viewed him with contempt.

"So somebody did some special effects or something?" Chuck asked.

Sam jumped from the ferocity with which Jockton leapt up from his chair to shout: "See?! It's not just me! He thought it too!"

Chuck looked up at the Sheriff in startled bemusement. "What the hell are you talking about, Don?"

"Wait till Morton gets back. I can't wait to tell him!"

"Is that your priority right now, Don?" Sam asked with clear annoyance in his voice. "We know it wasn't special effects."

"That's not my point, Sam. Morton thought I was being idiotic when I said it could have been. But Chuck here thought the same thing!"

"He doesn't know how and when the video was recorded. You did. That's the difference."

Jockton sat back down, frustrated that Sam had put a dampener on what he felt was a moment of victory.

"If I may continue," Chuck said. "This is either a joke, in which case: why? Are you bored? Do you not have an adequate social life? Is this how you get your kicks? Or you believe what you're saying, in which case I'll call my psychiatrist friend to come down and assess you both."

"There's only one way to convince you," Sam proclaimed, standing up. "Let's go to the laundromat."

"So many exciting adventures have started with a sentence like that," Chuck said.

Monday

8:18pm

Sam reckoned this must be how prosecuting attorneys feel when they drop a bombshell in court that cements their case.

He resisted the urge to smile when Chuck entered the laundromat and saw Nancy spinning, fused into the bloodstained steel column.

But he couldn't resist one dig. "Still want to call your shrink friend?"

Chuck heard him, but chose to ignore him.

Morton, who was standing with his back against the wall, frowned at the implications of Sam's remark, and unfolded his arms. "He didn't believe you?"

"No. And I showed him the video," Sam informed him.

Jockton saw his opportunity. "He thought it was special effects!"

Morton looked at the Sheriff and immediately understood why he appeared so euphoric. "OK, cool your jets, Sheriff. He didn't know when and how the footage was captured. You did. So your suggestion was still dumb."

"Un-goddamn-called for!" Jockton almost yelled.

"Don, can we please focus on what's important right now?" Sam pleaded.

"OK," Chuck said, his gaze fixed on Nancy, "I'll bite."

Sam proceeded to tell Chuck the whole story – his parents, the book, Mike, and the murders. When he was finished, he still feared the M.E. might get a psychiatrist down to assess them.

Instead, Chuck seemed rather blasé. He just ran his hand through his hair and said: "That's people for you."

"That's it?" Morton asked with genuine curiosity.

"I've always allowed for the possibility that aliens might exist in the universe even though we have no evidence for them. And–"

"Mike isn't an alien," Jockton said.

"If you let me finish, Don. I've always allowed for the possibility that aliens might exist in the universe even though we have no evidence for them. And if I can allow for that, I can accept the evidence you've shown me that demons exist. *A* demon, anyway."

"Got there in the end. Now we need you to help get Dirgle's body out of here," Morton said.

"Me? What am I supposed to do? You need to get someone in with a circular power saw to go to work on the column before we remove the body."

"We're trying to keep the number of people who know about Mike to a minimum," Sam explained.

"Why do they need to know about… Are we really calling him by his first name?"

"I don't think demons have surnames," Sam said.

"Just tell them some deranged killer disemboweled her and ran this column through her."

"No one's going to believe a killer came in, murdered Dirgle, and installed a rotating steel column into the floor and ceiling all in the space of an evening," Sam said.

"That's only if you get someone local, Mr. … What's your name again?" Chuck asked Sam.

"He's right," Morton said. "Who says we need to get someone who lives in Millvern? We get in a guy from out of town who doesn't know the circumstances and has no reason to ask about the column. For all he knows, it's always been there."

"Spinning?" Sam said.

"Well, Mr. Hain, I came up with the wind machine and vat of blood story. Why don't you think up something for that?"

"No, what I mean is how's the guy going to stop it spinning? He can't saw through it with Dirgle doing a merry-go-round. There's nothing even there to *make* it rotate. That's Mike's doing. No fucking story's going to explain that."

"He's right," Jockton said.

"Yes, thank you, Sheriff. When you have something worthwhile to contribute beyond stating the obvious, speak up," Morton declared.

"An explosion," Jockton said, overcoming his overwhelming desire to shout at Morton.

"What?" Sam asked.

"We don't get a stranger from out of town. We carry out an explosion to destroy the column. We tell the locals the killer left a suspicious package. That's the only way," Jockton said.

"Holy shit," Morton exclaimed in sincere astonishment. "That actually *is* a good idea."

"Thank you, Wallace," Jockton said with sincere delight.

"You're welcome. And I told you to call me Detective."

Jockton shook his head ever so slightly, just enough that Sam noticed it and felt sorry for the Sheriff. *Poor guy can't win.*

"What about Nancy Dirgle's body?" Chuck asked. "It'll be blown to bits."

"She's already mangled. And it's not like anyone's going to claim the body. She had no family or friends," Jockton said.

Sam looked at the Sheriff with surprise bordering on shock. "Look at you, Don! First you come up with a great idea, and now you're talking just like Detective Morton!"

"Please," Morton said with visible distaste.

"I wasn't trying to be cruel. It's just the facts," Jockton told Sam.

"OK, let's get to it," Morton ordered, stepping forward from the wall. "I'll continue to keep guard here."

"By the way, Chuck," Sam said. "We're the aliens."

"Come again?" the M.E. asked.

"You said you allow for the possibility that aliens might exist even though we have no evidence. But to any other beings in the universe, we'd be aliens. So, aliens exist."

"What I said was a perfectly reasonable statement, Mr. Hain. I said we have no evidence for aliens in the universe. In the absence of any, we're not aliens to anyone."

"Mars isn't inhabited. It's still an alien planet with an alien terrain. We and Earth are alien to Mars."

"Really? We're doing this?" Morton asked with exasperation. "A debate on astrobiology? Not like there's a dead woman spinning around."

Monday

10pm

Sheriff Don Jockton had always prided himself on being a man of integrity. He played by the rules and, despite many opportunities over the years, had never given in to the lure of bribes, kickbacks, and assorted other corruption.

So, it stuck in his throat that he was now having to do something he regarded as sketchy but some other cops would call routine. Since secrecy meant they couldn't involve a bomb squad to carry out a controlled explosion, Jockton had to resort to an inelegant but no less effective method of bringing down the column. He visited the storage facility where all weapons seized from criminals were held pending destruction and took a grenade. All it required was a quick amendment to the online record to state the quantity of grenades recovered was five and not six, as previously entered.

Jockton closed off the corner of the square where the laundromat was located and alerted the nearby restaurants and shops that Nancy's killer had left behind a suspicious package that necessitated a controlled blast.

With the area clear, Sam and Morton stood across the street and watched Jockton approach the laundromat entrance tentatively. Holding the grenade in the sweaty palm of his hand, he looked behind him. Sam gave him an encouraging thumbs-up, which caused Morton to utter a very slight gasp of exasperation.

Jockton opened the door, looked inside, hoping unrealistically that Nancy might have somehow fallen out of the column or that it had stopped spinning. When he saw her still doing the NASA centrifuge boogie, he took a step back, pulled the pin on the grenade, and hurled it. As soon as it left his hand, he spun around and darted out of the laundromat and blazed across the street to join the other two.

An explosion shook the laundromat and shattered all the windows, sending debris flying out onto the sidewalk.

The three men retreated back and covered their faces as dust and debris danced around in the air.

A few looky-loos just beyond the police tape watched from the outside of a restaurant.

"Get back inside!" Jockton ordered when he saw them. "This is a hazardous scene!"

"Then why are you there, Barney?" responded one guy standing with his wife.

"He's an officer of the law and you will address him with respect!" Morton shouted, flashing his badge. The guy went back into the restaurant with his wife.

Jockton couldn't believe his ears. Morton had actually come to his defense. "Thank you, Detective."

"Don't get excited, Sheriff. If I let him speak to you like that, it makes us all look bad."

Again, Jockton shook his head ever so slightly. *I can't win.*

The Sheriff got out his phone and called Chuck, who was waiting down the street in his car, as he didn't want to be close by when the explosion happened. While Chuck made his way over, the three walked across to what was left of the laundromat entrance and looked inside, covering their faces.

Through the swirling dust, they could see the wrecked remnants of the washing machines and dryers. In the center, the column had been ripped in two by the blast. Neither part was spinning.

Nancy's head lay atop of one of the few machines that wasn't destroyed. The rest of her decapitated and hollowed upper torso and arms had landed on a dryer door lying on the floor. The rest of her was nowhere to be seen.

They ventured inside, coughing as they stepped over the wreckage. The hideous possibility occurred to all three, albeit at different points in their tour of the ruins, that the lower half of Nancy's body might be buried under a pile of metal, wood, and plastic. Uncovering it would be a task beyond their abilities, and though bringing a clean-up team now wouldn't pose a problem in terms of having to divulge anything, they would rather Chuck be able to take her remains away this evening and just leave the debris for a crew.

"I'm here," Chuck called out as he walked in. "That was one hell of an explosion. It even made my... oh, Jesus!" He saw Nancy's head atop the washing machine to his immediate left. "That's gross!"

"She's getting the same reactions in death as she did in life," Sam commented.

"I can't find her," Jockton called out from the other end of the laundromat. "I'm gonna go into her office."

"You think the explosion propelled the other part of her body all the way into the office?" Sam asked.

"No, it's where she kept her whiskey. I need a drink."

The door to the back office had been blown off. Jockton stepped inside and froze.

The bottom-half of Nancy's body from the pelvis down had landed on the seat of her office chair in such a way that it was perfectly posed in a normal sitting position.

The other three heard Jockton throw up.

"Oh, he's found her," Morton said.

THREE MONTHS BEFORE

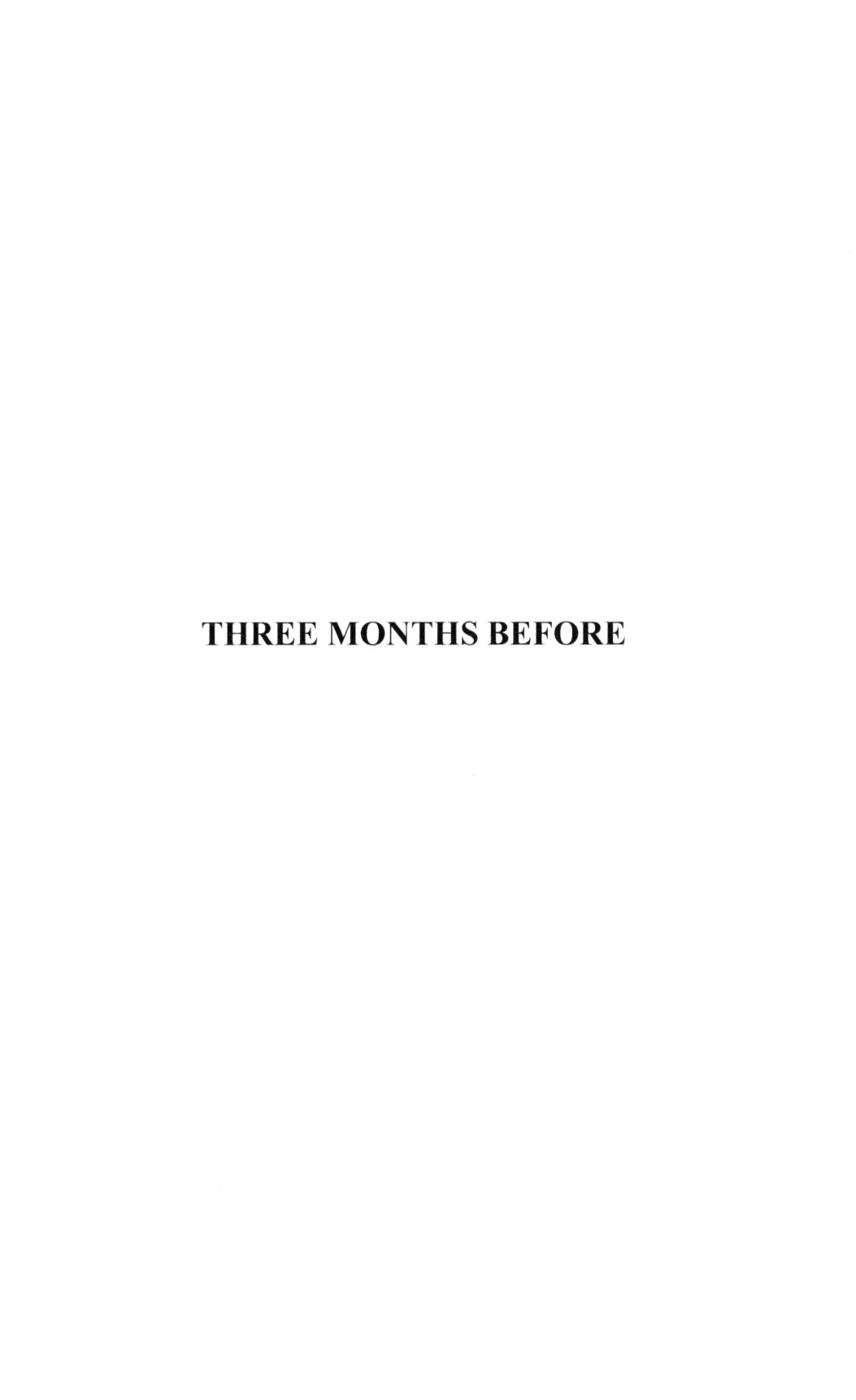

Credit Where Credit's Due

Leo and Polly were back in Sunderland for Mike's third kill order but, in their minds, would be their first real murder since summoning him. No longer would they rely on him to clean up any mistakes, because there *would* be no mistakes. They intended to make this a straightforward kill, authored entirely by them and all the kudos would be for them only.

A few blocks from where they'd killed Bloodworth, they selected another run-down one-story. This one was the last in a row of houses in an even more miserable, poverty-ridden road. Most of the houses had the typical signs of being long unoccupied. Windows that were either shattered or boarded up, trucks and cars that were missing wheels, windscreens, or windows – some all three - and one house that had a *Perot '92* sticker on a window.

The plan was simple, simplicity being at the top of their skillset. One shot to the head, no talk, no struggle, job done.

The Hains went up to the front door and rang the bell. Leo held his .38 behind him, finger poised on the trigger, waiting for his big moment.

***

At pivotal junctures in his life, Billy Nevill had had the misfortune of making the wrong choices, taking the wrong turnings, and giving in to his predilection for trusting people. No one chooses to become a heroin addict and live a miserable life of inertia and bad skin, but where Eddie Wynchover had been an asshole irrespective of his addiction, Billy had been a nice guy who was taken advantage of by people who actively sought out others' malleability to manipulation. So-called friends and girlfriends had exploited his goodwill, from pilfering his meagre earnings working at a fast-food restaurant to using his home as a 24/7 walk-in hangout for themselves and their buddies. Along the way, they'd got Billy hooked on smack.

Even as a junkie, Billy somehow retained his friendly disposition and his fatal weakness for trusting others. When he lost his job because of his problem, the poor guy actually thought his friends to whom he'd been so willing to give money whenever they wanted would help him out now that he was in need. They quickly proved their fair-weather natures to him when they advised him to go shoplifting and sell the goods to fund his habit and other living expenses. And poor Billy was still happy to let them use his home whenever they wanted, believing his kindness would eventually be repaid.

***

Billy never stood a chance. He had just shot up the last of his heroin supply and was in that space where everything was light and dreamy and tranquil. The 27-year-old opened the door and saw a guy on his doorstep. He wanted to ask the guy who he was and if he wanted to hang out. When the guy on the doorstep raised a hand, Billy could see he was pointing something at him. He wanted to tell the guy thanks for bringing him a gift and he'd repay the kindness. But before Billy could say any of that, he saw a bright flash. That was the very last thing he saw.

Billy dropped dead from a single bullet in the head. Leo looked down at his handiwork with pride.

"You did it! We did it!" Polly squealed with joy. "No mess, nothing!"

Leo nodded and proceeded into the house, followed by Polly, closing the door behind them. The house opened onto the living room, where they sat down on the couch and switched on the TV with the remote.

Although Billy had been a heavier junkie than Eddie, his home was paradoxically tidier. He at least carefully disposed of his needles and syringes. What there was instead was an unopened can of beer on the floor. Leo touched it and found it was nice and cold. He decided to toast his triumph. It was the least he deserved. He opened it and took a long chug, concluding with a loud burp. He passed it to Polly, who drank the rest, and ended with a chunky burp too.

"Wait till Mike sees!" Leo said proudly. "He can't say shit!"

"And you're basing that on what?" Mike asked, standing over Billy's body. No matter how many times he'd done that before, Leo and Polly jumped.

"We done good this time!" Polly proclaimed once she'd relaxed.

"Yeah!" Leo added. "No mess, no fighting, nothing! You ain't gotta do shit!"

Mike looked at them both, his face betraying no emotion. He glanced down at Billy's lifeless body, where a small pool of blood was forming, and then walked slowly towards the Hains. They found his measured pace ominous.

Mike came to a stop in front of them. He stroked his chin with the back of his hand and said: "Well, Leo, Polly. Apart from the transfer of fibers on the couch, your fingerprints on the remote and can, and DNA on and inside the can, yes, you've done tremendously well."

Polly looked confused. "So you saying we did do good?"

"No, you stomach-turningly repulsive troglodyte, you didn't do good. You did do bad."

"Son of a bitch!" Leo yelled in frustration. Panicking, he quickly added: "Not you, Mike. I wasn't calling you that. I'm just pissed… At myself."

"Much like your mother after she gave birth, no doubt."

"Huh?"

"Relax, Leo. Quite apart from the fact I don't have a mother, I can always discern when you're addressing me, because if you *had* called me that, I'd be force feeding Polly your heart by now."

"Sorry," Leo said.

"Don't grovel. It's disgusting. Now stand up and go over to the kitchen door."

Leo and Polly did as they were told. They watched Mike click his finger. The fibers on the couch, the fingerprints on the remote and can, and the saliva on and inside the can all disappeared.

He turned to face the Hains. "None of the other fucknuggets who summoned me needed me to do this for them."

"Other people summoned you and shit?" Leo asked.

"You're not the only morons who've cast that spell. And eventually, I will tire of having to do this and I'll just let the police arrest you. Then I'll visit you in prison to torment you."

"More than prison food?" Leo said with a chuckle that he wasn't able to complete because a gash opened up in his throat and the flesh on his face peeled off in strips that ran in rivulets towards his mouth and entered, followed by his eyeballs. Seconds later, the strips of flesh and eyeballs dripped out of the hole in his throat and landed on the floor, where they coalesced into a flattened version of his face.

Polly watched in silent horror, torn between wanting to stamp on Leo's face and wanting to scream at Mike to put her husband's face back where it was.

Leo was once again seeing Mike tower over him from this deranged perspective. He had learnt nothing from the previous incident when Mike warned him never to raise his voice again. Most people would have understood that that was a catchall encompassing more than just shouting, but Leo's comprehension being characterized by a tendency towards polarized thinking meant he couldn't foresee that making a joke out of something Mike said was no less heinous and covered by the same warning.

"Do you really want me to carve you up into a million pieces for Polly to eat? Because that's how it looks to me, human."

"No, sir – I mean Mike. I apologize. I won't do it again."

"No," Mike said, "this warrants a punishment." He stamped hard on Leo's face with one foot. Polly screamed, believing Leo was dead. "He's not dead, you piece of puke in human form." He raised his shoe to show Polly that Leo's face was stuck to the sole, albeit back to front. Leo was emitting a gurgling sound that made Mike laugh. "It's the first time he's made any sense."

Mike shook his leg and Leo's face slid off the sole of his shoe and onto the floor. Mike clicked a finger and Leo's face slid across the floor, ran up his body, and was sucked back into the hole in his throat. It re-emerged out through his mouth and spread back across his face to restore his ugly visage.

Leo touched his face to reassure himself he was back to abnormal, but when he tried to speak, he could only gurgle again.

"Oh, yes," Mike said, clicking his finger. The hole in Leo's throat closed and he gasped. He took large, heaving breaths, trying to regain equilibrium. "If you're going to do that, can you at least turn to face your wife, because your breath stinks."

Leo turned and put a hand on Polly's shoulder to steady himself. She wasn't sure which had shocked her more, seeing what just happened to Leo's face, or the anguish she felt when it looked like he'd died. After all, if her husband was to be killed, she should be the one to do it.

"I've been too easy on you to date," Mike said.

"We ain't dating. We're married," Leo replied.

"You see, this is what I'm talking about. You deserve far worse just for subjecting me to your squalid illiteracy. No more random kills. Next time, you'll have to murder someone important to you."

"There ain't no one not important to us," Polly said.

"No one? No family, no children?" Mike asked.

"We don't have kids and shit," Leo said, turning to face Mike.

"OK, I believe you," Mike lied, knowing about Sam. He'd keep that up his sleeve for the moment. No need to go there just yet. "I'll be in touch," he said and vanished.

Leo stood back from Polly and steadied himself. He turned and headed towards the couch. Polly reached out and grabbed him.

"Fuck you doing, Leo?!"

"I need a rest."

"You'll get your NDA all over the couch!"

"Oh, yeah."

Leo and Polly stepped around Billy's body to avoid the rim of blood around his head and went to the front door. Leo was about to open the door when Polly again grabbed him. "Stop!"

"What the fuck now?!"

"We ain't signed our names!"

"Oh, shit, yeah, you right!"

Leo dug into his pocket to retrieve the small paintbrush he'd brought with him. He kneeled down and dipped the brush into the blood. Standing upright, he daubed the wall in large red strokes, spelling out his name, just about the only thing he did know how to spell correctly. When he was finished, he handed the brush to Polly, who followed suit.

They stood back and admired the scene before them: Billy's dead body below the names *LEO HAIN* and *POLLY HAIN* written on the wall in blood.

"Now who's the floor-less mastermind and shit?!" Leo beamed proudly.

Wanted: Dead Or… No, Just Dead

Morton stood in Billy's living room, staring at the bloody names above the corpse. The Hains had left the TV on and Morton was struggling to concentrate over the offensive noise of a morning evangelical preacher demanding viewers send in donations for a personal prayer, with a starting minimum of $100 for the basic package and going all the way up to $1000 for the Gold Orison Package. He wanted to switch it off, but suffering from the strain of a recurring migraine since he began investigating impenetrable homicide cases, he forgot to bring a pair of gloves with him after he received the call about this murder.

Tuning the preacher out, he folded his arms and pondered whether these were the names of the killers written by the victim in his dying moments. Upon examining the body closer, he saw it would have been impossible for the deceased to have written anything, not only because there was no blood on his fingers but because he was killed by a single shot to the head.

That left the potential scenario that the killer was trying to frame these two people. Or perhaps the killer was being helpful by giving cops a heads-up on his next targets. One quick call to a colleague, followed by screenshots sent to his cellphone of the NCIC records on the Hains gave him the answer. And it was one that would never have occurred to him, or, indeed, anyone.

"So… The Hains murdered this guy and signed their real names for us to find," Morton said to his colleague on the phone. "That's… Well, that's a uniquely brain-dead thing to do."

Morton saw there were six warrants out for the Hains' arrest across six states for a series of crimes including murder and robbery. It wasn't uncommon for even the most low-down perp to evade capture for a long time, but normally they would do everything they can *to* evade capture. Committing murder and announcing themselves as the murderers ran contrary to that.

Back in his office, he read up further on the Hains, about their obsession with the occult and their fondness for using crystal meth, and the file notes written by cops on other cases who had made observations such as *Remarkably thick criminals*; *Should be locked up just for their poor hygiene*; and *In all my years on the force, I have never – I repeat never – investigated a more repulsive, backward, illiterate, odiferous, and dumb as fuck pair of shitheads.*

Now the signatures made sense.

Lightning Strikes Thrice

"One shot to the head at close range. Billy Nevill died instantly."

Morton stood over Billy's body in the morgue, listening to Judy, who was sporting pink streaks in her hair and was chewing gum.

"Finally, you got a simple, straightforward shooting, Walls."

"Not really."

"Oh?"

"The findings by the crime scene technicians. You didn't see it?"

"No, it looked a clean kill. I didn't think it was necessary."

Morton sighed so loudly, Judy thought he was going to pass out. "Job getting to you, Walls?"

"No forensics. No fibers on the couch, no fingerprints on a can of beer and TV remote, and no saliva on or inside the can. The perps could have wiped their prints. But the other two are impossible. No DNA on or inside *an open empty can of beer.* Not even the vic's. And no fibers on the couch. And I don't mean looking for something that didn't match the victim's clothes and coming up blank. It's like *no one* ever sat on it."

"Wow," Judy said, chewing. "That's freaky."

"Or maybe Billy just bought it that day and never got to use it," Morton said in a tone that Judy could tell was him making light of the case.

"Good to see more of that sense of humor you usually keep locked away, Walls."

Morton shook his head and went to stand against the wall, his hands in his pockets.

"Zero forensics. Again. Something impossible happened. Again. Sound familiar?" Judy asked.

Morton looked at her and realized what she was talking about. "Are you seriously saying the Hains did the Rance and Bloodworth murders? You said yourself there was nothing to connect the Rance killings to Bloodworth."

"That was before lightning struck for a third time."

"Again with the cliches, Judy."

"Hey, if the shoe fits, Walls. Yes, I do think the Hains did all three."

"I've read their case files. They're morons. They're total morons."

"Signing their names would suggest that, yes."

"No, I mean serious, lifelong morons. They're not capable of masterminding some amazing feat of physics."

"Says you. And says I. But the facts speak for themselves. Have you had any similar cases come in lately?"

"No."

"So, you can either believe three sets of random killings were carried out by three different parties, or you can accept that the Hains, as moronic as they are, managed to pull off these crimes without leaving any evidence. Except their names."

"I feel my migraine returning," Morton said, shaking his head yet again. "How do a pair of meth addled oxygen thieves do something that's beyond genius? And go to all that trouble and be mindless enough to ID themselves at the same time?"

"That's for you to find out, partner. I'm afraid I can't help you there."

Morton stared up at the ceiling, thinking over the details, and a memory came to him. He looked across at Judy. "You know, you summed it up best with something you said about the Bloodworth murder."

"Did I? That does sound like me."

"You said the perps started off like amateurs and ended like magicians. Two extremes within one crime scene."

"Maybe the Hains have someone helping them. A third person who cleans up their mistakes," Judy ventured.

"I doubt it. That would require someone intelligent, and no one intelligent is going to associate themselves with the Hains."

Intellectually Challenged

Leo and Polly were on the motel room bed, slobbering over each other in a rhapsody of ecstasy.

The TV was on, as it always was, in anticipation of a news report on their latest murder.

Leo would get out of breath fairly quickly on account of his weight and general poor health, which was one of the reasons he consented to his wife going out on occasion to fuck other men when he couldn't perform, but tonight, he was adamant about giving Polly what she wanted. This would mean her going astride, as he was too heavy to go on top and she didn't like him sweating all over her.

They were all set to undress and fuck when they heard the lead item on the news and stopped their slobbering.

Angie the newscaster was talking via live link-up to Gavin, who was reporting from outside Billy's house.

"What can you tell us about this murder, Gavin?"

"Well, Angie, police say the victim was Billy Nevill, a 27-year-old Portland native. He was killed with a single shot to the head. His body was discovered when a friend of Nevill's came by to visit in the morning and saw him through the window."

"And police have a lead on this murder, don't they?" Angie asked.

"Yes they do!" Leo squealed. He and Polly hugged each other in celebration.

"That's correct, Angie. The detective I spoke to said the killers left their names at the scene of the murder. And they have identified them to us as Leo and Polly Hain."

A photo of the Hains from about a year ago appeared on screen. The pair jumped up and down on the bed in celebration.

"The Hains have criminal records stretching back many years and there are currently six arrest warrants out for them across six states, and to that they can now add a seventh. The public are advised not to approach the couple and to contact the police if they see them."

"It certainly is unusual for a killer or killers to sign their real names at a crime scene, isn't it, Gavin?"

"That's right, Angie. The detective said none of the officers could understand or explain why anyone would want to identify themselves like this. It makes no sense. They do have one theory, though. When you look into the Hains' criminal history, something that becomes very clear very quickly is that this husband and wife are very, very intellectually challenged."

"Thank you, Gavin."

"Hell yeah!" Leo screamed, getting out of bed to walk around the room like an excited kid; an excited, unwashed, homicidal kid. "He said we're intellectual! I think that means smart and shit! And we're a challenge to the cops!"

When he didn't hear a response, Leo looked over and saw Polly was sitting motionless with a more vacant expression than usual.

"What's wrong with you, Pol?"

"They showed our pic. We gonna have to disguise ourselves now," she said quietly. "Maybe we shouldn't ain't never not written our names."

"No, fuck that! Mike ain't getting all the fame. We deserve it."

"We gotta go buy some hair dye and we gotta cut our hair so done no one can't not recognize us."

"That ain't nothing to worry about, Pol. The main shit is people know we did it and we're clever!"

He got back on the bed and went to put his arm around Polly, but she pulled away. "Hey! We was gonna fuck!"

"I ain't in the mood no more."

"Oh, fuck, Pol. Why you gotta be a buzzkill?"

Leo turned back to the TV, which was reporting on the aftermath of a school shooting in Tennessee. The Governor there was offering his thoughts and prayers.

"I think we should go back to the first two murder houses and sign our names. Then they gotta say we the ones who did the floor-less mastermind murders too!" he suggested.

"Are you out of your mind, Leo?! There gonna be cops all over those houses!"

"Oh, yeah, you're right."

"It was a dumb fuckass idea, Leo."

"I said you're right."

"Do you want us to get arrested?"

"Bitch, I said OK! Why you still talking about it?!"

"You getting me all hot and horny again, Leo," she said, licking her lips.

"I'm gonna eat you out like a homeless guy at a buffet."

"You always know what to say to get me all soaking."

Credit Where Credit's Not Due

After Leo gave Polly oral, they went into the bathroom to shoot up some meth.

Calling it a night, they returned to the bed to go to sleep. Leo pulled back the comforter and both he and Polly jolted with the agitated holler with which they always greeted an appearance by their tormentor.

Mike lay on the bed, looking up at the Hains, and asked: "Why did you sign your names?" Before they could answer, he bolted upright with such speed that they took a step back. Leo hoped this was just one of his meth-induced hallucinations and Mike wasn't really there.

Mike got out of the bed, and when his feet hit the floor, it caused a tremor in the fabric of the air that struck Leo with such blistering force that he knew this was no hallucination.

"No, let me rephrase that," Mike continued. "I'm shocked you two can actually write anything. Before, I'd have bet you'd write your names as a series of squiggles and smiley faces. Now back to my question: who said you could sign your names?"

"Uh…," Leo began sheepishly.

"Not *uh*. Who told you two fuckcherries you could sign your names at that murder?"

"I… I did it," was all Leo could muster.

"Say that again?" Mike asked. "You did what?"

"I killed him."

"Yes you did, Leo. Yes you did," Mike answered, taking a step towards Leo, smiling. His smile made the Hains relax.

And then Mike grabbed Leo by the throat and squeezed until Leo's face was a purple blob. Polly wanted to shriek but found herself mute. Like at the movie theater, Mike had put a block on her functions.

"Yes you did. But did you clean up the scene? Did you remove all the evidence of your having been there?"

Leo wanted to reply, but he was seconds away from death, so expecting a response was asking too much of anyone. His right eye bulged out of its socket. Mike squeezed tighter and the eyeball popped out and hit the floor.

Polly was in a state of silent fright that turned to panic when Mike stamped on Leo's eyeball. Mike raised the palm of his free hand in Polly's direction without looking at her and she slid backwards across the room until she hit the wall next to the bathroom door. He'd done enough finger clicks and it was time to switch up his style.

Mike loosened his grip on Leo's throat and let go. He collapsed to the floor, gasping for air with foul guttural grunts that threatened to segue into a mammoth upchuck.

"Do you *have* to make that disgusting sound?" Mike asked as he knelt down to pick up Leo's squished eyeball. Rolling it in his fingers, it sprang back into shape and he flicked it at Leo. The eyeball landed perfectly back in its socket. "I always nail that shot. I am so good."

Polly, finding that she could open her mouth again, came over and crouched down next to her husband and held his back.

"Awww. You make such a revolting couple," Mike observed.

Polly helped Leo to his feet.

"Go and sit on the edge of the bed," Mike ordered.

They heard what he said, expressed very concisely so that they could understand, but they nonetheless went to get back under the covers. Leo had barely lifted the comforter when Mike interrupted. "I said sit on the bed, not go take a fucking nap!"

Once they were sitting as ordered, Mike stood in front of them. He stroked his chin with the back of his hand and said: "Now do you want to answer?"

"What?" Leo asked.

Mike sighed. "Leo, I know you're at a disadvantage because of the contaminated gene pool you slimed out of, but are you seriously telling me you can't remember what I asked you two minutes ago?"

"Oh, that. Yeah. I mean, no. No, I didn't do any of that shit."

"That *shit* is what you two fucksticks are taking the credit for by writing your names. When did I say you could do that?"

"It's just that... That..." Leo didn't think there was an answer he could give that wouldn't result in him ending up on Mike's shoe or having the life choked out of him again.

"The news people was saying the murders was amazing," Polly explained, deciding to do the heavy lifting. "But the amazing stuff ain't us. It's the shit... the stuff that you did. But we did the murders. It don't ain't seem fair."

Mike stopped mid-stroke of his chin and stared at the Hains. He then burst out laughing for a full minute.

Once he stopped laughing, he resumed. "Let me see if I understand you correctly. You signed your names because you wanted the credit for murders that people were calling genius? Even though that now means the police know who to look for?"

"Yeah," Polly replied.

"I'm not often shocked, but, Leo, Polly, I can honestly say I am shocked. Truly. You two have got to be not only the dumbest people on this planet, I think it's safe to say you're the dumbest pair of shitstains in the entire galaxy. No. The entire universe. No, I apologize, I'll get it right this time. The entire multiverse."

"So you ain't mad at us and shit?" Leo asked hopefully.

Mike came over and sat on the bed next to Leo, which made Leo shiver. In the intonation of a parent comforting a sick child, he answered: "No, Leo, I'm afraid I can't say I'm not mad at you and shit. In fact, I'm very mad at you. I'm very mad at you and shit. But since I've already choked you this evening and you've given me a good laugh – indeed a hearty chortle – I'm satisfied to leave you with a warning not to do it again. Because I can't very well have a pair of dick-milkers like yourselves taking the credit for my work, can I now? No, I can't."

Mike got off the bed, and the dust and crumbs that his suit had picked up when he sat down vanished.

"So we're clear then? No more chasing fame?" Leo and Polly nodded. "Because if you do, I might punish you with something really severe. Like making you take a bath."

Tuesday

11:34am

In a rare moment of unity, Morton and Jockton agreed that neither of them should appear on camera for the task. Working in law enforcement, they couldn't risk their reputations by being seen talking to this individual and, by extension, lending credence to the topic of discussion. But as a private investigator who mainly followed cheating spouses, Sam could do it without any damage to his credibility.

So, once the online payment of seventy-five dollars had cleared, after Jockton assured him that Ronny would reimburse him before the end of the day, Sam sat in front of the laptop the Sheriff had provided for the interview. Morton and Jockton sat on either side of him at the station meeting room table so they couldn't be seen.

On screen, 34-year-old Orion Gorgo – a name that Sam was absolutely certain wasn't the man's real name – sat in his office, sporting sunglasses and a Van Dyke goatee with a handlebar mustache that ended in side curls. The walls of his office were painted black, and a pentangle necklace dangled over his plain black t-shirt. The image Gorgo wanted to present would have had more impact if it wasn't for the open bag of Funyuns and a glass of strawberry milkshake that were visible at the bottom right corner of the frame.

"Thank you for taking the time to speak to me, Mr. …" Sam fake coughed to stop himself from laughing. "Mr. Gorgo," he resumed. He could sense Morton, to his left, smiling wryly.

"Just so we're on the same page. If we go over ten minutes, I have to charge you five dollars per minute. I'm already giving you a special discount on my normal fee for an online consultation, so I'm not in a good mood, to be pretty honest with you, Mr. Howell."

All three had agreed Sam shouldn't use his real name in case this self-proclaimed expert on the occult whom they'd found online thought he was being mocked. As it would turn out, it made no difference.

"I'll get straight to it then, Mr. Gorgo. I'd like to know how to kill a demon."

Sam thought the connection had dropped, because Gorgo didn't move or say a word.

"Oh, shit, the screen's frozen!" Sam said.

"I don't like being mocked, Mr. Howell," Gorgo finally responded.

"Oh, you're still there. Sorry, what did you say?"

"I said I don't like being mocked."

"What makes you think I'm mocking you?"

"You want to know how to kill a demon? I'm a serious man, Mr. Howell, and my work is serious. I'm not here to be ridiculed."

"Look, Orion—"

"Mr. Gorgo to you."

"Mr. Gorgo, I don't know why you think I'm mocking you. My question is serious."

"Do you know how many people I get asking questions like that?"

"A lot?"

"None."

"Oh… Then what's your problem?"

"The only type of person who would ask a question like that is a timewaster trying to mock me and I won't stand for it!"

While Sam tried to think of what to say, Morton got a scrap of paper out of his inside jacket pocket and wrote something down. He turned the note around so Sam could see it and he gently tapped the table. Sam glanced down and saw it read *cognitive dissonance.* Jockton got up from his chair to try and get a look, but Morton angrily gestured to him to sit down, as he was close to being caught on camera.

Sam looked back up at the laptop. "Mr. Gorgo, your website says you're an expert in the occult."

"Correct. I am."

"And your website also says you can provide expert consultations on all matters relating to the occult."

"Your ten minutes is running out, Mr. Howell. There are no refunds."

"What a little prick," Morton muttered quietly to himself.

"I've asked for your expertise and you've accused me of mocking you. Aren't you showing a bit of cognitive dissonance there, Mr. Gorgo?"

"What did you just accuse me of?!" Gorgo stormed, slamming a clenched fist down on his desk, which caused one of the Funyuns to fall out of the bag.

"It suggests to me you don't really believe in the occult and you think someone asking you about it must be kidding."

"How dare you question my honesty and integrity! I do believe in the dark arts to the very core of my corporeal being!"

Morton had had enough. He grabbed the laptop by its edge and turned it around to face him. "Then just answer the fucking question, you tiresome prick!"

Sam threw his hands up remonstratively and sat back.

"Who are you?!" Gorgo snarled.

Morton showed his police badge and said: "Portland PD Homicide!"

If Gorgo had worn the white makeup that some of his associates did, he would have been spared the embarrassment of all the color draining from his face. "Homicide?!" he repeated with a palpable shake in his voice.

Now that there was no need to hide, Jockton felt he should add the imposing power of his authority too. He got up and went behind Morton's chair and peered down. "And I'm the Sheriff of Millvern."

Morton put himself on mute and said to Jockton: "What are you doing? Get back in your seat. Now."

"Hey, that is uncalled for, Detective! This is my station!"

Morton looked at Sam and asked: "Can you deal with him?"

"Don't talk about me like I'm not here!" Jockton protested.

"It's OK, Don," Sam said. "Just let him deal with it."

The Sheriff returned to his seat and Morton unmuted his audio. "How do you destroy a demon, Gonzo?"

"You can't. You can't destroy a demon. It's a demon. It's indestructible. All the books I've read are clear on that."

"Thank you very fucking much, Go-blo. You could have said that to begin with."

"Is that it? I'm not in trouble, am I?"

"No. Enjoy your Funyuns."

Gorgo looked down and realized his snack was visible. "Son of a bi–"

Morton closed the laptop and slid it back in front of Sam. "Well, that was worthwhile."

"Who were we kidding?" Sam said. "The dickhead is right. A demon is by its very nature not of this Earth."

"Then there's nothing else we can do," Morton decided. "We just have to live with Mike doing what he wants."

"And let him kill innocent people? Well, not Nancy. Or my parents. But the two guys in the laundromat were innocent," Sam argued.

"No one's even reported those men missing. They can't have mattered much," Morton said.

Sam looked at the Detective in shock.

"Unacceptable," Jockton muttered.

"I agree with Don," Sam said.

"Thank you, Sam," Jockton replied with a smile. The Sheriff had grown on Sam in the last few days, and his occasionally dense comment notwithstanding, he always meant well.

"Gallows humor, Mr. Hain. It's part of the job," Morton said, putting his hands in his pockets and staring up at the ceiling.

"How about we try and negotiate with him?" Jockton suggested.

"Gorgo said he won't give a refund," Sam answered without looking at the Sheriff.

"I'm talking about Mike."

"I thought you were. But I was really hoping you weren't," Sam replied in a tired voice.

"Case getting to you, Mr. Hain, or the Sheriff's ideas?" Morton asked, still staring at the ceiling.

"What's wrong with my idea?! You've got the spell. Summon him to talk."

"Don, we don't need to summon him. He's already around. I told you he visited me in my room at the bed & breakfast."

"Then call out for him to visit you again so we can all have a sit-down."

"A *sit-down?*" Morton repeated, giving Jockton a sideways glance but remaining reclined in his seat. "Did you just smoke some PCP while we weren't looking?"

"We just spent seventy-five dollars on an occultist. We all agreed on that, Detective Morton. Why is my idea any stranger?"

"You're talking about negotiating with a demon, Don. A demon. What do we have to negotiate with?" Sam asked.

Morton resumed staring upwards and muttered: "He'd probably offer Mike a pizza and a six-pack to go away."

"Hey!"

"No, it's very called for."

Tuesday

4:53pm

Sam pondered the absurdity of the situation he found himself while he ate a late lunch at Eat All Day. That the one responsible for the murders was an inhuman entity who couldn't be destroyed, and all he, Jockton, and Morton could do was wait for the next murder. And even then – what? Go through the formal motions as an end in itself with no further moves possible? Was Millvern now destined to just live under the perpetual threat of killings, all of which would have to be explained to the locals as random and, in time, unsolvable? And what if Mike chose to go public with a supernatural spectacular that couldn't be covered up?

Eating his sandwich, Sam looked out of the window and saw Rob and Lucy walking on the other side of the road, hand in hand. Just then, the doors opened and Drew entered the diner with Inessa. *Let's just chill and see what happens* she had said that evening at Samphire. And now he knew what happened, as they too were holding hands. The new couple took a corner table and the waitress came over to them. Seeing all this spurred a thought in Sam. The waitress must be so relieved she no longer had to suffer Nancy screaming her chicken dinner order.

No, that wasn't it. He wanted to call or text Chloe to suggest they meet. They last hooked up on Saturday night. Surely getting in contact three days later wouldn't come off as needy and desperate. If anything, she'd probably appreciate that he had waited that long.

Oh, what the hell. He decided he'd call her once he finished his meal.

Once he was out of the diner, he called Chloe. They exchanged pleasantries. He was still formulating how he'd broach the subject of them meeting up when she asked very unexpectedly: "So, were you calling because you want to give me another good dicking?"

Sam stuttered a series of *umms* and *ahhs,* completely at a loss as to what his response should be. "I've never said that."

"I know you haven't, Sam. It's how I like to describe it."

"OK."

"So? Are you?"

"This isn't a trick question, is it?"

"Don't disappoint me, Sam. You haven't so far."

"Then yes."

Tuesday

8:35pm

Chloe's apartment was very tidy, neatly organized, and welcomed visitors with the smell of sandalwood, which emanated from an electric diffuser.

Sat on the living room couch while Chloe put the finishing touches to her makeup in the bathroom, he could picture himself receiving a massage from her while the diffuser filled the air with its tranquil fragrance. Just thinking about it threatened to put him into a drowsy state like an ASMR aficionado watching a video of someone roleplaying as a soft-spoken librarian.

He snapped out of it when he heard Chloe's voice from the bathroom down the corridor. "How's the case going?"

It's a total disaster because we're faced with a demon who is unstoppable, and so these murders are just going to continue is what Sam wanted to say.

"Still going," he said. "I can't really talk about it." Sam hoped that didn't sound arrogant or self-aggrandizing like the type of men who wanted to appear more important than they were. Even if the case hadn't involved a demon, he still couldn't impart any sensitive information. He owed Jockton and Morton that much integrity.

As he lay back on the couch, he heard a chuckle. Sam sat up straight, looking really fucked off. He looked around the room, imagining Mike being there but invisible, or perhaps viewing afar on the demonic equivalent of a CCTV monitor.

"What kind of person do you think is doing this?" Chloe asked, turning on the faucet.

"Probably someone really sick," Sam answered, then raising his voice and tilting his head up to add: "and really immature, perverted, and pathetic. Really pathetic!"

The sound of running water stopped and Chloe finally appeared. Horny, excited, and eager was how Sam wanted to be feeling. But the thought of Mike doing his Peeping Tom act made him queasy.

He was still horny though.

She joined him on the couch and they kissed for a few minutes. Running her hand down his back, she said: "I've got some more of the white stuff."

"Great."

She took his hand and led him to her bedroom, which welcomed him with the smell of lavender, it too from an electric diffuser. He lay down on the bed and she grabbed her handbag and removed a bag of coke. Joining him back on the bed, she said: "I want to lick it off your dick."

Whether it was the soothing effects of the aroma diffuser or his relief that she had so enthusiastically suggested they meet that made him feel sufficiently relaxed to ask what he was about to ask, Sam didn't know. "Don't you ever do coke the traditional way?"

Chloe laughed. He'd gotten away with it. There had been the very real risk that she would interpret that as a vanilla-tinged question, and that would mean he wasn't the guy she thought he was when they first met. "Yes, I do. But you did lines off my clit. I want to do them off your cock."

"OK. I can't say no to that."

Sam took off his trousers and underwear and lay back on the bed. As Chloe went down on him, he shut his eyes.

She carefully laid out a line of coke on the shaft of his penis and proceeded to snort it. He so wanted to be in the moment, but he was distracted by the gruesome thought that Mike might be watching all this.

Chloe trickled out another line on his shaft, which she licked off.

Sam finally lost himself and moaned loudly.

What the hell. Let him watch. Better an invisible demon than some rando human pervert.

TWO MONTHS BEFORE

First Do Harm

There once was a doctor named Mark Giles.

Right from the start of his career as a General Practitioner, Giles never cared for that old-fashioned thing known as a bedside manner. He enjoyed the power and privileges his role gave him when seeing patients. Giles knew he could do pretty much whatever he wanted and that there was little-to-nothing patients could do about it. Very rarely would fellow doctors take the word of a patient over that of a colleague.

There was the patient who had suffered with sinus problems for a long time and had repeatedly requested a referral to a specialist. Giles repeatedly refused the request, insisting there was no problem. Until the day the patient came in and demanded a referral. On that occasion, Giles said he would do it, but added: "I think this is a waste of time."

The patient was seen by the specialist, who diagnosed him with chronic sinusitis. At a subsequent appointment with Giles, the patient mentioned this, to which the doctor said: "So it was good of me to refer you, wasn't it?"

There was also the patient who suspected he might have Parkinson's. He attended with his wife, who, through tears, explained her husband's symptoms. Giles told her to hurry up and get to the end. When she did, he refused to refer her husband to a specialist for tests to ascertain his condition. Giles said they should just keep an eye on things and come back in two months if there had been no improvement. When the wife tried to explain that this had been going on for several months already, he stood up and told them to leave as he had other patients waiting.

Most recently, there was the patient who was suffering severe depression. She asked for antidepressants. Giles refused. He said she should go for walks to feel better. She showed him the scars on her arms where she'd cut herself. Giles said it was the sort of thing attention seekers do. She told him she'd been having suicidal thoughts and was worried she'd act on them and please would he prescribe antidepressants. Giles refused. He said he doesn't do something just because a patient demands it.

On this evening, 39-year-old Giles was on his living room couch, talking to a friend on the phone, telling her he'd got the news earlier that day that the patient who'd wanted antidepressant medication had killed herself.

"I told her she was an attention seeker and I was right. You don't get more of an attention seeking act than suicide!" he said, laughing. "And get this, her parents are threatening a lawsuit. Fucking middle-income nobodies."

"How did she do it?" his friend asked.

"Slit her wrists in the bath. Maybe her parents will be so distraught, they'll kill themselves too before they can issue any suit." Giles laughed again.

"Can they use your notes against you?"

"What notes? All I wrote was she presented as moderately unhappy. I didn't include anything else. I cannot be held liable for something that I couldn't possibly have foreseen." Giles laughed again.

His friend on the other end of the line heard the laugh, which was so infectious, she too started laughing. And she was still laughing when she heard Giles's laughter culminate in a full-throttle *hah!*

Then the line went quiet.

"Mark? Were you laughing so hard you fell on the floor?! Mark?"

The exclamation the friend had heard wasn't a laugh. It was the sound Giles made when the bullet entered his mouth.

There once was a doctor named Mark Giles.

Once. But not anymore.

The Next Next Level

Now that they were on the news, the Hains dyed and cut their own hair to avoid being recognized by cops or the public. To that end, they were successful. But being inconspicuous they failed at comprehensively.

Leo let Polly cut what little hair he had. It resulted in a fully bald center that picked up again towards the back as a separate island, and the thinning hair on one side ended an inch above his ear but not on the other. And anyone could see his shiny jet-black hair wasn't his natural color, not least because he'd neglected to wash off the dried drops of black dye on his forehead.

Even though Polly would usually cut her own hair, she thought letting Leo do it would produce a significantly different result that would help evade detection, a decision she came to regret. The result was a saturnalia of jagged, alarming spikes, looking as though she'd been electrocuted and forgotten to do anything about it afterwards. But she was at least happy with her choice of dye, as she'd often fantasized about being a blonde bombshell, even if it didn't quite fit with an occult image, though an actual bomb would have produced less of an eyesore.

Together, they cut bizarre figures in public, and the looks they got from people only heightened their meth-induced periods of paranoia. Fearful of being spotted, they resolved to stay in their motel room and only go out for necessities like food and murder.

And it was the latter that had brought them to the home of Mark Giles in Southwest Hills. Hunting for a house, they came across one that had a street-level garage and a flight of steps that took you down to the front door. Once they got past the bitterness that some people owned homes that were so elaborate in design, Leo and Polly were thrilled that they could commit this murder out of sight of any passersby.

When they got to the bottom of the steps, they could see their target through the front window sat on his couch and talking animatedly on the phone. There would be no need to ring the doorbell. They could carry out the kill right where they were.

The pair quietly retreated to stand in the darkness against the shrubbery opposite the window so they couldn't be seen. Not that Giles was looking up anyway. He was laughing uproariously on the phone, reveling in his own enjoyment about the events he was recounting to his friend.

Before driving to Southwest Hills, Leo had agreed that Polly could do this kill, as he'd done Nevill and all but one of the Rances. Holding her new 9mm, having disposed of her last one, Polly took aim. She waited for the right moment. When that would be she wasn't sure, but she was certain she'd know when it happened.

And there it was. Giles was laughing so much, he shut his eyes mid-paroxysm and tilted his head back. She fired once. The bullet went straight into his mouth. The phone fell from his hand and a stunned look froze on his face. His mouth remained wide open and his head wobbled. His eyes glazing over, Giles swayed until his head slumped back.

"You did perfect, baby!" Leo squealed excitedly and they embraced.

Leo got out his new .38 to shoot the front door lock. They went in and straight into the living room, careful not to touch anything.

The Hains took in the upscale furnishings of the room. It wasn't as luxurious as the Rance house, but it was still exceptional. And it pissed them off. Leo eyed the 50in 4K smart TV and decided it shouldn't exist anymore.

It didn't occur to him to at least steal it to make use of it for themselves, so he just shot the screen.

Polly stood in front of Giles's corpse and said: "Hey, Leo. How about I fuck him?"

Leo was still marveling at his work on the TV and replied: "Who? One of your finger-fuck buddies you hook up with?"

"No! This asshole! I wanna fuck his corpse. Take our evil to the next level."

Leo turned to look at her as though she'd just said she wants to be a good person from now on. "Evil to the next... We ain't narcophiliacs, you crazy bitch!"

"Necrophiliacs, you asshole!"

"Oh. So you mean narco cops ain't going after people who fuck dead people?"

"Shut up, Leo."

To make up for her disappointment, Polly went to the kitchen to investigate. She grabbed a cloth to open the refrigerator door and jumped in fright when the smart fridge's AI said in a realistically female voice: *Good evening, Mark.*

"Fuckass fridge!"

"What's wrong?" Leo called from the living room.

"It's one of these fridges that talk."

"Can you tell it to make us a steak and shit?" Leo said, laughing at his own joke.

Polly saw a bottle of Prosecco and took it out. She returned to the living room, gulping it down straight from the bottle.

She stood, gazing down at Giles's body. "You want some?" she said with a grin. She poured some of the Prosecco into his open mouth and over his clothes.

"What are you doing, Pol?!" Leo yelled, standing awkwardly in a hunched pose, desperate to sit down but wanting to avoid any risk of leaving evidence. "I want some of that!"

"Quit whining!" She tossed him the bottle and he caught it. He took a drink of it and said: "Remember we gotta take this with us so Mike don't give us shit about NDA on the bottle."

"Well, you've certainly improved, if only a little bit. And it's DNA," Mike said, standing by the doorway. He waited for their customary shock reactions to his sudden appearance and proceeded into the living room.

"So you saying we done good this time?" Polly asked with sincere enthusiasm.

"No, I'm saying you were relatively less moronic on this occasion."

Polly stepped aside as Mike came to look at Giles's corpse. With a flutter of his fingers, the drops of Prosecco in his throat flew back out of his mouth, and along with the ones on his clothes, danced up into the air. Leo and Polly watched in astonishment as the drops swirled around above Giles's head. "Your DNA is in those drops," Mike told Polly.

"But I ain't made of wine."

"Saliva transfer, fuckface." Mike's demeanor immediately changed and he looked unsteady on his feet. He stared at the floor and clutched his stomach. "Oh. Oh, I shouldn't have said that."

Polly was so shocked by what appeared to be Mike apologizing, all she could say was a simple "Thanks."

"No, I wasn't apologizing for the name calling. As soon as I said it, I pictured your husband fucking your face and now I think I'm going to be violently sick. Oh, why did I use that phrase? I… I have to tell you, that image is so troubling, I think I may have to commit suicide to escape it." Polly could barely hide her delight, which Mike sensed without even looking up. "Don't get excited, goblin. I was being hyperbolic to make a point." He looked up and, as he had correctly assumed, Polly was just blinking blankly. "I was being rhetorical." Still she blinked. Sighing, he clarified: "I'm not going to kill myself." Polly could barely hide her disappointment.

Mike went and perched on the armrest of the couch. "I'm strong, but I don't think even I have the power to erase that image from my mind. I need to return home and see if I can combine my powers with one of my diabolical associates to wipe that horrifying picture from my memory for all time."

Mike then looked over at Leo, who was in agony from standing in a hunched pose for so long, desperate to park his ass on the couch. "Do you want to sit down, Leo?" he asked.

"Yes please."

"But you're worried about leaving fibers from your clothes?"

"Uh-huh."

"And you'd like me to remove all the evidence after you've had a nice rest?"

"Yes please."

"Because you're tired from standing and your feet are aching?"

"Uh-huh."

"Well, then. There's only one thing for it."

"Yeah?!" Leo said with sincere optimism.

"Yes. Stand there and shut the fuck up."

Turning his attention back to the immediate, Mike fluttered his fingers again and the dancing drops vanished. He then clicked a finger. Leo and Polly looked around the room in confusion.

"What that one for?" Polly asked.

"The CCTV on the exterior of the house that showed you two vomit-inducers arriving and shooting this man. The camera's now broken and all recordings wiped."

"Thanks," she said.

"Oh, you don't need to thank me. It's not going to make me treat you nicely. Now, even though you colonic cartographers signed your names last time, a good lawyer with no conscience could still get you off if there's no evidence to incriminate you and get it dismissed as an attempted frame-up."

"How's an unconscious lawyer gonna help us?" Leo asked, still hunched over.

Mike looked at him, then got off the armrest, slowly walked over, stopped, looked at Leo again, and gave him a smack upside the head.

"Owww!" Leo smarted from the strike and held the side of his head. He teetered and looked to be seconds away from falling over. Polly rushed over to hold him steady.

"Tell me something," Mike said. "Have you two ever met anyone who didn't want to rip your guts out and piss on your cadavers?"

Before Leo could say *no,* Mike vanished.

The pair began trudging across the room, heading for the doorway back into the entrance hall. Unusually for Leo, he remembered something important. "Wait!"

"You can't sit on the couch, Leo, you dumb fuck!"

"No, bitch! We ain't signed our names and shit!"

"Oh, yeah."

Leo took out the small paintbrush he used for the Billy Nevill murder. The husband and wife took turns signing their names in the dead sadistic doctor's blood on the wall above the wrecked TV.

U-Haul If You Want To

"What's her name?"

Judy brushed back her turquoise streaked hair, chewed her gum thoughtfully, and asked: "Who?"

Morton nodded in the direction of Judy's phone, which she'd put down seconds before and displayed a photo of her smiling with her arm around a woman, both of them holding cocktails.

"Steph."

"Is she another U-Haul?" Morton asked.

Judy, smiling faintly, replied: "U-Haul? I told you about that just one time, Walls, and you've gotta bring it up every time I start seeing someone new."

"You didn't tell me, I read about it online."

"What were you doing reading about lesbian relationships, Walls?"

"I have an inquisitive mind. Comes in handy in my job. And I was killing time. After you told me about your one experience," Morton said, putting his hands in his pockets and looking down at Giles's body on the mortuary slab.

"Well, she's not. You know me better than that."

"So it's you, then."

"How dare you, Walls!" Judy said, laughing.

"I'm just going by your phone's new wallpaper."

"Yeah, it's a reminder of a great night out. It doesn't mean we're living together. Do you want to know about the dead doctor, Walls?"

"There's nothing you can tell me that's going to come close to what I've got."

"Oh?" she said, intrigued enough to momentarily stop chewing.

Morton, sensing there was no need to go through the motions of standing over Giles's corpse, moved to stand against the wall as he told Judy of his own findings. "The CCTV camera on the outside of the house was smashed. Cracked lens. The enclosure that housed it was ripped apart. No prints anywhere. No ladders around the place, no way of getting up there, and I think we can rule out those assholes bringing a ladder with them unless they'd reconnoitered the house beforehand, which I think we can also rule out, given that requires planning and thought."

"That's still not in the vicinity of the impossible, Walls."

"I haven't finished. All the recordings go to a remote server. And they were all erased. And not just from that night. The whole week's worth."

Judy stopped chewing again. "Are you serious?"

"These two definitely have someone helping them."

"They murder random people with no connection to one another and they have someone with genius forensic clean-up skills and genius computer hacking skills helping them. In what universe does this make sense?"

Morton nodded. "My migraine is beginning to take up permanent residence." Taking his hands out of his pockets to fold his arms, he asked: "Any magic tricks with the dead doctor?"

"No. That's what I was going to say. All very clean and straightforward. One bullet in the mouth, shot from outside as you already know. I read in the forensics report that the Hains' signatures didn't just have Giles's blood, it had traces of Billy Nevill's too. I guess it's official. You've got yourself a pair of serial killers, partner!"

"We knew that already. And even if they hadn't done Bloodworth and the Rances, you know they have to off three to be serial."

"So you are going with what I said about them being responsible for the first two?" Judy grinned.

"They have to be."

"I hope that didn't hurt you."

"What?"

"Agreeing with my theory, partner!"

Morton desperately tried to stop himself from smiling. He saw it off by declaring rather redundantly: "I can't wait to catch these two and put them away."

"Hey, Walls, you free tonight?"

"Why?"

"I'm seeing Steph for a drink and I thought it time I start introducing her to my close friends."

Morton looked at her, processed her words to determine if she was being serious, and realized what she was doing. "You're funny, Judy."

"I am, Walls. I am."

Studies

Leo and Polly finished their dinner of takeout noodles, disposing of the empty cartons by flinging them across the room even though a wastepaper basket was right next to the bed.

The TV was on, as it always was after one of their murders. While they waited for a report on the Giles killing, they tried to think of ways to entertain themselves. They were too logy from the meal to fuck, and they weren't hankering just yet for another hit of meth.

"Let's cut one us other," Polly suggested.

Leo, wiping sweet and sour sauce from his mouth with the back of his sleeve, said: "Whatever you want."

Polly got out of bed and went into the bathroom. When she returned holding a small pocketknife, she was disgusted to see Leo's postprandial sluggishness had sent him to sleep. Undeterred, she sat down next to him on the bed, carefully lifted his jumper and, grinning in anticipation of his reaction, slashed about four centimeters across his chest.

Leo woke with a shriek and saw Polly laughing and then licking the blood off his wounded chest. He shoved her off him and pulled down his jumper, saying: "Fuck are you doing, bitch?!"

"You said *whatever you want,* asshole! I was doing whatever I want!"

"Yeah. When I'm awake and shit!"

"Oh, fuck you, Leo!"

"Now I'm gonna cut you."

"You know what gets me hot, Leo," she said, handing the knife over to him.

But before Leo could return the favor, both his and Polly's attention was caught by the TV, on which the newscaster Angie had local breaking news.

"We go live now to our reporter outside the home of Dr. Giles."

Leo and Polly jumped up and down with excitement as the news cut to Gavin the reporter at the top of the steps that led down to Giles's house.

"Thanks, Angie. I'm here outside the home of Dr. Mark Giles. We did try to get closer to the front door, but the police have that area taped off. Dr. Giles was a 39-year-old General Practitioner and a highly respected member of the local community. His body was discovered yesterday morning when his cleaner arrived for her weekly visit. Police say he died from a single gunshot wound."

"But this isn't just any murder, isn't that right, Gavin?"

"That's right!" Leo said. "We did that shit!"

"Yes, Angie. The officer I spoke to also confirmed that the signatures of Leo and Polly Hain were left at the scene, as with the Billy Nevill murder."

"Are the cops now treating this as a serial killer investigation?"

"Serial killers. There's two of us, skank," Polly grumbled.

"I did ask the officer about that and he said there have to be three murders before they can be designated serial killings."

Leo furiously pointed at the TV as he ranted: "We done seven!"

"However, police now believe the Hains are connected to two earlier murder investigations that resulted in five deaths, which would mean that, yes, they are officially serial killers."

Leo smiled and calmed down, saying: "You know it!"

"I told you we ain't didn't need to go sign our names at those two houses!" Polly said.

"And although there were already arrest warrants out for the Hains for murders in other states, they were isolated cases and not part of a series of pattern killings," Gavin continued.

"What he say and shit?" Leo asked.

"Something about something. I don't know," Polly replied.

"I understand there's something about this murder that has stunned the investigating officers," Angie asked.

"Yeah, 'cause we did it!" Leo said, putting his arm around Polly and stroking the bloodstained knife with his thumb.

"That's right, Angie. Speaking to me off the record, one officer told me that Dr. Giles had a CCTV camera installed outside his house from which recordings were sent to a secure remote server. And somehow all the footage from the night of his murder and the entire week leading up to it have been wiped."

Leo bounced back up and down in rage. "Motherfucker! They're talking about Mike again! That's his shit and shit!"

"It's not just the fact that it's been erased that's got the officers bamboozled," Gavin continued. "What they can't figure out is how two people as intellectually deficient as the Hains could have pulled off such a feat."

Leo smiled and calmed down, saying: "Hey, they said we're intellectual and shit!"

"He also said something about the fishing? We didn't do no fishing."

"Yeah, I don't know."

Leo turned back to the TV, which was reporting on the aftermath of a school shooting in Alabama. The Governor there was offering his thoughts and prayers.

Leo turned to look at Polly: "Ain't you mad?"

"About what?"

"They didn't say nothing about the way you wasted that doc with one shot. No NDA, no nothing left. They just talked about that shit Mike did."

"I don't care, Leo. Now you gonna cut me and lick my blood or ain't you?"

"You want to be cut? I'll cut you," Mike's voice boomed.

Leo and Polly first jumped in shock, and then looked around the room in confusion when they didn't see Mike.

"Where you at?" Polly asked.

The room was plunged into darkness. The Hains felt the bed beneath them vanish and they fell to the floor. They began to sit up, which proved quite the challenge for Leo. But they didn't get as far as standing. They felt themselves levitating, gaining in speed as they floated upwards. Leo and

Polly squealed and shouted, fearing their faces would be smashed into the ceiling.

Instead, when they reached the ceiling, they felt themselves penetrating through it. And rather than hard, it was soft and malleable. As they passed through, a soft white light illuminated their surroundings and they saw they were floating up through layers of the same almost weightless texture, each separated by a suffocatingly narrow interstitial space.

The light dimmed as they approached the next layer and everything went dark again. This time, however, it didn't feel soft. Not at all. They screeched and grunted in agony from the pain of penetrating this final layer. It should have been impossible to pass through what must have been hard concrete, but here they were, screaming their lungs out as their bodies were absorbed and their faces were at once mangled, reformed, mangled again, and reformed again by the harsh grit of the concrete.

A hot, smokey wind provided a mocking respite, giving the Hains air to breathe but stinging their throats and eyes at the same time. But where was it coming from? They were still encased in pitch black.

A faint light heralded what they hoped was the end of the tortuous journey. It grew brighter, the scorched wind hit their cheeks, and they realized they were somehow going to emerge into the outside world.

Their ascent slowed down and they passed through the uppermost part of the concrete layer, whereupon red sand fell on their faces. Choking and spluttering, the Hains wiped their faces and were astonished to find they were in daylight. They came to a stop and the ground beneath them sealed up. Wiping off the remaining dirt and grit from their faces, the Hains sat up. Astonishment turned to unspeakable revulsion and terror when they saw where they were.

The couple were surrounded in all directions as far as the horizon line by several hundred thousand naked bodies, all with their mouths stretched wide open and wailing in pain. The Hains realized they were at ground level of the terrain they'd flown over when they were taken to meet Mike.

Leo looked down and shuddered at the sight of entrails slithering around on their own accord. He screamed madly and tried to stand up, but found he was stuck to the ground and couldn't get himself ambulatory. One line of entrails wriggled over his legs and he wanted to kill himself.

Polly had panicked tears streaming down her face from seeing up close all these corpses with their black eyes blinking rapidly. The capacity for words had deserted her and, like her beloved spouse, all she could do was scream. She too found it impossible to stand up.

The dead man immediately to Leo's left raised a hand, reached into his mouth, and tore out his tongue, holding it aloft. Leo wanted to escape this deranged spectacle, knew he couldn't, and settled for banging the sides of his head with his fists as though that would somehow make it all go away.

Knowing she could at least still move her limbs on the ground, Polly turned over to lie prostrate to avoid seeing any more of this carnival of butchery. Leo saw her do this and did the same. Yet again, the Hains were letting themselves in for disappointment from their extant inability to reach conclusions or make judgments based on past experience with Mike.

Both were face down for no more than one second before levitating one feet into the air. Their eyes opened against their will and the Hains saw they were each face to face with a corpse below; Leo hovering above a dead man and Polly hovering above a dead woman.

The dead woman tore out her tongue, but rather than hold it aloft, she tossed it aside and roared into Polly's face. The corpse's vociferous cry somehow contained necrotic power, as, absent a visible force or element, the flesh on Polly's face began to melt away.

Leo got the same treatment his wife was getting. After tossing aside his tongue, the dead man roared into Leo's face, causing his flesh to melt.

The last of Polly's face dripped away, exposing her skull and leaving only her eyeballs intact. She turned to see how her husband was doing. The remainder of Leo's face sloughed off his skull.

The Hains hung in the air, neither able to emit any more screams or moans. Their designated corpses below had ceased roaring and gone back to wailing and blinking.

Simultaneously, Leo and Polly flipped upright and dropped down. As soon as their feet hit the ground, they found themselves in Mike's black room.

They touched their faces and felt the soft flesh of their cheeks. It was back, albeit reacting to the atmosphere of the Domain by jiggling a few centimeters adrift from their skulls.

Footsteps approached from behind and Mike appeared. "The least you can do is thank me for sparing you from Blood Volcano and the Corridor of Madness."

He headed towards his throne, paused without turning around, and raised his voice ever so slightly, which, for Mike, was substantive enough to cause a shiver in anyone at the receiving end, to say: "I said the least you can do is thank me for sparing you from the Blood Volcano and the Corridor of Madness."

"Thanks," Leo said.

"Yeah, thanks," Polly said.

"You're not welcome." Mike sat on his throne and continued: "Now, what am I going to do about you two jizz-divers?"

"What do you mean?" Leo asked.

"Leo. Oh, Leo. You know, I sometimes wonder if I'll ever miss these conversations with you after you die painfully. Of course, I won't. No one would miss having to talk to you two cum-cloths. What I mean is you ignored my warning and went and signed your names again."

"I'm–" Polly began.

"Don't apologize. It insults my intelligence."

"We're–" Leo began.

"Leo, you terminally tiresome shitstain, was my issue the apology or the lack of a plural?"

"Huh?"

"Twas ever thus."

Mike got off his throne and walked up to the pair, stroking his chin with the back of his hand. "There is no point in me threatening to hurt you again, as much as I do enjoy torturing you. So, here's what's going to happen. If you sign your names again, I will punish you by tormenting someone close to you."

"But we told you we ain't–" Polly began.

"Shut it. I know you're lying." Leo and Polly looked at each other, sincerely confused by Mike's words, because they both knew they really didn't have anybody close to them for whose welfare they would be concerned. "I'm going to be busy for the next few weeks and won't be around to clean up your next murder. I'm taking some time off to study religions and the Republican Party to learn how to be more evil."

Mike looked at Leo and gave him a sharp slap.

"Owww! What was that for?!"

"Do I need a reason?"

Wednesday

11:16am

Sitting in the sheriff's station meeting room, Sam drank his coffee, weighing up whether he should just quit the case and head home. He didn't know this was to be his last day in Millvern anyway.

The dead end that he, Jockton, and Morton had reached in the investigation was why he'd only just turned up to the station. Effectively, they were waiting for Mike to claim another victim, though all three were agreed that referring to Nancy as a victim in any context was a stretch.

The door opened and Jockton stepped only halfway into the room as if to emphasize the gravity of what he was about to say. "We just got a call from the local college about an attack. We're heading over now."

"You want us to go break up a fight between a couple of college kids? Send your Deputy."

"Kids? No, no, they're saying something bloody is happening."

"So?"

"*Bloody and weird* is what they said."

"Oh, Mike's back." Sam got to his feet, reached down for his jacket that was hanging over the back of the chair, and abruptly stopped moving.

"What's wrong?" the Sheriff asked.

The college. Where Chloe works. Sam felt searing panic in his stomach. What if she's the one being attacked? What if she hasn't been attacked but is in the building and is in danger?

He put on his jacket and asked calmly: "Did they say who's been hurt?"

"They didn't give a name, but it's some guy who was causing a ruckus."

Sam's hot panic turned to a cooling rush of relief that was as invigorating as his early morning sodas.

And then he felt guilty for his reaction, as there was still some poor guy being ripped apart at this moment. Sam would remember this thought later and laugh at the irony of his concern.

Morton had been making himself a coffee in the station kitchen when the call came through. He waited at the reception while Jockton went to alert Sam. The three of them piled into Jockton's car. Morton had wanted to go in his own car, but Jockton insisted they travel together and arrive in an official police vehicle. Morton's eagerness to give Jockton a hard time over everything had diminished, partly out of exhaustion and partly out of a willingness to see him the way Sam did, as a well-meaning goofball, though he knew the latter would most likely be very fleeting and he would, sooner or later, revert to his default, so he didn't bother arguing.

Sam wondered if he should call Chloe to find out if she was in the college, but feared that any expression of concern for her safety would come off as a sign of emotional attachment. It wasn't; it was, as far as he was concerned, a normal human reaction and he was perhaps overthinking this and should just call her. She may even appreciate it.

Then again, things had been going smoothly and he wanted to avoid doing or saying anything that could risk it.

"*Bloody and weird,*" Morton repeated in the drive over to the college. "If Mike has opened up his bag of tricks for a wider audience, how are we going to explain it to the local rubes?"

Sam, who'd reluctantly agreed to sit in the back after Morton insisted his position as a detective gave him the right to sit in the front passenger seat, asked: "Haven't you answered your own question by calling them rubes?"

Morton turned to look behind him: "We got lucky once." He turned back to face the road ahead and commented: "Poor guy whoever it is that Mike's killing or killed."

Wednesday

11:02am

Tony Harwood, the late eponymous founder of Harwood College, had been a man of ambitions that were disproportionate to reality. A successful, self-made businessman who took pride in having attained his wealth despite a lack of educational qualifications, as he was fond of letting people know on a frequent basis, he nonetheless couldn't escape the feelings of insecurity and inadequacy that arose when around business peers who boasted illustrious academic histories. He even often suspected that they mocked him behind his back. To him, it didn't seem fair or just to have made all this money and still fail to get what he thought should be the appropriate degree of respect. It was a source of immense frustration that his wealth had bought him everything he could want except a shift upwards in standing, something that was compounded by the more overwhelming sense of resentment at having been misled that attaining enormous wealth *could* get him everything he wanted.

As part of his philanthropic efforts, Harwood wanted to leave behind a legacy that would go some way towards compensating for this lack that gnawed at him constantly. In 1985, he announced that he would fund the building of a community college. But it wasn't enough to just create a college that would bear his name. Ambition collided with reality when he also announced that this community college would have its own coat of arms with a Latin motto, and he could not be persuaded that both were completely redundant for an institution of that type. His legacy would show them.

Unfortunately, Harwood chose to outsource the creation of the motto to his 17-year-old nephew, not having any children of his own. Together with his friends, the nephew came up with: *SUGERE, PUER MAGNUS.* Also unfortunately, neither Harwood or his associates bothered to find out what *SUGERE, PUER MAGNUS* meant. It was the word *MAGNUS* that gave him all the reassurance he needed that it had to be a motto of suitable grandiloquence. When other high school students discovered its meaning, they decided to keep it to themselves, and it had remained a private joke among subsequent generations of schoolkids. None of the adults had ever bothered to find out for themselves, as the motto didn't even register with them anyway.

Since Harwood College's opening in the fall of 1987, students, teachers, and visitors had been welcomed every day at the entrance by the American Eagle coat of arms and the Latin motto that roughly translated to *SUCK, BIG BOY.*

This should have been another normal day at the college, but that fell apart when Kenneth White stormed past the reception, ran upstairs, and barged into the college library, where he assailed the librarian, a sweet woman in her thirties who wasn't used to having a red-faced lunatic shouting in her face.

"Where are your books on evilution?!"

The few students who were in the library stopped and looked at the angry man who was ranting nonsensically.

"Excuse me?"

"You heard me! I want to know where your books on evilution are!"

"Sir, do you mean evolution?"

"Evilution!"

"If we have books on evolution, they'll be in the science section."

"Science. Of course your godless college would have science books."

"Are you even a student here?" the librarian asked skeptically.

"Of course not! I'm here to cleanse this library of evil books. And where are your fag books?"

"Excuse me?!"

"You heard me! I want to know where your fag and dyke books are!"

"OK, I'm going to have to ask you to leave. We don't tolerate language like that here."

"Of course you don't. I bet you're a dyke, ain't you?"

"If you don't leave, I will call security to remove you."

"Well, are you?"

"You are disgusting and inappropriate. It is none of your business if I am a *lesbian* or not."

"I'm just spreading the love of the lord, bitch."

"OK, I warned you." The librarian picked up her phone and dialed a number. White didn't move. "Hi, could you come up to the library. We have an intruder being abusive and threatening."

"You have a soldier of the lord speaking the truth," White said. "At least describe me correctly."

"Thanks," the librarian said and hung up.

"I'll just wait here then," White declared. The librarian ignored him and carried on with her paperwork.

White turned to address the students, who had since gone back to reading, working, and browsing. "Science is lying to you. Don't trust what these books say. They're the work of the devil. Evilution is a lie."

"Man, shut your bitch ass up," a male student said in response.

"The lord said evil people would turn away from the truth."

"Didn't your lord also say something about gluttony?" a female student asked.

White smirked and responded: "Your words cannot hurt me. I'm protected by the lord."

The double doors swung open and the college security guard, a lanky, pale guy in his late twenties who didn't look as though he could pose much of a challenge to a 9-year-old, entered. The librarian nodded towards White and the guard went up to him.

"Sir, you need to come with me."

"I'm not going anywhere until I've cleansed this college of all its evil books."

"Sir, you've been asked to leave. Please come with me now."

"No! I will not leave, you godless lib! I am a soldier for Jesus and I am here to wage war against science and homosexuals!"

The security guard put his hand on White's shoulder, but White pushed him back. "You can't deal with me, boy."

The guard came back for a second go, but White used his protruding belly to push him back. As the guard staggered back, White turned and ventured into the library proper, barking: "Where's the science section?!"

The librarian came around from behind her desk, clutching her cellphone, poised to call 911.

"Where are the devil's books?!" White screamed, randomly grabbing at books from shelves.

One male student ran up to White and grabbed hold of his arm, yelling: "What the fuck is wrong with you?!"

"I'm here to cleanse the library!" He struggled with the student, but found that he wasn't as easy to fend off as the security guard.

The librarian was dialing 911 when the library doors flung wide open. She looked up and saw the doors were somehow staying open despite there being no one there to hold them. While the student and White continued to grapple, she went to investigate, her curiosity aroused by this strange happening.

She heard White let out a bloodcurdling cry and spun around to see him sliding back across the floor towards the doorway, dragged along by an invisible force.

"I knew this college was evil!" he shouted.

The students and the librarian watched aghast, obviously not out of sympathy for the wretched man but out of shock at the sight of the inexplicable and impossible.

Once he had exited the library, the doors swung shut. The librarian immediately ran over, followed by the students, to see what would happen next.

She opened the doors, and this time they were held open by her and the male student who'd been fighting White just seconds before. They saw him slide back and to the left towards the door to the stairwell. The door opened and he went through.

The spectators ran on, but when the librarian tried to open the door to the stairwell, it was locked. She turned the handle repeatedly, but it was futile.

She looked through the glass pane and saw White now had his back to them and wasn't moving. She could just about make out that someone was standing at the top of the steps going down.

"I think someone's talking to the asshole," she said.

White couldn't move. His heart was pounding from what he'd just experienced and all he wanted to do was get out of this building, go home, and put on one of his favorite speeches by his favorite President. But he couldn't move, and even if he could, there was someone blocking his way.

"Horrible little man, aren't you, Kenneth?" Mike said, stroking his chin with the back of his hand.

"Who are you? And how do you know my name?"

"I'm Mike. And to answer your second question, I'm what you humans call a demon. Actually, no, I know your name because I heard the Sheriff say it when he interviewed you in the diner."

"A demon? Yes, you are. All of you godless science lovers are demons. I'm glad you admit what you are."

"No, Kenneth, I wasn't using that as a figure of speech. I am a demon. I prefer diabolical entity, personally, if we're using English."

"What?"

"*What* what?"

"Huh?"

"Not you as well. As if I didn't get enough of that from the Hains. Five months of that. Hideous. Truly hideous."

"What do you mean about figure of speech?"

"I'd have thought the way you exited the library would be enough of a clue, but OK, here's another illustration." Mike clicked his finger.

The huddled spectators were startled when the glass pane went completely black.

"What the hell?" the librarian said.

A male student pushed through the crowd of bodies with his hand and reached out to rub the glass.

"What's that supposed to do?" the librarian asked.

"I thought it was dirt."

White was often fond of telling anyone who would listen that men who show emotion are either gay, vegan, or both, and that he was proud to say he had never cried once in his life. None of his friends or family would ever know that, before he died, Kenneth White had, in fact, cried twice in his life. The first time was in the privacy of his home on the day of the inauguration in 2021, which he rationalized to himself as an acceptable reaction to an atrocity. The second was to be this day. When Mike clicked his finger, as well as blocking the onlookers' view, it also caused White's head to detach from his body, hover to the right, and bang into the wall repeatedly. White screamed so loudly, Mike thought the man was going to have a heart attack.

The librarian looked at the students. All were stunned by the volume and agony of the screams.

"Oh, I hope that's the asshole and not an innocent person," she said.

The woman who was currently on shift at the college reception on the ground floor heard the scream. She leapt out of her seat, came around her desk, and ran to the door that led to the staircase, but found it wouldn't open. Through the glass pane, she could only see to the top of the first set of steps, but the rest of the landing that led to the second set of steps up was out of view.

His face bloodied from the multiple blunt force impacts, White's head hovered back to his body and reconnected to his spinal column. He coughed and heaved and wiped some of the blood off his face. He continued to cry.

"Now, are we on the same page?" Mike asked.

In between sobs, White responded: "It's… It's you, isn't it?!"

"Yes, it's me."

"You're… You're him!"

"Him? You'll have to elaborate."

"The… The devil!"

"Oh," Mike sighed. "That cartoon character again. Look, you humans really need to stop believing in your silly little fairytales. No such fellow exists. I understand that many throughout your history have been killed for saying as much, which, if you ask me, is a perversely ironic reaction by people who claim to oppose evil incarnate."

White brought his crying under control and said: "Then if you're not the devil, who are you?"

"I..." Mike's shoulders sunk and he rubbed his forehead in exasperation. "I already told you, like, ten seconds ago. Why doesn't anybody listen? I told Nancy Dirgle and she didn't listen. Honestly, does it look like I'm trying to do the mysterious, enigmatic shtick? I could if I wanted to, but seeing as I just played the drum fill from *In The Air Tonight* using your head, that opportunity's gone. So, I say again: here I stand, a diabolical entity, telling you, Kenneth White, you truly are a horrible, hate filled little man. And it's time to bring your theft of oxygen to an end."

"Should we call the cops?" one of the students asked.

The librarian was about to answer *No, they might save that asshole,* but before she could, there was a scream so blistering, it threatened to shatter the glass, which would have been unnecessary, as the unfathomable black veil over the pane vanished and the group looked on in confusion, their brains trying to make sense of what they were seeing.

The librarian, being closest, was the first to realize what she was seeing. Caught between wanting to vomit and to dial 911, she fainted. A female student grabbed her before she could hit the floor.

The guy who'd exchanged blows with White took the librarian's place to get a better look.

"That's some weird and bloody shit."

The stairwell of Harwood College had a new indoor fountain. It was created seconds ago. But this fountain didn't contain water. And it wasn't built into a pretty, aesthetically appealing, and carefully designed and carved structure such as you might find in a hotel lobby. The structure was White's torso, which was hollowed out. Lying face up at the bottom of the first set of steps going down, multi-jets of blood danced up out of the hole to create a traditional dome pattern. Three central jets of blood arced high above the dome, the middle one rising highest, and it was this, reaching above floor level, that the gaggle could see from where they stood.

Wednesday

11:32am

"I heard a scream. I tried to go see what was going on, but the door wouldn't open. I don't know why, it wasn't locked," the receptionist told Sam, Jockton, and Morton when they entered the lobby of the college.

Sam went to see for himself. He turned the handle and the door opened. The receptionist looked embarrassed. "I wasn't lying! It wouldn't open!"

"It's OK, we believe you," Morton assured her.

"Yes, we believe you," Jockton added, again resenting the cop from Oregon usurping his established authority.

Sam slowly ascended the steps, followed close behind by the Sheriff and Detective. He held his gun as a precaution even though he knew that Mike wouldn't be there and, even if he was, bullets would be useless. But he couldn't rule out the possibility, however tiny, that the murder had been committed by a human being.

Approaching the landing, he slowed his steps, looked behind him, saw the other two also had their firearms ready, and turned to the right, where he saw Harwood College's new fountain. He was momentarily transfixed by the sight. Streams of blood shooting up from White's open torso into a dome formation, and the central jets completing the pattern that would have been rather picturesque had it been water.

He then noticed on the wall immediately above White's mutilated body the name *MIKE* scrawled in blood.

When Jockton and Morton saw Sam lower his gun, they relaxed and ran up the remaining steps. Morton was the first to see it and he shot out an arm to block Jockton from going any further.

"What are you doing, Detective?!" the Sheriff asked.

"We don't need you throwing up all over the crime scene again."

"Why would I throw up?"

Morton decided to be proved right and stepped aside to let Jockton see. The Sheriff immediately retched and turned around to vomit over the steps going down.

"There you go," Morton said matter-of-factly.

"I'll… I'm going to get some water," Jockton said and headed to the ground floor.

"Take your time," Morton suggested.

"Well," Sam began, "I must say it's considerate of Mike to save the most demented part of his set piece for our eyes only."

"There's that," Morton said, pointing to the middle jet that arced the highest. He followed the sight line from its peak and saw where it led. "Could you go up there and tell me what's going on?"

"I can, but what's stopping you?"

"I don't want to get blood on my suit."

"Oh. Priorities. I get it, Detective."

Morton let Sam's comment slide and replied: "Thanks."

Sam edged around the blood fountain to the second set of steps, trying his best to avoid the spray, but got a few specks on his jacket. He went up to the first-floor landing, where he found a group of faces huddled together behind the door. "Just wait there," he instructed and went back down to join Morton. "They're behind the door. I guess this is what they meant when they reported something bloody and weird. We'll have to come up with another cover story."

"You got any ideas?" Morton asked.

"What was it we used last time? Wind machine and a vat of blood, right?"

"Yes, that was my idea."

"Well... Can you think of another?"

Morton smiled faintly, put his hands in his pockets and leaned against the wall to think.

They heard footsteps and looked down to see Jockton coming up, drinking from a bottle of mineral water.

"You OK, Don?" Sam asked.

"Yes, thank you, Sam."

"Then why are you coming back?"

Jockton stopped. "What do you mean?"

"Why do you want to see the same thing that made you puke? Do you want to puke again?"

"Uh... Maybe you have a point."

"How about you get Chuck down here to remove the body without anyone seeing Mike's showmanship."

"OK, good idea, Sam." The Sheriff gulped some more of the water and went back down.

"Good thinking," Morton complimented Sam.

"Thanks. Come up with an explanation for the local rubes?"

Morton stepped forward from the wall, folded his arms and said: "We'll tell them the killer funneled the victim's blood through a mini sprinkler that he placed over his body."

Sam briefly ruminated over the idea. "You know, the human race is so fucked up, that's actually not so implausible."

Morton went into his pocket, took out a quarter and tossed it into the blood fountain.

Nothing happened.

"Again. Disappointing."

Sam looked down at White's face and he remembered something from the drive over. "Detective, what was it you said on the way over here again?"

"Which part?"

"About the victim."

"You mean *poor guy whoever it is that Mike's killing?*"

Sam laughed uncontrollably. Being a man who didn't like being the butt of jokes, or feeling he might be, Morton folded his arms and said: "As I recall, you thought it was unacceptable when I made a joke about the John Does. Now you think this is funny. Are you having a breakdown, Mr. Hain?"

"No, Detective. You weren't to know. And I'll admit, I too felt bad when I didn't know who the victim was." Sam didn't want to relate the real reason he felt bad at the time. "This was Kenneth White. You were lucky enough not to meet him."

"Because?"

"He was a far right, antisemitic, homophobic, misogynistic, creationist piece of shit."

"Oh." Morton looked at White's corpse. "Maybe this Mike isn't so bad after all."

Wednesday

11:55am

Since there was no way for Chuck to stop the fountain, they decided to forego the standard procedure of placing the body on a covered stretcher for removal, as the continual spray would create a mess. Instead, Chuck placed White's corpse into a body bag and zipped it up so that the blood would at least collect inside the bag.

Once he had departed with the body in the backseat of his car, the eyewitnesses were allowed to leave. But first they had information to impart and questions to ask. Morton had told Jockton what to say, but he stood by in case the Sheriff fucked up and needed rescuing.

The only problem was that the first detail they wanted to talk about was something Jockton, Morton, and Sam couldn't have known of in advance: White was dragged along the floor without anyone touching him, the library doors stayed open without anyone holding them, and the door pane went black.

Jockton looked at Morton. Morton looked pissed that he was expected to think up another explanation on the spot. A get-out came to mind and he said: "I'm sure you can appreciate this is still an active crime scene and we need to investigate. We'll report on our findings as soon as we can."

Sam, also thinking quickly on his feet, decided on a different approach. "Mr. White had histrionic and narcissistic personality disorder and he was given to attention seeking acts. That's what you witnessed. It was just him walking backwards and screaming. And we believe the killer rigged the doors earlier so he could open them with a remote control, and he also used a remote to slot a black slide over the door pane."

Jockton wanted to hug Sam, while Morton was both pissed off at Sam's unauthorized intervention and impressed by his improv.

Then the witnesses moved on to the part Jockton was prepared for. He told the librarian and the college kids that the killer had made copies of keys, which is how he was able to lock the doors on the first floor and ground floor. That lie was easily sold.

As to the bloody display, he explained that the killer brought a mini sprinkler through which he funneled the victim's blood. That lie didn't get purchase as easily.

"The killer did all that in two minutes?!" the librarian inquired, accompanied by murmurs and chatter among the students.

"Two minutes?" Jockton repeated.

"Yes, Sheriff. One minute they were talking. The next minute the guy's dead and the killer connects a sprinkler to his corpse? Is there something you're not telling us?"

"Well..." Jockton struggled to think of a response.

Again, Sam came to the rescue. "That's what was happening while you couldn't see what was going on."

"Oh. OK," she said.

"The killer planned all this in advance?" one student said. "What a sick fuck."

"Yes, and this is still an active crime scene, so we need you all to leave now," Morton commanded. Finally, and to the three men's delight, the group began making their way out of the building.

Once Sam, Jockton, and Morton were outside the college, Morton turned to Sam and said: "What the hell was that back there?"

"They'd have gone away and talked about what they saw and it would have been all over town by lunchtime. No amount of explanations then would stem the tide. Better to nip it in the bud when we can. You may be a cop, but I know how people think, Detective."

"Thank you, Mr. Hain, but I spend my days investigating murders, not following husbands giving their secretaries the hot beef injection or wives giving their gardeners hummers. When it comes to human nature, I think I just might have the edge over you."

Sam laughed. "I like you, Detective Morton. That probably puts me in a very short list of people, but I do. Anyway," he said, turning to Jockton, "Don, I'm afraid there's nothing more I can do here. I'm going home. I'm done with this case."

"What?" Jockton said with dismay.

"Yeah, me too," Morton said. "I have to conclude the Hains are dead. That solves my case. And there's nothing I or anyone can do about Mike. So I'm going back to Portland."

Jockton looked genuinely dismayed. And this caused, in turn, a reaction in Morton that the veteran cop could scarcely believe. He actually felt moved by the notion that Jockton was going to miss him. Despite the way he had spoken to the Sheriff, despite their many disagreements and insults, the latter entirely unidirectional, Jockton appeared to be sad at

Morton's prospective departure. This one single emotion by the Sheriff had succeeded where so many criminals, peddlers of suspicious alibis, and lawyers over the years had failed; where their attempts to be disarming had fallen flat because Morton saw right through them, Jockton had unintentionally triumphed in softening the cop's attitude by his innate sincerity in a moment of human transaction.

"Why don't you at least stay one more night so I can buy you fellas a farewell dinner as a thank you?" Jockton asked.

Realizing that one more night would also allow for the possibility of a farewell fuck with Chloe, Sam replied: "OK, sure. Sounds good."

Morton didn't want to be a buzzkill, so he said: "Why not? I can hang around one more night."

"Fantastic!"

"Just as long as it's not Eat All Day," Sam said.

"You got it, Sam," Jockton assured him. "How about Tex's Tex-Mex? Do you like Tex-Mex?"

"I'm always down for Tex-Mex."

"Detective?"

"Sure."

"Fantastic! Let me give you fellas a ride back to your bed & breakfast." Jockton went on ahead to his car.

As the other two followed, Sam looked at Morton with a grin. The cop sensed it and looked at Sam. "What?"

"Don't worry. I won't tell him."

"What are you talking about, Mr. Hain?"

"You've warmed to him. I can tell."

"Be quiet," Morton said, feigning annoyance.

"It's OK, Detective. It happened to me too. There's no shame in it."

Morton just smiled and didn't say anything.

FIVE WEEKS BEFORE

The Last Murder

Had Leo never met Polly, he would have been, in contemporary vernacular, an incel. That he had a spouse had not negated his trenchant misogyny, and it frequently surfaced regardless of whether he was with or apart from his beloved. And it was Leo's misogyny that resulted in the last murder being an unplanned kill, though no less chaotic and slapdash in execution than the ones they orchestrated with premeditation.

It came about because Leo felt inspired by a porno he and Polly had watched on the motel pay-per-view. In the film, the male lover placed an ice cube on the woman's nipples and rubbed it around her areolas in a circular motion, followed by licking the drops that trickled down. Leo knew he didn't and never could look like the ripped, six-foot stud with the six-pack in the film, but he could at least obtain ice.

While Polly shot up some meth, Leo left their room to go to the ice machine that was at the end of the landing. As he approached, he saw an attractive young brunette already at the machine getting ice for herself.

Sienna Logan, a 26-year-old lawyer, had come to town on business just for the day. The organizing was last minute and she couldn't find anywhere better to stay, and she figured she could cope with a shitty motel for just one night. Dressed in her formal attire of high heels, black skirt, tights, and white blouse, she looked up and saw an odd man barefoot and in stained and shabby clothes getting close. Or to be more precise, she smelled him before she saw him. Sienna put on her best friendly smile to disguise her revulsion at his odor and appearance.

"It's all yours," she said with the politeness that women have inculcated into them from a young age as an imperative when dealing with members of the opposite sex because: a) they should always be kind and considerate towards men, and b) what might happen if they're not kind and considerate towards them?

But as she turned to go back to her room, Leo said: "I'm with my wife. Would ya like to join us, honey?"

Sienna turned to face Leo and tried not to laugh. Again, deploying her best polite refusal, she answered: "No, thank you. I'm really tired and need to sleep. I've had a long day. Goodnight."

"Why you got ice if you gonna sleep?"

"I'm going to have…" Sienna stopped herself, wondering why she was explaining herself to this creep. But as she was now beginning to feel queasy, she thought it best to just finish explaining and then get back to her room. "I'm going to have some water before I sleep."

"My wife and me are real good in bed, girl. We got a porno on the pay-per-view and lots of drinks and meth. You'll have a real good time and shit."

Sienna was done talking to this icky slimeball. She just looked at him with disgust and walked off.

And that triggered the red-hot misogynistic fury inside Leo Hain. Who did this girl think she was? Did she think she was better than him? He was sick of women who turned him down.

He waited until he saw which room she went in and then he ran back to his room. Polly was laid out on the bed in a meth haze, fingering herself. Leo went into the bedside drawer and retrieved his .38 and attached a suppressor that he'd never had cause to use till now.

"Fucking bitch!" he muttered out loud as he left.

"What's that, baby?" Polly asked.

Leo marched all the way around the landing to the opposite side of the motel and knocked rapidly on Sienna's door.

Inside, Sienna looked through the peephole and was horrified to see the yucky creep. That was it. She wasn't going to be polite anymore. She opened the door and yelled: "I told you to get lost, you nasty–"

Leo raised his .38 and fired twice. Both shots hit Sienna in the forehead. She dropped dead to the floor. Leo closed the door and ran back to his room as fast as he could.

"We… We… go… Gotta go… now." All that exertion in such a short period of time had left Leo out of breath, and Polly struggled to understand him amidst his huffs and puffs.

"What you talking about, Leo, you asshole?"

Leo paused to catch his breath and continued: "We gotta leave this place now. I just killed a bitch."

That snapped Polly out of her haze and she sat up on the bed. "You did what?!"

"I killed a bitch who wouldn't come join us for a three-way."

Polly got out of bed, enraged. "You killed some girl by yourself without me? Leo, you greedy fuck!"

"We can't stay here! We gotta pack our shit and leave."

"Did you sign our names?"

"No."

"We've gotta put our names, Leo! Else the cops won't know it was us."

"It was me who done it."

"Fuck you. What's her room number?"

Polly fired at the lock with Leo's .38 and she opened the door and went inside, followed by Leo. She looked down at Sienna's corpse and grimaced.

"This bitch said no to you?"

"Yeah."

Polly, feeling it only right that she contribute to the scene, stepped into the spreading pool of blood and blasted three shots into Sienna's already deceased body.

"Now it's *us* who done it."

Leo, holding the brush that Polly had made him bring, kneeled down and dipped it into the blood, stepping foot into the pool as he did so. He wrote his name on the wall and handed the brush to Polly, who wrote hers.

Leo sat on the bed and rummaged through Sienna's handbag with his bloodstained fingers, tossing out the contents as he searched for anything valuable.

"Got anything?" Polly asked when she finished writing her autograph and went to join him on the edge of the bed. Leo tossed out some dollar bills and change. "Better than nothing," she commented.

Leo threw the handbag across the room. "Let's pack our shit and get outta here."

Polly got off the bed and stood over Sienna's corpse. She bent down and spat on her face. "No one says no to my Leo, you stuck up bitch!"

A Bonanza of Forensics

"They must have fallen out with whoever was helping them."

Morton had just entered the morgue holding a cup of coffee and looking tired. He pulled a chair forward and sat down. Rubbing his eyes, he took a sip of the coffee and said: "Judy, I'm tired and my migraine is killing me. Could you leave out the cryptic statements and just cut to the chase today?"

"OK, Walls, no need to get sharp with me. I'm talking about the CSI findings. They left behind a bonanza of forensics. So if the Hains *did* have someone helping them, he or she didn't show up for this party."

Morton drank more of his coffee. "Or maybe they had an extended psychotic episode that somehow made them intelligent and now they're back to being just their normal selves."

"Creative, Walls. That would be a first for a psychotic episode."

"I'm just trying to ignore my migraine."

Judy went to stand over Sienna's body on the morgue table. "Two shots to the head from a .38 less than a feet away. Killed her instantly. And then three shots to the abdomen postmortem. Overkill again, like the Bloodworth murder. And you know the rest. Bloody sets of footprints, fibers on the bed, the Hains' prints all over the place, and Polly Hain's saliva on the vic's face."

Morton put the cup down. "No evidence at the previous murders that would convict them in a trial. There were only the signatures at the last two that a good lawyer could say was a frame-up. And now they throw that all away by leaving enough shit to put them away for life or on death row. What was it you said about the Giles murder? *In what universe does this make sense?* You nailed it. In what fucking universe."

"Maybe they decided what the hell? They'd written their names, so they figure why bother?"

"After all that effort before? No, there's got to be an explanation for all this. And it's pissing me off not knowing."

Judy pulled a chair forward next to Morton and sat down. She chewed her gum quietly as Morton finished his coffee.

"How are you and the wallpaper girl?" he asked.

"Do you mean Steph?

"Yeah."

"*Wallpaper girl,*" she repeated with a laugh. "She hasn't moved in if that's what you're getting at."

"I wasn't getting at anything."

"What about you, Walls? Why don't you have anyone?"

"You know why."

"Yes, I do. Relationships aren't for you."

"So why ask?"

"People change."

"I'm 47. I think I'm pretty set in who I am."

"Then I hope you never change, Walls. I like you just the way you are."

"And I like you the way you are, Judy."

"Awww. Aren't we sweet together?"

Morton smiled and gave Judy an affectionate pat on the shoulder as he stood up. "Right. Now we know for certain it's the Hains and not someone framing them, it's time to get the public to help."

"How?"

"The one thing that appeals to all human beings and can turn former accomplices into helpful snitches. Money."

The Breads Rent A Cabin

"How long you folks planning to stay?" Walt Lennard asked.

The gray-haired 73-year-old had, against all odds, succeeded in maintaining his independent business renting out cabins in the wooded areas of Rhododendron, in Oregon's Mount Hood Corridor, in the face of competition from online-only booking sites and private homeowners renting out their abodes, the latter a trend he found particularly grotesque ("I wouldn't let no goddamn stranger into my own home when I'm away, who knows what they're gonna do?"). It had also provided him with solace since he was widowed at the age of 68. Having a place to go to every day where he could meet people and earn money was what kept him going and kept his faculties intact.

"About a month. Maybe bit longer," Polly said. She and Leo had built up savings over a long period from mugging, robbing, and pickpocketing people, and before they departed Sunderland, they topped up their cash reserves by robbing an all-night liquor store. They had stopped in at the first cabin rental agency they could find driving through Clackamas County.

"You folks nature lovers, huh?" Walt said with a smile, innocently assuming the couple sitting in front of him in Walt's Cozy Cabins were normal human beings.

"Yeah, we love trees and shit," Leo replied with typical class.

"Well, you've come to the right place!" Walt proclaimed with the same enthusiasm as when he first opened his business twenty-nine years ago. "I'll just need your names to start the paperwork."

"I'm Frank Brown and this is my wife, Maggie White." As Walt scribbled down the fake names, Leo preemptively added: "All our friends thought it was fucking hilarious me and my wife are Brown and White! They call us the breads!"

"Is that so?" Walt said, continuing to fill in details and wondering why the husband felt it necessary to disclose that information.

"Yes, sir!" Leo's feigned friendliness was beginning to creep Walt out, not least because the man's grin reminded him of cartoon drawings of the infamous 19th century British serial killer whose name he couldn't recall just at that moment.

Walt paused to take a tissue from the box on his desk and wiped his nose. "You folks will have to excuse me. I've got a bit of a cold." If Walt had known how foul these customers smelled, he'd have sung the praises of the virus that had given him anosmia by infecting his upper respiratory tract.

"We can move in today and shit, right?" Leo asked.

"You sure can, Mr. Brown. I'll need a deposit, one month's rent, and a debit or credit card number to keep on file, and I'll hand you the keys."

"We like everything cash. We don't ain't believe in no cards," Polly said.

"You don't have any bank cards?" Walt asked with suspicion.

"Cash all the way," Leo said, still smiling and still creeping out Walt, who felt reluctant to proceed any further with these customers. He always took card details for security. Anyone who refused had something to hide.

But then Leo lifted the backpack he'd brought with him, unzipped it, and showed Walt the wads of twenty and fifty-dollar notes inside. "Is this good enough and shit?" Leo asked.

382

"Well, slap my ass and call me a biscuit," Walt said, mixing his idioms, a habit his late wife had found lovable. Staring at the cash, in a matter of seconds he rationalized to himself why, in this age of tough competition for business, he should feel no inclination to ask his customers why they were carrying around so much cash. "Yes, that's good enough, Mr. Brown."

Walt finished the paperwork, printed out the rental agreement, and took the deposit and rental fee. "I just need one of you to sign the agreement and you're all set."

Leo took the pen that Walt held out, which pissed off Polly, who wanted to play some part in all this. Leo signed the sheet, which Walt placed on top of a pile of other paperwork.

"Right! Let's get you good folks your keys!"

The keys, a copy of the rental agreement, a receipt for the deposit and month's rent, and directions to the cabin in their possession, Leo and Polly got into their car and headed off to their new temporary home. During the drive, Polly called Leo a fucking asshole for not waiting to see if she wanted to sign the agreement. He called her a bitch. Their marriage was as strong as ever.

Sitting back in his chair and drinking a coffee with a dash of bourbon, Walt looked at the pile of cash on his desk. He wasn't a fan of breaking with basic business practice, but he told himself this is how things were conducted back during the American Frontier: good old-fashioned cash, no questions asked. So be it.

He put the money into a locked drawer for safekeeping until he'd deposit it at the bank. He then took the rental agreement off the pile of sheets and filed that away.

Even Killers Like To Be Cozy

Leo and Polly very quickly made themselves at home in the cabin next to the woods in Rhododendron. Upon arriving, they found a clean, shiny, and welcoming abode, with polished wooden floors, furniture, a kitchenette, and a roaring fireplace set in a marble mantelpiece. The bedroom boasted a king-size bed with fresh cotton sheets and pillows and a smooth, unblemished headboard. The bathroom was equally well maintained and spotless. It was the kind of place travelers wanting a cozy getaway would appreciate and make a concerted effort to take care of whilst staying there.

So, of course, within a day or two, the Hains had reduced the cabin to a shithole. But it was still their kind of cozy.

On their first night, they stopped off to get Chinese takeout and beer for dinner. They sat up on the couch to eat while they watched TV, immediately staining the leather in kung pao and oyster sauce. They wolfed down their food, eagerly awaiting the news about the motel murder.

Leo had a noodle hanging out of his mouth and glazed carrots falling on his lap when he saw a photo of Sienna Logan on the news. "Turn it up!" he yelled excitedly. Polly spilled some of her beer as she reached for the remote and turned up the volume.

Angie, in the news studio, spoke via live link-up with Gavin, who was reporting from outside the motel in Sunderland. "Gavin, what can you tell us about this motel murder?"

"Police have named the victim as Sienna Logan, a 26-year-old lawyer from Prineville who was visiting Portland on work. She was shot five times. Her body was discovered by a cleaner when she failed to check out of the Forest Creek motel by midday."

"Detectives have a lead on the case already, don't they?" Angie asked.

"Yes, Angie. They confirmed that this murder was committed by the serial killing couple Leo and Polly Hain, names that regular viewers will be familiar with."

Hearing their names never got old and both Leo and Polly whooped in jubilation. Leo whooped while he was still swallowing his food and started coughing violently. He spluttered and made a sound as though a drugged-up elderly hobo was living in his bowels and imitating a foghorn.

"Oh, Leo, you dumb fuck!" Polly complained, pushing him away on the couch.

Gavin continued: "Officers believe the Hains were staying at Forest Creek motel this whole time."

"Yeah!" Leo said, clearing his throat. "And they didn't know shit!" He immediately stuffed his mouth with more noodles.

"Now, I understand that police have some surprising information about this latest murder, isn't that right, Gavin?" Angie asked.

"That's right, Angie. The Hains signed their names again, like the previous two murders, but unlike the previous two murders, and the murders that detectives retroactively connected to the Hains, they left a ton of evidence behind when they murdered Miss Logan, including DNA and fingerprints."

"That's quite unusual, given what happened before, isn't it, Gavin?"

"Yes, Angie. One detective I spoke to said the previous murders looked like the work of intelligent perpetrators, which they couldn't fathom with the Hains being responsible, whereas this murder *does* fit with their profile. That is to say: sloppy, incompetent, and intellectually deficient."

"Hey! They said we intellectual again!" Leo shouted delightedly.

"But why they keep saying we gone fishing? We don't do no fishing," Polly said irritably.

"Do police have any leads on where the Hains have fled?" Angie asked.

"Officers refused to say if they have any information on the Hains' current location, but they repeated their call for anyone with tips to come forward."

"Yeah! They don't know where we are 'cause we always one step ahead and shit! They don't know about Frank Brown and Maggie White!" Leo yelled excitedly. He downed the remainder of his beer and let out a long, booming burp.

"That gets me so hot," Polly said, moving closer to Leo again on the couch.

"Yeah, baby. I'd rather pound you than that news bitch on the box."

Polly immediately pulled away from Leo, anger growing on her visage. "So you been thinking about that Angie skank?"

"No, Pol. I said I'd rather pound *you* than her. I wanna pound *you!*"

"Why even talk about her, Leo?! You gotta be thinking about her. You done wouldn't never not mentioned her otherwise!"

"I ain't thinking about her! I said I *don't* wanna fuck her!"

"Go play with yourself, you asshole! You ain't not gettin' no cooch tonight!"

"Oh, fuck you, Pol!"

Leo turned back to the TV, which was reporting on the aftermath of a school shooting in Mississippi. The Governor there was offering his thoughts and prayers.

Leo looked over at Polly, expecting her to be aroused as she always was whenever he said *fuck you* or similar, and was dismayed and not a little disturbed to see she didn't have the grin that always preceded her informing him she was moist. She met his gaze and got up off the couch with an angry huff. "You can whack off to the news skank. I'm gonna shoot up and sleep."

Once she was in the cabin bedroom, Leo turned his attention back to the TV. There were only five minutes of the news program remaining. He sat back on the couch and unzipped his trousers. On the table in front, he caught sight of the pile of napkins that had come with the takeout boxes. He leaned forward and grabbed a couple of them and sat back to begin jerking off. It had been a very long time since he'd used a tissue for the purposes of masturbation, so this marked a step up in his personal hygiene. Normally, Leo would just jack off and blow his load over himself or onto the carpet, as he had done at the motel. A neutral observer, if inclined towards generosity, might speculate that the pristine and relatively opulent surroundings had triggered deep in Leo's subconscious the stirrings of something comparable to respect – assuming Leo had ever felt it for anyone or anything for there to even be vestiges still lingering – or triggered a vague recollection that this was something he used to do. Even if either of these theories was true, he would have been oblivious to it.

This was all academic anyway, as Leo promptly defiled the cabin by tossing the napkin onto the floor upon finishing.

Jess Dalton

"Detective Wallace Morton spoke to reporters earlier today outside Portland PD Headquarters and announced the reward," Topher, the Los Angeles newscaster, said. The news program cut to a pre-recorded clip of Morton.

"We are offering $25,000 for any information that helps bring to justice Leo and Polly Hain."

Jess Dalton, 35, looked up from her cellphone. She was on her couch in her LA apartment, relaxing after a day's work as a casting assistant in the film industry. Hearing those names after all these years jolted her out of her emoji selection in the message she was writing.

"They are wanted for eight murders in the Portland area, as well as homicides and robberies in six other states," Morton continued. The news showed a photo of the Hains. Jess covered her mouth in shock. "If anyone out there knows where the Hains are or has any information about them that might prove useful in our investigation, please get in touch with Portland Police immediately. You will receive a $25,000 reward if your tip leads to their capture."

The Hains, on the loose and committing murder. What if they go after Sam? She and Sam had lost touch over the years, but she still felt affection towards him. And she knew the danger his parents posed from the time she and her family took him in. She had to call the cops to let them know these monsters have a son who could be their next target.

And $25,000 wouldn't hurt either.

They're Being Sarcastic, Right?

I

Casacide

If there was such a thing as murdering a place, the Hains had massacred the cabin in less than a week.

Empty beer cans and takeout boxes littered the floor, along with Leo's gruesome discarded napkins. In a meth-induced haze, they had stabbed and slashed at the wall panels with knives, and broken the two wooden chairs, in the process of which Leo cut himself and dripped blood onto one of the severed chair legs.

Not for the Hains idyllic creature comforts like dozing next to a fireplace, opting to jack up the thermostat and instead use the fireplace as a place to throw their used needles and syringes after each meth binge. And whenever there was a pause in their demented onslaught against the walls, they left their detritus on the mantel shelf.

The bedroom wasn't spared the Hains' casacide. The pillows and sheets were stained not just from their default uncleanliness but the hair dyes that they'd insufficiently washed out. The headboard was bloodstained from when they cut each other during a fuck. During one particularly exuberant session, Leo got carried away and fractured the headboard. Polly got so mad at him – having always envied people who slept in beds that have headboards – that she said they might as well go all the way and she kicked the headboard until it broke.

The bathroom was relatively unscathed; the shower part of it anyway, and only from lack of use. The toilet area was another matter and both looked and smelled how a toilet must have looked and smelled after the late Rush Limbaugh or late Jerry Falwell had an all-you-can-eat barbecue buffet.

On what was to be their last night in the cabin, they had burgers for takeout and watched TV. While viewing a true crime documentary about an unsolved murder, Polly wondered out loud if Mike was going to turn up. Leo replied "I don't know and shit." They also shared a laugh about how the murders they'd committed would also go unsolved.

They completed their night by shooting up meth and having mutually unsatisfactory sex on the floor next to the dormant fireplace before retiring to the bedroom, where they sat up in bed discussing where they should go to find their next victim.

II

Spacetime Shenanigans

Leo was in the middle of suggesting they kill the owner of the rental agency so they could continue staying in the cabin without having to pay when he found himself on the couch watching the true crime documentary. Polly was next to him on the couch eating.

"What the fuck?!" he yelled.

"Shut up, asshole, I'm trying to watch the show!"

"We was in bed just now!" he shouted and found himself in bed again, where Polly was suggesting they talk about where to find their next victim.

"What the hell just happened?!" he yelled.

"Why you shouting at me, you son of a bitch!" Polly screamed and she found herself on the couch watching the start of the documentary.

Leo was next to her gobbling down his burger and saying "You think they gonna make a show about our murders and shit?"

"What the fuckass is going on, Leo?!" Polly shrieked.

"I said you think they gonna make—"

"I ain't talking about that! Did I black out? Did you roofie me, Leo?!"

Leo picked up his bag of fries and threw them at her. Polly ducked and the fries landed on the bedside table. She was back in bed and Leo was saying they should kill the cabin owner.

"What the fuckass is happening?!" she screamed.

"Bitch, you said let's talk about who to kill next!"

"We was watching TV a second ago!" she insisted.

"That was two hours ago! Did you roofie yourself?"

Polly angrily shoved Leo and he fell out of bed and landed on the floor next to the dormant fireplace, where Polly was taking her clothes off.

"What the hell?!" Leo squealed in severe agitation.

"You said let's fuck, asshole!" Polly complained.

"We was in bed talking about who to kill!" Leo said, standing up and fearing the meth had finally made him insane. "This is really scaring me and shit, Pol!"

Leo turned and ran into the bedroom, where he saw himself and Polly in bed talking. Leo screamed; Leo and Polly in bed screamed; Polly joined Leo at the door and all four screamed.

The Leo at the door now found himself in bed screaming at his counterpart at the door.

The Polly at the door also now found herself in bed screaming at her counterpart at the door.

The ones at the door vanished.

Leo got under the covers and cried. Polly shoved him and thundered: "Stop that shit, Leo! We gotta go see what's going on!"

She got out of bed and pulled the cover off Leo, who was rocking his head and bawling. "Mike fried my brain, Pol!"

Polly dragged him out of bed and took him by the hand out of the bedroom. She froze when she saw Mike standing by the cabin's front door.

"I love fucking with you two."

III

Humans

Pointing at the mantelpiece, Mike commented: "That has some mighty fine Sylacauga marble underneath all the dirt. You didn't appreciate it. Of course."

Leo and Polly stood motionless, neither knowing what to say but both feeling the inevitable was coming.

He stepped further into the cabin, stroking his chin with the back of his hand. "As I said to you last time we spoke, I've been busy the last few weeks learning more about theology. I must say, my diabolical associates and I have got nothing on the religions! What a catalog! Committing and covering up child abuse, controlling women's bodies, starting wars, beheading non-believers, persecuting and murdering people because of who they're attracted to, flying planes into buildings, animal sacrifice, forced marriage. Tell me something. When religions describe themselves as being all about peace and love, they're being sarcastic, right?"

Leo and Polly didn't answer.

"If you ask me, religion was invented by the evil to control the stupid who, in turn, become evil. I'm almost envious. What an epic con-trick. Whooo! A supposedly all-powerful being creates an entire universe, hangs around for 13.8 billion years, and only then decides to communicate its existence, but does it via humans who declare, without any proof, their divine revelation to be the one and only truth that everyone must follow, except that, sometime later, other mortals declare *their* divine revelation to be the one and only truth that everyone must follow, also without proof, and sometime later, or even at the same time, yet more humans declare their divine revelation to be the one and only truth that everyone must follow, again without proof, and every single one of these divine revelations threatens vicious, sadistic punishment if you don't follow their precepts, no matter how inane and stupid.

"And this is my favorite part: which particular religion you choose to follow, and even which sect of that religion, since all the sects are at odds with each other, depends entirely upon where in the world you were born, at what point in history, and what language you speak, because if you were born 4,000 years ago in Athens, your choice of fairytales would differ vastly to your choice if you were born 2,000 years ago in Great Britain, and they would differ to the ones if you were born in Persia 500 years ago, the Amazon Rainforest fifty years ago, Japan ten years ago, or Kentucky last year. So, not only is your choice a lottery, it's a lottery based on factors over which you have no control! And people actually fall for this shit?!"

Leo and Polly shrugged and shook their heads, surprised that Mike wasn't in the state of fury they had expected him to be.

"Oh, I wasn't expecting you to answer. After all, trying to have an intelligent debate with you two would be like expecting Republicans to be compassionate. Or expecting Republicans to not be hypocrites who secretly pay for their mistresses' abortions while denying women their rights. Or expecting Republicans to stop hating anyone who isn't white and heterosexual. Or expecting Republicans to extend being pro-life to people who are starving or freezing to death. Or expecting Republicans to not appeal to white supremacists. Or expecting Republicans to not murder Black people out jogging. Or expecting Republicans to not celebrate when there's a mass shooting at a gay nightclub. Or expecting Republicans to not be evil."

"So, this mean you ain't mad at us and shit?" Leo asked.

Mike was speechless for the first time.

"This mean you ain't mad at us and shit?" Leo repeated.

"No, I heard you, Leo. I'm just trying to understand how you arrived at that conclusion when there's no clear correlation between the two. I'm even trying to empathize with your thought process by imagining how a mildly sentient bag of vomit would think. And, no, I'm coming up blank."

"It's 'cause you talking about other stuff," Polly ventured.

"Oh, I see! You were confused by someone able to talk and think about more than one subject! Of course! That's where I went wrong! Well, Leo, to answer your question: I'm afraid no, it doesn't mean I ain't mad at you and shit. I *am* mad. I am very mad at you and shit."

Mike clicked his finger and the walls of the cabin started bleeding black all over. The furniture and kitchenette vanished, along with the fireplace, followed by the door and windows. The floor turned black, the door to the bedroom disappeared, and long streams of blood rippled up and down the walls on either side of them that were now entirely black. The Hains realized they were back in Mike's world.

They looked straight ahead and saw Mike staring at them with a cold, fixed gaze. He didn't move and he didn't say anything. This began to unnerve the pair. They were used to Mike hurling insults or attacking them in some bizarre fashion. They weren't used to him being still and being silent.

He continued to stare at them, and his expressionless face disturbed them. Leo hoped Mike would soon call him a name or even choke him out again. Polly wanted to tell Mike to hurry the fuck up and say his piece, but she felt sick with nerves and was trying her hardest to conceal that from Mike.

When he finally spoke, there was no reprieve from their anxiety.

"You have lied to me for the last time. You have betrayed me for the last time."

Mike's voice had a timbre the Hains weren't used to. He'd been angry before, but this was something new.

"I warned you not to sign your names again. I warned you I would punish you."

Polly finally swallowed the reservoir of saliva that had accumulated from her desperate attempt to not show fear. "What are you going to do?"

"I'm going to torment Sam."

Leo and Polly looked at each other and broke into hysterics.

"Fuck him!" she chuckled in unwisely hasty relief.

Speaking up, Leo joined in with the premature jubilation. "Do what you like!"

Mike observed them laughing raucously without making comment. He did this until he could tolerate the moronic pair no more. "Oh, shut the fuck up."

In a flash, the Hains were dead, vacuous grins etched on their faces in a manner that would leave a neutral observer in no doubt that they had been profoundly stupid, annoying individuals.

Looking at the corpses, Mike sighed.

"Humans really piss me off."

He clicked his finger and the Hains' bodies vanished.

Mike himself then instantaneously returned to the cabin and went into the bedroom. He saw the state of the bed. "Oh, would you look at that. Disgusting people. Truly disgusting."

He went around to the other side of the bed. He fluttered his fingers and large globs of blood from nowhere hit the wall and, as though guided by an invisible pen, wrote the name *MIKE*.

Wednesday

5:32pm

Jockton sat at the station's front desk, drinking coffee, and looking forward to the farewell meal with his new pals. He felt comfortable thinking of Morton as a pal since the Portland cop had accepted his invitation without shoehorning a jibe into his response.

Deputy Ronny had popped out to the local store to stock up on refreshments for the station kitchen. Before the recent murders, Ronny's weekly shopping trip was the most exciting thing that happened around here.

Jockton laid down his coffee and picked up a copy of the local evening newspaper. He skipped the first couple of pages, as he wasn't in the mood to read about the police still not making progress on the murders of the two John Does, Nancy Dirgle, and Kenneth White. The paper's website had invited readers to post their tributes to Nancy and White and their personal recollections. The page was taken down after it was flooded with comments from locals about how much they hated them.

The doors opened. Without looking up, Jockton said: "Hope they had the biscuits I wanted, Ronny." When no reply came, Jockton put down the paper and saw a man in a nice suit approaching the desk who reminded him of the John Does. "Oh, I'm sorry, I thought you were my Deputy. What can I do for you?"

Mike gave Jockton a friendly smile. "You are such an amiable fellow, aren't you, Don? I can see why Sam likes you and your peachy personality."

"You know Sam? And my name? Sorry, who are you, sir?"

"There you go again. *Sir.* Impeccable, Don. Impeccable. Nancy Dirgle was so rude and uncouth. And, oh, that Kenneth White. Awful human."

"You must be a local if you knew all these folks, but I don't think I've had the pleasure before, Mr. ...?"

"*The pleasure.* You're just so polite, you should come giftwrapped and wearing a bow."

"Well, that's very kind of you to say, sir, but I really would like to know who you are and how I can help you."

"Of course, Don. And because you've been so nice, I will respond accordingly. My name is Mike."

"OK, Mike. And what can I do for you?" Mike looked at Jockton with a broad grin and the Sheriff felt there was a joke he was supposed to be getting. "What? What is it?"

"That name doesn't mean anything to you?" Mike asked, stroking his chin with the back of his hand.

"*Mike?*" Jockton repeated, picking up his coffee. "No, should it? I mean…" The Sheriff finally caught on and he dropped the coffee. The mug shattered, spilling coffee across the floor. "Oh no. It's you. You're the one who's been doing all the killing!"

"Well, that makes it sound like I'm a mass murderer. I've only killed two people in your town. And let's be honest, I think I did you all a favor there."

"Two? But there have been four victims."

"And to answer your earlier question, you can help me get Sam down to the morgue."

The last thing Sheriff Don Jockton saw before he died was Mike clicking his finger.

Wednesday

5:45pm

Chloe walked down the front steps of Harwood College. She debated whether to drop Sam a message about going for a drink later. She also debated whether to get the bus home or walk home.

In the middle of deciding on these two matters, her cellphone rang and she got it out of her pocket. "Hello?"

"Chloe, it's Sheriff Jockton."

"Oh. Sheriff," she said surprised. "I wasn't expecting a call from you. Do you need to interview me again?"

"No. But I do need your help. I need you to come to the county morgue right away. Can you do that?"

Chloe stopped walking, frowning both in confusion and curiosity. "Why do you need me to come to the morgue?"

"It's urgent. I can't discuss it over the phone, but it's to do with the recent murders."

"Do you need me to ID a body or something?"

"Please, Chloe. I can't tell you over the phone."

"OK. I'll get there as soon as I can."

She ended the call and carried on walking, deciding, if it's as important as the Sheriff says it is, she might as well order a cab on her phone's app to get there quicker.

As she opened the app, she realized something about the call she'd found odd but couldn't pinpoint at the time. The Sheriff had called her by her first name. He had never done that.

Chloe then thought to herself she was being ridiculously pedantic and it didn't mean anything. She ordered the cab and waited for it to arrive.

ONE MONTH BEFORE

The Breads Are On The News

Walt sat at his desk, having his afternoon lunch of a sandwich and light beer – he didn't think it professional to have regular beer during work hours – and absently watching the local news on the wall-mounted TV.

The news turned to the Hains and they ran the clip of Morton seeking tips. Walt's attention was caught when a photo of the Hains was shown while Morton spoke.

He got out of his chair to get a better look at the photo. Something about the two people looked awfully familiar. His ears had also perked up at the mention of the reward.

When the news moved on to the next item, he returned to his chair and tried to remember where he might have seen these people before. He shook his head, doing his damnedest to source the memory that the news had triggered.

Finally, it clicked. The Hains resembled the weird couple he'd just recently rented out one of his cabins to, except they had different color hair and maniacal hairstyles and were called the Breads. No, wait, that wasn't their name; that was the anecdote that the creepy husband had pointlessly related.

Brown and White! That was their names. Damn. It wasn't the Hains after all.

Walt resumed drinking his beer and stopped mid-gulp. *You stupid old coot! Why would two people wanted for murder use their real names?!*

"You're getting senile, Walt," he said out loud. Certain they were the couple wanted by the police, he opened the drawer where he kept all the rental agreements. The one for their cabin was top of the pile, as that was the last place he'd rented out. He looked at the bottom of the page.

Walt Lennard had seen a lot in his 73 years, but never in his life had he seen anything like this.

There, at the bottom of the page, in the line above the typed name, *Frank Brown,* was the signature, *Leo Hain.*

"Well, butter my butt and call me a monkey's uncle. That's gotta be the dumbest sumbitch in the world."

This Calls For SWAT

Morton was at his desk going through tip-offs sent in by the public when a colleague ran breathlessly over to his desk, clutching his cellphone.

"Morton, you gotta take this call!" Detective Perry Devlin said excitedly.

"I'm already wading through tips, Devlin. You do your share."

"No, Morton. I've got a guy on the phone who knows where the Hains are!"

"You mean some guy who's seen a couple he *thinks* are the Hains. Quit wasting my time, Devlin."

"No, Morton! This guy rented a cabin out to a couple using fake names, but the husband signed the rental agreement Leo Hain!"

"Yeah, that sounds like the Hains," Morton said, taking the phone from Devlin. "Hello, this is Detective Wallace Morton. Who am I speaking with?"

"I already told the other fella everything," Walt replied.

"Yeah, well pretend you haven't told anyone anything and start from the beginning," Morton said, grabbing a pen and pulling forward his notebook.

"Goddammit!"

"Yeah, I know it sucks, but what are you going to do?"

"Can't you just ask the other cop to fill you in?"

Morton waved Devlin away. Once his colleague was back at his desk, he said: "No, I don't trust any of them. Now, before you start, I need to make sure I'm not wasting my time and you haven't got some other guy who happens to be called Leo Hain. Can you describe them?"

"Yeah. Real ugly, real weird, and look like the people in the photo shown on the news. And I know it's the people you're looking for 'cause he said his name's Frank Brown and his wife is called Maggie White, but the dumb sumbitch signed his name Leo Hain."

"That's them alright. Now all I need is the address to the cabin."

Walt provided the address to Morton and then asked: "So when do I get the reward?"

"Cool your jets, Mr. Lennard. We haven't caught them yet. We'll go down there and if we apprehend them, you'll receive your reward."

"Sumbitch!"

"Yeah, we can't have everything we want, but what are you going to do?"

"Alright, but you call me when you arrest those sumbitches."

"I will. My first priority upon apprehending these serial killers I've been hunting for five months will be to phone you." Morton was about to end the call when he added: "By the way, Mr. Lennard, please don't get any silly ideas about trying to blackmail them in advance of us arriving."

"What are you talking about?"

"I mean don't be so impatient for your reward that you go to the cabin and demand money for your silence as though you haven't already spoken to us. These are dangerous people and they will kill you. In fact, I suggest you don't go into work for the next couple of days. Chances are they're already planning to murder you."

"Sumbitch!"

After the conversation with Walt, Morton left the office to make a call on his phone that he didn't want the other officers to hear. He called a friend in SWAT and told him he needed a unit to back him up in a raid in Rhododendron. His friend wanted to do things formally by having the request signed off by Morton's Captain and other detectives assisting in the investigation, but Morton argued this was a top priority time-sensitive case and he needed a team immediately. Eventually, his friend relented and got a SWAT unit assembled to join him in going to Rhododendron.

Morton felt relieved that this case would shortly be closed. He was looking forward to capturing these two foul murderers, but also getting answers to a lot of questions. Like how did two dumb fucks pull off such remarkable crimes, and had someone really been helping them?

Whatever the answers, at least the Hains would be in custody by the end of the day.

Interesting Reading Matter

"There are two possibilities," Morton surmised. "One: They've been kidnapped and are still alive. Two: They're dead. And we're looking for a rival serial killer who wants the world to know him as… Mike."

"So I guess you'll be calling on us again, hey, Detective?" the SWAT Commander asked.

Morton couldn't tell if he was being condescending, but he chose to accept it. "Yeah, sure, maybe."

As the officers filed out of the cabin bedroom, Morton decided to take with him the book he'd found.

On the ride back to Portland in the SWAT van, Morton sat with the Commander and other officers. The SWAT Commander, sat opposite, noticed the title of the book Morton was holding. "Interesting reading matter."

"It belongs to the Hains. I thought it might prove useful."

"Are you planning to use black magic or something, Detective?" the SWAT officer to Morton's immediate right asked.

Morton, ignoring the officer, addressed the Commander: "Real impressive intellect in your unit, Commander. A good thing their conception of deductive reasoning isn't actually put to use in investigations or a lot of innocent people would be royally fucked."

The thick-skinned veteran grinned and said: "My team are skilled where it counts. In the field."

Morton smiled at the Commander's backhanded compliment about his own men.

"Yeah! You hear that?!" the offended officer told Morton.

Morton, without looking at the SWAT cop, replied: "Yes. A pity you didn't."

Wednesday

5:51pm

Sam lay on his bed in the B&B, debating whether to call or text Chloe to tell her this would be his last night in Millvern.

He looked at his watch and got pissed at himself for leaving it so late in the day. It would now most likely be too short notice for them to have a final hook-up tonight.

In the middle of deciding on this matter, there was a series of loud, thudding knocks on his door. Sam immediately sensed there was an urgency behind the knocking, which triggered the same fear as when he first heard about the college attack. He opened it and saw Morton with a deadly serious look on his face. Sam's stomach lurched. Something must have happened to Chloe.

"I just got a call from Deputy Roony. The Sheriff is dead."

Sam looked down and shut his eyes. *Poor guy.*

Wednesday

6:02pm

Chloe was met at the entrance to the county morgue by Jockton, who beamed a smile and said: "Thanks for coming down, Chloe."

She followed him into the building, through a corridor, and down a long flight of winding steps to the refrigerated crypt where the bodies were stored. Walking down, the thing that had bothered her came to the fore again.

"Sheriff, may I ask you something?"

"Sure you may, Chloe."

"That's it. That's the thing. You never call me Chloe. You always call me Miss Katz. Don't get me wrong, I'm not offended. I don't mind you calling me Chloe. I actually prefer it. I just don't get why you've suddenly switched."

They had arrived at the bottom of the steps and the door into the crypt. Jockton looked at Chloe and said: "I switched because I know you prefer it."

"Oh. OK," she replied, unconvinced.

He opened the door and let her go in first. "Sit down and make yourself comfortable. I'll be back in a few minutes."

"No offense, Sheriff, but I don't really want to be in a morgue longer than I have to. Can you just tell me why you've got me down here?"

"I'll explain everything. Just wait here and I'll be back in a few minutes." Jockton nodded at her and left the room.

Chloe folded her arms and looked around the room in discomfort. She rubbed her upper arms in reaction to the chill of the crypt.

She looked behind her and saw the rows of cabinets in which the bodies were stored. She shivered and turned to look at the door, hoping Jockton would return soon, willing it to happen.

ONE WEEK BEFORE

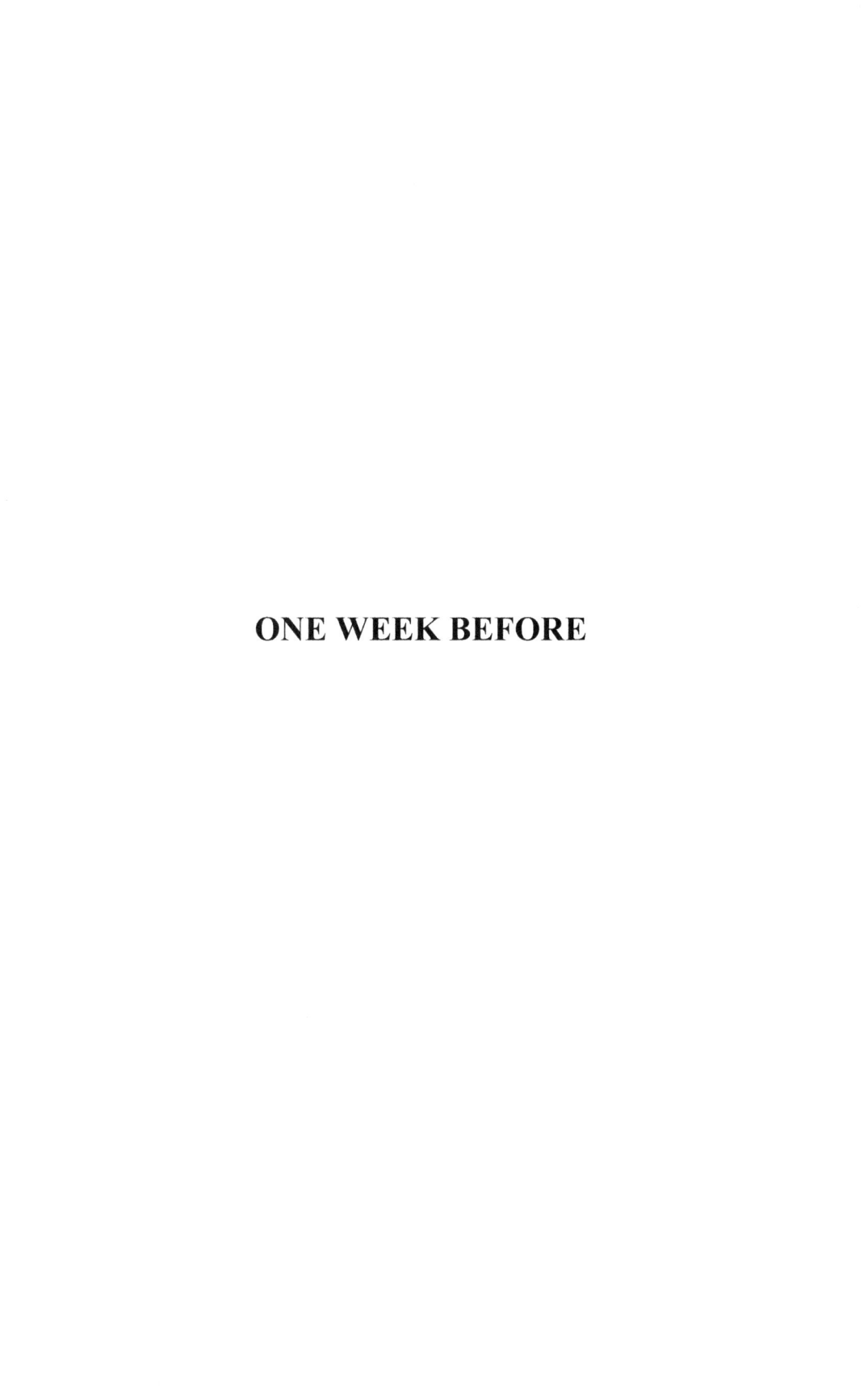

Going To Frisco

A month after the unsuccessful raid on the cabin, Morton was still sifting through tips from the public. The risk that always came with appealing for information, especially where a reward was offered, was the number of false leads, useless tips, and downright inane comments he and the other cops had to go through. Just that morning, Morton had read about a supposed sighting of the Hains at an art gallery in New York City, which he knew immediately to be erroneous, not only because the couple described by the tipster were well dressed, but because they were in an art gallery.

Another member of the public who'd called in wasn't even offering a tip as to their whereabouts. He was just convinced he'd met them in a bar twelve years ago and they owed him five bucks and asked if the police could get his money back if they ever find the Hains.

On the verge of throwing all the remaining tips into the wastepaper basket, Morton sat up in his chair when he read the next card. A woman called Jess Dalton from Los Angeles had called to say she knew the Hains' son and that she feared for his safety.

After shouting at his colleagues for failing to put this at the top of the pile of tips, he got on the phone to Jess.

"What took you guys so long?! I rang you, like, over a month ago!" Jess complained.

"Yes, sorry, Miss Dalton, but as I'm sure you can appreciate, this is a large-scale investigation and we have a lot of information sent in by helpful members of the public like yourself to work through. We try and get through them as fast as we can. Now, it says here the Hains have a son and you know him?"

Jess told Morton everything she knew: Sam escaping his parents when he was 17, their obsession with the occult, her family taking him in, their romantic relationship, where he went to college, his last known location in San Francisco, and eventually falling out of touch over the years. Morton wrote all of this down.

"Why did he run away from his parents?"

"He didn't go into detail. All he said was they tried to murder him."

"But he didn't even change his name?"

"He didn't want all the bother that comes with a new identity. And he was sure his parents wouldn't report him missing because of what they'd done."

"And why didn't he go to the police for what they'd done?"

"Sam said he couldn't be sure the cops would believe him. They might have just sent him back to his parents. Cops have been known to do that, Detective."

Morton stopped writing. "Yes, I know, but I haven't."

"Well, I'm glad to hear! Now, what are you going to do? They might go after Sam."

"If you don't know where Sam lives these days, I doubt his parents do."

"Detective! You can't know that for sure! His life may be in danger!"

"OK, calm down, Miss Dalton. I'll try and locate Mr. Hain and speak with him. See if he might be able to help."

"OK, good. So, when do I get my reward?"

Morton switched the phone to his other ear as a physical expression of his astonishment at her question. "Excuse me?"

"The $25,000 reward. When do I get it?"

"Miss Dalton, all you've told me is the Hains have a son called Sam. You haven't told me anything about where they are or how to find them. We don't give rewards just for any piece of information."

"Damn it," Jess muttered in disappointment.

"But I'm glad it made you pick up the phone to us anyway. This is the best lead we've had in a while. Actually, it's the only lead we've had in a while."

"Thank you for that little barb, Detective, but I would have phoned you people anyway. I'm worried for Sam."

"OK, Miss Dalton. I'll get on to it straightaway."

"If you do speak to Sam, can you pass my number on to him please. Tell him it would be great to catch up."

"Sure. Thanks again, Miss Dalton."

Morton got onto his computer with the details he had for Sam: his full name, age, where he'd gone to college, and his last location. Within minutes, the Detective had found him. The Hains' son was still in San Francisco and working as a private investigator. Morton didn't mind taking a trip to Frisco.

He looked at the name on the computer. Sam Hain. He said it out loud. "Sam Hain."

The penny dropped. "Of course. Fucking idiots."

Wednesday

6:10pm

Sam and Morton stared at the station front desk, numbed by the sight before them.

Jockton's upturned head lay on the desk, functioning as a plant pot filled with flowers. The name *MIKE* was written in blood on the paneling below.

Ronny was outside the station. Upon discovering Jockton's severed head, he'd run out and called Morton and remained there since. He couldn't bear to see his boss like that. But it also meant no one knew where the rest of the Sheriff was.

"Why'd you have to kill him, Mike?" Sam asked out loud.

"Is he here?" Morton asked.

"What?"

"I'm sorry, Mr. Hain, but people don't normally ask questions to demons, and since you seem to have a hotline to Mike, I thought you might know if he's here or not."

"I was just thinking out loud, Detective. But for all I know, yeah, he might be here. He's been around… at other times," Sam said, red-faced.

Morton went over to examine the Jockton flowerpot closer. He leaned forward and sniffed the flowers.

"What are you doing, Detective?" Sam asked, grimacing.

"These are real flowers. Actual real, fresh flowers. I thought they'd be fake, like the kind you see in a diner. But they're real."

"So?"

"That kind of attention to detail is just… Mike doesn't do anything half-assed. It's quite something."

Sam shook his head, still reeling from Jockton's sudden death.

Morton turned and went to the front door. He opened it just enough to stick his head out to call to Ronny. "Deputy Ralphie."

"It's Ronny," Sam corrected him.

"Yes, Detective? And my name is Ronny."

"Did you find the rest of the Sheriff's body?" Morton asked.

"No, Detective. I couldn't bear to look."

"Fine," Morton responded flatly. He closed the door and rejoined Sam. "Deputy Rudy said he couldn't bear to look. And he's supposed to be a cop."

"Go easy on the guy. The poor kid's probably never had to deal with anything more serious than neighbors arguing about driveways and garden fences. How would you feel if you came in to work and saw your Captain decapitated?"

"Well, for a start, it's been so long since he put a perp away, the first thing I'd feel is amazement that anyone who'd want him dead is even still alive."

"Interesting people skills, Detective. No wonder you told me you don't care what others think of you."

"Yes. Now do you want to get on with this or not?"

"Let's check out the meeting room," Sam suggested.

The pair went down a corridor to the main meeting room where they'd held all their discussions on the case. Sam opened the door and stopped so abruptly that Morton bumped into him.

"What the fuck," Sam said.

"What is it?" Morton asked, trying to get past Sam.

"Uh… Remember in high school when your biology teacher told you your small and large intestines laid out would be the length of a football field? Well, Mike's tried to put that claim to the test."

Morton shoved past Sam, declaring: "I don't need you to protect me, I can take it." Not being someone who was often shocked in his line of work, Morton was blindsided by what he saw.

Jockton's headless body lay in the middle of the long meeting table with what had become Mike's signature of a hollowed-out torso. But instead of being in a pile next to the body, Jockton's unfurled intestines were hanging on the walls and from the ceiling fan, and they were stretched along the floor all the way around the room, creating a circuit of viscera. The room was a tour de force of bloodletting.

"Now that is spectacularly fucked up," Morton commented in a tone that almost sounded like he was impressed.

The pair returned to the reception area, both looking and feeling downcast. Even Morton thought Jockton didn't have that coming to him.

Sam sat down on one of the reception chairs and shut his eyes. He'd had it with this case. He felt tired in his body and his mind. He'd see to it that Jockton's remains were taken to the morgue and then he'd be outta there.

His phone rang and he reached into his pocket slowly to answer unenthusiastically. He saw Chloe's name as the caller ID. If she was calling to arrange a hook-up, he'd meet for a drink, but he didn't think he'd be in the mood for sex.

"Hey, Chloe," Sam said.

"Sam! Where are you? I need you to come get me," Chloe replied in a frantic tone.

"Why, what's wrong?" Sam asked, alarmed by her voice.

"I'm at the morgue. The Sheriff told me to come down here for some reason."

"Oh, Chloe. I've got something to tell you about the Sheriff."

"He told me he'd be back in a few minutes, but I'm still waiting and the door's locked and I can't get out."

"You've been waiting for hours and you're only calling now?"

"What are you talking about? I've been waiting for about twenty minutes."

Sam felt the same ineffable horror he'd experienced when he saw the laundromat video, that emotion where it was like he'd stepped outside the bounds of normalcy and was teetering on the precipice towards insanity.

"Chloe, when did you last see the Sheriff?" Sam asked slowly.

"I just told you, Sam! Twenty minutes ago!"

"OK. Listen to me. Try and remain calm. I'm coming over right now with Detective Morton."

Sam ended the call and stood up. Morton saw the look on his face and walked over. "What's up?"

"I think I'm going to throw up."

"Oh, not you as well! Is this your idea of a tribute to the Sheriff?"

"That was Chloe Katz. She's at the morgue. She said she saw Jockton just twenty minutes ago."

"Oh, fuck."

***

They told Ronny to stay in his car, wait in the station, or go home; they were fine with all three. They'd made it this far without having to let the Deputy in on the case and they were determined to keep it that way.

After Ronny said he'd stay in his car while they went to investigate what Morton called a development in the case, Sam and Morton got into the Portland cop's car and sped off. Sam got out his handgun and checked the chamber. He knew a gun would be useless against Mike, but he felt he should have it ready anyway.

Sam sensed Morton looking at him. "I've got a license," he assured him.

"You need a firearm in your line of work, do you, Mr. Hain?"

"I investigate spouses suspected of having affairs, Detective. You don't think that can lead to a homicidal situation?"

SIX DAYS BEFORE

Thursday

8pm

Mike stood in the empty laundromat. The only sound came from the few washing machines and dryers that were still in cycle.

He went to one of the empty dryers and opened the door. He stood back and closed his eyes.

Mike's facial features distorted as though mangled by an invisible surgeon's knife, albeit bloodlessly. As his nose bent out of shape, his eyes slid to their respective sides, and his lips disappeared, a new face emerged.

But it didn't stop there. The new face continued to protrude along with an entirely new body emerging from Mike's limbs and torso, the flesh of both intermingled and stuck together like putty, until the new person had fully stepped outside of Mike.

Mike's face and body returned to normal. He stood facing the first John Doe.

John Doe turned and climbed inside the dryer.

Mike clicked his finger and blood appeared on John Doe's shirt where a stab wound had just materialized underneath.

***

Had Nancy turned around at that moment, she would have seen something to which her reaction would have been composed entirely of *fuck* and every variation thereof, including but not limited to *What the motherfuck, you fuck?!*

John Doe had turned his head and was grinning in Nancy's direction.

He turned his head, stopped grinning, and the light in his eyes went out, once again an empty vessel, an avatar of Mike.

Wednesday

6:36pm

Sam and Morton ran into the county morgue building, where they saw the receptionist, a guy in his mid-twenties called Dylan, at the front desk.

"Have you seen the Sheriff?" Sam asked.

"Yeah, he's downstairs in the crypt with some lady. Who are you two?" Dylan asked with suspicion.

Morton flashed his badge and asked: "When did he arrive?"

"Just before six. What's the problem?"

"Has he come back up?" Sam asked.

"I don't feel comfortable answering these questions. I don't even know who you people are." Morton raised his badge again. "Yeah, I saw that. You're Portland."

"Which way to the crypt?" Morton asked firmly.

"Look, let me call the Sheriff on his cell–"

Morton took out his gun and bellowed: "You are delaying a homicide investigation! Now tell us the way to the crypt or I will arrest you for obstruction!"

Sam and Morton barreled down the steps frantically, both with their gun at the ready. Sam got to the bottom first. He tried to open the door, but found it locked.

He saw Chloe through the glass pane run over to the door and a rush of relief upon seeing her unharmed cascaded over him.

"Is Jockton back?" Sam asked.

"No! Now get me out of here!"

"OK, Chloe, we need you to stand aside so we can shoot the lock."

Chloe nodded and retreated several feet.

"I'll do this," Morton insisted. "You don't have the authority."

"Fine, do it." Sam stepped aside and Morton fired twice at the lock. He opened the door and they entered.

Sam ran over to Chloe and put his hands on her shoulders. "Are you OK?" He immediately regretted his words and the way he'd run to her. He'd come this far without looking needy or sentimental and this would be a helluva time to fuck that up.

"Yeah, I'm just really confused what's going on. The Sheriff tells me to come here, saying it's real important, and then he disappears, leaving me in this cold, creepy place."

"I'll explain everything back at the station," Sam said, concluding he had no choice but to let her in on the secrets of the case.

"Alright, let's go," Morton said, holstering his gun. He went to the door and couldn't believe it when he saw it was locked again. "What the fuck. It won't open."

"You've gotta be kidding!" Chloe said with panic.

One of the morgue cabinets flew open by itself. They all spun around and were horrified to see the first John Doe, naked and pale, sit up on the stretcher and turn to smile at them.

"Son of a bitch!" Sam yelled.

"What the hell is this?!" Chloe shrieked.

"Chloe, get back!" Sam shouted as he got out his gun. She ran to a corner of the room and watched John Doe #1 leap off the slab. He ran furiously towards Sam and Morton and was met with a hail of gunfire from them both. The shots propelled him backwards, slamming into the stretcher.

A second cabinet burst open. This one held the second John Doe on its slab, also nude and deathly pale.

"Oh, this just gets better!" Morton said.

John Doe #2 sat up and turned his head to smirk at them.

"What the fuck's with all the grinning?!" Sam commented.

"Maybe they're happy to be alive?" Morton suggested.

As insane as it seemed to ask, Sam ventured anyway: "Are you guys OK? Are you happy to still be alive? Would you like medical assistance?"

John Doe #2 leapt off his slab and, together with John Doe #1, charged towards Sam and Morton, who fired again, but this time the bullets didn't slow the John Does down.

John Doe #1 grabbed hold of Sam and hurled him across the room with inhuman strength. Sam smacked into the wall and slumped to the floor.

Morton tried to reload his gun, but John Doe #2 got hold of him by the neck and slammed him against the door, causing him to drop his firearm. He began to pummel Morton with punches, smirking maniacally.

Chloe looked around for something to use as a weapon. She spotted a handheld electric saw on a shelf next to other autopsy tools. She ran to the shelf and grabbed it.

Sam got to his feet and saw John Doe #1 stalking towards him. He raised his gun and shot him in the head. He fell to the floor and black blood spewed from the bullet hole. Sam stepped over him to go and help Morton, but saw Chloe had got there first.

Armed with the saw, she switched it on and with great force rammed its oscillating blade into the back of John Doe #2's head. His grip on Morton loosened and he staggered back. Morton stroked his bruised throat and tried to recover his composure.

With the saw embedded in his head, Chloe ran it across John Doe #2's skull, creating a long gash from which black blood gushed out. She withdrew the saw and tossed it aside.

Morton picked his gun up off the floor and fired two shots point blank into John Doe #2's head, sending him to the floor.

The three of them paused to catch their breath and looked at the two motionless, naked corpses on the floor.

"Do you think they're really dead this time or just pretending?" Sam asked Morton. The Detective shook his head.

"Guys, unless there's a convention of necrophiliacs in town, please tell me there's a rational explanation for why there are two dead guys walking around with their dicks out," Chloe said.

"There is an explanation," Sam began.

"Good."

"Does it have to be rational?" he asked.

Morton kneeled to examine John Doe #2 closer.

"Careful," Sam warned, glancing at John Doe #1 on the floor directly behind him.

"It's alright, I think he's definitely dead," Morton said. "And I don't want to hear any cliché about famous last words."

John Doe #2's eyes shot open and he pulled Morton from his kneeling position face first onto the floor.

Sam and Chloe reacted with an anguished chorus of *No!*

John Doe #2 got hold of Morton by his hair and smashed his face repeatedly into the cold tile. Black blood dripped from his face onto Morton's back.

"Not the suit!" Morton cried out.

Chloe went looking for the saw she'd thrown away, while Sam reloaded his gun. But before he could rush to help Morton, John Doe #1 also came to life and clasped his hand around Sam's leg and pulled him back, which sent Sam crashing to the floor.

Chloe found the saw under the first slab. Grossed out by the prospect of getting under it, she shoved the cabinet shut and picked up the saw.

Morton managed to wriggle out from under John Doe #2 and reached for his holster. He emptied the remainder of the clip into John Doe

#2's face, reducing it to a bloody pulp and spraying the front of Morton's suit with black blood.

"It's over. It's fucked. There's no way I can wear this again," he said in resignation.

Chloe came running over with the saw, but Morton waved her away. "He's down for the moment. Go help Sam. I'll be sitting here mourning my suit."

She nodded and turned to see John Doe #1 was now on his feet and dragging Sam across the floor towards the wall by his neck.

Chloe ran across the room, the saw's blade whirring. Without turning around, John Doe #1 raised his free hand and that simple action sent Chloe sliding back across the floor until she smashed into a bare autopsy table at the opposite wall.

Morton wanted to help Sam, but the blows from John Doe #2 had been punishing and he was too battered and winded to get up, let alone provide help. He used the time instead to reload his gun and preemptively blast the entire chamber into John Doe #2's already heavily shredded face. More black blood decorated his suit, but he was past caring.

John Doe #1 pulled Sam to his feet and held him by the throat.

"Come on, you gruesome fuck!" Sam said defiantly. "Fucking do it! Come on! I don't give a shit! At least I'll have an interesting death. No heart attack or getting run over! I get taken out by a demon's murder victim who came back from the dead more than once! How many people have said a sentence like that in their lives?! None!"

Chloe frowned, certain she must have entirely misheard Sam.

"Come on! Do it! Fucking do it, you Ivy League, milquetoast looking piece of shit!" Sam taunted.

John Doe #1 let go of Sam's throat and smiled, but this smile was amiable rather than maniacal. "No, I won't do that," he answered in Mike's voice.

Morton and Chloe looked on, astounded that John Doe #1 could talk.

"Mike?" Sam said astonished.

"Who's Mike?" Chloe asked.

"Sort of," John Doe #2 said in the same voice, sitting up. Morton grunted and recoiled, reaching for his gun.

"Mike?" Sam repeated, this time to John Doe #2.

"Who's Mike?" Chloe repeated.

Morton took out a new clip to load into his gun.

"Quit it, Detective. I think we've established bullets won't kill Mike," Sam said.

"Who the fuck is Mike?!" Chloe asked in exasperation.

John Doe #2 stood up, his head a bulb of black blood from Morton's relentless gunfire.

John Doe #1 turned away from Sam and walked over to his fellow naked undead buddy. They collided with one another, merging into one person, no longer naked but dressed in a nice suit and with a different face.

Chloe covered her mouth, unable to comprehend what she was witnessing.

"Mike?" Sam asked.

"Can someone tell me who the fuck is Mike and how he just did what he did?!" Chloe shrieked.

"Yes, Sam. It's me. And I'm most impressed. Most impressed. You've done yourself proud. You didn't waver or cower. And that's why I'm not going to torment you any further."

"Who were the other two?" Morton asked, holstering his weapon and slowly standing up. Looking down, he shook his head in dismay at the atrocity that had been wrought upon his suit.

"Both me. Well, my avatars. Nonentities controlled by me," Mike explained.

"Umm, guys. Can one of you please tell me what is going on here before I lose my shit?" Chloe asked with controlled anxiety.

"She's right. She's entitled to an explanation. In fact, everyone is. Let's assemble at the diner and all will be revealed," Mike said.

"But you're not going to kill any more people, right?" Sam asked. "You're just going to explain?"

Mike laughed. "That's one of the reasons I like you, Sam. No bullshit. Direct, to the point, and courageous."

"Perfect. An endorsement from a demon. That can go down on my résumé," Sam said.

"From a what?" Chloe asked.

"Like I said," Mike answered, "all will be revealed. Shall we say 8pm at the diner?"

Wednesday

8pm

After paying off the owner to let them have use of Eat All Day for the evening, Sam and Morton went to collect the others whom Mike had demanded be present: Chuck, Drew, and Rob. The pair did query why the presence of those three was necessary and Mike explained that, since they'd been questioned over the first John Doe death, he felt it only polite they find out the truth.

Chuck had been home watching TV, Drew had been getting ready to meet Inessa for dinner, and Rob had arranged for Lucy to come over while his parents were out for the evening at a *Conservatives Against the Separation of Church and State* fundraiser. Chuck was brought up to speed on Jockton's death, and the other two were only told they had to attend because of a crucial new development in the investigation.

Chloe was also clued in on the Sheriff's death, though not the manner. Realizing what this meant about the Jockton she had met at the morgue, she felt faint, so Sam and Morton left out the rest of the backstory for Mike to explain, and they all assembled in the diner. Sam and Morton sat across from each other in a booth, Chloe and Chuck sat alone in separate booths on either side of them, and Drew and Rob shared a table near the entrance. Morton had wanted to change clothes, but there was no time to go and buy a temporary suit; temporary, because he'd only buy the real replacement, an Armani, back in Portland.

"Where's the Sheriff?" Drew asked.

"He can't make it," Sam said.

"Is he at the Cinemount? I noticed they're showing *Smokey and the Bandit* and I assumed he's the one who asked them to screen it."

"He's dead," Morton announced.

Sam shook his head at Morton's blunt intervention that made Drew and Rob look aghast.

"The Sheriff's dead?!" Drew said, immediately regretting having thought ill of him because of his taste in films and former British prime ministers.

"Murdered," Morton clarified.

"Jesus, Morton," Sam said.

"Mr. Hain, given what they're about to hear, I think we're way past concealing the truth."

"About to hear what?" Drew asked.

"Yeah, why you got me over here?" Rob asked. "I was gonna meet Lucy till you fake cops turned up and ordered me to come with you. And what the fuck is up with all the blood on your suit? Did you kill someone?"

"I'm not a fake cop, boy," Morton said, insulted. "I'm a homicide detective with the Portland PD. And no, I didn't kill anyone."

"No, you're just killing my sex life."

"Mine too. And you still haven't said why we're here," Drew said.

"We're waiting for one more… *person* to join us," Sam replied.

"Why do you say *person* like you're not sure?" Drew asked.

"You haven't got my parents and their lawyer coming, do you?" Rob asked.

"No, kid. Just sit and be quiet," Sam said.

"I imagine you all have a lot of questions," Mike said. Everyone jumped and saw the new arrival at the door.

"Where the hell did you come from?!" Rob asked. "The door didn't even open."

Mike walked slowly across the diner portentously and came to a stop in the middle, facing Sam's booth, and perched himself against a table, smiling.

"Private detective guy," Rob said, addressing Sam.

"It's Mr. Hain," Sam responded, not in the mood to go through the usual bullshit over his full name.

"Yeah, Mr. Hain, who is this guy?"

"Just be patient, kid. You'll find out."

"See, I knew this was gonna end up being some pedo shit!" Rob said, standing up.

"It's not pedo shit. Just sit down and you'll find out. Mike, do you think you could get a move on please?"

"Yes, Sam," Mike said in a pleasant tone. "Good evening, everyone. My name, as you've heard, is Mike. It's not my real name, but it'll do for now. And I am what you humans call a demon."

The diner fell momentarily silent. The quiet was broken by Rob: "Uh, Mr. Hain," – then looking at Morton – "Cop, is this, like, an intervention for your friend's emotional problems?"

"Just listen to what he has to say, kid. You don't want to piss him off," Sam said, glancing at Mike.

"Don't worry, Sam. Rob isn't in any danger. His comments don't offend me. I have a very thick skin. Do you want to see it?"

"No!" Sam said. "Just please get on with it."

"So, like, you're a badass at something?" Rob asked. "Like, you're a demon the same way someone is a demon on the electric guitar or a demon on the drums?"

"No, I'm an actual demon. Or diabolical entity, as I prefer it."

Rob looked at Sam and Morton again. "Are shrinks available at this time of night?"

"I understand why you don't believe me. I'll prove it to you," Mike offered. His facial features became freakishly misshapen and a new face began to emerge.

Rob, Drew, and Chuck screamed in reaction. Chloe was already numbed from her earlier experience in the morgue and just looked on impassively. Sam and Morton felt themselves veterans of this sort of thing and were equally nonchalant.

The new face, as well as a new body, poked through Mike's frame. This caused Drew to dive under the table, Chuck to back up along his seat until he was against the window and bring up his knees as some sort of defense, and Rob to run to the door, grabbing frantically at the handle, which wouldn't open.

The new man, similar in appearance to the two John Does, stepped outside of Mike. Rob turned around and looked at the new guy in terror.

"Relax, Rob. I'm not going to hurt you," both Mike and his vessel, in Mike's voice, said simultaneously.

"If you're trying to calm him down, you're going about it the wrong way," Sam commented.

Mike clicked his finger and his new avatar vanished. "Now take a seat," he ordered.

Rob looked to Sam, who nodded to reassure him, even though he wasn't actually sure any of them *weren't* in danger.

Rob went back to his seat, and Chuck went back to a sitting position.

"You can come out now, Drew," Mike said.

Drew emerged from under the table, embarrassed, but still nervous, and took his seat. His vow to himself after his experience with Sarah Shitblood that he wouldn't put up with crap from anyone still stood, since this obviously wasn't anyone.

"This is some special effects, isn't it?" Drew asked, wiping his brow.

"Yeah, demons ain't real. This gotta be some 4D CGI hologram or something," Rob added.

Sam and Morton looked at each other and smiled in remembrance of Jockton.

"I'm real. Or would you like more proof?" Mike asked.

"No!" Sam said. "Look, guys, as fucked as it seems, Mike's real."

"Demons ain't real," Rob said.

"Look, you can believe a private investigator and a cop from Portland have somehow acquired state-of-the-art special effects technology the likes of which the world has never seen and would have to cost a few hundred millions dollars. Or – *or* – you can wait patiently and see what Mike has to say and then understand what's going on." He looked at Mike and said: "Before you start, I just need to know. Are my parents dead?"

"Yes," Mike replied matter-of-factly.

"And you killed them?"

"Yes."

"Case closed," Morton said to himself with satisfaction. The others looked at him. "I just like it when I solve a case."

"And you killed Nancy Dirgle, Kenneth White, and – what am I saying, of course you did," Sam said.

"You murdered the laundromat lady?" Rob asked. "She pissed you off too, huh?" he said, laughing.

"But why did you have to kill Jockton?" Sam asked, feeling upset again. "He wasn't a bad guy."

"I'll get to that. But first I want to tell you all about the last six months and what I've had to put up with. I want to tell you all about two stupendously stupid assholes called Leo and Polly Hain. Even more stupid and even more asshole than Drew's old colleague, Sarah Shitblood."

Drew looked at Mike in astonishment. "How on earth do you know about her?"

"So, you remember the part where I told you I'm a demon?"

"You worked with someone called Shitblood?" Chuck asked.

"That wasn't her real name, obviously. It was a private nickname I gave her," Drew replied.

Mike walked over to Drew, who looked fearful again. Mike gave him two quick, sympathetic pats on the shoulder. "I'm sorry for what you had to go through. She's an awful person."

"Thank you."

"Would you like me to kill her for you?"

"What? No! No, I don't want you to kill anyone!"

"OK."

Mike returned to perch himself against the table. "Leo and Polly were Sam's parents. He ran away from home when he was 17 because they tried to murder him."

Except for Morton, who already knew his story, they all looked at Sam, stunned but also sympathetic. He appreciated the sympathy, but the attention made him feel uncomfortable.

"Man, I thought *my* parents are assholes," Rob said. "I mean, they *are* assholes, but… I forgot what I was gonna say."

"Can you not make this about me please?" Sam asked Mike.

"Wait," Rob interjected. "Your name is Sam Hain? Like, Samhain?!"

"Oh, we don't have time for this right now, kid," he pleaded.

"That's some gnarly shit, man!" Rob said.

"Then six months ago," Mike continued, "they used a book on the occult to summon me. Those two fucknuggets wanted me to do their bidding."

"*Fucknuggets?*" Sam repeated, laughing.

"Yeah, it's a great word, isn't it? I love using it."

"So they summoned you to go and murder people for them," Morton said.

"What? No, what gave you that idea?" Mike asked.

"All the people you murdered in Portland!"

"No, they were all murdered by the Hains."

Sam and Morton looked at each other.

"Please make this make sense!" Sam begged.

"How did his dumbfuck parents pull off ingenious murders?" the cop asked.

"Let me back up a second, because we're getting ahead of ourselves here," Mike said.

"Uh, demon?" Rob said.

"It's Mike."

"Yeah, Mike. Since we have to sit here, can I at least go get a drink from the kitchen?"

"What would you like?" Mike asked.

"I was gonna get a Coke. Does anyone else want anything?" Rob asked, looking around. They all shook their heads. "OK, cool." Rob stood up.

"Here you go," Mike said, holding up a bottle of Coke that he wasn't holding the second before.

"Thanks, but I want a real Coke from the kitchen, not something that's gonna eat me."

"This *is* a real Coke. I just used my powers to teleport it from the kitchen instantaneously."

Rob, looking at Mike with suspicion, stepped across to where he was standing and took the bottle. "Thanks. This, err, this doesn't have any demon stuff in it, does it? It's not gonna turn into blood when I start drinking?"

"I don't know where you get your information on diabolical entities from, but this is a normal Coke. Enjoy!"

Rob returned to his seat and sat down. Feeling a little more relaxed, he unbuttoned his black shirt and sat back, revealing the t-shirt he wore underneath that showed a winged monstrous creature flying above a tidal wave of blood washing over a hill of skulls.

"Hey, how did you get a picture of my last birthday party?" Mike asked.

"What?"

"Never mind. As I was saying, Sam's parents summoned me to do their bidding. What they wanted was for me to go and rob banks for them. Can you believe that? They summon me and that's the extent of their imagination."

"Yeah, that sounds like my parents," Sam said.

"So I decided to punish them. I would make them go out and kill on my command for as long as I wanted and they'd have no choice in the matter. The problem was that they were so fucking incompetent, inept, and backward that they left every crime scene with more DNA than a sperm bank. I had to clean up after every murder just to prevent the fuckpellets from being caught by the police so I could continue owning them."

Morton smiled faintly. Finally, he had his explanation for how the Hains appeared to have pulled off magic tricks. Finally, he knew, in Judy's words, in what universe their crimes made sense. He thought it was a pity he'd never be able to tell her about all this.

"But then they decided to get cunty. They wanted to be infamous. They started signing their names after every murder. They wanted credit for the fact people were saying these crimes were the work of a criminal genius. They were taking credit for *my* powers! And they didn't even use a moniker but their actual real names in full. How brain-dead can you get? A rhetorical question, because in their case, there was never a limit. Anyway, I warned them to stop. I warned them that if they did it again, I would torment someone close to them. And when they betrayed me, I told them I would make good on my vow. And that I would torment you," Mike finished by looking at Sam.

"Me?!" Sam asked incredulously.

"They just laughed."

"Yeah, because we were never close!"

"So they said. But I thought there was a chance they could be bluffing. Parental bond and all that human shit."

"You got the wrong couple for that, Mike. There was never any bond. But then why kill them if that was going to be their punishment?"

"Oh, that was just to shut them up. They were really pissing me off by laughing. I can bring them back any time I want."

"You can?!" Sam said, wondering how many more surprises Mike had lined up.

"Yes." And the doors to the kitchen opened and out came Leo and Polly, tied to chairs that were sliding along the floor, around the counter and into the dining area, where they came to a stop behind Mike's table. Unable to open their mouths, they squealed frantically.

Rob, Drew, and Chuck joined Sam, Morton, and Chloe in feeling that events had made them veterans of the bizarre and grotesque, so the appearance of these two didn't cause a new degree of shock among them beyond mild gasps of surprise.

"Fuck me," Sam said, looking down and shaking his head. "Family reunion time."

"Sam! Is that you?!" Polly yelled, now able to speak.

"That you, son?" Leo asked. "It *is* you! Sammy!"

"Sam! Help us, son!" Polly pleaded.

"Yeah, Sammy, we love you and shit!"

"Shut the fuck up. You don't need to pretend in front of these people. They all know you're a pair of sick motherfuckers."

"You still mad about that home movie we was gonna make, son? You done misunderstand what we was doing and shit!" Leo insisted.

"Yeah, you ain't not misunderstanding!" Polly added. "You read the name of our movie wrong. It ain't wasn't *Snuff,* it was *Sniff.* We just wanted to video film you try on some fancy cologne!"

"I'm going to mute them while I continue," Mike said, and the Hains were unable to speak once again. They resumed muffled squealing, but that too Mike shut off with a wave of his hand.

"What I'd give to have that power," Sam commented.

"Oh, and I've also muted their odor. You should thank me, because if you could smell them right now, you'd smash the windows and run away."

They all stared at Leo and Polly.

"I said you should thank me." Immediately, they all expressed their gratitude with assorted *thank yous,* uttered in varying tones of fear and agitation, except for Sam and Morton, who expressed their appreciation calmly.

Continuing, Mike said: "I intended to torment you and, when the time was right, bring them back to see you suffer in case they *had* been bluffing. My idea was to lure you into a nightmare case that was unsolvable, hence the non-existent John Does."

"That was meant to torment me?" Sam asked. "They each had just one stab wound. Hardly a bloodbath."

"I couldn't risk showing all my tricks at once, otherwise you might have just gone home the same day. I started soft to begin with. But I saw the unsolvable aspects of the case weren't having the desired effect, which is why I visited you in your room that night and showed you the image of your dead parents. Even that didn't disturb you. So, I took it up another notch by killing Nancy Dirgle. And then Kenneth White. There have to be *some* real murders in a murder investigation. And still you held it all together. Most impressive. You never appeared anguished. Even when you wanted to give up and return home, you kept going. And if you had given up and gone home, at least that's one place where I knew for certain you'd be tormented."

"What do you mean?"

"Oh, while you've been here, your apartment's been home to a family of crackheads."

"What the fuck!" Sam said, standing up and realizing there was nothing he could actually do to Mike. Sitting back down, deflated, he asked: "Why did you have to do that?!"

"Hey," Mike said, taking a seat and stroking his chin with the back of his hand, "why should it only be humans who get to be petty and childish? Besides, I'll have them out of there before you return. And that's the thing, Sam. I like you. I set out to torment you and you dealt with it all with guts and determination."

"Growing up with psychopathic parents hardens you," Sam explained.

"You *did* succeed in tormenting someone, just not the one you were targeting," Morton said. "Six months I had this case driving me nuts trying to figure out how the impossible kept happening with every murder. I've got a permanent migraine as a result."

"Well, at least someone suffered," Mike said.

"But I still have questions," Sam said.

"Uh, Mike?" Rob said.

"Yes?"

"If you guys are gonna keep talking, can I at least go get something to eat from the kitchen?"

"And that's why I like you, Rob!" Mike beamed. "Even though everyone knows what you really want is for me to just hand you something so you don't have to go to the kitchen, you still go through the pretense of asking me politely."

"I'm not sure I got any of that, but if you're offering, I'll have some fries and a slaw please," Rob requested.

Mike raised his arms to show a bowl of slaw in one hand and a plate of fries in the other. Rob got up and went over to Mike. "You're a cool bro, man," he said, taking the food and returning to his seat.

"What are your questions?" Mike asked Sam.

"The John Does. Why did you make them so alike and so bland?"

"When I first visited your domain, I went looking for the most common archetype of the human man, for myself to begin with and then later my John Does. I just went with the first ones I saw. They were standing inside the window of a store, dressed in nice suits, looking rather blank and inoffensive."

"Do you mean mannequins?" Sam asked.

"Is *that* what they were? I wondered why they weren't moving."

"Man, this is slaw is really good," Rob announced. "It's not as good as the apple slaw our chef makes at home. That's the best. Man, that apple slaw would be so good right now, with some onion rings and ranch dip too." Rob looked around the diner casually. When he was done doing that, he glanced furtively up at Mike and then away.

"Don't push your luck," Mike said. Rob resumed eating quietly.

"Yes, I admit I underperformed on that," Mike continued. "But I was just starting to learn about you humans. I'm still learning what makes you tick. Your form of procreation is most fascinating. After viewing you and Chloe, I can see why Doug's Emporium is so popular."

"Oh for…" Sam said, looking down and covering his face.

Chloe looked at Sam and then at Mike, with alarm turning to disgust. "You watched us having sex?"

"Why did you have to mention that?" Sam muttered without looking up.

"You knew?!" Chloe asked.

Looking up at her, Sam replied: "What was I supposed to say? 'By the way, Chloe, an invisible demon watched us having sex the other night'?"

"Man, you're living death metal lyrics in real life. I am so fucking jealous," Rob said.

Wanting to move to a different question, Sam asked: "But why Jockton? Why did you kill him in such a fucked-up way?"

Chuck sat forward in his seat and said: "Yeah. Don was my friend. He didn't deserve to have his guts hung up like tinsel."

Rob, Drew, and Chloe looked disgusted by the revelation. Sam was just glad they weren't talking about his sex life anymore.

"I needed to get you to go to the morgue knowing the Sheriff was dead when Chloe called you. That was my last stab at seeing if you'd falter or stay the course. I knew she's important to you and seeing the Sheriff dead would make you fear for her safety."

Sam went red and Chloe smiled.

"But I'd have gone there anyway," Sam said. "You didn't have to behead him and unfurl his intestines." Rob, Drew, and Chloe groaned in revulsion. "Oh, there's no point censoring it now, you've already heard it all."

"I had to make it particularly gruesome to see if you would go to Chloe's rescue without hesitating. Back to that human bonding shit," Mike replied.

"Wait a minute," Morton said. "If you cleaned up all the crime scenes, why was the last one riddled with so much evidence?"

"I wasn't around to clean that one up. I was away on a research trip. That one was all the work of these cumstains. I wouldn't have minded them claiming that murder, but I already warned them not to do it again and it was the principle of my threat that mattered. I do have my principles."

"What now, Mike?" Morton asked." Are you done killing people here? No more plans to be evil?"

"Hey, I'm just endearingly malevolent. If I wanted to be evil, I'd join a religion or the GOP."

"I heard that!" Rob said, grinning in concordance.

"But to answer your question, yes, I'm done killing people here. Though I was planning to kill the Hains again and make it permanent this time." Leo and Polly, still unable to make any sound, rocked about in their chairs. "What do you say, Sam? I know you want them dead. I can kill them for you right now and make it really spectacular. Blood, guts, and torn flesh, the whole showstopper."

Morton stood up with urgency. "Wait a minute. I've been on this case for six months. And now they're here, I'm entitled to arrest them and take them into custody. They have to face justice."

"Just let him kill them, Detective," Sam said. "What difference will it make to you?"

"And have this go down as unsolved? I have a strong record in closing my cases and I'm not about to have it spoiled."

"I will not let you put these fuckcherries on trial where they can take the credit for my powers," Mike declared. "That's what they'll do. They'll plead guilty and everyone will think these cumdrizzles are smart."

"Look, maybe there's a way we can work around this," Sam said. "You want a closed case," he said looking at Morton, "and you don't want them taking credit for your work," he said looking at Mike. "Fine. So here's what you do. Detective, you say the Hains only committed the last murder where they left so much evidence, and the other murders were frame-ups. You say clever murders were being attributed to them and in a fit of insecurity they did one to try and get the plaudits for real. A jury will buy it when they hear how brainless they are. You get your conviction and Mike has the integrity of his handiwork protected."

"That still leaves seven unsolved murders. No dice," the cop answered.

"You can't have everything, Detective. Be reasonable," Sam argued.

"Sam, you're forgetting something," Mike said. "It doesn't matter what Detective Morton says or charges them with. These two jizzbubbles will plead guilty to all of the murders. In the absence of another suspect, the jury will convict."

Leo and Polly rocked in their chairs as though to indicate they would do no such thing. Mike raised a hand and now the pair couldn't even move about anymore.

"Are they really going to plead guilty just so people think they're clever?" Drew asked.

"Have you even been listening to anything we've said tonight?" Sam asked.

"Guys, guys, demon, you're making this complicated for no reason," Rob said. "You got all you need in front of you. You just have to make a small change."

"What are you talking about, boy?" Morton asked.

"These two" – looking at Mike – "what did you call them? – fucknuggets got jealous Mike was getting credit, right? So you just say some killer was offing these people and they knew who was doing it. They got pissed the killer was getting props on TV, so they started following him and signed their names after he'd gone. They tried to do one on their own and that's the one where they left a shitload of their fingerprints or whatever. The killer got pissed they were stealing his likes for the other kills, so he tracked them down and wasted them. Cop here gets his case solved, and Mike don't need to worry about the fucknuggets taking his glory."

"I'm impressed, Rob," Mike said.

"A demon's impressed with me. That's some gnarly shit, man!"

"That actually works," Sam acceded. "And you say a killer called Mike, whose name you found written in the cabin, is the one who did it."

"I approve," Mike said, "especially as that part's about to become true."

"That solves the cases, but it still means there's a killer called Mike who hasn't been apprehended," Morton said. Sam gave him a harsh stare. Morton was about to respond indignantly when he sensed Mike also staring at him, which sent a chill up his spine. "Yeah, OK, I can live with that. Though I don't know how I'm going to make the case that the Hains knew this killer or about how we know he committed the other murders."

"Just plant some evidence and make some shit up. Don't you cops do that kind of thing all the time?" Rob asked with a scampish smile.

"Shut up, boy."

Mike turned around in his seat to look at Leo and Polly, who were now able to squeal and wriggle in their chairs again. "Time to say farewell to you two totally repulsive sacks of puke."

"Wait," Morton interjected. "Before you do that, I want to do something." He walked over to Leo and Polly, looked at them for a second, and slammed their heads together. They squealed in pain. "That felt so good," he said and returned to the booth and sat down.

"Want to say anything to them, Sam?" Mike asked. Sam shook his head. Mike looked at the Hains. "What about you two anal emissions?" He waved a hand, enabling them to speak.

"Sam, honey! Help us!" Polly pleaded.

"Yeah, son! We love you and shit!" Leo lied.

"Shut the fuck up," Sam said. "It's over for you two, do you understand?"

"You're asking them if they understand something?" Mike said with a laugh.

"We be good from now on, we promise!" Leo pleaded.

"Yeah, we ain't gonna not do nothing bad no more!" Polly lied.

"She should be killed for her illiteracy alone," Drew said.

"Now you see what I had to endure all those months," Mike said. He then stood up and turned around to face the Hains for the last time.

"Mike," Sam called, causing Mike to look back at him.

"What?"

"We don't need the gory showstopper."

"Are you sure?"

"Yes, I'm sure."

"Really? Because I can make it one for the ages."

"No!"

"OK, if you insist." Mike turned to face the Hains. "It's been awful knowing you two bile ducts. You are both incredibly loathsome and just so, so phenomenally dumb that... No, there aren't enough words in the English language or my own diabolical language to adequately describe your multiverse spanning imbecility. Fuck off forever." Mike clicked a finger and the Hains vanished.

Leo and Polly Hain found themselves in front of a tree in the woods next to the cabin in Rhododendron. They couldn't move, their feet stuck firmly on the soil. The husband and wife teetered forward at a forty-five-degree angle in an impossible pose that would ordinarily have seen them fall flat on their face. Three rows of three narrow vertical rectangular vents opened up on either side of their torsos, causing them to scream in agony.

Their internal organs were ejected from the vents in their backs, each organ partially mangled and sliced in the process of exiting, and hung momentarily in the air, still connected to their bodies by thin strings of viscera.

After a moment, all the organs were flung back through the vents and the Hains flipped backwards at a forty-five-degree angle, again frozen in an impossible pose, whereupon their organs shot out through the openings in the frontside of their torsos and were suspended in the air by the strings. Leo and Polly looked in horror at their mutilated and shredded hearts, kidneys, livers, lungs, pancreases, spleens, and stomachs right in front of them.

They uttered one final anguished, blistering scream, and the organs were pulled back inside their bodies and they collapsed backwards onto the ground dead, where their bodies were immediately submerged by soil until they were covered and sticks fell across the mound. A small red flag with specks of mud floated down and came to rest atop the sticks.

"If you return to Rhododendron, you'll find their bodies buried in the woods next to the cabin. Look for a muddy red flag on a pile of sticks," Mike told Morton.

"We done here? I might still be able to see my girlfriend tonight," Rob said.

"Mine too," Drew said.

"Wait," Sam interjected, which made Rob, Drew, and Chuck groan. "Just hold on a second. I need to know. Mike isn't your real name, is it?"

"No. If I told you my real name, it would make your ears bleed."

"So your real name sounds like Noel Gallagher singing?" Sam asked.

"That hurts, Sam. I have feelings too, you know."

"And the way you look?" Chloe asked.

"What about it?" Mike asked.

"What do you diabolical entities really look like?"

"If you saw my real visage, your eyes would bleed."

"So, in your real form, you look like the forty-fifth and forty-seventh president naked?" Sam asked.

"Just one more time, Sam. One more. I'm warning you. I won't take any more comments of that sort," Mike said calmly while furiously stroking his chin with the back of his hand.

"Didn't you say you're thick skinned?" Sam asked, feeling a tingle of fear.

"Well, yes, but even I have my breaking point."

"Just one more thing," Sam said.

"Enough already, Columbo," Rob said. "I wanna see my girlfriend."

"You said you prefer the term diabolical entity. But the book my parents used is literally called *The Demonian*."

"As I'm sure you've learned by now, Sam, that book changes itself according to its user. The original title was esoteric, which didn't cause any problems in the first few centuries of use. But as time has gone by, the masses have gradually got stupider, so at some point, the book took on its current name."

"So in your world, you're called a diabolical entity?"

"No. If I told you what we're called–"

"It would make our ears bleed. I can see the theme here. Thank you for answering my questions."

Sam got up, as did the others, who began gathering their belongings and stretching their legs.

"Poor Ronny. He was so shaken up by the Sheriff's death," Sam said, who then looked straight at Mike as though he'd just been struck by a bolt. "Hold on. If you brought my parents back…"

"I'm way ahead of you, Sam." Addressing the others, Mike announced: "Attention, humans. I'll only bring back one person: Nancy Dirgle, Kenneth White, or Sheriff Don Jockton."

"Don," Sam said.

"Show of hands for Dirgle," Mike said. No one raised a hand.

"Don," Sam repeated.

"Show of hands for White." Again, no one raised a hand.

"Just bring back Don," Sam said.

"And show of hands for the Sheriff." Everyone raised a hand – even Morton.

"OK." Mike clicked his finger and Jockton appeared sat at the table just as Mike himself vanished.

Jockton looked all around him. "What in the hell is going on here?!"

Wednesday

9:25pm

Nobody had to be told not to tell anyone about what they'd seen that evening. No one would believe them anyway, but more importantly, they'd risk getting committed.

Rob and Drew went home, and Chuck agreed he'd fill Jockton in on everything that had transpired.

Sam, Morton, and Chuck panicked when they realized Ronny had already seen Jockton dead. How were they going to explain away his boss's comeback?

Chuck called Ronny's cell to find out where he was first of all.

"I'm at the station. Where's the Sheriff?"

"What?" Chuck asked, wondering if seeing Jockton's decapitated head had made the Deputy lose it.

"I went to get biscuits and came back and he was gone. That was three and a half hours ago. He's not answering his phone. Is he OK?"

To their enormous relief, it appeared that Mike had wiped Ronny's memory of the earlier events and replaced it with a different recollection.

"Yes, he's been investigating an important development in the case. He's heading back now."

***

Chloe hung back while Sam, Morton, and Jockton said their goodbyes outside the diner.

"You sure I can't persuade you to stay for that meal I promised?" Jockton asked.

"Sorry, Don. I'm really tired and just want to go home," Sam said. As happy as he was that Jockton was back, he really wanted to get out of Millvern.

"Yeah, me too," Morton said.

"OK. Well, it's been a pleasure working with you fellas. Nice knowing you, Sam," Jockton said, shaking his hand. "And it was nice to meet you, Detective Morton." Jockton held out his hand.

"Call me Wallace," he said, shaking the Sheriff's hand.

"Really?! Thank you, Wallace! Well, I best get going."

Sheriff Don Jockton waved goodbye and walked off with a buoyancy in his stride.

"You know, I'm not sure what's more amazing," Sam commented to Morton. "Meeting a demon, or you getting to like Don."

Morton just smiled, and then remembered something. He reached into his inside jacket pocket and retrieved a folded piece of paper. "I almost forgot. I found out about you because an old friend of yours called us when we asked the public for help. She told me to give you her number and said it would be nice to catch up some time."

He handed the note to Sam, who unfolded it. "Jess! I haven't seen her in years. You're only telling me now?"

"I needed you focused when we first met. She told me you two used to date, and I didn't know if you'd run off to see your old flame before you could help me on the case. I meant to tell you later, I just forgot."

"You really are all business all the time, aren't you? It's not just Mike who thinks of it as human bonding shit, isn't that so, Detective?"

"Call me Wallace."

***

Sam and Chloe declined Morton's offer to give them a ride back to their B&B and home respectively, preferring instead to enjoy the evening air with a walk to Let Me Be Your BB. Morton drove on ahead to collect his belongings at the B&B and check out.

The walk gave Sam and Chloe a chance to talk about everything that had happened. They both agreed that, given Sam's emotional turmoil over the course of the day and Chloe still absorbing the gravity of what she'd witnessed, neither of them was in the right place mentally or physically for a farewell fuck.

Sam got his belongings from his room, checked out, and returned to his car. He hesitated about whether he should say what he was thinking, but figured what the hell.

"Look, I hope you didn't think I came off too, you know, attached or worried back at the morgue."

"Sam, you were being normal. I'd have been concerned if you *didn't* give a shit. I like a guy to be chilled, not sociopathic."

"OK, thanks." They embraced and had a long kiss.

Sam got into the car and rolled down the window.

"Next time I'm in San Francisco, I'll drop you a line," she suggested.

"That'll be great."

"By the way. I know men like to feel special, so I'm gonna tell you something so you can feel special on your journey home."

"Yeah?"

"You're the only guy I've let do coke off my pussy."

"Now *that's* something I wish I could put down on my résumé."

EPILOGUE

Sam locked *The Demonian* in a safe in the corner of his office. He knew it was pointless to try and destroy it, and would most likely kill him if he tried, and he wasn't going to risk it ending up in another psychopath's hands if he simply threw it away.

Taking out the note Morton had given him, he saved Jess's number on his phone. He would send her a text or just give her a call and suggest they meet. Los Angeles was a short flight away, so he could pop over there any time.

Relaxing in his office chair, Sam opened a beer and drank. Soon he'd be back to his usual bread and butter of following cheating spouses, dealing with difficult clients, chasing late payments for services rendered, and encountering lowlifes in the course of his work, as well as lowlifes more generally.

Sam sighed.

"People really piss me off."

SAM HAIN MIGHT RETURN

HE HASN'T DECIDED YET

Printed in Dunstable, United Kingdom